Quondam
An Ancient Mirrors Tale

With a touch
magick~

[signature]

Quondam
An Ancient Mirrors Tale

Jayel Gibson

Synergy Books

Quondam: An Ancient Mirrors Tale
Published by Synergy Books
P.O. Box 80107
Austin, Texas 78758

For more information about our books, please write to us, call
512.478.2028, or visit our website at www.synergybooks.net.

Publisher's Cataloging-in-Publication (Provided by Quality Books, Inc.)

Gibson, Jayel, 1949-
    Quondam : an ancient mirrors tale / Jayel Gibson.
    p. cm.
    LCCN 2007935897
    ISBN-13: 978-1-933538-83-9
    ISBN-10: 1-933538-83-X

    1. Mythology, Celtic--Fiction. 2. Magic--Fiction.
3. Science fiction. 4. Fantasy fiction.   I. Title.

PS3607.I268Q66 2008   813'.6
                QBI07-600244

Cover art, maps and internal illustrations © 2005-2006
Michele-lee Phelan, Art of the Empath
Cranebrook, N.S.W., Australia
www.ArtOfTheEmpath.com

This is a work of fiction. None of the characters or events portrayed in this
book exist outside the author's imagination, and any resemblance to real people and incidents is purely coincidental.

10 9 8 7 6 5 4 3 2 1

Awards

Dragon Queen: A 2007 USA Book News Best Books Finalist

The Wrekening: A 2007 USA Book News Best Books Finalist

Damselflies: A 2007 Writer's Digest Book Awards Honorable
Mention Title

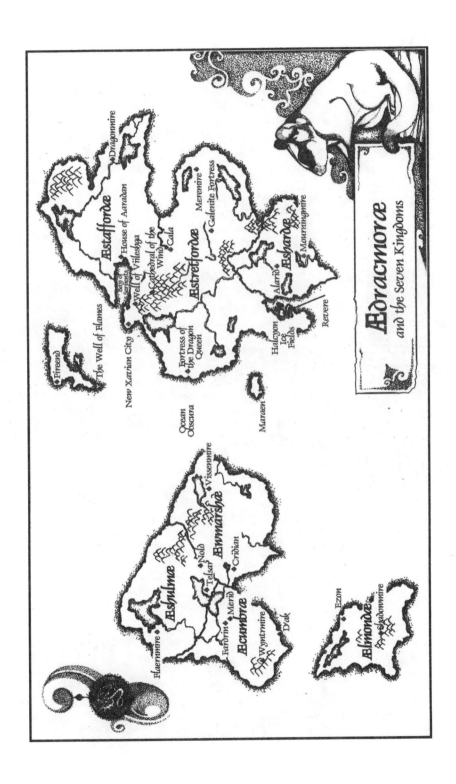

Ædracmoræ
and the Seven Kingdoms

Dragonmire

Estafforde

House of Aaradan
Well of Vrileshga
Cathedral of the Wind
Cala
Merenire
Galenite Fortress

Estretforde

Isle of Serpents
The well of Flames
Eshanoe
Fireend
New Xavian City
Fortress of the Dragon Queen
Alarid
Mourningmire

Ocean Obscura
Halcyon Ice Fields
Revere
Mataen

Flaernire
Ashulme
Nolb
Telsar
Vissenmire
Bwmarshe
Cridan

Ewianoe
Kaforin
Merid
Wyntrmire
D'ak
Ezon
Elmonoe
Shadowmire

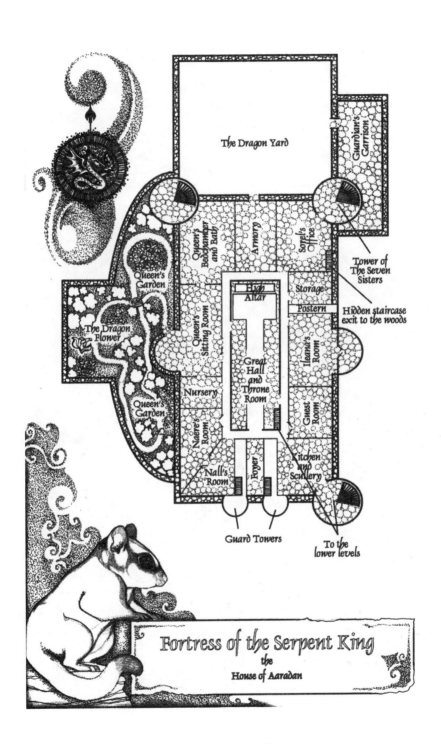

The Dragon Yard

Guardian's Garrison

Queen's Bedchamber and Bath

Armory

Sorel's Office

Queen's Garden

Queen's Sitting Room

High Altar

Storage

Tower of The Seven Sisters

Postern

Hidden staircase exit to the woods

The Dragon Flower

Ileana's Room

Nursery

Great Hall and Throne Room

Naere's Room

Guest Room

Queen's Garden

Nall's Room

Foyer

Kitchen and Scullery

Guard Towers

To the lower levels

Fortress of the Serpent King
the
House of Aaradan

Boak Mines

Alabaster Wastes

Serabia

Tyne's Mine

Quern's Crossing

Head Knock Narrows

Auriconica

The Dreadwoods

Emyute
Campsite

Ga's
Valley

Stonetel

Shattered
Spine

Fungal Shroud

Elder's Lake

Feverous Forest

Sanguine
Sea

Dragonfire

Malaia's Scar

Mount
Shadowmaw

Nestlewood

Shattered
Spine

Corusca

Boat
Dock

The
Nest

Nigrous River

Obsidian
Fan

Ruins of SuVgo

The Sea Beyond Us

The Barrens

Ruins of Eolia

QUONDAM
(West)

The Sea Beyond Us

Boak Mines
Boak Mines
Saedan's Sands
Bipa's Mine

Ga's
Valley

• Luminora

Ip's
Valley

Emyute
Campsite

Emyute
Campsite

Adumbra •
Emyute
Campsite

Nimbus
Lake

Mochla's Freehold

Ud's Valley

• Merfolk Caverns

Elder's Cave •

Dragon's
Heart

Sanguine
Sea

Sepulcher of
the Sorceresses

• Beom's Freehold

Islander's •
Cabin

Emyute
Campsite

Emyute
Campsite

Emyute
Campsite

Volite
Village

Achroma •
Endhaven •

Rider's
Cross

Emyute
Campsite

Ri's Valley

Fount of
Sorrows

• Downwind

Kraek's
Slaughterhouse

QUONDAM
(East)

Dedication

In remembrance of Bettye Cummings.
A thousandfold memories of joy and laughter and the priceless gift of true friendship.
And
With love and gratitude to my husband Ken, for his tireless support and endless encouragement.

Synergy

Any work of fantasy is a union of magic and madness that includes golden grains of potent sorcery from those who are sometimes totally unaware that their enchantment has rubbed off on the author. My gratitude to these and all my friends for their encouragement and touches of thaumaturgy.

The city of Port Orford, Oregon, my home, for her beauty, tranquility, and people—truly a writer's paradise.

Gold Beach Books (the coffeehouse bookstore) in Gold Beach, Oregon, for the wonderful inspiration of the rare book room, a quiet table, and lots of café brevés.

The South Coast Writers Conference for the encouragement they provide all writers, and Southwestern Oregon Community College for their sponsorship of this annual event.

Josephine Ballantyne of Wordwing Editors, a true member of the Errant Comma Enclave. It is with tongue in cheek that I assure you any errors you may find belong to her.

Collaboration

Sean W. Anderson has collaborated with Ms. Gibson in the creation of two characters mentioned in *Quondam*. The characters Nall and Talin are based on role-play characters originally created by Mr. Anderson for online gaming.

Mr. Anderson lives with his family in southern California.

Table of Contents

Prologue: Dragonseed

The men's angry voices rose in a crescendo as their nervous mounts squealed and shied away, fearful of entering the deep gloom of the spirit woods.

"Leave him!" the captain shouted. "His wound is fatal. We need not risk the wrath of the wood nymphs on a dying poacher!" He jerked his horse around, spurred it sharply, and led the king's soldiers away at a gallop.

The wounded man cowered, shivering in the chill of the shadowy mist. He waited until the soldiers' cries and the sound of pounding hooves grew fainter. When silence embraced him once more, he struggled to his feet, slipped, staggered, and then fell to his knees on moss-slicked stones beside a stream. Clutching his bloodied side, the dying man fought to regain his footing. Swaying on unsteady legs, he attempted to find his balance and stumbled forward only to drop face down in the shallow water. Blood swirled in an increasing eddy that tainted the sacred pool beyond, releasing a sudden coppery odor that sent a pure white stag fleeing in a cloud of apprehensive snorted breaths and shrill calls of alarm.

Choking as he ingested water, and quivering with the growing chill brought about by loss of his physical life force, the man rolled onto his back and drew up his legs as a painful spasm of blood-strangled coughing overwhelmed him.

Tendrils of thickening mist swirled at the bank of the stream, the nebulous vapor gradually shifting from shapelessness to indistinct form as the glowing life within the deepening twilight grew and revealed the forest's twin sentinels, Flida and Karid.

Flida gripped Karid's formless fingers, drawing her sister back beneath the trees. "It is a Man!"

Karid, tugging against her sister's hold, replied, "Aye, near death. I can feel his fear." Again Karid pulled against Flida's fragile grip and broke away, the energy from her effort casting a sudden bright flare.

"Stay back, Karid! Do not touch him!" Flida exclaimed.

"Why? I have never seen a Man, and are we not charged with easing the terror of death's claim?"

"In fern or fawn, but not in Man! Never in Man. Only the ancestral gods may accept the life force of a human and free a soul. You know it is so! Come back! Come away, Karid!"

Karid gathered the mist around her, drawing it in to give her form more substance. Kneeling beside the fallen man, she whispered, "You are dying."

The poacher's eyes flew open as his startled gasp brought on another fit of strangulated coughing.

"Do not fear me. I am the wood nymph Karid, a sentinel of these woods. Your wound is mortal, you are dying," she told the man as she examined him with growing interest.

Karid's soft words earned the man's feeble nod. He raised a bloodied hand and reached out toward the pale spirit, his movement dispersing the hazy outline of her delicate form. "Help me...end my suffering. Accept my soul...please..." he begged.

"No! You must not," Flida warned. "Karid! It is forbidden to any but the gods. Only they have the power to judge a man's soul. You know it! Our realm is here within the wildwoods and does not include the flesh of men. Come away! Leave him!"

Karid shook her head, and a cascade of glittering particles showered the dying poacher in a waterfall of light. "He came to *us*! Should I abandon him in his final moments simply because he is a Man? That would not be very charitable. I want to share his thoughts and feel the passion of warm flesh as he struggles to cling to life," Karid said, eager with desire. "Then I will send him gently on his way. Surely the gods will forgive my curiosity in the presence of such compassion."

"Karid! Do you mock the gods?"

Karid ignored Flida and cupped the man's face in her hands. Her wistful eyes claimed his, and her lips dropped to meet his mouth as she drew into herself his dimming life force and struggling soul.

She drew away with a rapturous cry. "Oh, Flida, there is such ecstasy in Man's flesh! The rush of blood and fearful pounding of the heart! It is unlike anything I have ever felt!"

Karid's ethereal image then rose, paused, and convulsed. She began thrashing about as if captive to a seizure, poisoned by the touch of a human. Flida screamed and shrouded her sister's writhing and contorted form, trying to tear away the flesh that was quickly taking possession of Karid's spirit. "No!" she wailed.

A thunderous roar followed the flash of the dark god's arrival. "Nymph, you dare to steal from us?" The smoky voice sent coils of sooty darkness around Karid, hiding her from Flida's anxious gaze.

Discomforted by the flesh that now covered her form, Karid huddled into herself, arms clutching her newly formed knees. "I meant no harm. The man was dying. I only wished to save him from the pain and fear of death, to ease his passage, nothing more. He came to us, came into our woods, into the realm of our rule."

"Save him? When did the gods grant you the power to save the souls of men? You lie, spirit!" roared the dark god. "I can see the truth behind your actions. Your desire was not for this man's wellbeing but was driven by your jealousy and pride and by the belief that we would not feel the tremor of your trespass."

"Surely my curiosity will not be judged harshly!" Karid pleaded. "What harm can come from taking a single human soul when the gods have so many?"

"You defy the gods and ask what harm will come of it?" the dark one asked with a burst of laughter. "You have betrayed your sister and the spirit world you serve, broken the laws that bind you to risk a moment in the pleasure of the human's flesh. Now, flesh-bound you will wander the earth beyond these sacred woods, revered by none and reviled by many."

"Do not take my sister!" Flida implored, her fragile image ice blue, pulsing in fear and sorrow, and her crystal tears falling to blanket the moss beneath her feet in glistening snow. "A single nymph cannot protect the magick of these woods! Karid's act was not one of disrespect. She was just curious. Take back the human form! Let her stay with me!"

"Loyal Flida, what your sister did was not done out of kindness. By her action, Karid scorns the gods. Her fate now lies within the flesh she so desired. Your tears cannot stop what has begun," the god hissed, a slow smile shifting the shadows of his features, "but if you truly believe Karid's protestation of innocence, perhaps you are compassionate enough to join her in the realm of men?"

Flida stared at the loathsome flesh that now engulfed her sister. "Karid...I..." she whispered and turned away, "I cannot find you innocent."

"I thought not," the god replied, fading in a bell-like peal of satisfied laughter and lingering accusation. "Even your sister finds you guilty, Karid, and unworthy of her sympathy. Go now from this sacred place. Until the bounty of the gods is loosed, here you will no longer have power. Here you will no longer be welcome. Let the gods see how you fare among men."

Karid rose and held out hands now enfolded in fragile flesh. She raised them to touch her newly formed face and stroke the long golden hair that fell like silk across her heaving breasts. Karid's luminous emerald eyes watched her tormentor disappear and then shifted their gaze to Flida. "Sister, you will soon wish you had not forsaken me. I will not bow beneath this curse. I will rise among the flesh-bound and lead them against you for shunning me this day. I will bring war to you Flida, and men will curse your name!" She flexed her fingers and closed them to form angry fists. "There is strength in this blood and bone, which the god has bound to the magick of my spirit. I will learn to love this beating heart and the breath of these lungs. From behind this shield of flesh, I will rule men with the breath of dragons. I may not be revered, but I will be feared and obeyed." She spun around and raced away toward the realm of men, the moonlight gilding the halo of her hair and flashes of pale flesh.

Flida watched the first dead, argent leaf drift to the earth nearby. "What will you do, Karid? And how will I stop you?"

4

-⚜-

Malaia, blood heiress to the throne of Quondam, dove against the toppled giant, an enormous knotwood tree that had been ripped from its anchorage in the frenzy of mating dragons. She pressed her face into the leaf litter, trying to make her body as small as possible, and clamped her hands over her ears to muffle the thunderous bellowing that threatened to deafen her. The earth came alive, shifting and shaking beneath Malaia's body, trembling under the weight of the massive dragons as they wrestled and battered one another, tails lashing and wicked jaws snapping.

Another tree crashed to the ground and sent a new shudder reverberating through the soil beneath the terrified woman. Suddenly the sounds were much closer, within the very glen where Malaia hid. She whimpered, oblivious to the possibility of alerting the beasts to her presence. It would be impossible for them to hear the faint sounds of her distress above their own deep-throated growls and labored breathing.

When the wizard Aenzl had approached her with the idea of saving the dragon's magick within the king's man-born bloodline, Malaia had felt indebted to the old man. It was he who had offered sanctuary when no other would. Even those most loyal to the king's reign fled ahead of Queen Karid's armies, condemned by association, warranted for execution by command of the new ruler. Queen—the use of the title caused Malaia to gag—Karid. She shivered as the name assailed her senses with images of razed villages, the smell of scorched earth and burning flesh, and the sounds of men screaming. The story of the former sentinel's betrayal and subsequent banishment from the spirit wood had traveled from mouth to mouth in the kingdom. It was the beauty of Karid's human form that had drawn Malaia's brother, the king, into a deception that ended in his murder. The king's death left Malaia to be hunted as the last mortal heir to the throne of Quondam and Karid its self-appointed queen.

Karid's armies also hunted the magick flames of the few lingering dragons so that she alone would possess their power, and soon her armies would extinguish the dragons' magick forever. Only the fulfillment of Malaia's promise to the wizard could prevent this loss and save the wildwoods and the realm of men from Karid's cruelty.

5

The wizard swore that Malaia's forbidden union with the magickal beast would be blessed by Flida, sister of Karid and remaining sentinel of the dying wildwoods, and that the planting of the great dragon's seed within Malaia's fertile womb would provide a powerful future ruler—a rightful blood heir, strong enough to challenge Karid and reclaim Quondam's throne for men. A beast born of Man and magick, a dragonspawn allied with Flida against Karid's false rule, would have the power to stop the decay of the sacred wildwoods.

A sudden shadow nearby caused Malaia's thoughts to return to the dragons. She had imagined dragons' mating to be similar to that of a farmer's cattle, with the cow standing while the bull covered her, grunting in his effort to inject his seed. Nothing she had ever seen had prepared her for the reality of witnessing the dance of the dragons.

Talons locked, the dragons swiveled and whirled overhead. Their broad leathery wings outstretched in a balletic pirouette of titanic proportion, they danced to a symphony of thundering dragon song before breaking free and crashing in meteor-like strikes that cratered the earth and sent missiles of grass-bound soil ricocheting skyward.

Malaia raised her head and peered between tattered branches, hoping to see just how close the monsters had drifted. In the small meadow beyond her desperately inadequate tree fortress, the dragons continued to drive against one another, the wings of the male beating furiously as he lifted off the ground and attempted to settle behind the female. The snarling and snapping increased as they charged and butted one another with such tremendous force that more trees crashed about them and the ground was set aquiver. The larger dragon, the female, was neither docile nor willing. She fought against the slightly smaller male, ripping scales and leaving great gashes along his heaving sides, but the male was stronger, or at least had more energy, for now that the female tired, he gripped her roughly just under her wings and behind her forelegs and thrashed about trying to place his greatly engorged organ into the shadows beneath her tail.

A final roar shattered the air as the male hit his mark. The great female gave a long, low groan and released a fiery breath, scorching the grass of the glen. The male pumped feverishly before suddenly going rigid and bellowing out his conquest. With a downward sweep of his great wings, he lifted from the female, spilling a bit of his precious life-giving seed. In a final gesture of dominance, he snapped his great jaws and was gone, soaring away over the great woods and calling out his victory.

The female dragon squatted and released a hot stream of urine, marking her presence in the glen, before rising into the air to follow after her mate and disappear.

Scanning the area for Karid's soldiers, Malaia cautiously climbed out from her hiding place. Reassured that she was alone, she pulled the small vial that the ancient augurer had given her from beneath a dirt-smudged cloak, but her hands shook so badly that she dropped it twice before finally securing it firmly in her grasp. What had she been thinking? To make such a deal with the old soothsayer now seemed beyond comprehension. What would become of her once the dragon's seed was planted? What beast would be born of the forbidden blending? But then again, what if she failed the wizard? Would he withdraw his offer of protection? What chance for her then?

Still shaking with fear, she hurried to the site of the dragons' mating to search the ground for her prize. There on the crushed grass lay the dragon's spill, viscous and still steaming, carrying the magickal beast's foul odor. Malaia knelt and scraped the sticky white seed into the glowing vial, stoppering it with the gauzy black leaves the wizard had provided. She watched, stunned as the fragile gauze stiffened and formed a barrier within the vial, securing the dragon's milt until it could be delivered. Holding the clear flask to the light, Malaia shuddered at the movement of the dark seeds within the thick, milky liquid. It was a potential for life that would, by the skill of a sorceress's midwifery, a wizard's will, and the blessing of a woodland nymph, soon be united with a seed of her own.

Malaia wrapped the vial tightly within a soft cloth and slipped it inside her shirt, between her breasts where it would remain warm and viable. Then with a last furtive glance about her to make sure she remained unseen, she hurried away toward the road and the village of Dragonfire, where the sorceress C'thra and the wizard Aenzl waited.

It seemed to Malaia that an eon had passed. The seasons slowly turned around her, from hopeful spring through sun-kissed summer and on to brittle autumn. All the while her belly grew greater, and she felt the life within battering against the walls of its membranaceous cell until she believed the beast would not wait to be taken by the sorceress but simply burst out of its fleshy confines.

Eventually the time arrived, and she lay in the pastoral midwifery area within the sacred boundary of the standing stones, feeling the great stresses of her muscles as they attempted to expel the unwanted creature, the creation of the dragon's seed and an ovum from Malaia's fertile womb.

Her body was bound to the birthing chair, the arrival of her beastly child inevitable and just moments away. Malaia tossed her head back and forth as long wails of agony burst from her throat, her white-knuckled fingers clutching the edge of the seat on either side of her thin, naked hips. Her flesh was slick with the sweat of pain and terror and the dreadful fear of the creature she had conspired to create—the creature that caused ripples across her swollen belly under the magick touch of the sorceress.

Shadows drifted around the glen, always just beyond Malaia's field of vision. She could only see the sorceress C'thra, whose eyes shifted from the dark V between Malaia's trembling legs and pain-contorted face as she issued a midwife's sharp directions. Hot tears of regret ran from the corners of Malaia's eyes, filling her ears and muting the sounds around her.

"Push, Malaia! Push!" C'thra's harsh voice demanded.

The mother-to-be bore down. The pain between her legs grew dagger-sharp, and she gritted her teeth to strangle the scream that welled up from deep within her soul. Suddenly the pain grew so great that she could no longer contain her cry. Her lips drew back in a hideous grimace, and her shrill voice rent the air, blanketing the glen with her words of anguish. "Death, take me, and curse this newborn demon! Set me free of this beast! Death, free me of it! Oh sweet death, what have I done?" With the third calling of death's name, Malaia's words trailed into silence as the spawn of her sin slid from the warmth of her womb into the chill of the world.

C'thra glanced to her left, giving a subtle nod to the others, who waited expectantly. No sound broke the stillness save the mother's soft weeping. Such were the exhaustion and fear that claimed her that she did not see her death approach. A gossamer veil of deepening darkness covered Malaia, stealing the breath of life and ending her days.

Aenzl, the aged wizard, drew forward. "Karid, go from here! Here you have no right to be! You are nothing more than the desperate distortion of a woman, not worthy of either gods or men. Your place is in the killing fields. It is there you will find the countless souls you must feed upon in order to renew your cursed flesh. You have no power over those within these sacred woods."

"Such cruel words uttered against a nymph and a lady!" Karid said as she stepped into the light. "I would expect a gentler greeting from a wizard of the mist. Have we not long shared this world in peace? Have I not made way for new life by the taking of the old? Can you truly fault me for twisting a curse into a blessing, Aenzl? Are you faulting me because I have learned to love the warm flesh of Man?"

"You, Karid, are no longer nymph—your betrayal makes it so—and you are certainly no lady. You dare to call your violent rule peace? No matter the splendor of your physical form, you are nothing but false flesh that fools no one except the humans you corrupt to do your bidding," the wizard scoffed. "You spoil everything you touch, and it is you who moved among men, deceiving the lawful king with false beauty before slaying him and stealing his crown. It is your desire to live in the flesh that has allowed the human blight to spread across our sacred lands, to claim the world and scar it all, leaving us naught but this small patch of dying woods. You are as false as a whore's cry of pleasure."

"One cannot rule Man with weakness. It requires a fist of fire. I rule Quondam. All save this bit of the Feverous Forest you call home, and soon enough I shall snatch even this from Flida's tenuous hold. My sister cannot save the forest alone, and she does not have the power or skill to call forth an ally. She is weakened by my absence, even as I am strengthened by Man's flesh. So too are you doomed, old man, as are all those who still believe that the magick of our ancestors will rise to save them. There is no magick. There is only the power of Man. And I control Man. Only a few black Noor who served the king continue to resist, and soon enough they will succumb to my promise of protection or die without it. Frankly, I do not care which they choose."

9

With an angry shake of his head, Aenzl swept around Karid and paused beside C'thra to place a pale, gnarled old hand on the head of the newborn. The wizard commanded, "Sever the bond."

The sorceress cut the binding cord, releasing the pale child from the attachment to its dead mother. C'thra lifted a white-hot iron from the glowing coals and touched it to the severed end of the still bleeding umbilical lifeline, causing the fleshy blue-purple cord to sizzle and the blackening blood to boil away. With soft cloths she wiped away the mucous of birth and stroked the softness of the infant's downy head. She whispered to those waiting to hear her words, "The perfect image of a human and not like a dragon. This babe is as perfect as I have ever seen—a flawless vessel to contain the final fragment of Quondam's sacred magick."

Karid stirred, her shadow looming across the glen. Settling near C'thra's side, the queen hissed in a voice as cold as glacial ice, "*This* is the challenger my sister sends? *This* is your hope for a future king to save mankind and the spirits of the wildwoods?" Karid spat her disdain. "And you dare call my embrace of the flesh a betrayal? My sister has betrayed you all!"

At the sound of Karid's voice, the child's eyes opened, locking on those of the woman who would hold his fate, and within his mind the echo of a small dragon's roar was heard.

Karid's form swirled away, trailing bitter laughter as her ghostly gray sleeve rippled in an expansive gesture. "His own mother summoned me to take her life and curse him, and so, as is my right, a curse I offer—that Man shall judge this child a beast, brand him, and exile him to a rock where his own blood will bind him. His very name will be forgotten, forbidden even as memory! I shall let you keep your dragonspawn for he is rooted in neither the realm of Man nor magick, and unless he is, he will never rule."

"Beware of pride, *lady* Karid, and of where your love of flesh and blood may lead!" Aenzl shouted.

There was a soft shuffling as the shadowy figure fled, leaving a chill, angry challenge in her wake. "A curse upon you all! Let the dragonspawn stop me if he can, wizard!"

"Beware your pride…" the wizard once again warned as Karid disappeared.

"My sister has grown harsh and bitter within the flesh." From deep within the gloom came a dancing light. In a shimmer as pale as silvery moonlight, the nymph Flida made her way forward and took the babe from C'thra's arms. Her eyes grew damp, and a single tear fell upon the child's brow. "It is fey fair you are, my little one, and with my tear I will temper my sister's curse. While I cannot dispel it completely, I can balance it with my blessing. For no more than ten generations will Karid's curse bind you upon a prison rock, and no dominion will she ever have over you lest you speak her name thrice.

"I will send a woman traveler, one born beneath the sign of serpent and dragon, a stranger to Quondam's shores. This woman will embrace you and set you free by the speaking of your forbidden name. Together you will go forth as legend to uncover the power within a tomb and free the bounty of the gods. Only then may you rise to challenge Karid and take from her the curse of flesh. From there you will be free to choose your own path within the realm of Man or magick."

Shaking the particles of light from her hair, Flida lifted the likeness of a hand, and her golden voice charged C'thra and Aenzl with the child's care and keeping. "Until death, I charge you, C'thra, with my legend's care. With no mother, he will know naught of himself, and so I entrust you with his nurturing and truth. Share my words and my promise, wrap him in your wisdom, and call him son.

"Aenzl, hard will be your service, for when Karid's men come to judge the dragonspawn 'twill be you who must sacrifice your freedom to see him safe. Bind yourself to him, and become his steward and teacher, his keeper and friend."

Flida gathered up the infant's tiny hand and brought it to her lips, her whispered kiss stirring wisps of red-gold hair about his fair and cherubic face. "You are the hope of our tomorrows. You will be a legend to those accursed by Karid, the redeemer of magick, and a king among men.

"I leave you now with these final warnings. Take heed of the depth of Karid's anger and her desire to keep the form of flesh, for she has betrayed the sacred trust of the gods again and again in order to keep its pleasures and its power. But no such life can be given Karid without the gravest sacrifice of others, and what my sister does in the name of Man is not of Man at all.

"Guard well this child when at last he ventures beyond the rock of Karid's promised prison. There will be many who would lead him astray."

Flida returned the child to C'thra's waiting arms, the luminosity of her presence fading with her final words, "My blessings upon you all."

As the dragon child grew, the world of men became warped and twisted, shattered in the self-destruction of the two warring factions—those whose fear-driven loyalty was to Queen Karid, and those who were devoted to Flida and the ancestral gods.

Karid's curse burst upon the dragonspawn in the first year of his manhood. Beneath the false queen's merciless gaze, a panel of judges declared the young man a beast born of a forbidden union and guilty of murdering the queen's prime elder. They branded him and sentenced him to a rocky prison, bound by the blood of his signature. His name was proclaimed demonic and forbidden even to the memories of men. For ten generations, the child born of the union between woman and dragon bore his punishment in silence, but that which was done to him in the name of Man was not of Man at all. It was of Queen Karid.

Chapter 1: Assassination

In a world not her own, and in the guise of another, Karid's fiery handmaiden slipped along the side wall of the tavern, pressing herself back into its deep shadow as sudden laughter erupted just inside the adjacent open doorway. Another burst of merriment brought a vision of her target swimming into focus. The air shimmered as her body temperature rose in preparation for the assigned task.

No survivors. The blood of the serpent must boil. No descendant of the House of Aaradan may be allowed to reach Quondam. Flida's promise of the dragonspawn's legend must never be fulfilled!

The woman nodded at her mistress's silent reminder. Invoking a veil of invisibility, she stepped into the crowded tavern, where the king of Ædracmoræ and his soldiers were celebrating their victory. She positioned herself near the center of the room, close behind the king.

"Sōrél of the House of Aaradan," she snarled, releasing the veil.

The king spun around.

Indigo...?

But caught in the first fatal flash of deadly heat, his silent disbelief was swept away. The flames raced outward from their source, swallowing him instantly in their fiery anger, the blistered flesh and scorched bone of Sōrél, king of Ædracmoræ, lost within the inferno.

The wall of fire rolled outward, engulfing those seated around Sōrél's table and beyond. Before they had risen to their feet, their lungs were seared and their clothing and hair were set aflame. The writhing men were literally roasted as the stomach-churning odor of smoke from their oiled flesh billowed its way through the burning thatch and up into the night sky.

Again the woman's heat intensified, destroying even the great timbers, cracking the hearthstone, and reducing the living to bubbling blood and baked bone waste. The tortured screams of burning men echoed off the steaming stones, drowning out the crackling sizzle of frying flesh.

Amidst a rattle of dorsal scales, the assassin stepped over what remained of the tavern's smoldering wall, her white-hot skin cooling to its unnatural deep blue and purple tones.

With a nod of her head, she addressed her waiting mistress, "Milady Karid, it is done. There is no longer a threat of the Aaradan seed being spread. Sōrél of Aaradan, bearer of the serpent's blood, and all those in his company are dead, returned as ash to the land of their birth."

The assassin's smile revealed sharp white teeth, the tip of her blue cleft tongue darting out to scout the air for threats before leaping through the glimmering mirror behind her mistress.

From the gloom of the nearby stable, Horsfal, the tavern's owner, watched the shadowy figures escape and the mirror fade away after them. Allowing his hands to drop, he gave voice to his stifled screams and fell to his knees, praying for the Ancients to protect him.

Yávië, queen of Ædracmoræ, upon hearing of her husband's success, celebrated this joyous news with the members of her court. The last of the death dragons had been slain, and Lohgaen of Lochlaen, ruler of Ædracmoræ's embittered third house, had been captured and imprisoned for crimes against the crown. King Sōrél and those with him were due back by star rise. Unavoidable affairs of state had kept Queen Yávië from accompanying Sōrél, but they had been cleared, and she was anticipating her husband's joyous return. Victorious friends and family of the crown would soon be safe within the walls of the fortress of the Serpent King, the House of Aaradan.

Eyes bright, cheeks flushed with laughter, Queen Yávië stood, chalice in hand, ready to offer praise to her valiant king, her husband. Without warning, darkness gripped her mind, followed by an image of her beloved, smiling Sōrél suddenly met by a wall of blue-white flame. A woman of fire, a Maraen, stood beyond the shimmering blaze. Vision blurring with horror and disbelief, Yávië heard Sōrél's unanswered question, *Indigo…?* Unconsciousness claimed her, and she fell, sending the blood red wine of her joy washing across the glistening white silk of the table covering.

"Mother!" Princess Sóvië leapt to her feet and dropped to the floor beside the queen, brushing Yávië's hair from her pale, damp brow before looking up into worried faces.

"She is chilled with sweat."

The sorceress Näeré knelt beside her niece and lifted the hand of her sister-in-law, Queen Yávië, gasping as she released it, and drew away in horror.

"My brother," Näeré choked. "Sōrél is dead." She turned, weeping into the arms of Nall, the guardian, a wordless wail of loss escaping her trembling lips.

"My father is dead?" Sóvië's strangled question jolted Näeré from her own grief and the guardian's embrace to turn to her young niece, casting a spell of deep sleep over Sóvië even as she urged the guardian to carry the girl to her chambers.

Grumbleton! Nall's sharp, silent word summoned the court's wizard healer.

Queen Yávië awoke beneath the warmth of heavy coverlets, her mind still foggy from the lingering effects of her wizard's spell. Sudden memory shattered the momentary calm. Her breath caught, and scalding tears streamed down pallid cheeks.

"Yávië…" the guardian Nall's deep baritone resounded through the silence of the stone bedchamber.

The queen turned her sorrowful gaze in Nall's direction. Her eyes were red, and her face was swollen from weeping. A shuddering inhalation sent her body into spasm. She gripped the guardian's extended hand, crushing it painfully between her own.

"Sōrél is dead," she cried, "murdered by the Maraen woman, Indigo. I heard him speak her name with his dying thought. Speak it—even as she burned him. I heard his silent accusation."

Sobs wracked Yávië's body as she fell back against the pillows.

"Sōrél is gone, Nall. He is gone. Lost to me beyond restoration, lost…" her words faded as the depth of her loss left her bereft of words.

She looked away from her trusted friend, gathering a fragile fiber of strength and squeezing the tears away behind closed eyes.

"The others? Those with Sōrél?" she asked, turning back to meet Nall's red-rimmed eyes.

Again Yávië glanced away, drawing in another deep, empowering breath, unshed tears glinting on her lashes as she blinked them away, but Nall's mournful silence was more eloquent than any words he could have uttered.

"How many died?"

"We will find those responsible, Yávië. I swear it to you. We will begin the search as soon as the funerals—"

"How many?" the queen repeated.

"Your guardians and Cwen's friends—Talin, Klaed, and the Feie wizard, Brengven—were all with Sōrél. Twenty-six in all."

The queen's clear gaze met his. "And Sóvië and Näeré?"

"Your daughter sleeps beneath the wizard Grumbleton's healing spells. Näeré paces and waits for your waking. She has no thoughts beyond revenge against her brother's killers."

"Have you told Cwen? Sent word that her uncle and friends are dead?"

"I sent a messenger. Cwen is at the cloister. It has been nearly five summers since last she saw any of us. I do not know how she will react, but I thought the courtesy of notifying…" Nall's words trailed away as he imagined his daughter's anger.

Yávië's eyes softened as she thought of her niece. Cwen was an undisciplined, willful girl, intolerant of loyalty and love, scarred by the betrayal of wicked men and hardened by the recent death of a lover. She was a girl who, on the one hand, disavowed allegiance to the crown and its demands, yet on the other, was bound to the crown by her Aaradan blood. A dangerous young woman, trained as a guardian, but not restricted by that station's pledge of restraint. A girl very much like Queen Yávië had been in her youth.

"Your daughter will react unreasonably, Nall, in the way she always reacts. Coming so close on the heels of the wound left by her recent loss of Caen, Cwen will forget in an instant the time and distance that has separated her from her friends. Her hurt will be great, and she will blame me for allowing them to accompany Sōrél. She will blame Näeré and you, and even Sōrél. She will snarl and turn against us before weeping for our dead and storming off to single-handedly avenge us all." Yávië sighed, a faint smile touching the corners of her lips, and she reached out to stroke Nall's cheek. "Cwen will bring the fury of her warrior's heart to us, even as we honor our dead."

Yávië slipped from the bed as the sad, softly soughing sound of silk against silk echoed her despondency. "Let us prepare to pay tribute to our lost ones. And then we will find and punish those who have dared to attack the House of Aaradan."

With a curt nod, the guardian Nall turned on his heel, leaving his queen to her grief and memories of her beloved husband, Sōrél.

Cwen of Aaradan, daughter of the guardian Nall and the sorceress Näeré, and niece to Queen Yávië, knelt in the center of the heavily misted glen, head bowed, eyes closed, and lips moving in wordless entreaty as she called on the power of the Ancients to guide her in her search for retribution. Thoughts of vengeance brought the image of Caen's face and a flood of memories—the often teasing wink above his smile, his strength, the passion of his kiss, and the warmth of his hands against her skin. He was gone now, ripped away at the hands of Lohgaen of Lochlaen in an abortive attempt to end Cwen's life. But she had not died, and she swore that revenge would be hers. Lohgaen was imprisoned, but Cwen did not intend to wait for the crown to execute him. That would be her pleasure.

Her thoughts shifted to her recent dreams—fog-filled dreams of a hooded man. It was always the same. From the mist of her dreams he strode, backlit by a dying fire, to stand before her and reveal his face, a face that had become as familiar as her own. Who was he? She prayed the fates would one day reveal him to her.

The thunder of an approaching rider dispelled the visions and brought Cwen to her feet, sword drawn to meet the possible threat. Not many were brave enough to challenge an acolyte of Belasis, but occasionally a group of foolish poachers or a thief wandered onto the grounds of the cloister in the belief that the group of women would be easy prey.

The rider leapt to the ground as a heavy warhorse skidded to a stop before the scarlet-robed woman. The beast was winded, chest lathered with sweaty foam and heaving heavily in an attempt to pull breath into its lungs. At the sight of Cwen's sword, the man dropped to his knees, head bowed in submission. "Prophetess, I bear a message from the crown."

"I am not a prophetess, merely an acolyte. I shall lead you to Belasis to speak to a prophetess if that is your need." Cwen said, sheathing her sword.

"Are you not Cwen of Aaradan, daughter of the guardian Nall and the sorceress Näeré of Aaradan? Are you not the niece of the crown?"

"Aye, I am."

"The message is for you, for Cwen of Aaradan. I was told at the cloister that you could be found here."

A sudden feeling of unease brought Cwen's hand back to the hilt of the sword, and her tone took on a sharper edge. "What is this communication you bring me, messenger? The last message I received from the crown was of death."

"Your father summons you to the fortress of the House of Aaradan. Two suns past, your uncle was murdered along with twenty-six others in Horsfal's tavern. The queen awaits your arrival, since several of the dead are your friends."

"And the names of these friends of mine?"

"Talin, the nephew of Lord Galen, Councilor Klaed of Drevanmar, and one called Brengven the Feie."

With sudden, irrational fury against this messenger, she sent him reeling with the back of her hand and sliding face forward with the impact of her boot upon his backside.

"You are fortunate I do not cut out your tongue!" Cwen shouted, leaping to the saddle, gathering the reins, and spinning the messenger's startled horse about. "You can collect your mount at the fortress!"

The messenger stood and tested his aching jaw before addressing the circle of scarlet-clad women who had been drawn by the commotion.

"I do not believe this acolyte will be returning to take her vows," he said.

Nall raced to intercept Cwen as she hurled herself from the back of the trembling horse. He held out his arms and smiled, for nothing was more important than greeting his long absent daughter.

Cwen charged forward and slammed into his chest with the balled fists to send him staggering back.

"She allowed Talin and Klaed to go into battle? Sōrél took Brengven into battle against Lohgaen of Lochlaen?" she accused.

Nall gripped her wrist. "No, Yávië and Sōrél allowed them nothing. They went in hopes of bringing Lohgaen into custody without bloodshed. It was their choice, Cwen, not the crown's order."

Cwen pried her father's fingers from her arm, throwing her hands in the air to warn off his further touch.

"They were not prepared for such a fight. They are not guardians, Nall. Talin is—was—competent with the axe, but he was no warrior. Klaed was a nobleman, a councilor, and Brengven feared his own shadow. How could she place them in such peril? How? And Lohgaen of Lochlaen, why does Yávië not hang him and be done with it? Why is he allowed his life? If I had done half of what he is accused of she would not hesitate to hang me! He killed Caen, Nall. My Caen—I will no longer wait for justice. I will make my own."

"Cwen," Nall interrupted. "Yávië and your mother have lost a husband and a brother. Ædracmoræ has lost its king. Talin was like a son to us, Klaed and Brengven shared our table. Lohgaen will be dealt with. Can you not see past your own grief and anger to share ours?"

His daughter lifted her chin and her cheeks flushed, as she recognized her impropriety.

"We shall settle this when the dead have been honored and their souls set free. I will stay in the garrison until then."

Cwen shouldered past Nall, leaving him staring after her, mumbling with despair, "She is the spawn of the abyss, and I am the demon keeper."

Swinging back, she called to her father, "And the tavern owner, Horsfal? Was he among the dead?"

"Nay, Cwen, he was spared."

Cwen's eyes narrowed. "You do not find that suspicious? A bit convenient?"

"He has been questioned. Your suspicions are unfounded. Horsfal was in the stable bedding down horses when the assassin came, and he has always been your friend. He thinks of you as his own blood."

"You know who killed them then?"

"We are not certain."

"You are lying, Nall. I see the moisture beading your brow. What is it you do not want me to know? Or do you merely find yourself gagged by the queen?"

"His silence is not by my order," Yávië's voice rang out at Cwen's shoulder. "Your father simply seeks to spare you a future of horrifying memories."

Cwen looked from Yávië to Nall and back again. "Tell me."

"Sōrél's last word was 'Indigo,'" Yávië whispered as she relived the flooding memory of fire.

"Indigo? There is no reason a Maraen woman would attack us— Sōrél must have been mistaken. It must have been some of Lohgaen's vicious supporters."

"We do know that Sōrél's last thought was 'Indigo.' I heard it clearly within my mind," Yávië answered with unbearable sadness.

Ignoring her aunt's reasoning, Cwen demanded, "I want to see the bodies."

Fearing that Cwen's fierce anger would only be augmented by the sight of the charred remains, Yávië replied, "You do not need to see."

Cwen rolled her neck to ease her tension, and her eyes slid to meet her father's before locking on the queen's. "I have lost Caen to Lohgaen of Lochlaen's hatred of the House of Aaradan, and now you tell me that you believe Uncle Sōrél, Talin, Klaed, and Brengven are lost to the Maraen women of fire. It is as if we are being exterminated!

"But, as Nall has reminded me, you have lost a husband, my mother has lost her brother, and the world has lost its king. I will see them, I will honor them, I will pay my final respects, and then I will go to Horsfal and find those responsible for their deaths."

Queen Yávië lifted a hand and gestured toward the fortress, following Nall and Cwen down the steps and into the long silent corridor toward the hall that housed the dead.

As she approached the bodies, Cwen's posture stiffened, her fists clenched, and her nails bit deeply into her palms. Taking a deep breath, she flung the covering back and stared at the twisted black cadaver, no larger than the body of a child. It was all that remained of Brengven the Feie. Along his spine, remnants of his leather satchel had curled and fused with flesh and bone. The horror and stench of the burned body left Cwen choking for fresh air.

Beside her Nall flipped back the sheet covering Klaed of Drevanmar, stepping quickly away to turn back the next sheet and expose the body of Talin. Both men had been Cwen's friends since childhood.

"Have you seen enough?" Nall asked.

"I would see Sōrél." Cwen's teeth caught her lower lip in a death grip, drawing blood as Yávië drew back the cover to expose the king's charred skeleton.

"He was struck first, by the full force of the Maraen woman's fury." Yávië's trembling fingertips stroked the skeletal ridges above the eye sockets that had held her husband's startling sapphire eyes. Now they held only ash. She turned her hand and stared at the cinders coating her fingers before raising them to draw the lines of sorrow across her ivory brow.

Cwen returned to stand beside Talin's body, staring at the ash-dusted skull as she tried to recall his face. "Too long were we parted, my friend. And now you are no more. I will avenge your death, find those responsible, and by my own hand steal the last breath from their lungs. I swear it to you, Talin. I swear it." As Yávië had done, Cwen lifted a sooty remnant of life and marked herself in mourning.

Nall took Cwen's arm and led her from the overpowering smell of death into the fading light of a chilly autumnal evening. "At least see your mother before you leave."

Cwen held up her hand to wave away Nall's words. "You soothe her. She will know no real peace until I have found those responsible for Sōrél's death and ended their lives. The search cannot wait. I will go to Horsfal's and find the one who did this."

"Cwen, we will find those who did this. It is the business of the guardians of the crown. Your search will only bring us into conflict," Nall entreated.

She shook her head and backed away, bringing her fingers to her mouth and emitting a single long, shrill whistle that summoned a snow-white, horse-like equus of Aaradan. "Already we are in conflict. This conflict began the day you and your queen sent Talin, Klaed, and Brengven into a battle that was not theirs to fight—when you forgot that they were not guardians in your garrison and failed to protect them. Follow her; follow your queen. I will follow the path of the assassin until it leads to the one who holds her leash. I do not believe it was a Maraen, certainly not Indigo. Sōrél must have been mistaken. I will return before Yávië lights the funeral biers."

Cwen swung about and leapt to the back of the snowy equus, gripping its mane and urging it forward, away from the House of Aaradan and on to the misted road that would lead her to Horsfal's tavern.

Chapter 2: Pursuit

Cwen flung herself from the equus and launched herself at Horsfal, her vision blurred from scalding tears. She plunged into a mountain of flesh, fists flying, sinking deep into the living tissue with incoherent obscenities and wild muffled screams before collapsing against the great man's belly.

Massive arms crushed her deeper into mounds of heaving flesh as Horsfal, though in considerable pain from her lashes, gripped Cwen to him, allowing her to release her crippling grief. As unintelligible cries became mumbled words, Horsfal pushed Cwen back and wiped her streaming nose with a large fleshy thumb and forefinger.

"I saw them, Horsfal! Saw their charred, stinking remains. Yávië says the Maraen slaver Indigo killed them. Why? Why would she hunt members of the House of Aaradan when they have never done harm to her or her people? We may have annoyed her by searching her tavern in the past, but the Maraen women have always controlled the fire of their bodies, and it would take far more than the occasional search for smuggled goods to bring on such an attack. The Maraen do not kill indiscriminately with their heat."

"I am not at all certain it was Indigo or even a Maraen," Horsfal admitted. "There was an odd shifting of the image as though the assassin was under a spell of transformation. And the assassin was not alone. There was another, Cwen. It was a woman's form, cloaked and hooded beyond my recognition. They fled through a mirror unlike any I have ever seen. A mirror that was summoned and then vanished after the assassins passed."

Cwen rubbed her eyes with her fists in an attempt to stop the flood of tears, and then pressed her fingertips against her aching temples as she tried to clear the images of death from her mind. "Who would dare to challenge the crown now that Lohgaen of Lochlaen is imprisoned? What race other than the Maraen has such power over fire? Who would have the power to control a Maraen?" She blinked away fresh tears and stared up at the tavern owner's guilt-ravaged face.

"I wish I had an answer for you. I wish I could have done something…I am not a brave man, Cwen," Horsfal answered.

Cwen reached up and touched the drooping jowls, "No, Fal, you are not, but—" Her words were cut short by a wind that whipped the air before subsiding into pellucid, rippling waters that calmed to reveal a linking mirror. From its center flowed a woman of fire who sent waves of ever-intensifying heat toward Horsfal and Cwen.

"Cwen of Aaradan, born beneath the sign of the serpent," the assassin hissed in recognition.

Horsfal threw his bulk between Cwen and the sudden brilliant flash of superheated air. He grabbed her by an arm and tossed her away as if she were no more than an offending piece of lint. Cwen landed hard on the far side of the remaining stone wall, rolling to a stop against the burned out tavern. Horsfal's screams and the sweet, acrid smell of burning flesh struck Cwen, and a rush of blue-white flame roared overhead, licking the air and singeing the tips of her flyaway hair as she pressed her face into the ash-covered earth. She leapt to her feet, called for the startled equus, and grabbed a handful of mane to pull herself up as the frightened animal pounded past. Crouching low over its withers, she urged the equus forward, away from the suffocating heat and Horsfal's agonizingly inhuman howls. Her face pale beneath its tear-stained layer of ash, Cwen desperately urged her terrified mount back toward the fortress of the queen.

Yávië gazed across the field of funeral biers at the soldiers awaiting her signal to toss the torches to set the dry wood ablaze, thus freeing the trapped souls to take their places amid the stars. King Sōrél, a man tormented by his past and Yávië's love since girlhood, was now gone beyond reclamation.

She raised her hands and gave the command, singing the ancient words that would send men's souls aloft.

Beside Yávië stood her daughter, Sóvië, and the wizard Grumbleton, their expressions grim with the task of burying a father and a king. When the bones cooled, it was their responsibility to sift the ashes and carry Sōrél's remains to the vault of Aaradan, leaving the king to rest eternally beside his ancestors. They were surrounded by the assembled guardians of the crown, mounted on dragons and pledged to serve and protect the king and queen of Ædracmoræ. Upon completion of their funereal duties, the guardians would hunt those responsible for the deaths, never resting until the murderers had been brought to justice.

As Yávië lifted a hand to brush away an errant tear, the shrill whinny of a frightened equus caused her to spin around. The flying copper hair told her it was Cwen returning from Horsfal's tavern.

"Run!" Cwen leapt from her mount and raced headlong toward the queen, causing guardians to draw weapons and dragons to shift uneasily. Reaching Yávië, Cwen crashed against her, grabbed the queen's wrist, and half-dragged her across the field away from the funeral blaze. "Stand up and run! Run, damn you to the abyss! The assassin comes! She has burned Horsfal. She spoke my name and the sign of my birthright! It is as if they seek to eliminate the entire House of Aaradan! Now run, damn you, Yávië! Sōrél's spirit will haunt me all the days of my life if I let them burn you."

The air crackled with the heat and strange fire that billowed after them, its temperature scorching, boiling, and baking the flesh of those behind.

"Näeré of Aaradan, mother of the one born beneath the sign of the serpent!"

The shouted words chilled Cwen. She pushed Yávië ahead and swung to look over her shoulder.

"Mother!" Her cry went unanswered, and she saw only the wall of flame that raced toward her as if it were alive. Fearsome noises issued from behind the towering inferno, screams of tortured men and dragons drowned within the rising volume of the deadly blaze.

No identifiable bodies could be seen through the dense, oily smoke, but the smell of death hung close.

"Sóvië!" Yávië's sudden shriek jerked Cwen from thoughts of her mother. Through a sudden clearing in the smoke, she saw her cousin Sóvië and the old wizard Grumbleton stumble and fall before a new veil of smoke surged across the meadow and enveloped them in its darkness.

The whoosh and crackle of a new threat spun them back toward the fortress. Eerie light flickered beyond it, and long fingers of dancing flame rushed up the portcullis, twisting and melting the iron hinges, cracking and blackening the surrounding stone. Above, the ancient icon of the dragon entangled amid the serpent's coils, the symbol of Sōrél and Yávië's joined houses, was engulfed in the blaze and would soon be destroyed.

A white-hot woman emerged from the failing fortress. Ablaze with the writhing flames of inescapable heat, she swept out her hands, setting the field on either side of her prey afire.

"Indigo?" Yávië's hoarse, uncertain cry once again spurred Cwen to action. She grabbed Yávië and yanked her back the way they had come, but the field now held only burning corpses and collapsing funeral pyres. There was no escape; the fiery death of the assassin's fury was all around them.

Yávië sank to her knees, tears of defeat spilling down her cheeks. "Leave me so that I may join Sōrél and Sóvië!"

"The abyss I will!" Cwen bellowed. "Cast a quenching spell. Call the rivers to defend us! You are the queen of Ædracmoræ, Yávië. Do something!"

Yávië shook her head, "Without Sōrél and Sóvië, I have no passion for the fight. Do you not understand, Cwen? They are dead—everyone is dead! Without them I am nothing."

"Look at me! I am not dead! I stand here, most likely the last blood of the House of Aaradan, and what I understand is that you intend to let me be roasted alive by some whore bitch pretending to be Indigo! Get up! Damn you, Yávië, get—"

Beneath them the earth trembled and rivulets of silver swirled. A shimmering surface reflected their images for an instant before their bodies slipped through the mirror into darkness.

❦

The women clung to one another, vision blurred and eyes still stinging, their flesh reddened and blistered from the assassin's heat, as their lungs gulped in the suddenly sweet, smoke-free air.

Cwen released her steadying grip on Yávië and examined the moonless nightscape. The pungent odor of ripe vegetation sprang from the disturbed soil, and the rich, peppery scent of willows mingled with water wafted over them from beyond the hillocks silhouetted in the distance.

"Are we somewhere below the Northern Mountains, perhaps?" Yávië whispered.

Cwen frowned and shook her head, starlight dancing on her copper hair. "The moons should be high and full, Yávië, but they are beyond our sight."

"Within a mountain valley then…?"

Again Cwen disagreed. "Water and willows are lowland signs."

Her youthful eyes adjusting quickly to the darkness, Cwen brushed past Yávië and said, "Wait here." She scrambled up the nearest rock-littered slope and stood staring across an unfamiliar landscape. Fields of dry, withered grain swept across a wide valley. In the distance a great, glistening walled city rose from the darkness, and beyond the city an endless expanse of glassy sea mirrored a moonless, star-filled sky.

Cwen blinked, hoping to clear away the seeming mirage, but it remained solid and unwavering in the crisp, clean air. A chill lifted the flesh of her exposed skin and sent her sliding downhill to rejoin her aunt.

"It is not Ædracmoræ."

Yávië rose from her seat on a stone and looked up the hill and back to Cwen. "How can this be? Show me."

Together they returned to gaze across the dying farmlands to the unknown city by the sea.

"We should find a place to rest." Yávië slid her hand around Cwen's, drawing her back.

"Rest?" Cwen asked, jerking her hand free. "We find ourselves in a strange land after nearly being roasted alive, and you want to sleep?"

"Cwen—"

27

"No! I am going to that city. I am going to find out how we got here and how to go home. Then I am going to find out who sent that murdering Maraen or whatever it was. You can sleep if you like, but I have no time for it!"

"You are young and brash and foolish!" Yávië exclaimed. "You will most likely draw death to us before night's end. We are exhausted by our wounds and grief and in need of replenishing our strength, and *that* requires sleep. Home is gone, Cwen, fallen beneath the assassin's conflagration, or have you so soon forgotten the stench of burning flesh and the screams of our family and friends?"

Cwen recoiled as if she had been struck, then swung about and headed toward the far off city.

Yávië stood frozen for a moment in the grip of angst and sorrow, as she watched her niece walk away, before turning to follow the scent of the willows. The gurgling of water breaking over stones drew her forward, and long tendrils of welcoming willow caressed her as she stooped beneath their protective canopy.

Sliding to the ground within a nest of tangled roots, the queen of Ædracmoræ hugged herself and wept—broken, alone, and unarmed.

Cwen quickly became lost amidst the rustling whispers of parched, feather-tipped grain stalks, crossing and recrossing her own narrow, wending path. Angry tears welled, and a stream of loud, foul curses spilled from her pouting lips, "Stupid bitch! Damn bit of dragon scat! Whoremongering witch!"

A sudden noise like the sound of scales on dry grasses stopped her tirade and instantly turned her to stone-like stillness. Ears tuned for the next intrusion, Cwen drew her sword stealthily from over her shoulder and swung around to meet the threat. Shocked disbelief at the creatures before her kept her from sensing the first blow from behind.

Chapter 3: Quondam

Cwen woke from her dream of the hooded man with a pounding headache and the coppery taste of blood in her mouth. She tried to rise, crying out at the blinding pain and gut-wrenching nausea that threatened to overwhelm her. Without lifting her head, she took quick, shallow breaths, swallowed the bitter taste of bile, and opened her eyes to find feet—gray, three-toed, and filthy—standing inches from her face.

"Stryvers," explained a cool feminine voice.

Cwen rolled her eyes in an attempt to view the speaker, but whoever it was stood behind her, out of range.

"They are stryvers—I believe you would call them 'slaves' in your language. Have you come alone?"

Cwen remained silent.

"Are there others? It is not safe for foreigners to wander alone beyond the city walls. It is a wasteland filled with Queen Karid's warring tribes, and our control of the stryvers loses potency outside the walls. Sometimes they revert to more barbaric behaviors when left to themselves. Did you come alone?"

With great effort, and without lifting herself from the ground, Cwen forced her body backward and stared up at her inquisitor. The woman was as ripe as a young goddess and tall, easily eight spans. Beautiful, curvaceous, and perfectly proportioned, her exposed arms and thighs were well muscled, and her flawless skin was deep golden brown with a patina that resembled the richly burnished dark oak of Yávië's finest furniture. Her eyes were startlingly pale, the blue of a fair-haired child, and while the sides of her head were hairless, a mane of thick black hair ran from high at the center of her brow to the base of her spine. Gleaming gold tattoos covered the left side of her bare, silken scalp.

"I asked if you have come alone. The longer you delay your answer, the more danger to any companions."

"Who are you?" Cwen croaked.

The woman's lips curved in a smile, revealing perfect teeth. "I am a Noor. Have you come alone?"

"No, not alone. The queen of Ædracmoræ—my aunt Yávië—remains beyond the fields. We fell through a mirror."

A sharp command followed by unknown words of authority summoned two dark men and then sent them away.

"My brothers will bring your companion. Would you like water and fare?"

"Yes, water. I do not know the word 'fare.'"

A small frown creased the Noor's smooth forehead. "Food," she corrected.

"No, I could not eat. My stomach churns with bitterness."

The Noor poured a cup of water and knelt to moisten Cwen's lips as she explained, "You drew weapons against the stryvers, and so they slammed—struck you—to avoid being harmed."

Cwen allowed her head to roll away from the Noor, and she stared up at the silent, gray being—the stryver. It had a steeply sloped forehead and was slack jawed, its vacant eyes seemingly unfocused. The creature was stoop shouldered and covered in scaly, ashen gray skin. Long arms ended in hands with fused digits and opposing thumbs, while its slender body sat on short, crooked legs supported on flat, three-toed feet.

Cwen turned back to the Noor. "How is it you speak my language?"

"I do not. I carry a sibilant stone, a speech evaluator—translator. It is not always correct, but I am learning to speak the foreign words without it as I encounter your kind."

"Do you have a healer or a wizard? Someone who can ease my pain?"

"Why would you choose to lose the pain of the lesson?"

"What lesson? I don't understand." Cwen clenched her eyes and pinched the bridge of her nose against the throbbing ache.

"You drew a weapon against the stryvers, and they struck you. If the pain is taken too soon, you will not recall the lesson learned and will make the same mistake again. Is this not the way of teaching beyond the mirror?"

"The mirror? I must find the mirror and return to my home. My people are under attack. Can you help me?"

"Always travelers ask this. What I know of mirrors I have learned from foreigners like you. I have never seen a mirror, and no one ever leaves Quondam. You will remain here among the Noor, as my father's guest. What should I call you?"

"I am called Cwen, Cwen of Aaradan."

"I am N'dia, fertile daughter of A'bach."

Cwen's curiosity over why a girl would announce herself fertile, as if it were part of her name, was interrupted by sounds of scuffling, shrill cries of anger, and broken snatches of the unknown language as the men returned with Yávië.

A squeal and a gasp left the queen on her hands and knees next to Cwen. "Cwen? Are you hurt?"

Cwen lifted her hand in acquiescence. "Aye, and it seems I shall remain so until my lesson has been learned."

"What? You speak nonsense, what do you mean?" Yávië leaned forward, examining the discolored lump above Cwen's right eye.

"Yávië, meet our hostess, the Noor. It appears that we are refugees."

Yávië stood, eyes rising to meet the probing gaze of the striking young Noor woman. "I am Yávië, queen of Ædracmoræ."

"Here there are no rulers except Queen Karid—only traders, boak miners, farmers, herders, nomads, and stryvers all at war with one another as they vie for the queen's favor. I would recommend remaining in the city and learning to trade, for it is the safest way to make a living and provides the most lucrative return."

Yávië pushed at her tangled hair, instinctively drawing a strip of leather from her wrist and tying the unruly raven strands back from her face as she demanded, "We will not be staying long enough to learn to trade, if you will be so kind as to show us the mirror that will lead us home. Our people will be searching for us."

"You have entered Quondam. There is no other journey, no passage home for you. You are not regal here. There is no realm over which you rule, and you have no people. This,"—elegant, well-manicured fingers stroked the serpent-encircled gem resting at Yávië's breast, the jewel of her birthright—"this has no meaning here. You are merely another stranger, a guest in my father's house. We will teach you how to trade and keep you safe within the city, but we cannot help you go home."

"That is unacceptable," Yávië replied. "We came here through a linking mirror of some sort. It must also allow return travel to Ædracmoræ."

Kindness softened the young Noor's face as she shook her head, and she lifted her hand to touch Yávië's blistered cheek. "Were you not snatched from the moment of your death? Your life is a gift that can no longer be lived beyond Quondam's borders. For some reason you have been spared. Now, I suggest that you rest, and tomorrow, if your wounds allow, I will show you the city and begin your teaching."

A wave of N'dia's hand sent the stryver scurrying away on all fours. "Come, I will show you to your room. The stryvers will bring a litter to carry your niece."

The room was opulent, filled with heavy furniture of polished dark woods with cushions of deep, soothing greens and pale, pleasing yellows. Two beds flanked doors leading to a sheltered terrace overflowing with unfamiliar flowering plants.

Yávië sat at Cwen's bedside, bathing her niece's brow with the cool, damp cloths furnished by the stryvers. A single tear slipped from Cwen's closed eyes.

"I am sorry I left you, Yávië. It was wrong of me, a stupid reaction to my fear."

"Cwen, we are afraid, lost and tired, grief-stricken and angry. I do not blame you. Tell me what you have learned. What are the gray beasts that lurk outside the door?"

Cwen frowned in an attempt to remember. "The Noor woman, N'dia she called herself, says that they are slaves. I think they are under some type of spell, for she told me that the Noor sometimes lose control of them outside the city. She said they could be dangerous to foreigners—foreigners, that is how she referred to us. The ability to bear young seems to be of great importance. N'dia introduced herself as the fertile daughter of someone. I forget the name."

"Did she take your weapons?"

"Aye, I have not seen them since I woke." Cwen's eyes closed again as a shiver of fear coursed along her spine.

"It appears our magick does not work here. I attempted to heal your head and the blisters on your face, but nothing happened. I cannot hear your thoughts. It is as if I had never learned spell-casting or mindspeak."

Cwen opened her eyes at her aunt's deep sigh. "We *will* find a way home, Yávië."

"Sleep, Cwen. We will need our strength if we are to escape this city." Yávië bent to kiss Cwen's cheek. "We are all we have, you and me."

"Aye, Yávië. Tomorrow, we will begin our search."

Outside the door, N'dia listened to the whispers of her guests' hopeless desire and turned sad eyes to meet her father's stern warning, "You must not help them, N'dia. If you do, Queen Karid will know. Her spies are everywhere, even here within our household."

"But Father, they were attacked by Karid's guards of fire. Their kingdom was burned at Karid's command! Surely we cannot stand by—"

"You must not help them, N'dia, or we will be the next to feel Karid's fist of fire."

N'dia's silent nod satisfied her father, and after emptying a vial of clear, odorless liquid over the fruits she carried, she slipped inside the room.

"I brought fruit and nectar. You should eat. It will help you regain your strength and heal your wounds."

"Are we prisoners here?" Yávië asked.

"No, of course not."

Yávië searched the woman's face for signs of deception.

"I could lie, and you would not know, for inscrutability is a characteristic of all Noor. But I am not lying. You are free to go at any time, though I must caution you against it. The Noor are city builders, master tradesmen favored by the queen of Quondam. As such, we can offer safety within these walls, but beyond the trade center confines there is much danger. Wild beasts, free stryvers, warring clans of nomads, and herders roam openly, all controlled by Queen Karid. It is said among my people that she is the godling of death wearing the flesh of Man. If that is not enough to make you cautious, you should also know that treacherous sands, deep canyons, impenetrable steaming forests, vast barrens, and impassible mountains mar the landscape in the West. There is only safety within the cities of the Noor. We would not like to see you harmed. Learn our ways, and live long, full lives. Do not throw away the gods' gift of life."

"What? What did you say?" Cwen struggled to sit up, gritting her teeth and gripping her gut against the pain. "A gift! To permit death's kiss would have been a kinder gift. Allowing us to fight our final battle and die with our kin would have been a gift! Our kingdom was aflame, attacked by a woman of fire. Do you know of them, a race with power over fire?"

N'dia's expression remained blank. "I have never heard of such a race."

"But—"

"I do not know them. There are others like you, foreigners, those who have been pulled from death in their home worlds and given the gift of continued life here in Quondam. Perhaps they may know of these fire women."

"N'dia!" The shouted name was followed by a string of unintelligible words.

"My father calls. I will speak with you in the morning. The new day will make things seem brighter. Eat and sleep and heal." She held a finger to her lips and added in a whisper as she backed away, "I am not the only one who carries a sibilant stone."

Yávië stared after her. "What was she mumbling about?"

"I think she was warning us that others may understand our words," Cwen whispered.

Nodding, Yávië poured cups of the thick, sweet, fragrant nectar, bringing one to Cwen. "Then let us eat and sleep and heal."

In silence they sipped nectar and nibbled fruit until Cwen slept and a deep, drug-induced drowsiness drove Yávië to quench the candle flame and retire to her bed.

Cwen shivered within the mist of dreams. As far as the eye could see the unearthly landscape was shrouded in shades of gray. Ahead the flicker of a dying blaze cast a warm golden glow behind the shadow of a crouching man. He rose and strode toward her, his heavy cloak flowing around him with each single-minded step. Cwen shivered anew in growing fear and anticipation. Her heartbeat quickened to match and then exceed the rhythm of the man's rapid footfalls.

He stopped at an arm's length distance from her. The fire was now hidden, but its faded blush silhouetted his towering frame. He raised a hand and pushed back his hood, revealing thick copper hair and held her in his keen, intelligent, golden-eyed gaze. Against the mist behind him arose the shadow of a dragon entangled in the dusky coils of a serpent. His silent words shocked her. *Come to me, daughter of the serpent.*

Cwen clutched at her throat and shot up in bed, her heart hammering, her breath catching painfully in her chest as she searched the unfamiliar shadows of the room. Neither man nor serpent-shrouded dragon loomed in the darkness. Yávië's soft breathing was the only sound. Cwen expelled the air trapped in her lungs and drew a deep quaking breath. Again the same dream. Even in the strange land of the Noor the cloaked man had found her. She drew her knees to her chest and hugged herself. Who was he? How did he know the sign of her birth? Why did he haunt her sleep?

Chapter 4: Introductions

Cwen awoke to a welter of aches and pains. She moaned as she maneuvered her body into a sitting position. A glance at the bed across the room showed Yávië missing, a supposition quickly confirmed by the sound of her voice calling from the terrace.

"We must be careful what we eat. We were drugged," Yávië said as she returned to their room through the terrace doors, dressed in a floor length, hooded robe. "And our clothing has been taken. I suppose we have been left with nothing but robes in their hopes of hindering our escape. A climb to the street below will be risky, but I believe it can be done."

"Aye, but even drugged my sleep was fitful," Cwen muttered and stood, examining bruises trailing across her ribcage, hips and thighs. "Let me recommend against drawing a weapon on the stryvers. Call it my first lesson learned. They may look harmless, but in a group and armed with cudgels they were quite effective in disarming me."

Cwen slipped the robe Yávië offered over her head and stepped through the doorway onto the terrace. "What did you see out here?"

"A grand city. It must cover several leagues. There," Yávië pointed, "across the channel you can see a second city, or a temple. I am not sure whether the water is a sea or a lake."

"It is The Sea Beyond Us. It surrounds Quondam," N'dia said, her voice startling her guests. "We are in the city of Achroma, a trade center. The cathedral in the distance is Endhaven, where it is said an ancient king once lived, and now it is home to Queen Karid's council of eldermen. My father and brothers are trade directors, overseers. They invite you to join them for morning tea."

"Will it benumb us like last night's gift of fruit, so that you can steal something else from us?" Yávië asked.

N'dia's eyes widened. "You have not been robbed! And I only gave you a bit of knotwood syrup. It has not harmed the others. I assumed your workings—your anatomy—to be the same as the other foreigners."

"And it is your policy to drug all of your guests and steal their clothing?" Yávië scowled.

"It was for your own good, so that you could sleep and heal. The first night is always the hardest for newcomers, and I left clean clothing to replace yours. Please come, share tea with us. I promise it will not harm you."

"It would be nice if we had our own clothes." Cwen lifted the hem of her robe, indicating its excessive length and volume.

"Perhaps tomorrow. Today you will rest and heal. Your bruises are deep and must be painful. Please come to tea—we can sit outside in my father's garden and feed the beasts. I am sure it will make you happy."

"Make me happy! We have been ripped from our home, mauled by your slaves, and had what little we own stolen! You think a bit of tea and feeding some animals will make us happy? You must be a foo—"

Yávië gripped Cwen's arm, interrupting her niece's outburst. "N'dia is right, Cwen. A bit of relaxation will do us good, and it would be impolite to refuse our host's offer."

N'dia smiled. "I am not fooled by your play—performance— Yávië, but maybe my father and brothers will be. Men are far easier to dominate, are they not?"

Cwen choked back a hoarse laugh and nodded to Yávië. "It is good to know the strengths and weaknesses of our enemies."

"I know that you believe I seek to harm you in some way, but it is not true. I only want your safety and happiness. You cannot go home again, and I know you will try to do so. Travelers always try for a time before they accept the truth. Some are lost, but most adjust and become quite content. Achroma is not a bad city."

N'dia opened the door and stepped back so that Cwen and Yávië could precede her into the hallway. "Left, then just follow the stryver."

Led by the silent gray stryver, the women wound their way through the residence and into a sunny courtyard where three robed men rose to greet them.

"Traders my ass," Cwen whispered to Yávië upon sight of the men. "Look at them, they are warriors and somewhere in this place there are weapons."

The tallest of the three bowed and indicated cushions. His pale eyes appraised Cwen, seemed to dismiss her, and moved on to Yávië.

"My daughter says you were a queen in your homeland," he acknowledged.

"She is still a queen. And that makes me a queen's niece and a woman of some importance," Cwen said with an overly bright smile.

"It is more likely that you are nothing more than a rude and impetuous, though valuable, child—much like my own daughter." To Yávië he offered his hand, engulfing the small pale one she extended in return. "I am A'bach, N'dia's father. Come, we shall sit there," he indicated a table some distance away, "and allow the children to become acquainted while we discuss their future."

"I am not—"

Stern looks from both Yávië and N'dia's father silenced Cwen. She dropped to a cushion before the low table where N'dia's siblings sat and poured a cup of tea. "If you drug me again, I will probably have to kill you," she said, looking at N'dia. She frowned up at the towering young man seated closest to her. "I am Cwen. And who are you?"

"I am J'var, and my brother is L'or. My sister is N'dia."

"I have already met your sister. She drugged me last night and robbed me."

Confusion wrinkled J'var's polished features, and L'or gave a deep chuckle.

"I do not understand," J'var confessed.

"N'dia brought our dinner. It was poisoned. Then she stole our clothes."

"Cwen teases, J'var. I only gave her a bit of knotwood so that she could sleep—"

"And heal," Cwen finished, sipping her tea and looking up with wide-eyed innocence. "What are your father and my aunt talking about?"

J'var's frown deepened. "They discuss your future."

"No one discusses my future without my presence." Cwen rose, clutching her ribs as the pain from their bruising reminded her of yesterday's beating.

"You are hurt?" J'var reached out to steady her, only to have his hand slapped away. He turned to look at N'dia in hopes of some explanation of the foreigner's behavior. His sister spent many hours studying newcomers and professed to understand their ways.

A tittering sound, almost a giggle, made its way past the fingertips N'dia had pressed to her lips. "She is not like the others. I don't understand her at all."

A sudden rustle in the flowering shrubs caused Cwen to spin around, her hand reaching for her missing sword. A broad smile spread across L'or's face, and he slapped J'var on the back. Several sharp gestures punctuated L'or's long stream of unintelligible words involving the repeated use of Cwen's name. J'var's response was low and soothing.

"What did they say?" Cwen looked from the men to N'dia and back again. "Are they talking about me?"

A small stag-like beast pushed its way forward, stretching out its neck to lip the hem of Cwen's robe.

"L'or says you want to fight. He offers to serve as your opponent when you are ready." Again N'dia hid a giggle behind her fingers.

"Give me my weapons, and I will be happy to fight your brothers."

"Oh, J'var does not wish to fight you. He says your scent is sweet, and it would be better—"

"I said that I found you lovely," J'var interrupted in a slow, cautious cadence. "It is not often our home is graced by such a beautiful and fascinating woman. You hair is aflame with sunlight, and your eyes glow like rare polished gems. Now, if you will excuse me, I have a meeting in the city."

Cwen stared after J'var's broad back, startled when he turned back to her and added, "Beware of my brother. L'or only pretends he wants a fight."

L'or's deep laughter drew Cwen's attention, and at his shrug she added her own. "It is far wiser that I see the threat than be blindsided by your competing ardor. I know that you are both warriors." She reached out to tap L'or's bulging bicep. "Just where *do* you keep your weapons?"

"You are far too beautiful and fragile to burden yourself with weapons," he replied. "It would be more appropriate for you to spend time with N'dia. Our father has raised his sons to admire women, not to raise weapons against them. Perhaps N'dia will let you attend her woman's training after you have healed."

As L'or excused himself and left the garden, N'dia grabbed Cwen and hugged her gently, laughing at the copper-haired girl's uncomfortable resistance. "See? Men are so easily manipulated. All you have to do is smile, look through lowered lashes, and touch the tip of your tongue to your lips, and they will allow you anything."

Yávië turned her head slightly at the sound of Cwen's laughter. "Your sons and daughter seem to have amused my niece."

A'bach returned her smile. "Your niece is unlike anyone my sons and daughter have ever seen. Most of the foreigners who pass into Quondam are men, and the few women there have been are not nearly so fair and definitely not as fierce and challenging. Have you found it difficult to control her?"

"Cwen has never been controlled by any, not even her own parents. She has not lived with us for many summers. She only came home for the funerals." Yávië swallowed a rising bitterness, and her eyes grew vacant as death's dark images overwhelmed her.

"You mourn the dead, and in my eagerness to know you I have been impolite. I should have recalled my own grief at the death of my wife. Please forgive me. I should allow you to rest," A'bach apologized.

"I don't need rest, A'bach. Your kindness is appreciated, but I need to go home. We need to go home. Our kingdom is under attack and without its leader. Please help us."

His ice-blue eyes were startling in the darkness of his inscrutable burnished features as they searched Yávië's sorrow-filled face. "Did my daughter not tell you? If you were swept into Quondam, it is because you have no home, no life beyond our borders. Always those saved are taken from certain death—always."

"How can we know that? We did not see my…my daughter was left behind." Memories of Sōrél's final word and the assassin's fierce heat made Yávië weak. The image of Sóvië falling behind the fall of flames and the screams of burning men grew within her mind and drowned out the cheerful chirping of the many small birds near where they sat. She clasped her hands and allowed her eyes to close against the brilliant dappled light that played within A'bach's garden. Taking a deep breath she looked up at her host. "I must try and find my way back. I must see for myself, I must know that there were no survivors. I must know if my daughter lives."

A'bach tilted his head and examined his guest. "We cannot help you. It is forbidden by Queen Karid, Quondam's ruler."

Yávië nodded and stood up. "I believe it will be best if my niece and I leave your home as soon as possible. Our determination can only bring unpleasantness to your family, and that is not our wish. You have been very kind. Now, if you will allow us our clothing and my niece's weapons we can go on about our business."

A'bach called to N'dia in the sharp, clipped tones of his own language, pointing a finger as she frowned and shook her head.

"My daughter believes she should save every foreigner, even though I have told her it is not possible. Some of you insist on making your own way. I will have a stryver return your clothing. It has been cleaned and the burn holes mended. Weapons are not allowed to women, so they have been confiscated." He reached out and took Yávië's hand. "I do wish you well. I cannot imagine what it is like to be ripped from all you know and cast into all this strangeness. Beyond these gates there is little civilization left until you reach the next Noor trading center. The closest is Adumbra. You may be able to hire a guide or travel with one of the guarded trade caravans headed that way. Today I must insist you rest and allow your niece's wounds to heal. Tomorrow I will have N'dia accompany you as far as the tavern where you will find a woman who can help you. N'dia may not enter the tavern." His eyes rose to meet his daughter's unhappy glare and waited until he received her reluctant nod of agreement. "Is this acceptable?"

At Yávië's whispered, "Aye," A'bach bowed and left them.

"If you do not find what you seek, you will always be welcome here," N'dia said as she padded ahead of them down the long hallway, her bare feet whispering on the stones. "Many have gone in search of a way home and then returned to us. On our way to B'rma's Tavern I will show you how to buy goods. I am not allowed inside the tavern because it is…" N'dia searched for the correct word, "improper—for a director's daughter of marriageable age to be seen in such a place. Many foreigners congregate there though. Perhaps we will meet others from your world." She chattered to cover the sinking feeling settling in her stomach. In truth they never came back. Those who left in search of the mirror to take them home always vanished. She did not wish to lose Cwen and her aunt to whatever fate awaited them beyond the city walls. There had to be something very special about such a fierce, fire-haired, golden-eyed girl, one willing to take on N'dia's arrogant brothers. One that Queen Karid wanted dead.

Dressed in her scrubbed and patched clothing, Cwen paced the room looking less than ever like the niece of a queen. Yávië sat on the bed feeling foolish in her mended funerary gown.

"I can make the climb," Cwen insisted. "You can remain here and cover for me in case anyone comes snooping about. I don't trust them. They may have no intention of letting us go tomorrow, with or without N'dia. And speaking of N'dia, that girl is up to something. I could hear it in her voice. And those brothers of hers treated me as if I were a tart delivered for their entertainment. What is wrong with these people? No weapons allowed to women? What could possibly be the reason for that? How do women settle disputes? What is it these people fear, Yávië? Yávië…?"

Yávië looked up, her face worn with sorrow and worry. "Go Cwen. You will not be happy until you try. I am very tired—too tired to argue about a climb down the wall. All I can think about are those we left behind. What of Sóvië? What of your parents, the wizard Grumbleton, and my guardians? Are they all dead as A'bach says? I have to know,

Cwen. I must see for myself. Until I do, my mind cannot focus on anything else. Find us a way out of here."

Cwen sank to the bed beside her aunt. "I am not without compassion for those we left behind, Yávië," she said, the admission bringing a new flood of regret and anger. "I will take you home, and I will punish those who killed Sōrél and the others beyond anything they can imagine. I will flay the very flesh from their living bodies. I will help you find Sóvië. But I cannot just sit still and wait for someone else to decide my fate—not even for you, Yávië."

Placing a hand on each side of her niece's face, Yávië smiled. "You have always been your own guide, Cwen, and you follow your own mind, always. I told your father you would come in a fury and stay to avenge us all, and I believe you will, no matter what we may find at home. We are much alike, you and I—fiercely protective of what is ours, though your life has been so shadowed by brutal, deceitful men that your heart has hardened and you cannot see the good in any. Go, find us a weapon and see if you can get me something more practical to wear. Tomorrow, one way or another, we will leave this place." She dropped her hands to her lap. "Go."

Cwen stepped out onto the terrace and examined the wall to the right of the railing and then the street below. The nearest torch was distant enough so that only a faint shadow would be cast as she made the descent, so long as she remained below the overhang of the terrace leading off their room. There was another terrace offset to the left, but it was empty, the doors to its room closed and the windows dark. With a deep breath, Cwen swung her legs over the stone and lowered herself until she hung in a vertical position. Grimacing as she flexed her sore muscles, she released her right hand and lowered it to grip the edge of the terrace floor between the stone balusters. She reached out with her left foot and sought a toehold. Her soft leather boots, worn with age, made no sound as her foot flexed within to grip the rough stone. She eased her weight onto the wall, freeing her left hand to find a crack in the mortar. Bit by bit she worked her way downward, keeping to the right to remain in the shadow of the terrace. Her right hand found a broad, sturdy vine, and she swung herself onto it and, amidst a rustle of leaves, inched her way toward the street below. A backward glance revealed the soft earth supporting the roots of the trailing plant, and she let her body drop, landing with a soft thud on the soil near the base of the wall.

"Might I be of assistance?"

Cwen swung around with fists already balled and ready to strike, then dropped her hands and released a soft, deep chuckle.

The man before her no longer wore his morning robe. He was naked to the waist, his bulging bare arms folded across a massive chest. A deep green cloth was bound about his loins and fell to the mid-point of heavily muscled thighs that flowed on to knotted calves. His feet were bare and the golden tattoos along his polished scalp and chest shimmered in the moonlight. Beneath their arched brows his pale blue eyes examined Cwen with open curiosity.

"Is there no escaping you? J'var, isn't it? Where is the other brother?"

"Aye, I am J'var. L'or has gone to Endhaven on an errand for our father. Where is it you wish to go? I will be happy to escort you."

"Oh, I was just feeling a bit restless and thought I would take a walk."

"Good. We shall walk together." He gestured to the street and reached out to take Cwen's arm.

"Stop it!" She shook off his hand. "I can walk without help. I am not an invalid, and the bruises given me by your ill-mannered stryvers no longer hurt."

The man's hand shot forward and gripped Cwen's waist, causing her to cry out as strong fingers found her bruises.

"Well, they don't hurt much," she hissed, pushing at his hand and shifting to ease the ache. "I have been hurt worse."

J'var withdrew his hand and walked along beside Cwen for several paces before speaking. "Who would hurt you? And why?"

Cwen shrugged. "I have a lot of enemies."

"I too have enemies." J'var scrutinized the small woman at his side, his eyes following the flow of her coppery hair as it billowed about her face. "My enemies seek to steal my position within Queen Karid's directorate, to defame me before our ruler, but I cannot imagine why a woman would have enemies unless she had committed some crime."

The laughter that burst from Cwen filled the silence of the dark street and caused J'var to frown and look around to see if it had roused anyone.

"Where I come from, even honest men and women can have enemies. And when someone attempts to steal something from us or burn us to death, we settle it with swords."

"Or daggers?" J'var reached to the small of his back and withdrew Cwen's slender dagger from his waistband. "This is what you seek, is it not?"

Cwen stopped and held out her hand. "Give it to me."

J'var smiled, his strong white teeth a startling contrast to the rich brown color of his skin. Laughter lines crinkled the corners of his eyes. "If I do, will you kill me with it?"

"No. I will climb back up the wall and into my room, where I will sleep with it under my pillow. Now, give it to me."

His intense assessment made her uncomfortable, and she pushed her hand forward for emphasis. "Give it to me. And where is my sword?"

He flipped the dagger over and handed it to her hilt first. "If you are caught with that you will be taken before the magistrate and sentenced to work in the laundry for the rest of your natural life. Even men are not allowed to carry weapons within the city walls, and women are not allowed weapons at all."

Cwen tucked the dagger into the sheath at her waist and looked up at the solemn, bronze-skinned man. "Just what are women allowed?" she asked indignantly.

"Come, you need not climb the wall. I will take you in through the courtyard." J'var swung back toward the residence.

"You didn't answer me."

"Husbands. Women are allowed husbands and homes, babies and laundry. Now come, your pillow awaits that tiny dagger, and N'dia worries that I have failed as a man and let you become lost."

"Why you arrogant son of a slitherwort-infected bane boar bitch! How dare you order me about! I am not one of your stryvers or your sentimental sister! I will do what I please and go where I want!"

Cwen screamed her rage and leapt toward J'var with dagger drawn only to be met by his steel-like grip as he wrested the blade from her hand. Without a word he slipped the dagger back in his waistband and swung Cwen up over his shoulder. The protesting screams from his charge brought people wearing nightclothes to their windows and out onto overhanging terraces to see what the commotion was about.

"J'var!" a voice called from a nearby balcony. "J'var, is she the one? The one rumored to carry the serpent's blood? I see she bears a weapon!"

Yávië's pale face appeared at the terrace railing, her cries of concern drifting to the street below.

A surly grunt was J'var's response to the sudden chaos. He flung open the gate to the courtyard and stomped inside to be met by N'dia, pacing back and forth in her agitation.

"N'dia, this girl is a menace and an embarrassment," J'var said, his eyes glinting with anger. "Father will surely have your hide for bringing her here when he hears about this. I will leave her in her room. See that the door to the terrace is locked and a stryver stationed below it with orders to break her legs if she climbs down the wall again. Director V'ran saw me manhandling a dagger from her right outside the house, and you can be sure he will tell Father when he sees him. Already he spreads the nomad's tales about her ancestors. If Queen Karid hears them, there will be no safe place for her. As soon as it is daylight, take Cwen and her aunt to the tavern. Leave them with B'rma, and tell her to find them passage on a wagon headed out of Achroma. A wagon headed out in any direction!"

"J'var! You don't mean that!" N'dia exclaimed.

He glared at his sister. Cwen's howls grew louder as she dangled down his back, clawing in an attempt to reach her dagger. He jerked her down and wrapped her in his arms, crushing her against his chest.

"Hush! I mean it! Before I gag you!"

Cwen froze and bit off a squeal. "You wouldn't!"

"Why wouldn't I? You have brandished an illegal weapon in front of our neighbors. A weapon you used to attack me after I was kind enough to give it back to you! We will be lucky if we don't both end up in a cell awaiting sentence." He released her and shoved her away from him. "I thought you so very beautiful, a fertile gift from the gods, and you *are* fair and fragile, but like the deadly fire thistle, you are filled with venom! Take her, N'dia—get her out of my sight and out of earshot! I no longer wish to hear her voice!"

Cwen stood beside N'dia, mouth agape with confusion, staring after J'var's retreating back. "How would you know I am fertile?" she asked.

"I can smell it in your blood," he threw back over his shoulder.

"I want my dagger!" Cwen howled after him, backing up as he swung about and returned, his furious scowl focused directly upon her.

He stopped a hand's breadth away, breathing heavily and flexing his jaw against gritted teeth, neck muscles corded with tension. "If you want it, take it from me."

"Stop it!" N'dia snapped, grabbing the dagger from her brother's waistband and holding it out to Cwen.

Cwen leaned forward, brushing against J'var as she reached for the blade. His hands snaked forward and gripped her upper arms, forcing her against the wall. "Do you think you can fight me and win?"

She squirmed in his grip, kicking against unyielding shins.

"Do you?"

"No!" she cried out.

He jerked his hands away. "I do not know where you came from, but you cannot win a fight against a man here. And if you try to fight, you will die. Don't be a fool!"

J'var snatched the dagger from N'dia's hand and slapped its hilt across Cwen's palm. "Don't be a fool," he repeated. Pulling the sibilant stone from around his neck, he tossed it to N'dia and stalked out of sight.

"He likes you," N'dia murmured, "but he really does not wish to hear your angry words."

"What are you talking about? He threatened to gag me and have a stryver break my legs. He hates me."

"Perhaps you do not know as much about men as I thought you did." N'dia linked her arm through Cwen's and handed her the sibilant stone. "Come, I will take you to your room. You should sleep if you plan on leaving in the morning. The stone will help you communicate in the city."

Yávië met them at the door, deep worry lines etched into her forehead. "I thought you had been killed!"

"She merely annoyed my brother, and he overreacted. I will leave you now. Sleep. Tomorrow will be tiring."

Cwen waited until N'dia disappeared behind the closed door before pulling the dagger out and showing Yávië. "N'dia also gave me this." She dangled the sibilant stone by its chain. "Apparently all one has to do is wear it to receive its benefits of translation. It should come in handy as we travel about."

Yávië was staring at the new bruises appearing on Cwen's upper arms.

"J'var doesn't believe women should bear weapons. He thinks I am a fertile gift from his gods and should bear babies and wash clothes." Cwen shrugged. "He warned me against being foolish. Maybe I should heed that warning. It does seem that everyone I meet can best me, even the stryvers. He said I could be put in prison for carrying a weapon and that it is against their laws."

"Cwen, we must be careful. Listen and learn the ways of these people if we are to gain their trust and secure their help. Do you understand?"

Cwen sank to her bed. "Aye…we must play a game if we are to win. Their game, a game for which there are no rules," she said, her brow furrowed.

"There are rules, but we just don't know what they are." Yávië walked over to her own cot, pulled back the covers, and slipped beneath them.

"Sleep, Cwen. N'dia's is probably right. Tomorrow will most likely prove to be long and exhausting."

Cwen, Yávië, and N'dia sat together at a table, A'bach and his sons at another, over a morning meal of rich pastries, fresh fruits, and soft cheeses.

"Has it always been like this?" Cwen asked, casting a furtive glance toward J'var only to be caught in his direct gaze.

N'dia looked confused.

Cwen shrugged and Yávië explained, "I think Cwen is disturbed by the fact that women and men seem to be kept separately, have different tasks, and are not seen as equals. Where we come, from men and women live and work together and are equals. Ability is all that limits one's choice of tasks."

"Men bear children?"

"No, but neither do women unless it is their choice."

"In Quondam a woman who can bear a child has become rare," N'dia explained. "We are looked after and worshipped for our ability to give life. No man can do that. Ask J'var or L'or. Each of them seeks a woman to bear his child, but neither of them has enough strength—power or position—within the directorate to secure such a woman."

"I would hate to be locked up in a house with nothing to do all day but chase children and wash clothing," Cwen mumbled.

N'dia chuckled. "Fertile women do not do laundry. They have a stryver to do it. One day I will choose a man of position, bear his children, supervise his house, and make my father very proud. One day, but not now—now I wish to find adventure—but how could anything be better than love?"

"That's not love, N'dia! It is servitude."

"Cwen, have you loved a man?"

Cwen looked away. "No. I don't know, perhaps I did."

"If you do not know, then you did not truly love. My mother told me of love. It does not end, not even in death. It climbs higher than all the stars and clings to life beyond the death of the body." N'dia's eyes grew moist. "My mother so loved my father. And I believe your aunt feels this as well for the husband she lost." She reached out and touched Yávië's sleeve. "I have heard you weep. No sorrow but the loss of an eternal love could pain you so deeply."

Yávië drew a deep breath and attempted to smile, tears pooling beneath her closed eyelids and slipping down her cheeks. "You are a very observant young woman, N'dia. And your mother was right. Love lives outside of our mortal existence. Loss should never be as permanent as mine. If I cannot go home, I have no hope of reunion with my husband when I die…"

"B'rma the tavern keeper once told me of a soulbinder. A person who can find lost souls. Apparently they are never really gone, merely misplaced—hidden—from us. Perhaps he can find your husband's soul."

"Yávië?" Cwen wondered aloud. "Is there a possibility Sōrél's soul could be recovered here on Quondam?"

"No. I would not know how to begin or where to look," Yávië replied. "The words to free the men's souls were not spoken. The ceremony was not finished, there was not time before you came for me and everything was burned."

"I believe there is always hope." N'dia stood up and called to her father, "We are going into the city. I will return before evening tea."

"Stay out of B'rma's tavern." A'bach shook his finger at his smiling daughter. "Going in the back door is just as inappropriate as going in the front."

"Father! I merely stopped to ask B'rma a question. I only leaned inside the door."

"Ah, but who saw you leaning? Director V'ran. And I shall never hear the end of it. He brings it up at every meeting of the directorate. Oh, he smiles and laughs, but it is quite clear he is no longer certain you will make a worthy wife."

"Good. I never intended to marry V'ran anyway. I find him disgusting," N'dia assured.

A'bach shook his head and watched his daughter gather the strangers and exit the gate. "Follow them, J'var. Do not let them come to harm. I would not like to lose the golden-eyed girl because of her arrogant determination to ignore Queen Karid's laws."

J'var nodded and without a word slipped out after his sister and her guests.

Chapter 5: Achroma

The city gleamed in the light of the new day, gold and silver glinting from the towering polished granite walls of its buildings. N'dia had slipped a sibilant stone over Yávië's head and assured her that it would make the day less confusing.

"Ours was the race chosen to keep peace and to care for the others after Queen Karid's Great War ended. We have been city builders ever since," N'dia said, chattering on as they walked. "For ten generations the Noor have controlled all trade on Quondam, and never has there been a rebellion within our city walls. Beyond the cities are dying farms and burned pasturelands of the herders. If it weren't for the Noor collecting and distributing food there would be much more death from starvation.

"Outside the city walls the nomads still war for control of the overland trade routes. Some nomad clans bring in spoils from raiding in the West, beyond the inland sea. There is a great barge used by the clans at Quern's Crossing. It is said to be an amazing feat of engineering, controlled by locks and levees. Someday I would like to see it."

"What lies beyond the inland sea?" Cwen asked.

"I do not know. The director of Stonetel reports that strangers do occasionally come through the mountain pass to trade, so he must know. No one goes into the barrens or wildwoods of the West." N'dia lifted her shoulders and said, "No one goes to Dragon's Heart at the center of the sea either. It is said to be inhabited only by beasts."

At the mention of Dragon's Heart, Yávië suddenly took interest in the conversation. "There are dragons in Quondam?"

"No. There is no danger of that. They were killed off long ago, exterminated by Karid's army generations ago. The tales are quite fantastic, though. A woman supposedly conspired with an elder wizard to create a monster by…" N'dia shuddered and wrinkled her nose. "It is too awful to think about. Anyway, you are definitely safe from dragons."

"And there is no magick practiced here? No fey or enchanted beings, no wizards?" asked Yávië.

"No. Not since very long ago, before Karid's rule. My mother told stories of small winged men and the sacred wildwoods of the West. Our valleys are supposedly named after several of these 'fireflies,' but they no longer exist, if indeed they were ever more than faery tales told to children. And the sacred woods are dying, giving up more and more of the forest to the barrens in the south and the dreadwoods in the north."

"N'dia, we come from a world where magick abounds." Yávië sighed as her mind wandered back to her home. "A touch can heal a wound. Dragons and men work side by side. Flying men and women are everywhere. Both Cwen and I learned spell-casting, but here it does not work. Are you saying that no one in Quondam uses magick?"

"No, no one, it was decreed forbidden and punishable by death at the end of the war. Perhaps B'rma will be more helpful. She is quite old and knows a lot of secrets," N'dia encouraged. "She talks to lots of travelers and traders, even nomads and miners who come into the tavern. I think that is why my father fears our friendship. He thinks B'rma will lead me astray with her scandalous rumors and fanciful tales. He has forgotten how whimsical my mother's stories were." N'dia raised her voice to be heard above a sudden argument at one of the vendor's stalls and pointed to a group of robed men leading tall, sturdy looking, long-legged, hump-backed, curly-haired beasts. N'dia explained, "Emyutes, nomads, the last race to hold true memories of the war. It is said they worship Karid in her human form. The beasts are droms. A drom can carry great burdens and travel long distances without tiring, though it is said they smell quite foul."

"Karid? She is your queen?" Yávië asked.

"She is said to be a horror, a flesh cloaked nymph and a souleater. Supposedly, she binds men's souls and steals their flesh," she replied with a grimace. "There is also rumor that she was once a sentinel charged with caring for the sacred wildwoods, that the flesh she wears was a punishment for some offense she committed against the gods. At least that is what I have heard. I do not know for certain, because I have never met her, so I speak out of turn. Her palace is far from here, in Serabia across the river from Quern's Crossing."

Swinging about, N'dia pointed down a side street toward a group of men who were covered with red dust. She spoke quickly to disguise her discomfort. "Saedans, they mine the boak mines and provide Quondam with what little fuel they find."

A herd of bleating goats crowded around them, followed by a short man and woman dressed in leather clothes. "Volites, they are herders from the valleys. Each year the flocks grow smaller as the queen's demand grows greater."

Grabbing Cwen and Yávië by the hand, N'dia rushed them to an open stall.

"Bread for the foreigners, Cudge."

The small woman touched her chest and gave her name, "Cudge, I am Cudge. Try soft bread. It is very good today."

"This is Yávië, and this is Cwen. They arrived two days ago and have been staying with us. Cudge is an Orpin, a farmer. She wears a sibilant stone and is licensed to sell to foreigners. See the sign?"

Cwen and Yávië smiled their acknowledgement and accepted the warm, soft, gauze-wrapped bread, taking note of the sign bearing a set of three wavy lines intersected by a half circle.

"Any shop bearing such a sign will have someone who understands you and can help you." N'dia sighed. "I am worried for you. J'var believes you will be killed if you leave the city."

"We will be cautious, N'dia, and we will listen to those who can help us," Yávië said.

Looking less than convinced, N'dia added, "Never talk to nomads, they cannot be trusted for they are superstitious and warlike to the very root of their souls, and there is not a one of them who does not do Queen Karid's bidding. Never talk to a free stryver either. They pretend they are civilized and do not need masters, but they are evil and cruel and prey on foreigners foolish enough to try talking to them. They cannot speak. Run if you see stryvers outside the city."

Distracted, Cwen watched as a man piled parcels wrapped in paper and gauze into the arms of the stryver beside him. She noticed the wide, bulky collar the stryver wore. "What do the collars do?"

"They do nothing. Only remind the stryvers of the agreement with the masters," N'dia explained. "We do not harm them. They are fed and cared for by their masters, and in return, they work."

Cwen frowned, "Rather like women with husbands?"

"No," J'var slipped up behind and whispered from beside her elbow, "women receive collars of gem stones and gleaming precious metals."

Caught off guard by J'var's sudden appearance, Cwen said, "I thought you gave up your sibilant stone so you would not have to hear my voice."

"I have reconsidered. Why should I suffer the loss of such beautiful music, just because the music box is—?"

"J'var!" N'dia exclaimed. "What are you doing here? Father sent you to spy on me?"

"Wait, let him finish. Just what is it you believe is wrong with me?" Cwen glared up at N'dia's eldest brother.

"You are arrogant, undisciplined, and unaware of the dangers that surround you, even here within the city. There!" J'var gripped Cwen's shoulders and turned her around, pointing to an Emyute nomad leaning against the wall. "See that glint of metal at his side? Manacles for a woman he believes he can sell to someone in the West or trade to Karid for a favor. He believes you a threat to his queen, and nomads do not like threats. He also believes you may be magickal, and you would not like the way a nomad takes a woman's magick.

"You act like a man because you are afraid to be a woman," J'var accused. "Your heart pounded like a trapped bird flailing against a cage when you were alone with me. But you *are* a woman, Cwen, and as a woman you are in great danger. Beyond the city walls, only Queen Karid's armies and nomads are safe. Even boak miners, farmers, and herders have begun to hire guards on their trips to and from the city. Be careful Cwen!" he warned sternly, walking away.

"N'dia, Father says to stay out of the tavern!" J'var called back as he disappeared around a wagonload of grain.

"He is—"

"Right," Yávië finished. "You are undisciplined, Cwen, and have always fought out of fear and anger, not out of real strength." She held up her hand to stop Cwen's annoyed retort. "Without weapons and magick we are totally unprepared to exist in such a strange world. Let us see if N'dia's tavern owner can really help us."

"N'dia, why are you not in danger?" Cwen asked.

N'dia's eyes widened with surprise. "Because I am Noor. The Noor are favored by Karid. We are allowed fertility in return for our obedience and service." She swept her hand before her. "Look around you, Cwen. How many fair-skinned, fire-haired women do you see?" She smiled to ease the sting of her next words. "Every man in this city wants to possess you because you have the ability to bear young and are a prize unlike any they have ever seen. Even my father wished to befriend Yávië in the hope of binding you to one of my brothers, but my father will not hold you against your desire. Beyond these walls there are others who may not be so kind. It would be best if you choose your fate before they do. If you select someone, the others will honor your choice, and the directorate will protect you. If J'var is right, if you are seen as a threat to Queen Karid and you leave the city…I am sorry Cwen, but I am afraid there is nowhere to run."

Cwen stared at N'dia, speechless at last. Yávië covered her eyes, already exhausted by her sorrow, the stress of the day, and their inability to take action. N'dia took their hands and led them around a building, down a narrow walkway and through the back door of B'rma's tavern.

The woman behind the bar was also a Noor. Tall and imposing, her central mane of hair was deep blue, highlighted with the silver streaks of maturity. Unlike N'dia's, her scalp was free of golden familial tattoos, though her upper arms bore marked circlets of glittering symbols. Pale eyes looked up as the trio of women entered behind the bar, but the rise and fall of her cleaver against the side of meat never faltered.

"N'dia," B'rma acknowledged between the fleshy slaps of the blade.

Tables were set in the shadowy recesses of the gloomy room, and around them the noise of loud conversation and male laughter filtered through the smoky dimness.

"I bring foreigners. They need your help. Cwen has drawn the attention of the nomads and will not be safe unless we hide her."

A sidelong glance at the copper-haired Cwen brought a nod from the tavern owner. "So this is the one causing all the commotion. She *is* rather noticeable." B'rma slid the thick wedge of meat a bit closer and proceeded to hack it into smaller chunks. "A drab robe and a head covering will do for a start, but shaving the hair and veiling those golden eyes would be more effective. Sending her into Stonetel or Dragonfire might save her—if the nomads could be avoided along the way. Recently foreigners have fled to the West. It is said they are protected within the Feverous Forest, as the queen's armies do not yet wander the wildwoods."

"I don't intend to shave my head, and I cannot walk about hidden beneath a veil. I—" Cwen glanced at the silent Yávië, "*we* want only to find a way to return to our world. The mirror that brought us here must be somewhere, and once we discover where, we will go home. We want nothing to do with these 'armies' everyone keeps referring to, or your queen. We just want to go home."

Without warning, B'rma lifted the cleaver and let it fly end over end, flecks of fat and bloody flesh spattering Cwen's face as the blocky blade whistled across the room to land between a nomad's fat fingers where they gripped the door jamb at the tavern's exit.

"I would not leave without settling your debt," B'rma shouted, wiping her hands on a stained apron and leaping over the bar to quickly cover the distance to the door, hand outstretched to receive her payment from the hooded man examining his fingers.

Coaxing the cleaver free with a jiggle and dropping the coins in her pocket, B'rma returned to her task at the bar, tossing Cwen a rag to wipe the blood off her face.

"What you want has nothing to do with it," B'rma continued as if they had not been interrupted. "Karid rules Quondam with an iron will, executing all who challenge her. If you are discovered outside the city walls, you will become personally acquainted with Karid's armies or the nomads who serve her—of that there is no doubt. I can get you on a wagon headed for Adumbra. From there you can make connections with someone to take you on to the West. Or you can be sensible and marry J'var and remain in Achroma. I understand there is a blazing heat in his loins for you."

Eyeing Cwen's open mouth, the tavern keeper smiled for the first time. "You could do worse. He is as strong as ten droms, is a member of the directorate, and his family's women are among those allowed to keep their fertility because of A'bach's loyalty. Most women would be willing to kill for such a match."

"I am willing to kill to avoid it," Cwen admitted, pointing to the cleaver and adding, "I thought women weren't allowed to carry weapons."

B'rma pulled the cleaver free and turned it over, laughing, "This? This is no weapon, merely a kitchen tool."

Suddenly, an avalanche of sharp words from B'rma brought a serving wench scurrying to replace her at the bar. She led her guests to a private room and indicated they should sit. Pouring a thick, steaming, green-black liquid into small earthenware cups, she offered a toast, "To the safety of the red-haired stranger." Each tossed back her drink, Cwen and Yávië gagging at the hot bitterness.

"What is it?" Yávië gasped with a shudder, choking and coughing in an attempt to ease her burning throat.

"Fermented gall oil," N'dia smiled. "It is an acquired taste."

B'rma rummaged through a pile of clothes and pulled out coarse gray, hooded robes, tossing them to Cwen and Yávië. "These will cover your hair and most of your skin, but if you refuse to wear a veil I cannot hide the young one's golden eyes. The best I can do is give warning against you making eye contact. Most have become used to foreigners among us, but never has one had hair or eyes like yours. It is as if you are marked by Quondam's legends and already superstitious rumors spread like wildfire among the nomads. To the west, in the forests beyond the Sanguine Sea, there are others who are, well…different. There you will not be so much at risk."

"What do you mean, different?" Yávië asked.

"It is said they bear the mark of a demon's curse. Talk among the nomads says perhaps you bear this curse as well."

"I am neither marked nor cursed!" Cwen jumped to her feet.

B'rma lifted her hand in warning, slipping to the door to peer outside. Then she stepped onto a crate at the window, looked out into the alley and drew the window closed. "I caution you, do not draw attention to yourself by any action. Fear makes men angry, and fearful, angry men commit unspeakable crimes in Queen Karid's name."

"Fear?" Cwen snapped. "Haven't you heard? I am just a woman. A woman from beyond the mirror, but there is nothing frightening about me. I could not defend myself against J'var, even when I was armed with a dagger. I offer no threat and have no magick. Why would they fear me?"

"Your pale skin, your hair and your eyes. Because of these they believe you may be a legendary beast escaped from its prison. The beast is rumored to bear eyes of gold and hair of fire and take a human form. Other rumors are far worse and say you are the woman born beneath the sign of the serpent who will set the beast free. Either way, you are feared by the nomads and hated by the queen."

Cwen sank into a chair and stared at Yávië. "How can we defend ourselves against such superstitious fools? Fools who believe in tales of cursed beasts."

"Not all of us are fools," N'dia admonished. "Those who live within the cities do not believe the tales of the monster, but the Emyute nomads are a superstitious people and have shared their tales with other weak-minded races—stories of hideous dragon-headed, flesh devouring, shape-shifting beasts that are only kept at bay by the nomads' offerings of human flesh."

Yávië stood and slipped the rough textured robe over her tattered gown. Reaching out, she gripped B'rma's arm. "Help us get to this place called Stonetel. It seems our only hope."

Below the window the lurking nomad smiled and backed away, hissing to his companion. "Send word to the queen. We have found the women she seeks and will have them in our grasp within a fortnight. Both will be dead before the moon hides her face."

Chapter 6: Nomads

Buried for the twenty-third day in a wagon bed beneath tarpaulins and grain, Yávië and Cwen rode in bone rattling discomfort and stifling heat toward the city they hoped would offer sanctuary. Their savior was a herder with a sibilant stone, who was on a return run from Achroma to Mochla's Freehold, a slowly failing cooperative farming community. He had assured B'rma and N'dia that the nomads would not suspect such a humble man of treachery, and he could see the strangers safely to the trade center of Adumbra before he headed homeward with the load of ripened grain that B'rma had provided in payment and as camouflage.

The incessant lurching of the wagon over the rut-filled road combined with the stench of the draft cattle and the suffocating heat finally forced Cwen to sit up and throw back the tarp. She brushed away the grain and drew the slightly cooler air deep into her lungs. Tugging her hood forward, she shielded her eyes against the sun's glare and searched the wagon bed for the near empty water flask. Finding it, she handed it to Yávië.

Cwen knelt behind the driver and shouted into his ear, "How much further to tonight's camp?"

"Darkfall."

"And to Adumbra?"

"Two, maybe three days. Here there is danger. There is an Emyute camp on the cliffs south of Adumbra."

Cwen glanced up and judged darkfall to be several shadow's passing if Quondam's star cast shadows at the same pace as the one on her home world. The wagon gave a jolt and threw Cwen against Yávië, spilling precious water and wetting Yávië's robe.

"At least I shall feel cooler until the wet spots dry. What did the farmer say?"

"He said we would reach camp by darkfall. I judge that to be three shadows, no more. Another two or three days to the trade center." Cwen took the offered flask and wet her tongue with a swallow of the remaining water. "You would think we would pass more travelers along such a well rutted road."

"I don't believe we should be looking to meet others, Cwen. I am concerned about your safety. Perhaps it will be best if we can find a place to hide you in Adumbra. I can go on to Stonetel and return for you once I have located a way home."

But already Cwen's head was shaking in disagreement. "There is no way I am going to remain behind. You can do the talking. I will keep my eyes downcast to avoid detection, but I will not be left behind."

Sudden shouts and the sound of galloping animals sent the women diving back beneath the tarp. Cwen reached out to toss grain over the exposed edge, but the driver's strangulated, breathy hiss and the spattering of blood across her exposed skin told Cwen they had been found. The cattle bawled, and the wagon was dragged to a halt.

"There is nothing we can do," Yávië whispered. "Just do what they ask, and don't make trouble."

"I have the dagger."

"No, it will only get us killed more quickly." Yávië gripped Cwen's arm. "They will kill me, Cwen. They have no use for me. Only you have value, you are young and fertile—they value that. Just do as they say, and perhaps you will live. Cwen, promise me if anything happens to me you will still search for Sóvië. Swear it."

"I swear it." Cwen nodded as the tarp was pulled away, exposing them to a circle of nomads.

The nearest man leapt over the side and into the bed of the wagon, jerking Cwen to her feet, pushing Yávië away as she tried to grab her niece's hand. A swift slice of his curved dagger relieved Cwen of her robe, releasing her hair to the wind as the nomad swept the hood away.

"I have it! I have the demon!" the nomad shouted.

A nomad on horseback pushed his way between the men and stared in disbelief at the woman before him. "Bind it and bring it."

"No!" Yávië rose, jarring the man who gripped Cwen with a swift shove before she collapsed under the strike of a second nomad's cudgel. She remained motionless, blood seeping to mat her hair and pool in the bed of the wagon.

"Yávië!" Cwen's cry was stifled as three men dragged her out face down, two grasping her legs as the other drove his knee into her back, wrenched her arms behind her and manacled her wrists. They released her and stepped away, laughing as she struggled to stand.

"Let me see my aunt!" Cwen screamed and tried to scramble back into the wagon bed. "Yávië!"

The horseman knocked her off her feet with the shoulder of his mount and then, with shouted commands, had his men bring her to her feet again.

"Do you understand me, demon?" His words were thick with the Emyute accent. At her failure to respond he slid from the horse and stood before her. His fierce slap rattled her teeth and left blood trickling down her chin. "Do you understand?" He gripped her face, grinding the wounded lip against her teeth. "Do you, demon?" His knee slammed between her legs, spreading them as he forced her back against the wagon. "Do you understand me?"

"Yes," Cwen hissed, eyes rolling in search of movement from Yávië.

"You are mine until I decide otherwise. Do you understand?"

His hand dropped, fingers biting into the flesh of her breast then slid up to grip her throat, his thumb squeezing off the blood traveling to her mind as she thrashed against him.

When she went limp he allowed her to slide to the ground, the hidden dagger falling free of its scabbard.

"Drag it." He pulled the ornate ring from the demon's finger, picked up the blade, and threw it into the brush.

Salt air stung Cwen's dry, cracked lips, and the scent of the sea assailed every breath. Suspended from manacled wrists that ended in inflamed broken fingers, she balanced on the bloated toes of bound feet and saw nothing through the crack beneath her blood-caked lashes but her own battered breasts—bruised and torn by brutal beatings. She could not open her eyes beyond narrow slits, as they were far too swollen, and even if they had not been so, she had no strength to waste on lifting eyelids. Cwen knew she bled within, she could feel it, sticky upon her legs. It was the only reason the nomads had abandoned her torture. They seemed revolted by a woman's blood, though Cwen was uncertain if hers was the natural bleeding of the moon's cycle or the blood of some wound the Emyutes had created within her. She had lost track of the moon. Many days ago she had fallen into a stupor, locking what little remained of her sanity somewhere in the darkness of her mind. A tangle of hair hung across her right eye, and she could see a droplet of glistening blood clinging to its end. Her cursed hair was even redder now.

There was a sound. It was the Emyute nomad, Master Buul. Cwen recognized the jangle of his chains and keys. He was her jailor, the possessor of the fair, fire-haired prize—a prize he had shared with many.

A breath hiccoughed its way out on the malodorous air that reeked of vomit. *Fair?* Cwen knew she was no longer fair. Hopefully, she was not far from release, the moment when the cloak of death would free her from pain.

"Still you can laugh demon?" Master Buul no longer bothered with a sibilant stone. His beatings had taught Cwen to understand.

She croaked her denial, the "no" unintelligible as it escaped her abraded throat. In her mind she screamed it and begged in silence not to be hurt again, to be allowed to die without further anguish.

"Men said your eyes were more beautiful than the golden sun setting on the blood-red sea, but there is naught that is beautiful about you now, is there? There is no hint of magick left in you, demon, and the strength of the serpent within you flees through the flow of your blood." He allowed his ragged nails to rake the side of her scab encrusted breast, laughing as pain and terror caused a trickle of urine to spatter Cwen's feet.

"Take it down," he snapped at the man who approached. "Throw it into the sea."

"I would keep it," Lien mumbled.

Buul laughed. "It is dead. Already it begins to stink of death. It is of no further use. What little flesh remains would not even satisfy the hunger of a dog. Any threat of magick is gone. Throw it into the sea, Lien. Let the cold darkness claim it so that I can tell Karid the task is done."

Lien allowed Master Buul to cross beyond the fire and enter his tent before hissing into the young woman's ear, "Unlike Buul, I do not fear your blood. There may be a little magick left in you, demon, and I want it."

He unlocked the manacles and pulled the once beautiful girl to the ground, raised his robe, and knelt over her, taking her with quick, urgent thrusts in the hope of gathering the last of whatever magick she possessed. He rose, rubbed her blood from his body, and then wiped his bloodied hands along the damp grass. Lien dragged the woman to the edge of the cliff and rolled her off the escarpment, listening for the faint splash as the body struck the water far below and the silence that followed as the sea claimed her.

Wearing a satisfied smile, Lien went to tell Buul the demon was dead. As he approached the Emyute leader's tent, the chill night air grew warmer and the glow from within brighter. In the antechamber a rattle of scales and a surge of increased warmth hit him as a blue skinned woman of fire, one of Karid's guards, stopped him with a raised hand.

"You have good news for your queen," the fire guard growled, "news that will save your clan?"

Lien wiped the sweat that trickled near his left eye as he stuttered, "Y…ye…yes, the demon is dead. I killed her myself at Master Buul's command."

"Buul's command?"

"As was ordered by Queen Karid."

"A better answer, nomad. A far better answer. Enter and share the good news with your queen."

The fire guard lifted the flap and motioned Lien to pass, then followed him to take up her station near Queen Karid.

Lien saw Buul, the clan leader, silently kneel in the center of the room, head bowed in submission before the beautiful and enigmatic queen. As Lien neared, Karid tilted her head, swept the train of her ebony silk gown out of her way, and seated herself in Master Buul's dragon ivory throne from where she summoned Lien to approach. "I hope your news is good. Buul does not seem to know for certain," she said, brushing a heavy golden lock away from her face and trailing slender fingers across the swell of her breasts, breaking the Emyute's lustful stare. "He merely gave me this ring and said it belonged to the demon woman. What can you tell me?"

Lien looked up, trapped in Karid's green-eyed gaze.

"Well? Is there good news? I grow tired of waiting for someone to tell me that I have been obeyed," Karid said, her voice rising.

Lien cast a sidelong glance at clan ruler Buul, who still cowered wordlessly in his own chamber. Returning his full attention to the queen, Lien coughed to loosen frozen vocal cords and squawked out a yes.

"Go on. I want details," Karid demanded. "Did the woman suffer? Was the magick beaten from her as I instructed?"

"Y-yes, sh-she was b-b-beaten daily until her d-d-death, just m-m-moments ago."

"You seem a bit uncertain. What is your name?"

Another glance at his cringing leader gave Lien a feeling of power. It was he who had the knowledge the queen sought, not Buul. It was Buul who had failed Karid. Lien raised his chin and continued, "I am Lien. There was no time that I allowed the demon woman peace or painlessness. Even though Buul told me not to, I beat her one last time. I beat her as you commanded, Queen Karid. I killed her and tossed her onto the rocks below the escarpment, then came directly here."

A low sound, half snarl, half grunt, came from the center of the room.

"Hush Buul, you will have my full attention soon enough. Now, you, Lien, tell me, how was the woman killed?" Karid leaned back and smiled. "Convince me that she is dead."

Lien swallowed, his thoughts scurrying about as he sought to recall the moment of the prisoner's death. "I cut her throat," he lied. "I beat her one last time before I cut her throat, then I watched until there was no sign of life and threw the body into the sea."

The queen nodded. "What is your name again, Emyute?"

"Lien, I am Lien your highness."

Karid rubbed her hands together. "Yes, of course, lean as in hungry. Are you hungry, Lien? I like you, Lien, and I need men who I can depend on to follow my orders precisely. You have completed the task I assigned to Buul. He swore it would be no problem, but for some reason he was not willing to see to the chore himself. Perhaps he no longer has the stomach for such work," she said, her steely gaze shifting to Buul. "Stand up Buul!"

The Emyute clan leader rose, his eyes still locked on the sand floor.

"Look at me!" the queen commanded.

Buul looked up at Lien, his lips twisted in bitter anger.

"Look at me! Not at Lien! Now, give Lien your scepter. He is the new ruler of this clan. You will return with me to Serabia where we will discuss your unfortunate disobedience and agree on a consequence."

Buul's startled, disbelieving gaze swung toward Karid. "Your highness, you cannot mean—"

"Do it Buul! Before I sever your hand from your wrist and do it myself!"

Buul held out the scepter with a trembling hand. In a low, threatening whisper he spoke to Lien, "You had best hope my consequence is death."

Lien snatched the scepter, struck Buul a vicious blow, and earned Karid's laughing praise.

"Come Buul, before your new master looses his temper and deprives me of seeing you roasted alive. Guard! Let this man taste your kiss of fire."

The fire guard grabbed Buul's face, twisting and squeezing until his flesh began to sizzle and his jaws opened in a scream. She lifted her other hand and blew crystals of dragon's fire into the Emyute's mouth, scorching his tongue and throat and cutting off his cry.

Lien watched Buul collapse and the guard drag his body outside, and he was startled when Karid linked her arm through his.

"Come Lien, walk me to my coach."

At the coach, Karid cupped Lien's face and kissed him on either cheek. "You are the youngest and certainly the handsomest clan leader in the East. Tonight, Master Lien, celebrate with your men and enjoy the ripeness of your women. On the morrow, by your queen's command, expand the Emyute rule to the north, beyond Ga's Valley. Using whatever force you must, you will take command of the boak mines within Saedan's Sands. I am told Eipa's mine is particularly rich. Take it in the name of your queen, and report to me when the task is done."

"I will my queen."

"Of course you will, Lien, for you would not want to suffer Buul's fate." Laughing, Karid climbed into the coach, which lurched heavily as the horses sprang forward under the driver's whip.

Lien kept his eyes locked on Karid's coach until it disappeared, then raced back to the escarpment and searched the sea below for any sign of the dead girl's body. Finding none, he blew a sigh of relief and called his wives to prepare a feast in honor of his new position.

Chapter 7: The Gift

Riding song-filled waves, the merfolk raced upward, eager to see what Man had cast into the sea. Often they found treasures of wood and metal that were fit to offer the islander, but as they neared it, the scent of human blood made them fearful and drove them back. Interfering with humans would bring punishment.

Deathly white against the crimson waters of the Sanguine Sea, a body drifted downward, tangled knots of hair fanning out from its head and partially covering the face. Shadowy bruises dappled the flesh, and black blood eddied around the still form as the twisting current carried it through the water.

The sounds of the mermaidens mewling and moaning filled the sea around the mermen as thoughts were cast between them. *What have they done? What should we do? Is it alive? If it is dead, we will be blamed...*

Pushing forward, a large merman reached out and gripped a wrist to stop the body's downward course. He drew it nearer to him and, with slender webbed fingers, pushed the hair away to reveal its face. *It lives. Its heart still beats within its breast. We shall take it to the islander. We cannot give it back to those who cast it away, and it must not be found within our waters.* As one, the merfolk gazed toward the towering cliffs and the lands beyond that were peppered with men and campfires.

Together they held the human, keeping the face above the water as their cool webbed hands and strong, broad flukes propelled them toward to the sands of Dragon's Heart.

The merfolk called out with sorrowful song until the pale light of a lantern sliced the darkness along the narrow trail leading from the headland to the sea. They watched the light swing to and fro, dipping with the movement of the jogging islander. As the first rays of lamplight touched the human, the merfolk withdrew, bobbing in the sea, their bright eyes mirroring the lantern's glow.

The islander expected it to be a gift—a wooden crate or a metal box cast away by Man but treasured by the merfolk and offered in homage to the islander. Or perhaps this time it would be a large fish or some ripe kelp or sweet algae. They always came just after sundown on moonless nights. As he knelt, a frown erased his smile, and he looked up to see the pale faces watching him closely. In horror he realized it was not a gift, but a dead woman who lay on the blood soaked sand. And if not a dead woman, one so near death that he doubted she could be saved. He stood and walked to the edge of the cooling shore, the warm red waters lapping over his feet.

"I will bury her," he called to the merfolk, "no blame will come to you."

One by one the bobbing heads dropped beneath the sea, leaving the islander to the dangerous task of disposing of a woman's body. Once again he knelt at her side, leaning close, holding his cheek above her torn lips, checking for any sign of life. Uncertain, he placed his hand on her chest and tucked his fingers up under her left breast, feeling for a heartbeat. Still not sure, he raised the lantern and lifted a swollen eyelid, watching as the pupil grew smaller within its golden iris as if trying to avoid the light. The islander scooped up a handful of sea water and rinsed the dark blood from the woman's hair, revealing burnished copper lights that shimmered in the dancing rays of the lantern. Recognition flickered behind his amber eyes. He exhaled deeply and lifted the woman in whose dreams he had so frequently wandered and carried her homeward, wondering what he would say to the elder who shared his prison isle.

He laid the girl gently down upon his cot and, encouraged by a soft moan, placed strong herbs and tallow in a kettle. He sat beside her cleaning wounds, sewing torn flesh, and setting broken fingers as he waited for the healing mixture to boil. He paused to examine more closely a wound at the side of her left breast, a brand bearing the dragon's track, identical to the one he bore. He dipped cloth strips in the foul smelling mixture and wrapped the wounded girl in the hot, greasy rags, covering her with blankets to hold in the heat as the herbed tallow drew out the poisons of infection. She was a mass of abrasions, bites, and deep bruises, and blood seeped from between her legs. He wondered if it were by nature, at the moon's calling, or from internal injuries. Frowning, he gently bathed away the blood and padded her with soft cloths. Hourly he removed the tallow bandages, replacing them with fresh poultices. At the first rays of daylight, the islander changed the cloths once again and let himself out of the cabin, securing the door with a heavy lock.

He effortlessly ran the nine leagues to the holy man's cave and ducked inside. "Elder!"

The rattle of a stick on stone announced the crippled old man.

"Why are you here?" Elder asked grumpily.

"I need you to look at a woman."

"I have seen them. And those that offer themselves to you are never beautiful."

"Not a whore, a woman from the sea."

The elder stopped and scratched the tangled threads of his beard. "They cannot exist outside the sea. They get their air from the water. Gills, like a fish." He held up his hands on either side of his face, tapping his first fingers against his thumbs in the rhythm of gill breathing. "I thought you knew that, you have seen them often enough. They treat you as if you were a god. And a mermaiden won't offer you any relief. They can only mate with their own kind. Now, get out of here, and let an old man die in peace."

"You have been dying for the last hundred years, and I don't mean a mermaiden. This woman was washed up on the shore, a flesh and blood human woman, and I fear much of her blood has been lost. The merfolk brought her. Will you look at her?"

"No! Now go away, Islander!"

"She may die," the islander pleaded.

"Then bury her—far from here. Do you know what will happen if our jailors find anyone here they haven't brought themselves?"

"I am willing to risk it."

"Well I am not! I want to die in peace, not of rat bites in some prison."

"Elder, this is a prison."

"Aye, well, it offers great freedom. It is better than what I deserved."

"Is it better than I deserve?"

"Stop it! Since when did you start feeling sorry for yourself?"

"Since I discovered I am responsible for what was done to this woman. They beat her to within a breath of death. And do you know why, Elder?"

"No, but I am sure you are about to tell me," the elder replied, rolling his eyes.

"She has fair skin, hair of burnished copper, and eyes of gold. They burned her with the dragon's claw."

The old man's lips quivered, and he sank to the ground, knuckles white around his cane. "They thought she was you? Thought she was what you are, or the one sent to save you?"

"Aye, and she has paid dearly for it. It was my dreams that summoned her you know? I found her and slipped into her sleep where I knew that not even the hate of Karid could follow. Night after night I visited this girl's dreams and showed her my face. Elder, the unseen chains that bind us have never bound the power of my dreams. I saw this girl's kingdom fall. Saw the symbol of her ancestors—a serpent, Elder, a serpent embracing a dragon. I think she is the woman that Flida promised. Do you remember the words, Elder? The words of Flida's promise? You spoke them to me often enough. 'A woman traveler born of the sign of the serpent will embrace you, speak your name, and set you free.' Do you remember those words, Elder? That promise has kept me alive, kept me searching ten thousand dreamers within my sleep. But I found her, Elder, and I planted the seeds for her salvation within the dreaming mind of my deviant brother, the queen's spawn who manipulates the mirror. He snatched this girl from a fiery death at the hands of Karid's assassins, only to have her tortured on Quondam! Now, will you look at her?"

The elder shook his head. "Go home, boy. If she isn't dead, kill her and bury her far from here. No good can come of this, no good at all."

"I can't. She has no power. If she had the power of magick do you believe she would have allowed anyone to defile her so? Don't you understand? This is *my* fault, Elder!"

"Get out!" the elder screamed.

"I will not let it go unpunished," said the islander, standing his ground. "I will send word to the Noor directors. They will offer her sanctuary and find and punish those who did this. They have no love for the Emyutes or Queen Karid and her armies."

"You would only send her to her death. 'Tis better you kill her yourself."

"What do you mean old man?" asked the islander with disbelief.

"The Noor," the old man spat, "will not defend this woman! They are too afraid that Karid will withdraw her protection from them. And they will not punish anyone. They never protect the mirror's travelers once they leave the city. This girl has made men remember our prison, made them remember you. The Noor might want the woman for her uniqueness or possible child bearing ability, but they would fear her potential power and the reprisal of Queen Karid far too much to keep her. Death is a fearsome enemy boy, and the Noor are not brave enough to cross Karid and lose their lives. It was most likely the Noor who sent the girl out of the city and allowed the nomads to commit these crimes against her so they would not have to bear the guilt themselves. The Noor are cowards.

"Brilliant plan though," the old man continued, thinking aloud, "and left alone it would have worked. The girl would have washed up on some distant shore. A horrible murder committed by deadly merfolk. Oh, the Noor would have hunted and killed a merman or two to even the score, then the whole thing would have been forgotten. But no!" he exclaimed in fury. "The merfolk dragged her here. Now she is in your house, and you are in mine! You seem to be forgetting that the Noor directors are abed with Queen Karid and that mirror is death's doorway, nothing more!" The elder wrinkled his nose, clutched his head, and stared at a stalactite directly overhead, willing it to fall and end his miserable life. But it did not fall, for the sentence of the court and his pact with Karid's directorate withheld his magick by the blood of his signature.

"Then I will keep her here."

"You cannot just 'keep' a woman. She is a person. Not like you. She will only fear you. Besides, she will most likely die."

"Not if you help me. And I know how to handle women. They like me," the islander confidently replied.

The old man shook his head, his lower lip jutting out, and his eyes rolling skyward. "You know how to handle the whores who come to relieve you as the agreement dictates. Whores like anyone for a bit of coin. Their laughter is as false as their rapturous screaming. They aren't real women. And women who have been abused by men don't take kindly to men at all."

"Then I will protect her. I won't ask anything of her. Elder, have I ever asked you for anything?"

"No. And this is not a good day to begin, boy. Go, and come back when you want nothing more than to borrow a bottle of sweet berry brandy." The old man grunted and turned to leave.

Disappointment shadowed the islander's golden eyes as he stared after the wretched elder.

"I can't believe that after what you've done, you will not help me."

The old man whirled. "What I've done! What *I've* done! I saved your life, boy!"

"Saved me? Do you think I cared if I was saved? My life was spared, but it isn't much of a life is it? Listening to an old man's caterwauling echo across the hills as I work everyday to grow stronger and more skilled, knowing my strength and skills are wasted here. I relieve myself with whores under the watchful eye of my jailors, but have no hope of knowing the love of a real woman. I am not even allowed my own name. No, it isn't much of a life you've saved, Elder. And you can keep your brandy."

"Boy!" the elder called after the islander's retreating back. "Boil the black mushrooms with a bit of gall oil. It will help. And that's not caterwauling! It's prayer! A little of it wouldn't hurt you!"

Chapter 8: Magick

In the trade city of Luminora, J'var knelt before Yávië and extended the dagger. "I found it in the brush, not far from where I found you in the wagon. It must have been taken from Cwen and simply tossed away."

Visibly shaken, Yávië asked, "Is there no word? None at all? I cannot believe that no one has seen her. Someone must know where she is. Thrice your full moon has brightened the sky. They cannot have kept her for so long without being seen somewhere."

"I do not doubt they have been seen or that someone knows where she is, Yávië, but farmers and herders are afraid to anger the Emyutes. The nomads are fiercely loyal to Karid and quick to punish those who offend or threaten her rule."

"And Cwen? Would she offend or threaten?" Without waiting for his answer Yávië stood and paced the room. "I cannot wait any longer. You must find someone to take me deeper into Quondam," she said, running her fingers over the map before her, "to the West, to Quern's Crossing and across Head Knock Narrows."

"There was blood."

Yávië looked up, staring into J'var's eyes. "Where? How much blood?"

"In an Emyute camp, near the great escarpment, enough blood to lead me to believe Cwen is dead."

Yávië swung on J'var, punctuating the air with an angry finger. "Bring me her body! When I see her lying on the cold stones at my feet, then I will believe she is dead."

"Yávië, you have questioned everyone who would listen from Achroma to Luminora, and no one has admitted knowing anything about Cwen. Stop, and let her rest in her death. Do you not feel the stillness that remains in the wake of her passing?"

Her steps faltered, and Yávië sank into a chair. "It is not death. I know it is not."

"But you have felt the stillness. You know my words are true."

"No." She dragged her fingers through her hair. "I do not know your words are true. In fact, I do not believe they are. Why do you hinder my search? Cast stones upon my path and make men lie to me? Why J'var? Is it you who holds Cwen captive? Does your father?"

Yávië watched the darkness of anger settle on the young man's features, tightening his jaw and lips, narrowing his pale eyes.

N'dia's voice was cool as it drifted across the room, "The Noor do not hold women against their will."

A deep, shuddering breath brought Yávië's apology. "I know that is true, N'dia. What I don't know is why your family will not help me."

Behind them, A'bach spoke, "I will find help for you, Yávië. Wait here with N'dia and be patient. J'var, come with me. We will seek the wisdom of the council of eldermen."

Within the ancient cathedral on Endhaven, eleven grayed and timeworn men sat around the golden table in the Hall of Hallows. The Noor director A'bach and his eldest son stood before them.

"It has been months since the girl disappeared, and the woman is becoming a threat!" cried the youngest, most outspoken of the ten white-robed eldermen, his eyes darting to the blind stryver laying out the morning tea. The elderman lowered his voice to a murmur, "We must do something. This woman's failure to give up the search and accept that the young one is dead will lead to the discovery of our prisoner. She is bound to talk to someone who has heard the legends and who is curious enough to pursue the possibility that they are more than mere tales."

"No. I will guide the woman and keep her from the curious," A'bach swore.

"In the same way your eldest son and daughter guided the young one?" the youngest elderman snapped. "For a thousand years the secret of the dragonspawn has been kept, known only to this council, the Noor directorate, and Karid herself, all magick silenced by the blood of the pact's signing. We cannot risk it. Let the Emyute nomads—"

"No!" The black-robed prime elder at the head of the table shot to his feet. He staggered, his palsied hands gripping the table to steady him. "The death of one innocent is enough! Enough! We do not know for certain the cinnamon-haired girl was the one promised to the dragonspawn." He sank back to his chair. "I will not hear of another death at the hands of the nomads' brutality—at least not without some proof that we are threatened!"

At the prime elder's harsh tones, the blind stryver cringed and shrank away from his task. Only whispered prayers had been heard to cloak the hallowed halls for so long that such sudden anger jolted the tranquility of the stryver and set him listening to seek an explanation for the sudden dissonance.

"But, Prime Elder," the youngest elderman replied, "if the people learn that the beast is more than a superstitious Emyute tale, they will go to Dragon's Heart in search of the truth. For a mortal to step on the sands of Dragon's Heart is to break the pact with Karid that exempts us from death. Only the Noor bloodline of H'san is free of the pact, and then only to deliver the beast's supplies and the women who act as salves for its lust. A broken pact would free the dragon's wrath. It is only secrecy that keeps it bound."

"Do not lecture me on our pact—I was there when Karid and the dragonspawn signed it! Moreover, it is the elder wizard imprisoned there who binds the dragonspawn."

"The imprisoned wizard weakens. Years without magick have taken their toll," another elderman advised.

"Send Yávië back."

All eyes focused on J'var.

"My young director, you know that is not possible. Our agreement with Karid clearly forbids interference with the mirror keeper," the prime elder replied.

"Then send Yávië on to her husband," J'var suggested. "I have seen her suffering. She wants to reunite with her husband more than anything else. She would give up the search for her niece if she were offered reunion with her king."

Heads turned as each elderman sought the wisdom of the others, their curt whispers of disagreement charging the room and drawing the listening stryver closer.

"You believe the woman would willingly choose to free her soul?" asked the prime elder.

"I do, if it means the eternal reunion of their immortal spirits," A'bach said, supporting his son's idea. "She is alone. Without her niece or any hope of returning home there is nothing left for her. She may be determined, but she is not a fool. Her sorrow has taken a great toll, she knows she is weak, and the promise of paradise with her husband will offer eternal solace, a hard gift to refuse."

Again heads bowed, and discordant mumblings filled the room.

"It would mean releasing the soulbinder from his oath, allowing him to search for this man's soul. We would risk someone feeling the tremors from his presence as he worked his forbidden magick," one of the eldermen cautioned.

"Not someone!" another shouted. "Karid! Our pact with her prohibits the use of magick by this council. If we break the pact, Flida's dragonspawn is no longer bound. He will be free to seek the power of his magick, and Karid will turn her fury on us!"

The youngest elderman leapt to his feet and paced in agitation. "If only this council had killed the dragonspawn, none of this would be happening, and we would not sit here today contemplating this unthinkable risk!" he wailed.

"Silence!" the prime elder demanded. "Sit down!"

The youngest council member sat with a sigh of exasperation and disgust.

"Your behavior is not fitting a member of this council!" the prime elder chastised. "We could not kill what Flida's magick had created and blessed. Do you forget that it was by the command of a sentinel of the sacred woods, a sentinel still favored by the gods, that the last of Quondam's magick was hidden in the beast's blood?"

"He may have been created at Flida's command, but Karid's curse gave us dominion over him, did it not? It was madness to let him live after he killed your predecessor," muttered the youngest elderman.

The prime elder's furious glare silenced his subordinate. "You are too young to remember the dragonspawn's trial and the pact we signed with Karid, a pact that expressly forbids the use of magick by any man or beast and provides us with the queen's protection. Karid could not kill what her sister Flida had created as a sentinel of the sacred wildwoods. She did not have the power to do so. Not even the heretical nomads have been brave enough to attempt to kill the sacred beast. So, our queen could only curse the spawn, and with the help of this council and the Noor directorate, find him guilty of crimes against men, and lock him away, stripped of his potential power.

"We must be cautious, for if we allow the use of magick and the dragonspawn is freed, the queen will turn her sting on this council and the Noor directorate." The prime elder turned to the youngest elderman and asked, "Is that what you seek? Death for every member of this council and the directorate?"

The belligerent elderman dropped his gaze, his silence was answer enough.

"Nay, I did not think so!" the prime elder snapped. "It is by our agreement that the dragonspawn lives, and if it were freed and united with the human girl from the House of Aaradan, its potential would be limitless. But the young woman has been murdered by the nomads, freeing us of her threat. Therefore, we will heed our pact with Karid, and there will be no more talk of the beast or the use of magick."

After a long silence, A'bach offered, "In the tombs beneath the Fount of Sorrows the soulbinder's magick could be safely practiced. All words are silenced beneath the Fount, and the moment of magick would be muffled by the body of the earth. We would be rid of the woman, and everything would be as it was with no further threat of the dragonspawn's release or Queen Karid's anger against this council."

"Where is the woman now?" the prime elder asked.

"She awaits our return in Luminora, Prime Elder. We could have her here within a lunar cycle."

"Very well, bring the woman to us," the prime elder finally agreed. "Bring her, and we shall see. If she does not agree to release her soul and join her husband, then seeking the assistance of the nomads with this problem will be our only choice."

A'bach and J'var bowed and backed away as the blind stryver slipped out behind the curtains in the corner of the room, his thoughts churning with the eldermen's words.

A'bach and J'var returned to Luminora and collected Yávië and N'dia. A lunar cycle's journey took them overland from Luminora to Achroma where N'dia was left under the supervision of L'or.

From there, in the company of A'bach and J'var, Yávië crossed the restless sea between Achroma and the cathedral at Endhaven to reach the Hall of Hallows and stand before Queen Karid's council of eldermen.

"I am the prime elder, spokesman for this council," the ancient, black-robed man addressed Yávië. "We are sorry for the loss of your niece. The nomads responsible for her death will be punished according to our law. Since the girl was under the supervision of Quondam's directorate when she was kidnapped, this council feels some responsibility, and we wish to offer you compensation," the black-robed prime elder proposed.

Eyes fixed on the mural behind the golden table, Yávië lifted her hand to point at the fading images of dragons. "Once there was magick here, and there were dragons filling your skies. Where are they now? What happened to your magick?"

"It is true, once the skies were filled with dragons, but Queen Karid—" A stern look from the prime elder cut short the younger man's response.

"We did not bring you here for a lesson in Quondam's history," the prime elder continued. "We would like to end your sorrow. We have taken it upon ourselves to bend the laws against magick and allow our soulbinder to practice his art just once in order to reunite you with the mate you lost. Already the soulbinder has located the spirit of Sareel. That is your husband's name is it not? Sareel?"

Yávië forced the name away, ignoring the prime elder's mispronunciation of Sōrél's name and the deliberate bait. "First, you did not bring me here. I came of my own free will. I seek your help in finding my niece and nothing more. As for your offer, I believe it is nothing but another stumbling block deliberately pushed into my path to stop my search for Cwen."

"We have found a soul lost within death's chasm in a world called Ædracmoræ, your world I believe. It is the soul of a husband and father, the soul of a warrior and king. We do have the power to reunite you. Perhaps before you cast this opportunity aside you should see the truth of our offer."

"Already I have suffered the days of darkness that came with the loss of my husband," Yávië admitted. "I have no desire to experience the hurt of whatever deception you have planned. Through your seasons of planting and harvesting I have wandered this world in search of my niece, and in the end I stand here before old men who make false promises to reunite me with a dead husband."

Yávië turned to go, only to find her way blocked by A'bach and J'var.

"And you? Do you scheme with this council? Shall I follow docilely to my death? Is that your plan?"

Neither answered, and A'bach merely gestured that she return her gaze to the eldermen. Swinging about, Yávië spat her words at them, "Then let us get on with it! Show me your illusions!"

In single file they threaded their way along the narrow, winding staircase that plunged beneath the cathedral and entered a chamber aglow with candlelight. Overhead a tangle of dripping roots embraced the stone buttresses of an ancient well, the hidden foundation for the Fount of Sorrows that spilled its waters across the sacred island above this almost forgotten subterranean cavern.

"Soulbinder!" the prime elder called, drawing a man from the shadows. "Show the woman what you have found."

"It is dangerous, Prime Elder. I would be remiss if I did not remind you of the risk. The moment of magick will echo through the earth in a wave of tremors. It is possible that Queen Karid or another sensitive may take notice and mark it for what it is. If so, they will know we walk a forbidden path."

"Just do it. The decision has already been made."

Bowing respectfully, the soulbinder disrobed and moved to the center of the cavernous room, directly below the Fount of Sorrows. With a throw of his arm and a flash of his fingers, the soulbinder unveiled a brilliant shaft of light, and there within stood the shimmering image of Sōrél, king of Ædracmoræ.

"It proves nothing." Yávië remained apart, arms folded across her breasts, fingers digging into her own flesh to stop herself from screaming Sōrél's name. "Only that your jester is a well-trained illusionist."

"I assure you, madam, that this is no jest," the prime elder reassured. "Speak to your husband, go to him. You need only step into the shaft of light to join him for eternity."

"No. It is a trick. It must be a trick."

"I cannot allow the use of magick for more than a few moments." The prime elder's voice tensed. "We break our vows to our queen in our desire to help you. Go to your king now, or lose him."

Yávië felt Sōrél's warmth as his thoughts entered her mind, and she closed her eyes against the intruding eldermen. Sōrél's silent words, a whispered caress, pulled her closer.

Yávië, I did not believe the soulbinder's promise. I never thought I would see you again.

Yávië looked up, searching the ethereal face, the deep sapphire of his eyes. "Are you not just an illusion?" she whispered, sinking to her knees beside the pulsing light. "I have lost so much. Ædracmoræ is gone, burned by the same assassin who murdered you. I have lost Sóvië and Cwen. Everyone was taken. Oh Sōrél, I have lost Sóvië! I have been so alone."

Our daughter was not taken. Sóvië is home, safe with the wizard Grumbleton. I have touched her mind and felt her strength.

"Sóvië lives? You know this? You know that she is safe?" Comforted by Sōrél's words, relief eased the lines on Yávië's face. "But Cwen… Sōrél, she is lost, taken by the nomads. Somewhere in this world she waits to be found." Tears flooded Yávië's eyes and a sob, forced up from the depths of her soul, stole her breath and broke her heart. "Oh, Sōrél, I thought you were lost to me, forever lost…"

Sōrél's hand reached out, resting just beyond the edge of the light, fingers splayed, and awaiting Yávië's touch.

There is a great hidden magick in Quondam, my love, magick enough to summon my soul from the chains of death's abyss. I am here in the brilliance and beauty of the gardens of eternity, freed by this soulbinder and the will of this council.

The Queen of Ædracmoræ rose to stand on trembling legs and addressed the prime elder. "What will happen if I accept your gift and join my husband?"

"Beyond is the garden of purity, a place of eternal rest for the souls of Quondam's royal bloodline. It is a place beyond the trials of mortal life, where you will be with your husband. Your physical shell will remain behind and be given a resting place here among Quondam's nobility."

A sudden shudder along the cavern walls and drifting dust brought a scowl to the prime elder's face. "Time escapes us. I cannot allow the portal between these realms to remain open much longer. Tendrils of magick reach out beyond this space, and we risk detection. Whatever your choice, make it quickly."

"What of my niece? What of those left behind in my home world?" Yávië pleaded for an answer that would set her free, her eyes searching those of the prime elder.

Do you trust me Yávië?

Sōrél's private words stirred within Yávië's consciousness, pulling her back to him.

Another cares for Cwen. He frees you of that burden. With the power of the dragon, he frees you to come to me. If you refuse, this council will soon realize Cwen lives and hunt her to her death at the command of their queen.

She lives? Cwen lives, Sōrél? You know that this is true, know that she is safe? Yávië beseeched him silently.

Aye, Yávië, she was near death, but I have felt the presence of her healing soul. The day of our greatness has passed. Our enemies and allies have gone on to their punishments and rewards. Cwen and Sóvië remain to serve another. Their path is not ours. Sóvië's reign lies beyond a future of sorrows and defeats, wars and victories, both here and on Ædracmoræ. And Cwen will only be safe if you come with me. Your very search endangers her. Come with me, my love. Are we not at last entitled to our rest? Give Cwen the power. Allow Cwen and Sóvië to meet their challenges. Yávië, come to me.

In a slow and deliberate movement, Yávië placed her hands on the jewel that joined her power with Sōrél's and lifted it over her head. She looked at J'var and held it out to him. "If you should find Cwen, give this to her. It binds the blood of my house to the blood of Sōrél's. It binds the power of the serpent and the dragon. It will give her the strength…" Words suddenly failed her.

J'var lifted the serpent-encircled sapphire stone from Yávië's trembling palm and placed a hand on her shoulder to give it a gentle squeeze of understanding.

A single, faltering step took Yávië to Sōrél. "I trust you," she whispered as her hand broke the light and pushed against Sōrél's waiting palm. Their fingers entwined as he drew her to him, enveloping her in his eternal embrace. Behind her, outside the shaft of light, the eldermen watched as Yávië's body slid to the stone floor, an empty vessel—the final vestige of the warrior queen from a fallen world.

A'bach and J'var watched until the souls of Yávië and her king were lost from sight in the intensifying light. It winked out as suddenly as it had appeared, the magick sending out a final faint, shuddering pulse throughout the depths of Quondam before returning to the silence of its former dormancy.

A'bach knelt and lifted Yávië's body, tenderly smoothing the hair away from her brow. "She was a brave and noble woman, fit to rest among my ancestors. I will see to her resting place." Without a backward glance, he and his son began the upward climb.

No one noticed the small gray stryver pressed into a hollow in the stones. None saw him flee ahead of them, nor was he caught on the eldermen's boat as it returned A'bach and J'var to Achroma with Yávië's body. When the blind stryver crouched outside B'rma's tavern, those passing by believed he waited there hoping to gather scraps. As light left the skies and gloom cloaked the alley, no human eye noticed other stryvers join the first. In any event, a meeting of stryvers was ludicrous, for it was known that stryvers could not speak.

Their dull eyes shifting nervously, the group of stryvers slunk along beside the walls and slipped into the sewers that ran below Achroma. Outside the city walls they stripped away their collars and dropped to all fours, racing away into the night, free to share the newfound knowledge that the beast of the nomads' tales was held on Dragon's Heart Isle.

Chapter 9: Awakening

The old man stood watching from the doorway as the islander bathed the silent, copper-haired girl. "Just because a body breathes does not mean there is life," he snorted. "Just because the bruises have faded and the bones have knit does not mean the girl will wake, yet you act as though she can hear you!"

"There is life. She merely sleeps. Still I see her wandering in my dreams. She comes to me, Elder. And she bears the brand of the dragon."

"Bah! From dreams one can awaken, but this is the death of the mind. From that there is no recovery, no matter how long you care for the body. If she were your promised woman she would have wakened long ago. And the brand was merely burned into her as part of the torture. Just like yours. It does not mean she is the promised one."

Islander disregarded the elder's words and worked the girl's legs, arms, and hands, paying close attention to her fingers, massaging them and flexing each joint with gentle determination. "I saw the first snowflakes fall today beyond the ridge. I will take you there when you awake." He spoke in low, companionable tones, as if to an old friend. "Each day the merfolk have waited in the surf and watched for you, but they will go now until the spring."

"Daft is what you are!"

The islander continued to ignore the elder's rudeness and asked, "Will you stay with her while I go for the supplies? I will fetch yours as well and carry them to your cavern."

Sniffing and shuffling his displeasure, the old man shifted his weight to relieve pressure on his lame leg, thinking of the long trek from cave to boat and back again and the surliness of the Noor jailors. The offer was a good one, even though it might leave the elder emptying the woman's chamber pot. "How long?"

"A day, no more. I will want to spend a few hours with whatever woman they bring. It will be the last boat before spring, and I want to borrow a bit of woman's clothing for this golden girl. I hope this whore is thinner than the last."

Islander had collected quite a sampling of women's undergarments in the months since the girl had washed up on the shore and had even managed to convince one visiting lady of pleasure that she had lost her shirt.

The elder frowned. "About that *borrowing* you've been doing. Eventually one of those loose women will notice she's missing her woolies and cry foul to the jailors."

When the islander reached for a jar of herbal salve, the elder held out a small, cloth-covered pot. "Use this instead. It will draw the redness from the scars of your sloppy sewing."

"Why should we worry about scars on a woman who will never wake?" Islander quipped.

"Don't bait me, boy! If she ever does wake you can bet her first act will be to drive a bolt through your gut. You are stupid to leave weapons lying about."

"Daft and stupid—it is a fine man you have raised, Elder." A smile tugged at the corners of Islander's mouth. "You know that she will wake and that it is only because I have cared for her that she heals. Be here by daybreak. I want to be waiting at the dock when they arrive. I don't want the Noors to have any reason to seek us out. Besides, it amuses them when they believe I am desperate for the women they bring."

"And are you not?"

"Elder, I will not deny enjoying the company of willing women or the relief they provide the flesh. False or not, a woman's laughter is a far better sound than your voice. But desperate I am not, and not one of them has ever stirred the dragon in my soul."

The elder grunted and pursed his lips. "Must be another of Man's misconceptions then. They say you are a ravenous, uncontrollable, insatiable, voracious, rapacious—"

"Enough. I have gotten your point."

"—beast, and if you were not restrained, you would despoil their fair women, rip out men's throats, and eat their children."

"There is never any hushing you, is there? And I prefer turnips to children. Turnips have more virtue."

"It is why they keep you sated with working women."

"Yet look what they have done." Islander traced a raised, red scar along the unconscious woman's cheekbone.

"I am never satisfied. There is always a feeling of emptiness inside me no matter how many women they send. And I am bound by Karid's curse and the blood of my signature, just as you are bound by yours. No more, no less. Come, Elder, I will give you some turnips, pull your cart, and let you ride."

On the far side of the island, Islander waited as two Noor jailors disembarked from the boat, one shouting at the cowering oarsmen to bring the supplies ashore. This trip's harlot was Y'ithe, not unattractive for a middle aged woman who sold favors. She wore a heavy cloak against the bitter chill and reminded Islander of her preferences before reaching out to take his hand. "Come aboard. It is too cold to disrobe outdoors. Make it quick. I have no desire to be chilled any longer than necessary."

"It won't be necessary."

"What?" she swung back to him. "You have no need?"

The nearest jailor looked up from his chore. "Found yourself a mermaiden, Islander?"

"No, I merely meant Y'ithe need not disrobe completely. There is no need for her to be chilled unnecessarily. Don't you find that chivalrous of me, jailor?"

Laughing and shaking his head, the jailor pointed to a large empty crate. "There will do. No need to taint the boat with the stench of a beast. It is bad enough we are forced to travel with the odor of a whore."

Islander looked away to hide the flush of anger that rose above the collar of his shirt.

Huddled in the crate with Y'ithe, he stopped her hand as she reached for the drawstring of his trousers. "It is too cold. I will simply rock the crate. If you will cry out your pleasure, they need never know you did not earn the coin."

When he emerged from the crate, the islander ignored the jailors' jeers and provocation. With stoic disregard, he gathered the supplies and loaded them into the wagon that he would pull the twenty leagues to the elder's cave and thence another nine to his cabin. As he walked away, he was pleased by the thought that there would be no threat of jailors again until spring.

It was the depths of winter. Flurries of sleet had followed the drifting, powdered snow and drove the old man deep beneath the earth to warm, snug chambers. The islander had returned from delivering the elder some grain and a few dozen onions and tossed another log on the flickering fire.

"Are you warm enough?" Islander asked his unconscious guest as he dragged her bed as close to the fire as he thought safe and covered her with extra blankets that nearly hid her small, still form. Each day Islander worked the girl's muscles and joints, shifted her position to keep her comfortable and avoid the sores that the elder swore would surely come. He faithfully applied the salve to her scars and watched as they faded. In the past few days, she had been vomiting up the mashed and blended gruel, gagging at the very touch of meat against her lips, and so the islander began to strain the soups, offering the girl only the purest broth.

"Tonight there is a rare pale broth made of fowl and seasoned with herbs that Elder sent. He says your sickness is a good sign, though I am not sure he really knows."

Islander dropped to the chair beside the bed. He placed the bowl within easy reach and lifted the girl to rest against stacked pillows. She was so very pale, her skin fine and soft like the petal of a wild rose. The scars were barely visible, no more than raised white threads. Gold lights were woven though her hair from the fire's warm glow. "Beautiful," he whispered. "You are beautiful, and I feel as if I know you. So often I have stood before you in your dreams. Now here you are, a golden girl washed from a ruby sea. Eat your broth so that you can grow strong and wake to talk to me." He held the cup to her lips and watched them part, as if of their own accord, to accept the broth.

When the cup was empty, Islander filled it again and followed the same simple method, making sure she swallowed and blotting her mouth with the tail of his shirt when the cup emptied the second time.

"Shall I read to you?" He opened his only book—stories filled with tales of Man's conquest of the wickedness of magick and the deaths of the dragons. It was all he was allowed.

Islander passed the days in pleasant conversation with the silent girl. At the center of the room he sat and cleaned a starved hare while he waited for the kettle to boil.

"When I was young, the elder taught me how to behave as a man. I learned to string a bow and affix fletches so as to make an arrow soar. I am a good hunter, though there is little to hunt in winter. The sorceress C'thra taught me the many languages of Quondam and the manners of the court of the Noor. I believe I could pass as a very well-bred nobleman in Queen Karid's court if I did not bear the fey fairness of the dragon."

He poured tea and carried it to the bedside, pushing the bed a bit further from the hearth and turning back the top blanket. "The air warms. Perhaps spring will arrive early this year." As he always did, he lifted the girl and plumped the pillows behind her back, nestling her body into them to keep her upright. As Islander raised the cup, he noticed movement behind her eyelids, not the movement of a dreaming sleeper, but the movement of a woman trying to feign slumber. He saw a shiver run through the girl's body and the rigid set of her arms, her trembling fingers curling into her palms, so he put the cup back on the bedside table, stood up, moved away, and went back to cleaning the hare.

Cwen could not stop shivering. From somewhere close, the scent of sweet tea reached her along with the sound of another's breathing. Slowly sliding sideways against an unrecognizable softness, she waited for the pain. When the trembling increased and threatened to topple her from the bed, Islander stepped back to steady her.

"I know you are afraid," he whispered as he settled her back against the pillows, careful not to touch her or make any contact that could seem threatening. "You should drink your tea." He brought the cup to her lips and heard her teeth rattle against its rim before she allowed a bit of the sweet liquid into her mouth. She swallowed and opened terrified eyes.

Eyes as wide as a startled fawn and golden as a sunset in an autumn haze stared into those of Islander. As Cwen's gaze shifted focus to take in the rest of his face, she saw that the eyes looking at her with such concern belonged to a man—not Master Buul nor any Emyute nomad, but a man who was clean and from whom the scent of soap emanated. He was fair and wore his copper hair tied back in a braid. His eyebrows were arched questioningly above dark amber eyes, and his mouth held the hint of a smile. Cwen did not smile in return. She knew smiling was not allowed, that a smile was only a trick to make her forget the rules. She did not speak, for speaking was not allowed. Staring was not allowed either, but it was far too late not to stare, so she simply lowered her eyes and waited for the man to strike her.

Her shaking rattled the rails of the bed, and Islander smelled the release of the girl's urine. He stood and checked the water in the kettle, adding to it and moving it over the flame. He got a clean nightshirt and returned to the bed. "You have soiled yourself and need to wash. I have clean bedclothes and a nightshirt."

She did not move except for the bone-rattling of her fear. The islander sighed, wrapped her in the topmost blanket and carried her to his own pallet, lowering her and watching her fold into a shivering ball. He quickly stripped her bed and remade it, deciding that a quick change of her nightdress would be less traumatic than worrying her further with bathing.

"I am going to change your clothes. I will not touch you anymore than I must," he said gently. At his touch her shaking increased, and he swiftly lifted the soiled gown and replaced it with the clean one.

Again he carried her, observing that she made no move to stop him or grip him out of fear of falling. He settled her beneath the blankets and tucked them tight around her.

"Can you even look at me?"

Cwen closed her eyes more tightly, clinching them painfully against the possibility of offending him with her gaze. She knew the question was a trick, because looking was not allowed.

He turned away, murmuring sadly, "And men call me a beast."

◈

The elder seemed to be of special interest to the girl. While she never looked at him directly, Islander caught her glancing furtively toward the old man whenever he visited. Since the first terrified opening of her eyes, she had not made eye contact with either man.

"It is the conditioning of the nomads, boy," Elder explained. "Within their camps no woman is allowed a direct gaze, an expression of joy or displeasure, or a voice. Even those bound by marriage are rarely treated with more favor than a much valued dog. A girl like this, a foreigner they believed to be a demon, would have been a challenge to break. To reduce her to this level of obedience must have taken many beatings."

"Even the sound of my footsteps sets her trembling, and my touch terrifies her. What can I do, Elder?"

"Cover the floors with rags to dampen the sound. Don't touch her and don't talk to her. Perhaps with time a bit of curiosity will return and salvage some small portion of her sanity. Fear is an odious bedfellow and the only one she has."

Silence returned to the islander's cabin. His heavy tread whispered on cloth covered floors, every movement became slow and deliberate, and he withdrew his touch. They developed a routine within the silence. Each day Islander left the cabin to run the hills and practice the blades, and Cwen rose, wrapped in a blanket, to sit on the edge of the bed, pressing the soles of her feet against the floor and forcing them to bear a bit of her weight until at last she stood alone, gripping the edge of the headboard. In the belief that he would know and beat her for such insolence, she examined nothing and touched none of the young man's possessions. She ate whatever he placed before her, drank her tea, and rubbed salve onto her scars with trembling hands, never questioning her position.

When the air warmed and the smell of spring flowers wafted in upon the breeze, Cwen staggered to the open doorway in her owner's absence and stared out across the land. Step by tremulous step, she let herself down the stairs of his porch and lifted her face to the sun.

Islander came to an abrupt halt on the hill above the cabin and stared down at the woman standing in his yard. A breeze lifted her copper hair, creating a playground of rich, red-brown shadows wherein the golden sunlight danced. Her nightdress billowed around her bare feet, and her hands were held out as if in reverent supplication for the sudden warmth of the day. Her face remained expressionless, but it was without the tension it bore in his presence. Islander sank to a squat, a clump of berry brambles hiding him from discovery.

It was the unexpected cry of a falcon hunting overhead that sent the beautiful girl stumbling up the stairs and back to the security of her covers.

Torrential spring rains kept Islander inside, and the girl turned away from him, huddled beneath the protective layer of blankets. After the third day of inactivity, Islander cleared a space in the center of the room, dragging the table and chairs noisily across the floor, causing the girl to snuggle deeper into her defensive nest. He fetched the ancient wooden practice sword, warped and out of balance, and wished again he had taken the time to carve a new one. He placed his feet in position, raising the sword to guard. Slowly, he brought the sword to the left, sliding it into a smooth backhand stroke, each movement of his feet causing a floorboard to creak. He kept his back to the girl, except on the turns, and even then he did not look in her direction, but kept his gaze focused on the practice blade. As his muscles warmed, he moved more quickly, the wooden sword's slice audible as it cut a swathe through the air. After an hour he exchanged the sword for a staff and worked until hunger nudged him.

He set about preparing supper, slicing root vegetables and a slab of salt pork with practiced precision. Scraping them into the pot, Islander hung it over the fire before grabbing the pail and going to fetch more water. On his return, he froze in the doorway. The girl stood, stock-still in the center of the room, holding the practice sword across open palms.

Islander searched her face, but it was blank, and her eyes remained on the blade in her hands. Sensing the young man's presence, her hands began to shake, and fear circled her mouth in a white line. Her hair cloaked her face as her head bowed in submission, and she dropped the sword to the floor.

Islander set the pail beside the doorway and stepped forward to pick up the sword.

"There is no balance," the girl whispered, almost inaudible.

Startled by the sound of her whispered voice, the islander jerked upright, sending the girl scurrying to the far side of her bed where she dropped from sight, clutching herself against certain punishment.

Islander moved forward until he could see her crouching body. "What is wrong with the balance?" he asked, his low, even tones matching her whispered statement.

Cwen turned her head slightly, a single golden eye glancing up through a veil of hair before quickly looking away.

"Tell me. I would like to know."

She glanced up again, wetting her lips and swallowing to release the words over unused vocal cords. "It is old, the wood weathered unevenly."

"And you have some knowledge of swords?"

She nodded, silence reclaiming her fleeting lack of caution.

"Will you tell me how to correct the balance?"

But the momentary memory and the bravery that came with it were lost, and like a wounded bird, Cwen merely tucked her head against her shoulder.

When the stew had simmered long enough and the cabin was filled with the delicious aroma of fresh herbs and bread, Islander set the table for two, rather than placing the girl's food at her bedside. He sat alone and ate slowly, waiting for hunger to draw the girl to the table. As he wiped his bowl clean with a last bite of bread he heard the whisper of her bare feet. She circled widely, keeping as much distance between them as the cabin permitted, poised for flight back to her haven if this change in routine proved to be a trick.

She pulled back the chair and sat sideways, not trapping herself behind the table. She grabbed the spoon and shoveled the soup into her mouth, watching his hands suspiciously over the rim of the bowl. Her hand darted out and snatched a bit of bread, but her eyes never left their lock on his resting hands. Islander was certain that if he so much as curled a finger she would flee, so he simply sat silent and watched a moth flutter near the lantern.

When Cwen had finished eating, she carried her bowl and spoon to the pail, washed them and set them in the drying rack. She stood, hands hanging loosely at her sides as uncertainty claimed her. At last she shuffled to the table and claimed Islander's empty bowl and spoon and repeated the simple chore of cleaning up. When Islander stood, she froze and watched as he scraped the remains of the stew into a covered bowl and placed it on the counter furthest from the heat of the hearth. She looked away as he passed her on his way to wrap the bread and put it in the breadbox.

Without another word, Islander went to his pallet, stripped down to his woolens and slid beneath his blanket, turning his back to the girl.

"She spoke." Islander raised his voice to be heard above the splintering of wood. "And she eats at my table and takes on simple chores, cleaning up and weeding the garden."

Elder nodded, stacking the split logs against the woodshed. A glance at the cabin revealed the girl sitting within a ray of sunlight, shelling beans.

"Elder, she knew the old sword was not properly balanced. How could a woman know that?"

"Perhaps she had brothers or a husband. It is hard to know with foreigners. She is well past twenty summers, far beyond the marrying age. Most likely there is a husband somewhere, maybe even in one of the trade centers. It could be that one so exquisite belongs to a Noor director. What do you intend to do, boy?"

"Care for her. Keep her safe. Teach her to defend herself."

The elder snorted his disgust. "If you arm her, she may kill you."

"I doubt if she has the strength to beat me to death with a wooden sword. Besides she has shown me no aggression. I go out of my way not to alarm her."

"Boy, as she grows stronger and has time to recall what brought her here, she will become a danger to us. Of that there is no doubt. She will try to escape, even if it means swimming the sea. It would be best to let her go. Just show her the door, and tell her she is free. Let her make her own way. Give her that rotting raft you built and hid in the caverns of the merfolk."

"Do you fear her, Elder?"

"No. I fear what Queen Karid will do when it is discovered we have harbored her. Have you forgotten your trials? The pain of the rack and the whip? The burn of the brand? We have broken the pact, Islander. The jailors will report this to Karid once they discover the girl, and Karid will not risk having you set free by some female traveler."

The islander lowered the heavy axe, the sheen of sweat glistening across his bare chest and arms. "Did you feel the earth tremble, Elder? Perhaps we are not the only ones who test the chains."

"Aye, I felt it. Distant it was. Far to the southeast."

Islander wiped the sweat from his brow with the back of his arm and swung the heavy axe again, striking the wedge and sending the split logs flying.

"Endhaven?"

"Perhaps," Elder said in an exhalation of wheezing breath. "I think it is best we forget that we felt a ripple of power. Pretend it was nothing more than the natural grumbling of the earth. Now go, see to the woman. She stands beyond the porch."

The girl wore a pair of Elder's cloth trousers. They were held snugly at the waist with a drawstring, the legs rolled up to her ankles, and a shirt stolen from a whore. Islander found her more beautiful than sunset on the sea. Her arms were crossed protectively across her breasts, and her eyes remained focused somewhere beyond Islander's shoulder as she spoke. "Master, might I bathe?"

He did not answer aloud, but simply gestured to the rain barrel at the corner of the house and turned back to his work. Her next words stopped him and brought him back to her.

"Did you buy me from Master Buul?"

"No."

The goose bumps of fear rose along her arms, and he heard her teeth chatter as the uncontrollable shaking took hold of her. "If you stole me from him, he will come for me." The words rattled as her body shook back and forth.

"I did not steal you. Sit down."

Obediently, Cwen sat.

"No, not in the dirt—there, on the porch."

Cwen scrambled to get to her feet, sucking in a scream as he grasped her arm in an attempt to help her up.

"I am sorry." He released her arm and pointed to the porch. "Please sit."

Clearly panicking, Cwen took five strides to the porch and dropped to the step, hugging her knees. Islander sank down beside her and watched as she shrank away from him.

"The merfolk found you in the sea. It is they who saved your life by bringing you to my shore. That was nearly a year ago. I do not know anyone called Buul, but I can assure you that he will not come here."

Her hair fell forward, shielding her from his view as she whispered, "I have no memory of it, no memories of my days before Master Buul. You are my new master?"

"I am no one's master. I am a prisoner here, as is my elder. You are a free woman stranded on an island prison. I am called Islander, the old man is Elder."

"You give me freedom?" Her sudden disbelieving sobs tortured him, and he ached to comfort her. Feeling useless and overwhelmed by anger at the young woman's tormenters, he returned to chopping wood with a newfound force that strained his muscles and sent the elder ducking from the flying chip projectiles, cursing in irritation.

After the wood was stacked, the elder left with a final warning about a woman's fury, and Islander slipped past the still weeping girl to the rain barrel and washed away his sweat. He pulled a clean shirt over his head and went inside to cook supper.

He ate alone and left the girl's dinner on the table.

In the morning the girl was gone. Islander cooked breakfast and ate it on the porch in the hope that the smell of food would bring her back. He did the morning chores and loaded the wagon with firewood to take to the elder, slipping into the harness and setting off at a jog.

He stacked the wood in the elder's shed and gave a shout, hoping for a bit of a chat and the offer of fermented gall oil.

"Elder!"

"In here!"

The call drew him into the elder's living quarters where he discovered the cowering girl.

She backed away, nervously twisting the tail of her shirt as her eyes darted to the door and back again.

"Master, you said I was free."

Islander shrugged and poured himself some of the hot, bitter gall, drinking it in a long, single swallow. "I am not your master, and you are a free woman."

"I imagine it took her most of the night to find me. I've told her she can't stay here. That there is a shack near the boat dock," the elder said.

"She can't stay there. It isn't safe." Then, turning to Cwen, "They will find you there," Islander explained, looking at the girl. "It is one of the places the jailors search when the boat brings our supplies. I leave pelts and badly made arrows and snares for them to find. It keeps them away from my cabin. Makes them think they are a step ahead of me. Don't go there."

"I cannot stay in your cabin." Her words were soft, a test of refusal as well as freedom.

"Why not? You have been there almost year, and I have done nothing but care for you. I fed you and bathed you and emptied your chamber pot. I kept your muscles strong, but never did I touch you inappropriately. I gave up my bed and slept on the floor. Not once since your awakening have I demanded anything of you, yet suddenly you feel there is some impropriety?"

A blush of shame flooded the girl's cheeks, and she wrung her hands to stop their trembling. "I am not ungrateful. You have been kind, but—"

"The fates have dealt you a heavy blow. Stay with me," the islander interrupted, "until I can build you a cabin of your own. Stay where you are safe, where the jailors never come. Share my chores. Make polite conversation. I will help you rebuild your strength, and I swear I will not touch you."

"You would build me a cabin?"

"I promise it."

"And sharing your chores would be sufficient recompense? You will not beat me?" She closed her eyes against the horror the next words brought, "…rape me?"

"I swear to you, my hands will bring you no harm. Just share my chores. I will make no other demands of you, and I will craft you a practice sword. You told me once you had some knowledge of the sword."

Uncertainty creased her brow. "I have no memory of it," Cwen whispered, as her eyes flooded with the tears of loss and confusion, "neither of telling you nor any knowledge of using a sword."

"We will practice together and see if your arm remembers what your mind does not. And I swear before Elder, I will not ask more of you. I will not touch you. Tell me your name to seal the pact." He held out his hand.

"You'd best take that hand, Missy. You won't get a better offer on this island. And the boy would not swear before me and break his word," the elder said.

The girl looked up, her eyes directly meeting the islander's for the first time since her terrified awakening, and she realized that his golden eyes held the same quizzical expression as before and his mouth the same soft smile. "In my dreams I hear a woman speak my name. She calls me Cwen." She extended a trembling hand and sealed the pledge.

"Then Cwen you must be, for our dreams do not lie." The islander held Cwen's hand between his, warming away her icy chill and silently swearing he would somehow end her fear.

Cwen stepped from the cabin to find Islander seated on the porch with a limb of seasoned wood and a hand axe. Around him lay a growing pile of shavings as he expertly trimmed the branch into a practice blade.

"It must fit your grasp." He extended the end destined to be a hilt. "Take it, two-handed."

Cwen reached out, left hand first and gripped the stick. Islander leaned forward and examined the grip, nodded, then reclaimed the wood and resumed whittling. They repeated the process several times before he was satisfied the finished hilt would be right for Cwen's hands.

"Did I know you long ago?" Her question surprised him, and he looked up to find Cwen gazing at him with a puzzled expression.

"I feel as though I did," she continued, "but I cannot recall it. I cannot recall my life at all." Her words held the ache of loss.

"The memories will come. You were deeply wounded, both in body and in mind. It is no surprise that your soul has hidden its precious memories away. Focus on regaining your physical strength." Islander traded the small axe for a wood rasp and began smoothing out the new sword's roughness.

"But did I know you? Did you know me? Do you know anything about my life?"

He did not look up, afraid she would see the half lie in his eyes. "No, Cwen, until you awakened here on the island, you and I had never met."

"But," she hesitated as a deep, shuddering sigh wracked her body, "I am certain I have a memory of you. You sat in a misted glen beside a dying flame, and then you rose and came to me. You pushed back the hood of your cloak and revealed yourself. How could I have this memory if I did not know you?"

"A dream...?" The sound of the rasp paused as its scraping against the wood came to a halt.

Cwen picked at the skin along her thumbnail and worried the fragile memory in her mind, finally giving a slow nod. "Perchance it was just a dream."

Islander pulled on a glove, lifted a handful of sand, and began polishing the edge of the wooden blade. "Now, Elder and I are all you know, and your mind tries to make new memories to fill the void of those lost to you." Another handful of sand whispered against the wood.

"There is also a woman in my dreams. Tall, raven haired and violet eyed, she seems to know me. She whispers my name and soothes my mind when I am fretful. Who could she be?"

He recalled the woman from his dreams as well. "Perhaps someone from your past? A relative? Your mother?"

Islander extended the sword and squinted down the blade at a distant sapling and satisfied himself it was straight and true. He flipped it over and handed it to Cwen. "Test the grip and the weight."

She took the wooden sword, two-handed, her feet intuitively moving into base position as she pulled the blade to guard.

"It would seem your body knows the sword." Islander stood and moved to touch the tip of the blade. "Follow my hand. Keep the blade against my fingers." He led her through a simple exercise and back to guard, watching her feet move and her balance shift to compensate for the sword's movement. "Good. Your mind may not recall the skill, but your body does." He reclaimed the sword and returned to his seat, taking up the sand again and rubbing it into the wood, smoothing and polishing as he wondered who had taught such a small, fragile woman to wield a sword.

Chapter 10: Rebellion

N'dia's nostrils flared, and her eyes flashed an icy blue glare. "How could you go along with it? Now, Cwen stands no chance at all!"

"The girl is dead. J'var found her blood in the Emyute camp and on the escarpment. She was thrown into the sea. The Emyutes have admitted as much. She was beaten to death and her body disposed of in the hope that the merfolk would be blamed," A'bach explained for the third time.

"Then why are the Emyutes not punished! Where is Cwen's body? It must have washed ashore somewhere. Bring it to me, and I will believe you."

"You sound just like her aunt! It is over, N'dia! I will not have my daughter wandering about asking questions that accomplish nothing. The Emyutes have brought complaints to the eldermen. The trade directorate has publicly censored me. Your spending money will be less because of it."

"The eldermen killed Yávië," N'dia replied. "Without provocation or cause, they sent her to her death. And you helped them! You buried the body without even letting me pay my final respects. She was my friend! I should have told her the truth! Told her that you lied to keep Queen Karid from our doorstep! Cwen lives! I know she does!"

A'bach slapped N'dia, knocking her to the floor. "Your disrespect has become intolerable! Go to your room!"

N'dia held her face and stared at her father, ignoring his command. "I know Cwen lives. B'rma told me so."

"A superstitious tavern owner spreads lies, and you believe them over the truth of your father? You are too old to play such games, N'dia. No more taverns, no more foreigners, no more freedom. The time has come for you to wed. I think with a bit of coaxing Director V'ran can still be convinced to marry you. It is a good match, and you will bear him fine sons. And it will advance your brothers' positions in the directorate."

"Father! I do not want to marry V'ran! He disgusts me!"

"You will do as you are told. Allowing your freedom has brought me nothing but heartache and shame."

Tears flooded his daughter's eyes, and she fled the room, calling back over her shoulder, "Mother would never have allowed this! None of it!"

"Guard her door!" A'bach snarled at the stryver crouched in the corner, flinging his teacup at it when it hesitated. "If she opens the door, use your cudgel!"

A'bach rubbed his face and stared at the broken cup shards, a teacup from the West and a gift from the mirror guarding deviant to A'bach's wife, the sorceress D'lana. N'dia was right, her mother would never have allowed what had happened, but her mother was dead, because she had defied Karid's orders and practiced magick. Now A'bach feared he might lose his daughter. "Damn B'rma and her twisted tales," he thought aloud.

J'var stepped out of sight at the sound of his father's angry voice and N'dia's weeping and went to wait in his sister's room.

She entered clutching her face, her eyes swollen with tears that overflowed at the sight of her eldest brother. "J'var, Father says I must marry, and I do not want to marry V'ran! I said horrible things to Father."

"He will forgive them, he always does. And I do not want you to marry V'ran either. He's a drom's ass. I have always hoped you would marry someone from Stonetel or Corusca so I would have an excuse to visit beyond the pass."

N'dia sniffed. "It is easy for you to make light of it. You can marry whomever you choose. I had hoped you would choose Cwen and that she would choose you." A new flood of tears overcame her.

"Father says that the Emyutes have admitted beating Cwen to death and casting her into the sea. And now Yávië is dead, and we will never know the truth."

"Yávië chose to free her soul and join her husband. I saw their reunion. N'dia, it was…it was almost beyond description. Her husband's spirit was aglow with strength, and he drew her to him with such longing. They are together N'dia, and I do not believe Yávië made the decision to free her soul without knowing the truth about Cwen. There was much whispering between Yávië and her husband's spirit. I believe he spoke to her of Cwen." J'var withdrew Yávië's jewel from his pocket. "She gave me this, to give to Cwen."

"Then what is truth? Cwen is dead, or does she live?"

"I do not know, but I have been thinking about it. What if the nomads believe they killed her, but they did not?"

"That is stupid. The nomads have certainly killed enough women to know when one is dead."

"No. N'dia, listen to me. What if they tossed Cwen into the sea while she still lived, and she washed ashore in a place where someone helped her?"

N'dia shook her head and argued, "A fall from the escarpment into the sea after the nomads' brutal beatings? She could not survive it. And if by some chance she did, she would drown in the sea. It is too far from a place where one could climb out, and there are no settlements near."

"Dragon's Heart. What if she washed up on the isle of Dragon's Heart?"

"It is too far, and even if she did, she would have died there, alone. You are mad."

"No, I don't believe I am. You see, I know that someone lives there."

"J'var, you are making this up to humor me." She frowned at her brother's solemn expression. "How would you know that?"

"Every high-born in the trade directorate knows. Call it a leadership secret."

"Then who lives there?"

J'var held his breath, a vision of Cwen's fiery eyes and flowing hair filling his head, and then exhaled and whispered, "The dragonspawn."

N'dia backed away, shaking her head, "It is a myth. An Emyute tale left from the Great War. One of those that Father says B'rma makes up to entertain the drunks."

J'var remained silent and waited for N'dia to feel the truth.

"If it lived it would be ancient. If the tales are to be believed, the beast would be ancient."

"Aye, N'dia, for a thousand years it has been fed and sated by the sacrifice of the Noor clan H'san. But it is not alone. An elder wizard, the one responsible for the dragonspawn's birth, was imprisoned with it."

N'dia shuddered, recalling the tales B'rma told. "It is a monster, a hideous beast of insatiable appetites, part dragon and part man. J'var, it is too impossible to be true."

"L'or and I could go. Father is sending us to Adumbra in a few days. A side trip to the island is not beyond all possibility. Then we would know for sure."

"You would go and leave me here? Leave me to V'ran and his meddling mother? To the prenuptial ninnies who will flutter about? No. If you go, I will go. Leave L'or behind to deal with Father and his wedding plans." N'dia raised her chin and glared. "And we will take Mother's sword."

J'var rested his arm across N'dia's shoulders and laughed. "And just how do you propose we get a sword that only exists in B'rma's mind?"

"We will ask B'rma. She would not lie about Mother. And," she flattered her brother, "surely a young director so well trusted that he knows there is a dragonspawn imprisoned on Dragon's Heart Isle is smart enough to recover such a sword."

"And if I were to locate this mythical sword, you would not be afraid of encountering the beast of Dragon's Heart?"

"I am not afraid of anything when I am under your protection, my brother," N'dia praised. "And with Mother's sword we would be practically invincible, at least according to B'rma. Besides, even death at the jaws of a monster would be preferable to a life married to V'ran." She shivered. "He is nauseating. But Father meant it, J'var. If you leave me behind I will be wed before you return, forced into a marriage I do not want, bound to a man I do not love. You wanted

Cwen because she was free, and even now you are willing to search for her. Can you not respect me for the same qualities and honor my wish for the freedom to choose my life? Give me this, Brother. Take me with you."

J'var hesitated, and N'dia continued, "Please. Let us try to find Cwen. You know that she is special. You feel it here." She tapped J'var's heart. "Do we not owe her that much? She was lost when we were supposed to be protecting her."

"How is it, N'dia, that you are able to twist the most unlikely possibilities into seemingly rational actions?"

"It is because I am your baby sister and you only want what is best for me. And you know marrying V'ran is not best." N'dia put on a charming pout. "I just want a bit of adventure, J'var. What can be the harm?"

"Come then, I will take you to B'rma's, and we will ask her about this sword. Then you will stay there until I return for you." J'var opened the door on a startled stryver, sending it scuttling backward. J'var frowned. It had appeared to be listening. He shook his head and growled, "Get out of here! Go!"

But the stryver stood its ground and pointed to J'var, making a series of squeaks and gestures, finally reaching up to touch the sibilant stone hanging at the black man's throat.

"Get out of here, you moronic beast!" J'var snarled, slapping away the malformed hand. The stryver shook its head as if it understood and again pointed at J'var.

"Wait, J'var. What can he want?" N'dia knelt and watched with fascination as the stryver's usually vacant eyes focused on the sibilant stone. "Give me your stone," she beckoned J'var, taking the stone and slipping it over the waiting stryver's head.

Deep, bold words poured from the stryver's mind. *Come, daughter of D'lana. I take you to the mother's sword. Long it has waited.*

Blue eyes wide, N'dia whispered to J'var, "It speaks our mother's name and of her sword."

The stryver backed away, beckoning with fused fingers. *Come, come, Lady N'dia…hurry, hurry before the father sees.* Dropping to all fours it scampered a few paces before stopping to see if N'dia followed.

"You cannot trust a stryver, N'dia." J'var gripped his sister's forearm when she moved to follow.

N'dia looked ahead to the stryver and back at her brother. "Do you have any idea where Mother's sword may be? If not, I am going with this stryver for it says it knows."

"It says? Do you hear yourself, N'dia? If anyone else hears you, they will lock you away."

"No. It speaks. It does. Not aloud, but in my mind. I heard the words, J'var! Let us follow it. What can it hurt? It is just a stryver."

"Stay behind me," J'var ordered with a shake of his head and set off after the anxious stryver.

The stryver led them outside, away from the residence, along narrow side streets and into a rather squalid section of the city. At a curtained doorway behind a sausage vendor, they slipped into the shadows and followed a winding pathway that descended into the sewers below.

J'var gave a disgusted grunt and shouted at the stryver, "Our mother would never have come into such a place, not even to hide an illegal weapon. We go no further, stryver! N'dia this is a trap or at the very least mere foolishness. Come, we go to B'rma's."

"But I am here, J'var." B'rma stepped out from the darkness and said, "There is much about your mother you do not know, much that your father has withheld out of a misdirected desire to keep you safe. Your mother was my friend. To you she was Mother, but to most she was the sorceress D'lana, a weaver of spells and a conjurer of great skill. It was your mother's failure to accept the laws against her craft that brought her death. She wove into your childhood tales as much of the truth as she dared in the hope that you would one day come to understand. Since the day N'dia first came to me in discontent, I have waited for her to call the sword. It belongs to N'dia, though accepting it will bring her challenges you may not wish her to bear."

J'var stepped between N'dia and B'rma. "What harm would you bring to my sister? She is allowed no weapon. She has no skill, no experience with swords or bows. "

N'dia reached out and rested her hand on J'var's arm, feeling its tension. "That is not exactly true."

"What?" J'var whirled around to stare in shock at his sister.

"J'var, I have studied a bit with the sword. Here beneath the city in the ancient arenas of the old masters. B'rma taught me. I know I should have told you, but I feared—"

"And fear you should! It is a death sentence, N'dia! Karid forbids all women to bear weapons! You are not some foreigner, to be sentenced to the life of a scullery maid. You are the daughter of a trade director, an exemplar of womanhood. What if you had been caught?" He backed away, his angry voice echoing off the stone, "It is over, N'dia. Father is right. It is time that you married and forgot these childish fantasies. This is not just a bit of adventure in search of a missing traveler. This is dementia, passed through the bloodline of our mother if B'rma is to be believed. I cannot allow this foolishness. B'rma misleads you, and the punishment will be severe." He turned back the way they had come.

"J'var!"

He swung about to see his sister armed, a short sword held loosely at her side. "Why is it Queen Karid so fears a weapon in a woman's hand? I can no longer bow to laws that forbid me the power I know should be mine. You can stand with me or against me, but either way I intend to find the truth about Cwen. I should have told her the truth in the beginning, stayed with her, and offered my skill." Completely at ease, N'dia awaited her brother's response.

A ragged breath escaped his lips. "Karid does not fear a weapon in a woman's hand, only that the woman might cut herself!" He cast a contemptuous look at B'rma. "You will surely be the cause of my sister's death, but I cannot simply stand by and watch it. N'dia, I am coming with you, but at the first opportunity I will disarm you and carry you kicking and screaming to V'ran. I swear I will! But until that day, I will look after you. What else can I do but follow and protect you from this foolishness?"

N'dia's eyes sparkled with mischief. "You will never give me to V'ran, so you would do best to stop your blustering and arm yourself." She tossed the sword to J'var and claimed a hooded cloak from B'rma. "Follow the stryver. Let us see if we can find Mother's sword and begin our search for Cwen. A bit of adventure will do us good, J'var."

Chapter 11: Seasons

Side by side in the autumn sun, Islander and Cwen lifted the final plank into position. "Privacy within calling distance and still safe," the islander had promised Cwen. He had watched her grow stronger as they built her cabin. Her skeletal features had filled out, and the too thin arms and legs had taken on a woman's firm, lightly muscled roundness. The backbreaking labor and the pure air seemed to cleanse the shadowed recesses of her mind and leave her free of paralyzing nightmares.

He looked up to direct their next task, but words suddenly failed him at the sight of the thin white shirt clinging to her full, sweat warmed breasts. Cwen met his gaze briefly, then looked away before reminding him, "You promised—swore it."

"Aye..." He released the breath he had unconsciously been holding. "But I never promised not to think about it, or want it, only not to act. It is natural, Cwen, for a man to desire a beautiful woman. And I assure you, you no longer resemble a desiccated corpse. You have grown very beautiful."

"When will the jailors bring your woman?" Cwen reached up and pulled her hair forward to cover the raised scar on her cheek, imagining its ugliness.

Islander flung his axe to the ground. "Do you believe it is only the service of whores that keeps me from forcing you? Do you?" He reached out and gently pushed the hair back from Cwen's face, tucked it behind her ear, and frowned as she flinched. "That scar is only a memory. It is the hurt in here," he tapped her chest softly, "that has not healed. There lies the pain that betrays you and keeps you fearful, keeps you from separating good men from evil. I believe you have had that wound for a very long time."

He picked up his axe and attacked the limbs sprouting from a log destined to be a chair. Cwen moved away and sat on a stump, staring into emptiness.

"They killed my aunt. The nomads killed her when she tried to keep them from taking me. I have seen it in my dreams. The raven-haired woman was my aunt. Do you know what they did to me?"

The islander remained silent, sitting down in a squat as he waited for Cwen to share her terror-ridden memories.

Cwen's breath came in ragged gasps and her face paled, but her jaw hardened. "Again and again I tried to run away until they finally chained me, like a beast. They beat me for speaking and not speaking. They beat me for looking and not looking. They beat me for listening and not listening. They beat me so many times I cannot recall. But I did not die."

"No," Islander whispered, "you did not die."

"I had a dagger when they captured me. They beat me daily at daybreak to remind me I had possessed it, to remind me that a woman may never touch a weapon. I did not draw it when they attacked us, but I should have." She brushed away tears with an angry hand. "I should have risked it."

"It would not have mattered. You were a woman against men. Sometimes one simply cannot win against a superior strength. I could not win against those who imprisoned me. Like you, I was beaten and branded."

Cwen looked at him, her pale golden eyes meeting his deep amber gaze across a fallen log, and said, "Death would have been better than what happened to me."

Her gaze turned away and regained its vacant stare. "Why are you here? What was your crime?"

He dug in the earth with the axe handle. "I killed a man, a member of the eldermen's council."

"Why?" Her eyes again met his.

"They said I went mad."

"And him?" Cwen glanced toward the garden where the elder worked.

"He saved my life. Agreed to become my permanent keeper, if they would let me live."

"You have been here a long while?"

"Aye, a very long while."

"Have you never wanted to leave this place?"

"I have never considered it. I am bound by my oath in blood. At the time of my imprisonment, the lives of those I loved depended on my obedience, on my acceptance of this prison isle. The island has become my home. It is a life, Cwen. Perhaps not the best of lives, but it is a life nonetheless. My life, the only life I can expect."

Cwen nodded, considering his words. "And now it is my life, my prison as well." Her chin trembled, and she stared at him in a moment of fearful defiance. "But I will never willingly come to your bed, never. If you believe there is any hope of that, you are wrong. I know I owe you my life, but there is no debt great enough to make me pay that price. Are you still a man of your word, or do you intend to force me?"

"I will never force you, Cwen. You need not be concerned, for I have sworn it. But I will not promise not to look, not to want you. I am not a celibate. If it makes you uncomfortable to know that, I am sorry. It is simply the way of men."

"I learned the way of men." She stood, her mouth a tight line. "Men took what they wanted by force until I was left with nothing but worthlessness and fear." The tone of her voice was one of desperate hopelessness, and after a moment's silence she whispered, "I will go and prepare our meal."

Islander watched her walk away, a frown creasing his forehead. "She will leave you soon," the elder said, limping to his side. "As soon as she is confident of the sword in her grip, she will hunt the nomads. She does not fear death. She would embrace it, and I fear she will pursue it until it catches her."

"No, she is stronger than you believe. I will convince her to stay, at least through the fall and winter. Winter is no time for travel, and I will use the lure of the sword."

"You fool yourself, boy. She will choose death, because she cannot feel life. Look at her. She is as empty as the shells left at a raven's feast."

"Then I will tell her what I am and go with her. She cannot fight her demons alone." Islander turned to stare at the old man, daring him to speak a warning. But the elder held silent, simply staring toward the distant sea.

"Elder, have you not felt the power coursing through your veins in the days since the earth's trembling?"

"Boy, to use the power will bring—"

"I did not say I had used it or that I would, only that I have felt its return. You feel it too—I know that you do. Do you not even wish to test it?"

The old man stared straight ahead, knuckles growing white where they gripped his cane. Overhead the leaves began to tremble, dry and brittle, their rustling like so many angry whispers as they brushed against one another. "There! I have tested it, now let it go! They will kill us, boy, and your Cwen as well."

"Men have broken their pact with Karid. They allowed the use of magick when she expressly forbade it. They have broken their word. It frees us."

"Damn you, boy! We will never be free!" the old man replied in vexation. "If the eldermen realize that we know what they have done, they will send the Emyutes, and no amount of my pleading will save you this time."

Islander nodded his agreement. "For now, I will let it go. For now I will go and meet the jailors, and catch a fish for our breakfast. Will you be here when I return?"

"Nay, I will steal a few cabbages and leave you to contemplate your fate." The old man limped toward the garden with the islander staring after him.

The sun warmed Cwen's face, but beneath her eyelids wrestled dark, angry visions—visions in which Master Buul hung in chains as Cwen flayed his flesh. The image was dispelled by the scratching sound of stick on stone, and she opened her eyes to see the elder limping toward the porch.

"Islander has gone to meet the supply boat and spend time with his woman," she told him.

"Aye, 'tis why I have come. They will kill him, you know, if he continues to refuse the whores they bring. And if you force him to follow you from this island many will die. Would you want that on your conscience?"

"I—"

"Hush and listen to me, girl." The elder sank to the steps beside Cwen. "He sought you out, touched you in your dreams, and somehow brought you here. I don't know how, and I don't know what he sees in you, but he wants it desperately. The gods know that I have done everything I could to dissuade him. I begged him to kill you when you washed ashore, even gave him the black mushrooms that should have done it. I warned him you would never be whole and you won't, but can you not feel sufficient gratitude to spare his life? Are you so cruel that you would draw death to him after all I have done to save him?"

Elder's watery eyes searched Cwen's face. "He is precious, the very last of our royal blood," he said. At Cwen's blank expression the elder shook his head. "I waste my time. You are nothing but an empty shell, a branded body without heart or soul. I do not blame you for it. 'Tis the fault of the fates for allowing you to live."

"Elder, you make no sense. If you have something to say speak it plainly."

"Islander bears the last seed of Quondam's royal magick," he began. "He is the dragonspawn. Years ago, before Karid was queen or even human, she served beside her sister Flida as a sentinel, a protector of Quondam's magick and the enchanted wildwoods. It is said that Karid took a man's life, helped him with the release of his soul within the sacred woods, something forbidden to the sentinels for as long as the ancestral gods have ruled the universe. Her punishment was to become one with the flesh she thought she desired. Karid was forced to leave the woods and live among men, forever seeking men's souls, feeding on their life force as a souleater to maintain the youth of her human form."

The old man emitted a sharp, hoarse laugh. "But this was no punishment to Karid. She found that she loved the passion of the flesh and the power her body held over men. She lured our king to her bed, turned his soldiers against him, and murdered him. Karid feared her sister Flida, the remaining sentinel, would use dragons' magick to rise against her for this wickedness, so she slaughtered the royal dragons and stole their flame, but not before a foolish wizard and a sorceress had planted the dragon's seed in the womb of one of Man's royal bloodline. Islander is the spawn of that union, born of a human mother and fathered by the dragon's seed, the perfect image of a man. He is our only hope for any future king strong enough to challenge Queen Karid. Karid's attempt to create a spawn ended in the deviant who controls the mirror that brought you here. Do you know the power of magick, girl?"

Cwen shook her head. "Why are you telling me this? What would you have me do?"

"Go. Go now, while he is away," he pleaded. "Free him of your woman's spell."

"He has been nothing but kind to me, and I wish him no harm, but where would I go? How could I leave?"

"There is a raft hidden in the merfolk caverns. It can take you to the far shore. Islander built it, believing he and I would one day leave this island and live free. He is a foolish boy." Tears flowed unchecked down Elder's cheeks. "When he killed, the men tried him and found him to be a beast, too dangerous to live. I swore I would stay with him and see he was never free again. I am his jailor."

"I have seen only kindness in him. Why would he kill anyone?"

"He killed a prime elder. The one he believed murdered his mother," Elder explained. "Islander's mother was no threat to anyone, though as the time of the birth arrived she became fearful...afraid she had spawned a demon. In her fear, she cried out for death. Someone told the boy that the prime elder had ordered his mother's murder. I don't know who, and the boy would never tell, not even the beatings and branding could make him speak the name. But it was not true. Karid killed his mother, because his mother begged for death."

Cwen stood up. "I do not understand any of this, but if it will save his life, I will go. I owe him that."

"No."

Islander stood at the edge of the garden, his face expressionless, with his single utterance carrying a soft yet unmistakable warning. "You betray me, old man. You would take the only happiness I have ever known." He stepped forward, stiff-legged like a cat stalking prey. "Get out and do not come back."

Elder rose on shaking legs and stepped away from porch, his hand outstretched in pleading. "Boy, I do not betray you. I only seek to see you safe."

"Safe," Islander snapped. "I have seen you wish for death in your own misery, Elder. Yet what you seek to do would tear out my heart and leave me nothing. Go! Before I do something I will forever regret." His gaze shifted to Cwen. "You would truly leave me?"

"Boy—"

The islander's hand shot out and grabbed the old man, shutting off his words. He snarled and shook the elder and flung him into the soft soil of the garden. The islander crossed the field in a humanly impossible leap, the dark dense shadow of a dragon rippling across the earth and withering a row of beanstalks. He landed heavily and loomed over the fallen elder with clenched fists. "I warned you!" he growled.

Cwen raced to the elder and found him dazed and struggling to rise. After helping the old man to sit, she turned and placed her hand on the islander's chest, feeling his steely muscles heaving with each angry breath. "Stop this! It is not you but the beast they have put inside you. Is what the elder said true? That you no longer accept the women the jailors bring to serve you?"

Islander's eyes were fixed on Cwen's small hand where it rested on his chest. "Since you came, I cannot. I do not want them. I have no need. So far, the whores have held their tongues in order to collect their coins from the jailors. For how long that will continue, I do not know."

"And did you speak the truth to the elder? Do I bring you happiness?"

Islander's eyes shifted from Cwen's hand to her pale face, from her trembling lips to her wide golden eyes. "Aye." He lifted his hand to cover hers. "You hold my heart in your hand. You have since first I saw you in my dreams." He dropped his hand to his side and looked toward the elder. "I should take the old man home."

Cwen nodded, afraid to speak, not knowing what to say. She drew her hand back and curled it into a fist against her own heart, closing the islander's heat into the palm of her hand. "I will prepare supper," she said, turning to walk to the cabin.

Islander watched her, his eyes riveted upon the womanly sway of her rounded hips.

"I have never seen such a fool," the elder muttered as he gathered his cane, struggled to his feet, and stumbled to stand beside the islander. "There is nothing there for you, her heart is a stone."

Islander leaned forward and brushed the dirt from the old man's clothes, steadying him with a hand on his shoulder. "Already she has given me a reason to hope. A moment with her hand on my heart was more than I believed she would ever give. It is enough."

"Does this mean you forgive me?"

"No, I do not forgive you. You had no right to tell her of my birth." Islander gave the elder's shoulder a soft shake. "And do not try to take her from me again. Henceforth, I will decide what is right for me. Come now, I will take you home."

The glen was filled with the smell of Cwen's cooking when the islander returned. He paused at the door, took a deep breath, and prepared himself. Awkwardness would now lie between them, but awkwardness was far better than loss. His throat constricted with the thought that he had nearly returned to find Cwen gone, lost to a rotting raft on the sea because of the old man's fear. Islander knew he should not have shown his anger or spoken his feelings aloud and made Cwen even more wary and uncomfortable, but the elder had been wrong to tell Cwen the secret of his birth, to tell her what he was.

When Islander entered the cabin, Cwen's back was to him. She was working at the kitchen bench, kneading the dough for bread, and he imagined a smudge of flour on her cheek where she had brushed it with the back of her hand.

"Can you bear to look at me after what you have been told? Can you forgive me what I am and what I have done?"

"Supper will be ready soon."

"Can you Cwen?" he persisted.

She did not turn, but he heard her whispered words. "Give me a little time."

It was a deathly silent supper. Afterward Cwen undressed and went to bed, leaving Islander to the cleaning up.

A small sound, the padding of bare feet across the wooden floor, woke him in the blackness of the night. Islander stiffened beneath his blankets and waited for the creak that would tell him Cwen had opened the cabin door, but it did not come. Instead, he felt the warmth of her nearness.

In a quavering whisper she spoke, "I will give you what you want."

He turned over to find her kneeling beside his mat, the glow of a single candle backlighting her slender form beneath the worn nightshirt. Without thought he reached out to cup her face and felt her flinch.

"No." He withdrew his hands. "Not like this."

"But your need—" the sharp edge of panic heightened the pitch of her voice.

"No, Cwen. There is no need I have that should draw you to me out of pity or a feeling of indebtedness."

He reached up and smoothed her hair, tucking it behind her ears. She felt the tremor in his hand.

"Why am I so afraid? It is not as though I were an unblemished virgin. I am quite familiar with the act." Her words were bitter.

"No, you are not unblemished, nor am I. We are forever maimed in a way that others cannot see and we can never forget. Each of us is covered in a filth that cannot be washed away, tainted by the wickedness of others through no fault of our own. Through this," he touched his heart and then hers, "our union will be our redemption, Cwen. When it comes, it will not be brutal or frenzied or desperate. It will be calm and tender, a salve to soothe our shattered souls, but it will not happen until you are ready, until you come to me freely."

In the flickering glow of the candle, he saw the shiver that passed across her shoulders. He sat up, wrapping the blanket around them both and holding her as she wept. His hands did not go where she would not want them—not that his thoughts did not go there—and his touch was light as he stroked her hair, the first soft contact with her fragile trust. When her sobbing subsided and became no more than gentle tremors, she shifted against him, and he released her. She stood up and stepped away, using the back of her hand to wipe beneath her nose and then her palms to brush away the tears from her cheeks. "What if I am never ready?"

"The day will come when you want to take back your life, to wrench it from the hands of those who hurt you. On that day, when your pain and anger turn to need, I will be here."

"How can you be so certain?"

In the gleam of candlelight she saw his eyes grow moist.

"Because Cwen, it is what has happened to me."

Chapter 12: Release

The elder leaned on the handle of his hoe and watched the dance of the swords. Each stroke was met by counterstroke, each turn matched by the other's mirror image. Islander led Cwen through the attacks and counters, breaking occasionally to tap the girl's elbow or position her shoulder or foot. It concerned the old man that the girl never smiled, never laughed, and that her gaze remained distant as if focused far away. He worried that the whores would tell the Noor jailors that they no longer performed their services for the prisoner and that the Noor jailors would report it to the eldermen at Endhaven. But what the old man feared most was that Queen Karid would send her soldiers for the boy.

The raft was gone, burned. The elder had seen the smoke the day after the boy struck him, and he knew that the girl would not be leaving on the sea. Islander seemed at ease, there had been no recurrence of his anger and no further sign of the dragon's shadow. The elder positioned the hoe handle under his arm and scrubbed his face with his hands. When he looked up, Cwen stood before him and the islander was nowhere to be seen.

"Are you going to kill me?" the elder chuckled, pointing to the wooden sword dangling from Cwen's hand. "No smile, not even for an old man's jest?"

"Is it jest?" Cwen's eyes were clear and calm. "Or do you still believe me a threat to Islander?"

"I won't deny it. I don't believe you have anything to offer him that he could not get from whores. The only difference being that you torture him by withholding it as if you still held some priceless treasure."

The crack of Cwen's hand against the old man's face staggered him and only a quick grab at the hoe handle kept him from falling.

"You know nothing of what we do!"

"I know you do nothing!" The elder rubbed his cheek.

"He knows I am not ready." Cwen looked away.

"And just how many seasons do you think the boy should wait?"

"And just what is it I am waiting for?" Islander rounded the corner of the house, hands hidden behind his back. He looked from Cwen's blush to the elder's scowl and back again. "Ah, that…it would be best if you allowed Cwen and me to deal with that, Elder. I doubt any experience you might share would be of much use." He tossed a blade to Cwen, not a wooden practice sword, but one of polished steel stolen from the jailors' boat. "A gift from the Noor."

Cwen dropped the practice sword and caught the steel sword's hilt smoothly and stared wide-eyed at the islander. "You stole their sword? The jailors' sword? They will find it gone! They will come for us."

Their sword…the jailors…us…Hearing these words, Islander knew that in that moment Cwen saw herself with him, and he could not hide his smile.

"It is not funny! Why did you take it?"

As light as a feather, his finger traced the line of her jaw and noticed that in her alarm Cwen did not shy away.

"Because your house is finished, your bed is made, your fire is laid for cooking, and tonight, for the first time, you will be alone. If they should come for us I want you to be armed with more than a wooden stick. So—are you going to invite Elder and me for the first supper in your new home?"

The sword drooped, and Cwen gnawed at her lip. "Of course. Yes. You are both invited to supper. I'll go wash up and get started." She took a step and paused. "Thank you. Thank you for the sword." In a flash of gilded hair, gray trousers, and white shirt, she was gone.

"By all that is holy what have you done?" sputtered the elder, his wrinkled face scarlet, and his eyes bulging in near apoplexy.

Islander shrugged and patted the old man's shoulder. "I have stolen several swords over the ages. None was ever missed. As for what I have done, I have given an angry, frightened woman a means to defend herself. And in doing so, let her know I trust her. Now, finish the weeding, and I will fetch a bottle of your precious blackberry brandy for the celebration."

The elder's scowl deepened. "Do you intend to get her drunk?"

"You are worried about her honor?"

"Nay! I am worried about your hide being bloodied with that blasted sword!"

"I assure you both honor and hide are safe. It is not my intention to break her trust, or allow her to skewer me with her sword. Now, get to work, and see if you can find the last of the turnips and a few onions somewhere in that sorry soil. Give them to Cwen, and tell her they are your gift for the pot." Islander winked and sent the elder into a fit of grumbling. With a lift of his hand he set off to fetch the brandy.

When supper was finished and the slightly tipsy elder sent on his way, Cwen and Islander sat at the table with the dirty dishes between them. He filled his cup and, with a lift of an eyebrow, held out the bottle of sweet brandy.

"Nay, I believe I have had plenty."

"Not even for a final toast?"

"I do not think it would be wise."

Islander smiled a lazy smile, and Cwen shook her head. "No."

"Then we shall get on to your housewarming gift." He stood and she made to follow but stopped as he waggled a finger at her. "You stay here, and I will fetch it."

Cwen watched him leave and then gathered the plates and cups, dropping spoons into the pail of soapy water. She washed a plate, humming a nameless tune as she rinsed it and set it in the drying rack, feeling at ease, at home. A loud thud startled her, and she spun around in time to see the islander rolling in a large wooden tub.

"Your bathtub, milady."

Cwen's fingers flew to her mouth.

"All you need to do is heat the water." He flipped back a tarp to reveal a row of water-filled pails. "Elder and I brought up the water while you were doing morning chores. It is our gift to you—no more washing in a cold rain barrel."

Tears filled Cwen's eyes.

"Don't cry. It was meant to make you happy. I guarantee it will not leak and ruin your floors. I tested it myself. And here, look at this." He closed her door and slid the bolt home. "You need not worry about uninvited guests. And now I shall leave you to it. Just shout if you need me." He lifted the bolt and opened the door, glancing back to see Cwen standing with a dishrag dangling from one hand and the other knuckling her lips.

"Do you need help with those dishes?"

A slow shake of her head and more tears slid down her cheeks.

"Cwen?"

She swung away, back to the pail and the dirty dishes, attacking a plate with the rag, slapping it in the rinse water, slamming it into the drying rack.

"Good night, my lady."

She heard the whisper behind her and the soft tap of the door closing in its frame. Dropping the rag in the water, she sank into a chair beside her table, crossing her arms over its smooth surface and resting her head. "Why didn't you stop him you stupid woman?" she mumbled. "What are you so afraid of? Get over it. He is kind, and generous. He was right here, and you let him go. Stupid, stupid, stupid."

She lifted her head and wiped her eyes on her sleeve. Spying the half empty bottle of sweet brandy, she grabbed it and jerked open her door to find Islander sitting on the steps.

"You knew?"

"I hoped." He came to his feet but stayed on the step. "I could do the dishes and help you heat your water."

Cwen gave a series of tremulous gasps followed by a sudden silence.

"Breathe," Islander reminded her and was rewarded by another quick gasp.

Still neither moved, but at last Cwen broke the silence with her quavering words, "I am so afraid."

"I know." He held out his trembling hands, "As am I," shrugging when her eyes met his. "Soft and slow and we will stop if you change your mind." Met by another silence, he added, "Or I can go."

"I do not want you to go. Elder is right. I torment you with my refusal and for what? Because I am left with nothing but nightmarish memories, because I am too afraid to act?" She closed her eyes and held out her hand. When he took it, she whispered, "I don't want to be afraid anymore."

He slipped the brandy bottle from her hand, and ran a finger inside its rim, then touched her lips with its sweetness. At his touch her breathing quickened, becoming a low uncertain moan as his lips met hers and drew up the sweet liquid. Her hands came up against his chest, and he lifted his head to search her eyes.

"I cannot breathe," she gasped.

"Come inside where it is warm while you catch your breath."

She paused on the threshold, her eyes wide. The hair around her face darkened as it became damp with perspiration. "I am not sure if I can do this."

"It does not matter, Cwen. Shall I go?"

"Yes...no."

"Come inside, Cwen, before you get chilled. Sit by the fire and warm yourself. I will bring you a cup of tea."

She stepped inside, leaned against the wall beside the door and watched him close and bolt it. A clammy dizziness claimed her in the clutch of a new wave of uncontrollable anxiety, and she sank to the floor as her legs betrayed her. Islander lifted her and settled her in a chair near the fire. He pulled a blanket from her bed and wrapped her in it and then knelt before her to rub her icy hands.

"W-what's wrong w-with me? I know y-you would not hurt me. I t-truly do."

"Aye, but you are afraid to begin what you fear I cannot control." He tucked her hands beneath the blanket and picked up the cast iron kettle to hang it on the chimney hook above the fire. He filled it from the water buckets and pushed it over the flames with the iron poker. "I will heat your water, and then I will go."

Cwen closed her eyes and rested her head on the back of the chair, listening to the sound of tea being poured behind her.

"It is not hot, but it is still warm." He tucked the cup into her hands, smiling when she did not bother to open her eyes. Behind her he loosed the leather that held her braid, separating the plait and running his fingers through the hair to set it free.

Cwen lifted the cup to her lips and sipped as Islander's fingers found a tight muscle along her neck. A small sigh escaped her as he kneaded the tension away. "Sore," she murmured, letting her head fall forward as his fingers moved over the top of her left shoulder. "I am so tired."

"Aye, fear can be exhausting."

She opened her eyes and leaned back to look at him. "I am not afraid now."

"No?" He took the cup from her hands and placed it on the floor, circling the chair to stand before her. "Shall I kiss you again?" He saw her lace her fingers to stop their sudden shaking and knelt between her legs to take her hands in his. Hers were icy. "Liar," he teased.

"I am sorry," whispered Cwen, hair veiling her face as she bowed her head.

"The act is not as important as the reason behind it. I will wait, Cwen, until the time is right for you. If it is not tonight, that is all right. If it never happens, that is all right too. What is important is that you know I want to be here with you. Do you understand?"

She nodded, tugging at her lip with her perfect teeth as she wept. She reached out and pulled him to her and held on tightly, burying her face against his chest. At last she pulled back, sniffled, and wiped her eyes on her sleeve. "I should do the dishes."

He remained where he was, blocking her way, very aware of her legs against his hips. Knowing only a beast would take advantage, he rose, held out his hand, and pulled her to her feet.

"I could help you with the dishes, or they can wait until the morning. We really need to do something about the muscles of your sword arm." He lifted his hand to touch her left shoulder.

Cwen did not shrink away but allowed his touch, and he heard another sigh as her shoulders dropped a little, relaxing under his soft massage. Her eyes reflected the glow of the firelight, and she moistened her dry lips with the tip of her tongue. Islander lowered his hand to her waist and felt her shiver, but she did not move away, even when his hand moved lower, cupped her lower hip and pulled her closer. His other hand moved up her back, over her shoulder and down the soft skin of her throat and the swell of her breast. His eyes held her in his gaze as both hands began to fumble with the laces of her shirt.

"I want you, Cwen. But I do not want to push you into it. You decide." The shirt fell away, and the sight of her stole his breath. "You decide." The shirt slipped off her shoulders, a whisper of fabric against the floor. No skinny waif now, her breasts were round and full, and the nipples stood out like tender buds against their pallor. Despite the warmth from the nearby fire, gooseflesh rose across her chest.

"Cwen?" His eyes slid to her mouth. "Take back your life from those who harmed you. Tell me what you want." He let his hands slide up her naked back and kissed her very softly. "Can you breathe?" he whispered against her lips, kissing her more deeply as she nodded, and he felt her breath against his lips. He brought a hand forward to cup her breast.

She froze. "They cut me."

"And me." He lifted his shirt off over his head, took her hand in his and together they traced a long curved scar along his ribs and another on the left side of his chest. Still holding her hand, he used her finger to trace the scars on her breast and felt her quiver. "You are beautiful. The scars are an adornment, a part of you. Beautiful to me." He traced her scar with the tip of his finger. "Will you lie down with me?"

Her eyes shifted to the bed and back to his face. Without a word she went and slipped beneath the covers, face to the wall and her back to him.

Steam billowed from the water boiling in the fireplace, and Islander swung the hook out a bit so that it would not boil away and ruin Cwen's kettle, thinking her bath might come much later.

He joined her on the bed, and she tensed as it shifted with his weight but then relaxed under his hands as he rubbed her back, shoulders, and arms. When he finally turned her toward him, she came without trembling, her tear-filled eyes searching his face.

"They hurt me so."

"I know, and I will never let anyone hurt you again." He rested his hand on her stomach a moment, testing. When she finally took a deep shuddering breath, he loosed the drawstring of her trousers and eased them down over her hips and under her feet, tossing them to the floor. His feather-like touch trailed up the outside of her thigh, over the roundness of her hip and into the hollow of her waist before he palmed her breast and stroked her nipple with his thumb. Lips lowered to taste her skin. As he slipped his hand between her legs, she gave a startled cry and arched away, so he tucked her against him while he one-handedly fumbled with the last of his clothing. Cwen's breathing quickened, and she pushed against his chest with her hands. He released her, exhaled a deep breath, and watched the gamut of emotions reflected on her face.

"There is no hurry, Cwen."

"I know." She swallowed and leaned forward to rest her forehead against his chest.

His hand came up to stroke her hair, and he traced her spine to the small of her back and up again. "I can wait. I have waited for nearly two years, and a little longer will not hurt." He grimaced at the ache between his legs, glad she did not see and released another audible breath. "Would you like some brandy?"

"No." Her voice was small, muffled against his chest, and her arms wrapped around him and hugged him tight. She shifted with sudden decision, rolling and pulling him over her, her eyes widening as she felt him against her.

He held himself back, weight balanced on one elbow as his other hand cupped her face. "Cwen, if you want me to stop, tell me now."

Cwen's eyes reflected fear, uncertainty, and tears, but she shook her head. "No," she said, "if I stop you now, I may never have the courage to be with a man again."

He eased into her with the last of his control and pulled her tight against him, rocking, slow and gentle. His mind screamed for caution, reminding him of her fragile trust, as his body begged for release. His too-long denied body won, and it was over far sooner than he had wanted. But part of his power had been shared with Cwen, and his feeling of urgency had diminished. Still holding her close, and afraid he was too heavy, he rolled Cwen on top of him.

"Are you all right?" he whispered against her hair and was answered by an almost imperceptible nod.

"Did I hurt you?"

"No." A soft sigh as her arms tightened around him and she pressed her cheek against his chest. "No." He felt her tears, hot against his skin. She watched as the soft candlelight cast the dragon's shadow across the wall and ceiling. "You have a name, I know you do, and it is not 'Boy' or 'Islander'—tell me what it is." The breath that carried Cwen's soft words chilled the dampness of her tears and sent a shudder through the islander.

A name not spoken in a thousand years, banned from the lips of the living. A name to call the power of magick home to Quondam—a name to free the dragon. He pulled her closer, drew her up until he could look into her eyes. "It is forbidden."

"And *this* was not?" Her fierceness made him smile.

"Aye, everything I have done since your arrival seems to violate my pact with Quondam's queen, each act another forfeiture of my life. But the speaking of my name will be…felt. I am not sure to what magnitude."

"You have done something to me. My blood burns with it. I can feel it against my skin as certainly as a candle's flame. Speak your name to me and finish whatever it is you do."

"Cwen, the risk—"

Her fists slammed against his chest, she threw off the blanket and leapt to her feet. "Finish it!" she demanded. "I knew the risk! I accepted it! And by what you have done, so have you! So…have…you." Her finger pointed at his chest in accusation, and he could not look away.

The firelight cast a warm, burnished glow over Cwen's naked skin, mellow gold beneath the rainbow of flaming reds within her tangled hair. She hugged herself and whispered, "I know you are not a man. Tell me who you are!"

He reached out and grabbed her wrist, pulled her back to the bed, and rolled her beneath him supporting his weight with straining muscles. Cwen's hands were iron fists between them and on the wall the dragon's shadow grew dense, its scales prominent and wings extended.

"We have been bound by the fates since the days of our conception. This union merely begins our quickening. Already there are signs of transformation." He rolled to his side and touched her breast, drawing her eyes to his fingers. "Our scars fade, our bodies renew, and the dragon likeness marking you a traitor of the human race will appear and stain you." He traced the first rising lines of an indistinct image emerging on her shoulder. "But these are things we can still cover and hide. If I speak my name, there will be no turning back. We will be forced to flee this island, hunted by Karid herself, forced to fight for our freedom, fight for our lives and the lives of others."

He gripped Cwen's waist and pulled her atop him, wrapping his arms and legs around her and murmuring in her ear as she struggled against him. "That is the risk that I ask if you are willing to take, Cwen. Are you willing to risk all of that for nothing more than the sound of my name whispered against your flesh, for the ecstasy of speaking it with your own breath? Will it make your life worth living?"

Cwen stopped struggling. Exhausted and trembling, she relaxed against Islander's warmth, her words a soft admission of her need. "Your name is all that I desire. I must know who you are."

His words were hushed against her skin.

"I am D'raekn…"

As he spoke, the brilliance of lightning blinded them and thunder boomed across a turbulent sky.

"…conceived in the royal womb of the woman Malaia…"

Across the land a million night birds took to the air in a sudden storm of wings.

"…from the seed of the dragon lord, Brug…"

The merfolk dove to the coldest depths, and fishes leapt from the sea as the surface waters boiled.

"…and reared by the sorceress C'thra and the wizard Aenzl."

The earth roiled, and the mountains cracked and trembled with the power of D'raekn's words.

Nestled weary and heavy-eyed but safe within his arms, Cwen managed to breathe the name, "D'raekn…" before sleep claimed her.

D'raekn brushed the hair from Cwen's shoulder and kissed her as she slept, murmuring against her neck while allowing his eyes to close. "Perhaps it is time I challenged Quondam's false ruler…"

They made love again during the night. D'raekn was uncertain who started it. Cwen might have, but he was sure he had needed little encouragement, just her close against him. He was slower, more controlled, less urgent, and he took the time to give her the pleasure she had missed earlier. When she threw back her head, cried out his name, and clung to him breathing hard, there was nothing false about it.

As he drifted back to sleep, dark dreams of ice, fire, and dragon speak claimed him. The great dragon lord Brug spoke, his words burning within D'raekn's mind. *Not all were lost, dragonspawn. Karid did not claim every dragon's life. Some sleep deep within Quondam's bosom, against the sacred heart. In the end, your deviant brother, spawn of my loins, disfigured by Queen Karid's wicked womb, will see the golden-eyed woman to your side."*

D'raekn shifted restlessly as the dragon in his dream drew closer.

As my heir, you will take my power, bear my countenance, and end the false queen's rule. You will free those bound by her enchantment and release the sleeping dragons.

The dragon's warm breath cloaked D'raekn, and his sleep deepened. The precious words and images of the dream slipped into the depths of his consciousness.

A pounding on the door woke them from their tranquility. D'raekn wrapped a blanket around his waist, pulled the bolt, and threw open the door. Brilliant sunlight on newly fallen snow momentarily blinded him until the elder's head and shoulders blocked it from view.

"It wasn't good enough for you to scream your name to the heavens! You just had to let her speak it as well?" The old man said, his eyes seeking Cwen and glaring at her.

Hair tousled and mouth in a grim line, Cwen clutched a cover to her chest, daring the old man to speak.

"And you, woman! Suddenly took my advice and let him have it—fools! Now what are we going to do? You spent part of last night planning our escape, I hope. Good gods! Wipe that smile off your face, boy. One would think you'd never—"

Cwen stood up, naked, and felt some satisfaction at the elder's sudden silence. "One would think *you* had never seen a naked woman." She drew trousers up over her hips and pulled a clean shirt over her head, tying the laces and almost smiling at D'raekn's appreciative stare. "D'raekn, what is this old man's name?"

"Aenzl."

"Aenzl." Cwen stepped closer to the elder. "Thank you for keeping D'raekn alive."

"Sore lot of good it will do now. She'll be sending the soldiers. Queen Karid's attention you have drawn to us! Did you see what you caused?" The old man pointed toward the door.

Cwen walked out onto the porch and frowned at the destruction. An uprooted tree had crushed D'raekn's cabin, leaving it open to the night's snowfall. She shrugged. "I guess breakfast will be here today. What caused that to happen?" She rubbed a hand across D'raekn's bare chest and up the side of his face, fingers twisting in his hair, the night's shared power making her bold. "Your name or your passion?"

D'raekn stared across the clearing, his hand reaching out to stroke Cwen's back. "I do not know, but now I have nowhere to sleep."

"We do not have time for this!" As Aenzl slammed the porch with his staff, a shower of light like a dozen fireflies fluttered to the floor. "Magick," he mumbled, "your god damned magick!"

"The gods never damned our magick, Karid did. The time has come to set that right."

"Boy—D'raekn, they will skin us and boil us and stake us out for an insect feast. Crows will peck out our eyes, and the Noor will feed what is left of us to the nomads."

With strength driven by panic, Cwen gripped D'raekn's forearm. "Promise you will not let the nomads take me. Say that you will end my life before you allow it. Swear it to me!"

"Did he not warn you about speaking his name?" the old man asked, scowling at D'raekn.

"Aye, he did. Just promise it. Both of you swear it to me."

"You need not fear, Cwen. I will drive my own sword through your heart before I will allow the nomads to take you." He caressed her hair before giving the elder a dirty look and returning inside to get dressed. Everything was different now. Quite unexpectedly, D'raekn had something to live for and something to lose.

Cwen sank to the snow covered step and rested her head on her knees. She had been at peace for a moment in the wee hours of the morning with a man who wasn't even a Man. "I should have gone when you asked me to, Elder. I am sorry I did not listen."

"It would not have mattered." The old man's voice was suddenly kind. "The boy would have followed you, and I was a fool to think it could be any other way. D'raekn believes the two of you are fated, and perhaps he is right. He says you were born to a royal house under the sign of the serpent, the very serpent that embraced a dragon." He reached out and touched Cwen's cheek where the day before a scar had been. "If you are the chosen one you will change, your body will renew and grow stronger, and your mind will grow bolder. Together we might just have a chance to make things right. At least this way there can be a plan, a chance at victory against Karid. She cannot come at D'raekn directly, for she cursed his birth and gave Man dominion over him. But unfortunately, the council of eldermen and the Noors and nomads that serve her will be after you every step of the way. You will have to get D'raekn to the village of Dragonfire beyond the canyons of Malaia's Scar and find the sorceress C'thra. From there she can take you on to Mount Shadowmaw, the birthplace of Quondam's magick. 'Tis there the boy will find the power to challenge Queen Karid."

D'raekn squatted behind Cwen, hands working her still tense shoulders. "The jailors will not come before first thaw, because the boats are trapped in their harbor. When they do come, we will steal their boat and the horses they will bring to search the island. The path to the dock is already pitted with traps enough to take out a dozen or more men. On that day the two of you will remain in the safety of Aenzl's cavern."

"No." Cwen's anger flared. "I can be useful with the bow, the way you taught me. Dispatch a few men from a distance. I will not let you face them alone. Do not ask it of me."

A loud crackle, a blue-white flash of light, the smell of sulfur, and an explosion of dirt, loose and in clods, rained down around them as Aenzl turned to D'raekn. "*You* are the one who did it! *You* gave us back the power, and I will be damned if I will not use it against the jailors. Traps are fine, but a good archer," Aenzl patted Cwen's shoulder, "and a bit of wizardry are even better. We will be coming with you, D'raekn, when you go to meet that boat."

"Aenzl, you may want to practice a bit with that stick. A rain of dirt will not have much effect on our jailors," D'raekn replied.

"Boy, you may be a thousand years out of practice, but I am still skilled and a damn sight better than a handful of Noor jailors. Just you wait and see if I do not have them running and screaming into the sea! As for Karid and her threat of death, find the source of your power, and she will have no sting."

"A thousand years?" A reverent whisper slipped unbidden from Cwen's lips. The color drained from her face, and she shook off D'raekn's hands, stood, and backed away, casting a quick wondering glance toward Aenzl before locking her gaze on D'raekn. "The nomads told me that only gods and demons are everlasting. You have the face of the divine. Just tell me you are a god, and I will believe you. Do not say I have allowed a demon to possess me." Step by wary step, Cwen continued to back away. "Tell me."

A single leap from the porch closed the distance between them, the dragon's shadow looming as D'raekn moved into the sunlight. "Would you have me lie to you? I am not a god." Cwen's knees buckled, and he caught her around the waist. "But can you possibly believe a demon would care enough to heal a woman and wait for her to come to him, be foolish enough to speak his name to her? I do not think so. I may not be a mortal man, Cwen, but I am no more a demon than you."

He set her on her feet and steadied her a moment to be sure she would not fall. "And we are not everlasting, only very long lived."

"How long is very long?"

"Oh, five or six thousand years I would expect."

"Are you going to cook us breakfast now?" Aenzl called from the porch.

Cwen paled again, swaying, and D'raekn reached out to grip her arm. "But I—"

"Cwen, by our union and the speaking of my name the power is shared. Whatever life I have, so have you. The fire you felt was your new life taking hold. I do not believe the fates would have sent you to me if you were not the promised one."

"You are saying I had no choice but to accept you?"

"The fates merely set events in motion. It is we who choose our paths. At every fork you made a choice and received a reward or paid a price for each decision. Those choices led you here. You are a free woman, Cwen, and the choice to stay or go will always be yours."

"Can we eat while you think about all this?" Aenzl whined, and Cwen laughed out loud, a sound as pure and joyous as the peal of golden bells to D'raekn's ears.

"If you will grind my corn, old man, I will cook you breakfast." Cwen paused and rested her hand on D'raekn's arm. "I did not sleep with you because I care for you. I did it because I was afraid, and I do not want to be afraid. Please do not think last eve was love, or that it has given you unlimited reign over me."

D'raekn stared after Cwen and watched her walk into her new house ahead of the elder. He knew that no matter what she chose, he would always cherish the first day he heard Cwen laugh.

A long day of heavy work followed breakfast. D'raekn checked old traps and set new ones, staked pits and set braces of logs to roll downhill. His thoughts returned again and again to Cwen—the warm softness of her skin, her lingering natural fragrance. He had frightened her with the truth of their coupling, left her mind in turmoil and disbelief. His morning weapon instruction had not been gentle, and his voice was sharp at each less than perfect center in the targets he set for Cwen. "You cannot miss, Cwen. The jailors will not wait for you to take a second shot. While you are fumbling with your bow they will be dragging you off in chains. There is no longer room for error."

The angry hurt in her eyes left him sick, but no more than the thought of her death because he had not made her ready. Another month, perhaps two and the jailors would be upon them, and Karid would know that Cwen had freed D'raekn.

Chapter 13: Signs

"What is that, B'rma?" N'dia tugged on J'var's sleeve to draw his attention to the birds that wheeled overhead. It was no small flock. There appeared to be thousands of the night birds, so many that the sky was hidden by their flight. In the company of a growing band of stryvers, the three Noor had crossed the river west of Beorn's Freehold and were now nearing an uninhabited place called Ud's Valley.

B'rma pointed a finger at J'var. "Do you remember the tale your mother told of the dragon and the serpent?"

"Aye, it was a tale of promise. The dragon had no mate, and so the nymph Flida promised him that one day a serpent would embrace him and set him free. It was a silly story, meant only to put a boy to sleep, for it is well known that while a dragon's heart is passion, a serpent's heart is stone."

B'rma smiled. "Perhaps within a heart of stone can rest the greatest love. It was a promise from the day of the dragonspawn's birth, spoken by the sentinel Flida to the boy himself. After the dragonspawn's trial and imprisonment, when it was no longer safe to speak aloud of magick, the sorceresses passed it down as a children's tale to keep the promise alive. You should be ashamed, J'var, that you did not pay your mother more heed. Do you remember her death?"

"Nay, only that she left with an elderman and never returned home. Father told us that she was dead, her body lost. It was not until much later that I heard the ugly rumors of how she had been

135

arrested and executed for practicing the forbidden craft, for betraying Queen Karid."

Tears filled N'dia's eyes, and she swiped at them with the back of her hand. "Even I believed Mother had left us, until I began hearing the truth from B'rma."

"You have the magick in your blood, both of you, and L'or as well." B'rma pointed toward the birds. "And that is the sign that the dragonspawn has found the promised serpent, and she has freed him by embracing him and speaking his name. It is only the beginning. The power will return to Quondam, and as in the days of old, Man and magick will be forced to choose their allies and enemies in a struggle to find balance. You know the dragonspawn is not evil? He is not a demon, but a savior if you believe your mother's tales. He is sent to free us from Karid's rule"

The earth trembled and drove them to the ground as lightning claimed the sky and sent the birds fleeing in every direction. When the ground stilled, B'rma rose and dragged N'dia and J'var to their feet. "Let us find your mother's sword—our strength will soon be needed."

Ahead a cluster of grass covered tels peeked through the low ground mist, creating the illusion of islands floating among the clouds.

"What is this place?" asked N'dia, her whispered squeak barely containing her excitement.

"Ud's Valley. Below lie the cities of the Old Ones, fallen to ruin long before the rise of Man. Now they are home to the bones of those lost in Karid's Great War. Your mother is buried here in the sepulchre of the sorceresses. There also rests her sword." B'rma touched the shoulder of the closest stryver, sending it forward into the fog. It was one of several dozen that had joined them along their journey.

"Perhaps I should go first?" J'var had begun to wear a perpetual frown, annoyed by the trust B'rma placed in the idiot stryvers and irritated that even N'dia had begun to believe the dull, gray beasts were something special.

"Nay, the stryver holds the key to the tomb."

"Hmph! And just where does it hide this key? Since it obviously has neither purse nor pocket, I am fearful of hazarding a guess."

"Not all keys are cast in metal, J'var. The key is your mother's words, and it was the stryver she chose to hold them. One day you will see the stryvers for what they really are, but until then just a bit of respect might earn you their favor."

"Oh, I definitely want to be favored by a bunch of stryvers. It has been my lifelong goal!" J'var scoffed.

"You can go back." N'dia's words were soft and without reproach. "Father and L'or must be frantic by now. You could ease their minds and let them know I search for Cwen in the company of B'rma."

J'var stood silent, appraising N'dia. She seemed taller and stronger, confident of the rightness of her decision to search for Cwen.

"No, I will continue on with you. And I will hold my tongue regarding stryvers. Lead off, B'rma, show us Mother's magickal sword."

They trekked forward between the first two earthen mounds along the path the stryver had taken, drawn forward by a lantern-like glow. As they drew nearer, the glow became a pale winged man, his fair, silken hair billowing about a face with bright, quizzical eyes, a turned up nose covered with a sprinkling of burnished freckles, and a cherubic mouth. A pair of pointed ears tipped forward as if in eagerness to hear.

At the scrape of J'var's sword leaving its scabbard, the winged man spoke, "You need not arm yourself against me, for I am summoned by the dragonspawn's dreams to wield worry on the wicked Emyutes who despoiled the daughter of the serpent's blood. I honor you, son of D'lana with the mark of the woodland warrior." The man swept forward across the grass and placed the flat of his right hand against J'var's chest, on the left between shoulder and heart. As the winged man pulled away, N'dia gasped, for there on her brother's chest glowed a small, fiery handprint.

"Does it hurt?"

J'var looked puzzled and then shook his head. "No, just feels a bit cool." He reached up and rubbed the mark, frowning when it did not wipe away.

The winged man chuckled and bowed respectfully. "I am Ud, a firefly and servant of your mother, the sorceress D'lana. 'Twas with her death that she saved my life, and it is now my honor to serve her heirs and Man's future king." Ud's gaze shifted to N'dia, and he fluttered his wings to land beside her. "You come for the sword?"

"Aye," N'dia whispered, glancing again at the handprint on J'var's chest and taking a step back from the small, winged man. But he was not to be deterred, and he rose with rapidly beating wings, reaching out to place his hand against the left side of N'dia's face. "Wear the mark proudly, there for all to see that they might know the daughter of D'lana is a warrior for Flida, the woodland sentinel, and a defender of the rightful king."

N'dia raised a hand to her face and felt the cool imprint of Ud's small, magickal hand. A mischievous smile tilted full lips as she imagined the stark, fiery mark against her chocolate cheek and the shocked disbelief it would cause in Achroma. Her eyes met J'var's, and she couldn't stop a giggle. "Father will kill us both, but surely I need no longer worry about marrying V'ran."

Ud's eyebrows rose, and he looked to B'rma for explanation.

"It is just a jest among siblings, Ud, nothing that need concern any of us anymore."

J'var grimaced. "I would say your chances of marrying anyone have just declined sharply. Cwen and this magickal sword had better be worth the price we are paying. What about her?" His chin jutted forward to indicate B'rma. "Is she not worthy to be marked as well?"

B'rma shrugged off her cloak and pulled her shirt up over her head, standing, bare-chested and proud. The glowing handprint splayed across the top of her left breast, just below the shoulder. "I have born the mark since long before your mother wed your father." She threw back her head and laughed. "My ancestors served Quondam's last king, so I suppose that makes me your superior, J'var."

The scowl that marred J'var's chiseled features deepened as he expelled an exasperated breath. "How can you take all of this so lightly, B'rma? N'dia's life is as much as ruined. She will never be more than an outcast among our own people."

B'rma's finger waggled in J'var's face. "You don't even know who your people are!" She swept around to glare at N'dia. "Do you know? Do you have even the faintest idea of whom we are?"

N'dia looked away, suddenly embarrassed by her ignorance. Her mother's stories were a confused melee within her mind, without any clear meaning. "No, B'rma, I do not. I only know that my mother died for something she believed in so strongly she was willing to be taken from her children. And I know that Cwen is of great importance, that she is someone very special, and if she has given herself to the dragonspawn, he can be nothing but just and kind. That is how certain I am of Cwen."

B'rma smiled and squeezed N'dia's shoulder. "That will suffice for now." Turning to Ud she asked, "Is there news of Karid?"

"Aye, she has reduced the Emyute Buul to ashes and appointed another in his place. They war in Ga's Valley over Eipa's boak mine. The Saedan miners are outnumbered and poorly equipped, so my brothers Ip and Ri and I will join Ga against the nomads. Show those ignorant Emyutes a taste of magick like they have not seen since the Great War."

B'rma leaned forward and kissed the small man on the tip of his nose. "Good journey and good luck."

Without another word, she waved farewell to Ud and stalked off into the mist, followed by N'dia and a subdued J'var.

Ahead the stryver waited, crouched before an open tomb. Above the doorway, carved in the six languages of Quondam's races was a promise: *In the darkest days, when the stryvers speak and the hellwing flies, these swords will once again be drawn to defend the blood of kings.*

Beneath it were three columns of names, six in each. One was headed by the name D'lana, another by B'rma. The other names had no meaning to N'dia or J'var.

N'dia stretched up to finger the letters of her mother's name. "I wish that you had told me," she whispered reverently before ducking to enter the crypt.

A match flared, and B'rma lit the nearest wall torch, revealing an earthen path curving out of sight ahead. As N'dia's eyes adjusted to the muted light, she led the way forward, ever downward until the path ended in a T junction.

"Left," B'rma indicated, taking the lead at a quicker pace, drawn by the sword's song, a low hum that was not only heard but felt around the heart as a rather pleasant vibrating sensation.

"Do you feel it?" B'rma's eyes were bright with anticipation, and she was pleased to see her excitement reflected on the faces of J'var and N'dia. "It is the awakening power of the dragonspawn that has set the sword to singing. Word of his freedom will draw the loyal to Dragonfire. We will join them once N'dia bears the sword."

They stopped before a stone door. A sudden shuffling of footsteps brought a small, gray stryver. It stood on hind legs and rested deformed hands and misshapen head against the cool rock. With a great grinding, the door swung inward and revealed the resting place of the sorceress D'lana.

"Mother," whispered N'dia, and she stepped into the room to kneel beside the heavy oak casket with its swaddling of cobwebs and dust. "Help me." She looked up at J'var, and he drew his sword and forced the edge between lid and box, prying gently to lift the cover. As it gave way, he shoved it back and revealed their mother's remains wrapped in the green silks of her bloodline. Atop lay her sword, bound to her body by a golden cord tied with a wizard's knot. J'var and N'dia looked at one another, overcome by remembered grief and forgotten happiness. They hugged one another tight, their tears mingling. At last they parted, and N'dia reached out and touched the knot. They watched it withdraw its intricate golden strands to release the radiant crystal sword.

"Take it," urged B'rma, "long has it awaited your hand."

N'dia gripped the hilt and lifted the sword from its scabbard to read the blade's inscription: *And an army of fire shields shall follow her into battle.* The shimmer of the blade intensified, and the carved adornment of D'lana's name glowed white-hot as the letters shifted and changed to reflect the name of N'dia. "What does it mean?"

"That now 'tis truly yours, and you must make haste to Dragon's Heart."

N'dia and J'var stared open-mouthed, for the deep voice that spoke these words belonged to the stryver still waiting on the threshold. Its eyes were no longer a listless, clouded gray but the dazzling, ice blue of N'dia's own.

The stryver's gaze met J'var's, and a frown creased its brow. "Oft you have spoken harshly, Master J'var, but we know it was only out of ignorance, and we forgive you this offense." With a wink at N'dia and B'rma, it beckoned them to follow. "Come quickly, Lady N'dia, the dragon lord cannot wait. You can hire a boat at the harbor near Rider's Cross."

J'var caught hold of B'rma's hands and in a voice gruff with emotion admitted, "I have misjudged you, B'rma, and my sister as well. Thank you for the gift of my mother's truth. I will not doubt your word again." He spun about and hurried after N'dia and the stryver.

B'rma knelt and kissed the stone of her ancestors and lifted her own sword from its encasement before following the others.

Chapter 14: Karid

The Emyute Lien had been summoned from the battlefield in Ga's Valley. He assumed the queen was dissatisfied with his clan's progress against the Saedan miners. Even armed with little more than stones and clubs, the Saedans had proved difficult to overpower. They held the higher ground and used rolling braces of logs and great barrels of flaming fuel to hinder the advancement of Lien's troops.

Now Lien knelt before Karid, remembering Buul's failure and swift punishment. The queen paced impatiently, drawing away and then near. Each time she approached, Lien flinched and tucked his chin into his chest, careful not to look at her.

"I trusted you. I gave you Buul's power and a simple chore, but not even that has been accomplished." The crack of her booted footfalls neared. "Have you seen the storms? Did you feel the earth tremble? See the night birds flock?"

"I have not seen the birds your highness," Lien replied timidly, "but I did feel an earthquake, and the weather has been violent of late."

The queen threw up her hands. "Oh, if only it were just an earthquake and a bit of bad weather! Why did you lie to me?"

"I have not lied. The Saedans hold the high ground and have—"

"The Saedans? The boak miners? You believe you are here to discuss boak miners? Look at me!"

Lien drew a breath and looked up. Karid seemed to tower over him. "I have not taken command of the mines, but I will. It is only a matter of—"

The kick to his face was brutal, throwing him onto his back. Karid circled him, her lips curled downwards in a snarl of distaste. "Tell me again how you killed the woman."

He spat teeth and blood, wiped his mouth and stuttered, "W-w-woman?"

Karid kicked him again, this time in the kidneys. He screamed and twisted away from her, only to meet the boot of a waiting fire guard. "Shall I burn him?"

"No." Karid waved the woman off. "He will answer me." She knelt beside the moaning nomad. "Tell me how you killed the golden-eyed woman, the fire-haired demon. You did kill her, did you not? You told me she was dead."

Lien nodded and struggled to his knees. "I swear she is dead. I rolled her off the escarpment onto the rocks in the Sanguine Sea. She was dead. No one could survive such a fall."

"So you are certain she is dead?"

Lien nodded again, and Karid's boot slammed into his gut, doubling him over and leaving him gagging. Her spittle sprayed across his eyes as she gripped his cheeks and shouted into his face, "That earthquake you felt and that wicked storm, they were signs of the dragonspawn's release. If the woman is dead how did she free the dragonspawn?"

"I d-d-don't—"

"You're damned right you don't! You let the woman live! Set her free to speak the beast's forbidden name! Now he is loose, and I must have him hunted down and find a way to execute him! Do you know how inconvenient that is?"

"Inconven—?"

Karid grabbed Lien's hair and jerked his head back. "Not only did you let this woman live, but now my oracle tells me there is another daughter of Aaradan—another woman bearing the blood of the serpent—one who escaped my assassins' fire on their home world. Now there are two of them free to get in my way and complicate my plans."

"This close," the queen said, holding her fingers up and measuring a hair's breadth. "I was this close to ending the fulfillment of Flida's promise to the beast, and you single-handedly destroyed all my efforts.

But I will not let my sister win. Since I am now forced to hunt down the dragonspawn and, because of your carelessness, some Aaradan whore, you will find the other."

The nomad choked on blood and tried to shake his head.

"Oh yes! You will. I do not have time to kill you and select another for the task. You will go with one of my assassins. My deviant spawn will allow you passage through the mirror and into the land of Ædracmoræ. You will find the Aaradan woman and bring her to me. Deceive her if you must, but do not harm her. I will use her to draw the golden-eyed one to me. Show her this!" With a flick of her wrist Karid tossed Lien a small signet ring, then swung about and without another word, stalked out of the room.

Lien struggled to his feet, pocketed the ring, and looked around for an escape, but one of Karid's assassins blocked the only visible exit.

An indigo mirage of shimmering heat, the assassin beckoned him forward. "We must go. Karid will not tolerate our failure or a lengthy absence, and I do not think you want her to send someone after us."

Lien scowled, shook his head, and followed the woman into the cool dimness of the lower palace toward the deviant's hall of mirrors.

Chapter 15: Sóvïë

Sóvïë levered the long flat stone up and sneezed in the sudden fog of old ash that swirled about, dusting her face and arms. She stood up, drank from her flask, and scanned the distance, listening for a repeat of the rustling she had heard earlier. There was nothing except the cheerful gurgling of the nearby brook and the distant call of a bird overhead—perhaps the shiver along her spine and the prickling of her scalp were unfounded. Since the loss of her parents during the attacks on the House of Aaradan, Sóvïë had become hypersensitive to the world around her. She shook off the moment of unease, lifted her long dark hair, twisted it into a knot, pinned it, and went back to work, levering up another of the great stones that blocked the entrance to her ancestral home.

The crack of a twig beneath a careless boot was not her imagination. Sóvïë kept working, bearing down on the iron bar to lift the stone, pushing hard to shift it away from the growing opening. There was another sharp snap, this one closer. She spun around, the iron bar flung away and her sword drawn in a single fluid movement.

Before her stood an indigo woman who shimmered as though she was an illusion. Sóvïë's mouth went dry, and gooseflesh peppered her exposed skin. She recognized a fire woman, one similar to the assassin who had destroyed Ædracmoræ in a search for the blood of the Aaradans. At first glance, the woman appeared to be Maraen, but as the image shifted beneath the distortion of the heat another became visible.

"I knew you would come, knew that the death of my parents, aunt, and cousin did not give sufficient Aaradan blood to satisfy whatever master holds your chain. For some reason we cannot be allowed to survive."

Sóvië felt the burst of heat. With no more than a momentary surge in her brightness, the assassin sent a pulse of air hot enough to redden Sóvië's cheeks and cause streams of perspiration to flow.

"Do not make me disable you. Queen Karid requests your presence. You will come with me," the voice commanded in tones akin to that of a serpent slipping through sand. The woman's image wavered—into a race unknown—and then reverted to Maraen-like and familiar again.

"And if I refuse? What if I just tell you that I know no Queen Karid and choose to return to my work?"

"You will not refuse." A man, hooded and cloaked, stepped from the shadows. "I am the Emyute Lien."

"Sóvië?" a young man's voice interrupted, startling the assassin whose aura flared, heating the surrounding air and burning off the dust motes.

"No!" Sóvië threw herself in front of the approaching man and the small wizard who followed. "Stop!"

The assassin held up her hands in agreement, allowing the air around them to cool. "I was startled. I mean you no harm, but the daughter of Aaradan must accompany me to Quondam. I will kill the others if I must."

"Just kill them and take her!" Lien blurted.

"Ha! You are not a Maraen, but a poor attempt at transformation by someone with little skill is what you are," snorted the short, wild-haired wizard Grumbleton, stabbing the air with a stubby finger for emphasis. "I have served the House of Aaradan for a very long time, and there is no way some badly disguised, flaming barbarian will be taking Sóvië anywhere!"

"Shut up, old man!" Lien snarled. "We will be taking her. Whether you are alive or dead when we leave is of no import."

"Hush, Grumbleton, no one will be taking Sóvië anywhere," Xalin said, looking expectantly at the girl he intended to marry. "What is this, Sóvië? Who are these people, and what is a quondam?"

Sóvië twisted the ring on her finger before placing her hand on Xalin's arm. "She is one of the assassins—"

Xalin swept Sóvië out of the way, pushing her to the ground as he drew his sword.

"No, Xalin, no!" Sóvië scrambled to her feet and clutched Xalin's sword hand. "Please, please." She felt his muscles relax, and the sword lowered a fraction. "Please…"

He sheathed the sword. "Tell me why I am doing this."

"Because she will kill you, she will kill you with the power of the flame. I could not live with that, Xalin. I have lost everything except your promise to share vows with me. I refuse to lose that."

"Bah! Do not be stupid, Sóvië!" the wizard Grumbleton flailed his arms. "We will not let them take you! I will call the rain!"

"Do not make me burn you. I need only the woman. Your quenching spell may work for a time, but we will not go without her."

"The other—your fire-haired sister—is there, in Quondam." Lien dealt the winning card. He held out the ring Karid had given. "She lives among our people. If you come, we will take you to her."

"Cwen?" Sóvië frowned, accepting Cwen's signet. "You are telling us my cousin Cwen lives? It is not true. I saw her fall behind a wall of fire. She and my mother perished in the same flames. Perhaps you stole the ring."

Lien coughed, hawked up a wad of bloodstained phlegm, and spat it at his feet. "I do not know her name. Only that she is an Aaradan who lives. My queen spoke of it"

"He speaks the truth," the fire woman hissed. "There is another alive on Quondam who bears your blood. It is why our queen seeks your help."

"My help? My cousin Cwen is quite capable of helping herself. She has never needed anyone."

"If she is to be saved, you must come. Think. If we had come to destroy you, why would you still live?"

Xalin leaned close and whispered in Sóvië's ear, "Sóvië, they are lying. Can you not feel the waves of their deception?"

She nodded, her hand cupping his face and her words a soft breath against his lips, "But they do not lie about Cwen, for this is the signet my mother gave to her, and it hums with life. On that they speak the truth, and if Cwen lives, perhaps my mother does also. They were together, for I saw them together beyond the flames.

"Trust in me, Xalin. Am I not the most fearsome swordsman you know? The most perfect marksman with a bow? Is my magick not as powerful as the wizard's apprentice? Am I not heir to the joined thrones of serpent and dragon? I cannot forsake even the most fleeting possibility that my mother lives. I must go with them." Her lips touched his, opening to receive his warmth.

Xalin looked up and addressed the assassin and the man beside her. "She will accompany you, but I will come along to see her safe."

"And I!" chimed the wizard Grumbleton.

"No! Only the woman!" the Emyute Lien cursed and paced anxiously. "We are running out of time. Your cousin is running out of time."

"Only the one who bears the serpent's blood may accompany us through the deviant's portal," the assassin spoke to Sóvië. "I promise your safety, but the others must wait here for your return."

"Call your portal—give me a moment." Sóvië drew Xalin and Grumbleton to the shadows beneath the crumbling fortress wall. "I cannot explain it, but I trust that woman."

"By the gods, she's an assassin, Sóvië! You cannot truly mean to go with her!" exclaimed Grumbleton, his eyes wide with fear and anxiety.

Sóvië dropped to her knees and hugged the little wizard in a fierce embrace. "I have to go and find my mother. Trust me, Grumbleton, you have taught me well. Keep Xalin safe until my return."

She stood and gripped Xalin's hands. "Wait for me." Then she raced to the swirling silver mirror and passed through into Quondam between Lien and the assassin.

As she stepped beyond the mirror and into a stone-walled room in Quondam, Sóvië caught a glimpse of a creature whose scaly flesh appeared to have melted. An eye rested on a cheekbone, the nose and lips were twisted, exposing misshapen teeth. A stream of stringy slime dripped and pooled in the matted hair of its sunken chest. Sóvië tried to reverse her forward motion, but a blow to the back of her head sent her reeling, and she collapsed in the litter of bones and skin that covered the floor.

"If she is dead, so are we! Karid will kill us both and anyone else who bears a drop of our blood." The assassin dropped to Sóvië's side and rolled her over, checking for a pulse before she looked up at Lien and said, "You could have killed her! Karid said no harm!"

"What are you looking at?" Lien slammed his club across the gawking deviant's shoulder. "Do your job! Close the portal!" To the assassin he merely mumbled, "She is not dead, just easier to transport."

Lien took Sóvië's sword and dagger, grabbed her by the hair, and dragged her out of the hall of mirrors, along the dim hallway, and into Queen Karid's antechamber. He dumped her in a heap in the middle of the room and dropped the weapons beside her.

"Well? Summon Karid!" the Emyute demanded. "We have done what she asked."

The assassin stood her ground and stared at Lien. "You are filth, a despicable breed without honor or loyalty," she spat at him before turning away. She prepared herself and then pulled the cord to call Karid.

Sóvië moaned, sat up, and rubbed the back of her skull and neck.

"So you are the other daughter of Aaradan. I was unaware that there were two."

"There are not." Sóvië let her head drop forward, then rolled it right and left, finally raising her eyes to look at the owner of the voice. "I assume you are the queen of whom my captors spoke?" she asked, struggling with a bit of dizziness before standing up. She extended her hand in greeting, "I am Sóvië, daughter of King Sōrél of Aaradan," allowing it to drop when it was not accepted. "The other woman you have captured is Cwen, my cousin. I am considered quite civilized compared to her."

"But you are dark, and she is…"

"A halfling—it is a long story, but I can assure you that one half of her *is* Aaradan, the other half is extinct thanks to your assassins and their efficient use of fire. What place is this? Why am I here? And who is that huddling in the corner?" Sóvië pointed toward a gnarled old woman crouching in the shadows. "I know your assassin and the man who cracked my skull."

"You are very bold for one who may die at any moment. This place is my palace in the city of Serabia. And you are here because I command it." Karid circled the girl with mild interest and thought her pretty in a dark sort of way, but dressed in leather breeches and a soiled shirt, she did not look like the daughter of a king.

"Your threat came as no surprise," Sóvië said. "I have been expecting the return of your assassins since their last visit, though I did not expect the club to the back of my head." She glared at the waiting man and reminded herself to kill him at the first opportunity. Sóvië held up the signet. "Is my cousin alive, or was that just a ploy to get me here?"

"She lives and has the potential to cause me a great deal of trouble. You are going to stop her."

Sóvië laughed, then looked at the serious expression on Karid's face and laughed again. "You cannot be serious!" She wiped the tears from her eyes. "You brought me here thinking that my presence would somehow control my cousin's behavior? I have not seen her in years. We do not even like one another! She is a rogue and a thief, not worthy to be called an Aaradan, and I assure you she would rather cut my throat than speak to me. Someone has definitely misinformed you."

Suddenly Sóvië's hand shot out, summoning her sword. It was Karid's turn to laugh. "Your magick is of no use here. It was gone the moment you stepped through the portal. Quondam has no magick. What little there was has faded, diminished to the occasional glimmer within the wildwoods of the West. And I will soon put an end to that as well. This cousin you speak of has fornicated with a devil and freed him from his prison. I believe when she hears you have arrived, she will come for you and leave the demon weakened."

Her thoughts a confused jumble of possibilities, Sóvië stalled. "What are you talking about?" *Could it be that creature I saw?* "How did my cousin come in contact with your devil?" *If Cwen is held by some demon, can my mother be with her?*

"Your cousin was believed dead, but recent events have proved otherwise. She has become the concubine of a dragonspawn and loosed him within my kingdom. He will destroy us if he is not stopped. Help me draw her away from him, and I will set you both free."

"My cousin was not alone. Another woman traveled with her, a dark woman, older, but very much like me. Is this woman also with the demon you speak of?"

"Another daughter of Aaradan?" Karid's voice rose, and she turned toward the oracle crouched in the corner.

"There is no other your highness. The bones spoke only of this one and the fire-haired girl," the oracle droned.

"Then who is this other woman?" Karid demanded.

"One touched by the gods but not of Aaradan blood," the oracle added.

"Your oracle is correct. The other woman is my mother. She does not bear the blood of Aaradan, but that of the Sojourners, creators of my world. On Ædracmoræ she is called the Dragon Queen, one favored by the gods."

Karid kicked the bones that lay before the oracle and screamed, "You knew this and did not tell me!"

"My queen, you asked only that I seek those bearing the blood of the serpent," the oracle reasoned. "You did not ask for those endowed by the gods!"

"Well I am asking now, you toothless hag! Where is this Dragon Queen? Find her! Find her right now!" Karid shook her fist toward the heavens and wailed, "Why am I surrounded by the dimwitted? I have won! Stolen Man from you! They worship me, obey my every command! Why do you still haunt me?"

"Perhaps I should go and let you deal with your staff," Sóvië picked up her weapons and sheathed them. "It is obvious that they require some additional instruction, and you are very busy."

The air grew hot around her, and Sóvië looked up into the flaming eyes of the young assassin. "I cannot let you bear arms, and I cannot let you go." She extended her hand, and Sóvië gave up her weapons.

"No, I suppose you cannot." She gave a gentle smile. "Do you have a name?"

"Assassins are not allowed names!" Karid snapped before turning to a shimmering fire guard. "Take this woman to a cell, and see that she remains there. Any problem and your clan's blood will be held accountable. Is that clear?"

"Yes, my queen, very clear."

"Oh, and *Master* Lien," Karid said, stroking the waiting nomad's cheek and purring, "while you were away I was forced to replace you. Your wife's brother now commands your clan." Suddenly, she whirled away, beckoning the oracle to follow.

"But I did your bidding! I did what you asked! Why do you punish me?" Lien cried, trembling with shock and disbelief.

Karid paused and turned to examine him. "You lied to me. This entire fiasco is your fault. I cannot abide liars."

"What will become of me?"

"I need a messenger. Take a message to my commander in Stonetel, and tell him to ready my troops to march on Luminora. Can you handle that, Lien? Take a message to Stonetel?"

"Aye, my queen," Lien murmured, relieved to be leaving the palace with his life.

Chapter 16: Discontent

Aenzl did not stay for supper, the growing storm between woman and dragonspawn being sufficient reason to send the elder off to prepare his own. Cwen's resentment over D'raekn's harsh instruction earlier in the day left the woman waspish and the dragonspawn churlish. D'raekn tried to explain that he only wished to prepare her adequately for the coming battle, but Cwen's fierce pride prevented her from accepting his explanation.

Cwen slammed plates and sawed through the day-old bread with a vengeance. She snapped, "Outside," when the stew was heated through, and they ate their meal on the porch in a good deal less than companionable silence. Cwen's hurt and anger were thick enough to spoon up along with the hearty soup they were eating. As soon as D'raekn's bowl was empty she snatched it from his hands and went inside, slamming the door behind her. She returned after a few moments of banging about in the kitchen, a rolled mat in her arms. "I will not have you in my house! You can sleep on my porch if you wish." She flung the mat toward him and slammed the door again. This time the slamming was followed by the crash of the bolt being driven home.

D'raekn stood mutely, staring at the door and feeling a fool for assuming she would take him to her bed again. He gave a low snarl and considered breaking down her door, but what would he do then? Force her? No, not that. Beg her forgiveness for behaving like a man sensible enough to fear the future? When boiling oil froze he would!

In a vile temper, he threw the mat down and growled at the hardness of the porch as he stretched out upon it. He drew his legs up in an attempt to fit his body to the uncomfortable woven straw, dragging his cloak over him in annoyance as he glared out into the yard. "I should have told her I was a god," he muttered, "or acted the demon she believes and taken what I want." Neither thought soothed him, and he lay sleepless, listening to the sounds of Cwen filling her bathtub and visualizing every gentle splash as her body sank down into the warm water.

When he could no longer stand it, he jumped to his feet and ran the path from the headlands to the beach and sat on the sand where he had first found her, grinding his teeth and cursing his luck. If he had known how brief his joy would be, he would have stuck to the whores.

In the deepest hour of night he returned to find the cabin dark and the remains of the blackberry brandy next to his mat. Disgruntled beyond belief, he ignored the cup and tossed back the rest of the sweet liquor before huddling on the mat, plagued by dreams of dragon deaths and Karid's destruction of Quondam.

Behind his eyes, dragons screamed and fell like rain, butchered for the elements used to transform ordinary flesh into Karid's fire assassins.

D'raekn tossed restlessly as the foul visions continued.

Karid drew men to her armies with promises of wealth and the immortality of the flesh. Her armies stormed across Quondam in a wave of destruction, killing all who would not bow and stealing fertility from women of childbearing age with the barren-making potion created by the royal alchemist.

Eventually the flood of images ceased, allowing the dragonspawn a few hours of uninterrupted sleep.

The twang of a bowstring's release woke him, and he arose, sore and sullen, to find a steaming cup of tea beside the mat. In the yard, Cwen prepared to loose another arrow, her arm steady as she sighted down the shaft. *Thwack.* Dead center of the straw man's heart. Again, the whistle of the arrow and the tear of the straw as Cwen's shot found the perfect mark. "Is there nothing you want to say to me?" Her voice matched the cold fire in her eyes.

D'raekn lifted his shoulders. "You are better today than yesterday?"

"Aye, while you snored on the porch, I have practiced. You are not responsible for me or for what may happen to me just because we spent one night in the same bed." A jerk of her head and another angry arrow hissed into the straw.

He sighed and shook his head, sank to the step and watched the grace with which she nocked the arrow, no fumbling, just fluid motion from quiver to bowstring. "I am responsible, whether you like it or not. One night shared, or a hundred, we are mated you and I. You may tell me it means nothing to you and walk away, but it does mean something to me. I did not take you lightly, Cwen, just to satisfy the flesh." He sipped the tea and watched a tremor claim her hands and send the next arrow wide, into the trees. "Is that a trembling from fear? Or something very different?"

She ignored him and went to look for the arrow, tramping through the brush beneath the trees and parting the grasses with slaps of her hands. Tears stung her eyes, and she blinked them away. "I do not want you!" she shouted.

"Leave the arrow. Come here."

She looked back over her shoulder with a furious "make me" expression on her face.

"Come here, Cwen." His voice was low, soft, and determined as he met her stare.

For a moment it seemed they were stalemated, and then she walked unhurriedly back to the porch and stood before him, looking up to meet his gaze. "What would you have me say? That I love you?"

"Not unless you do."

"Well, I definitely do not," she swore aloud. The acid of the lie churned in her gut, and the truth plagued her mind. *I cannot allow myself to love you. It would hurt too much to lose you.*

D'raekn shrugged. "There is nothing I can do about that, though the porch was a hard, cold way to let me know. But it does not change my feelings or make me any less responsible for you. I have cared for you since I found you near death on the beach, and like Aenzl, you are my family now. That means I will make you strong and sure with your weapons, even if my demands anger you and make you turn away."

He got to his feet and threw the last of the cooling tea into the dirt. After setting the cup on the handrail, he lifted Cwen by the waist to place her on the porch behind him. He took the water flask from its hook on the wall. "I am going to the dock—in case Aenzl asks."

"Why? Do you expect a boat so soon?"

"No, just some things I want to do."

"I could come with you."

He swung back to her. "Cwen, do not play games. I have no energy for it today. I did not sleep well, remember? If you want to come, come and I will put you to work, but we will be gone overnight."

Without waiting, he took off across the yard. Cwen stared at the tree line where he had disappeared and then started after him at a slow jog.

It was near dusk, and the sun was falling toward the red horizon in the west by the time they reached the dock.

"What is over there?" Cwen sat down and dangled her feet over the edge of the dock.

D'raekn dropped to a crouch beside her and stared across the sea. "Another world—the trade center of Corusca where our enemies wait. A vast, wet forest that hides a tangled web of canyons that bear my mother's name, and a mountain range of dragon bones said to hold the key to my...*our* power. Somewhere beyond the sea we will find the woman who raised me and people who will help us."

"The sorceress C'thra in the village of Dragonfire—Aenzl told me."

D'raekn stood and pulled Cwen to her feet. "There is a sulfur spring up the path behind the shack. I will cut brambles, and you can drag them to the pond and dip them. Then bring them back, and lay them out alongside the shack to dry. Before we leave tomorrow, we will place them inside and create a fire trap."

By the time D'raekn called Cwen to quit, her arms and hands were a mass of angry, bleeding scratches, but a stack of sulfur-dipped brambles reached the roofline of the old shack. He led her inside, lit the lamp, started a fire in the tiny hearth, and put the kettle on to boil. When he looked back, Cwen was sitting, back against the wall, arms folded across her knees with her head resting on them. D'raekn pulled a sack from the shelf and poured what was left of the dried vegetables and rice into the pot, adding a few dusty herbs for flavor.

"Cwen," he whispered, touching her shoulder, "you should eat something before you sleep, and I need to look at your scratches."

With a sigh she lifted her head and held out her arms, too tired even to speak. D'raekn rubbed salve into her wounds and examined blisters on the palms of her hands. "Why did you not tell me you needed to stop?" He brushed a tangle of hair away from her face and tilted her chin up to make her look at him.

"I did not want you to be sorry I came," she mumbled, leaden eyelids closing with a will of their own. "I don't want you to think I am weak."

"I do not think you are weak. Foolish maybe, but not weak."

Cwen managed to stay awake long enough for a cup of broth and vegetables, though she ate most of it with her eyes closed. When she pushed the cup aside and laid her head on the table, D'raekn stood and arranged a pallet on the floor. He carried her there and tucked an old wool blanket around her. "Sleep well." His kiss brushed her brow, and she mumbled something unintelligible as her breathing settled into the gentle rhythm of deep sleep.

He bedded down across the room and let his thoughts wander through the ages to allies of long ago, bloodlines sworn to protect Malaia's son. The bloodlines of the houses of B'rma and D'lana, long allied with the house of C'thra through the practice of their magick, were now hidden among Quondam's races. His eyes closed, and he saw the sorceress C'thra clearly, wearing her cloak and fevered with the need to tell him he would live to rise to power. Patience, she had urged in the darkness of a stinking cell beneath Karid's palace, patience and caution until the serpent embraces the dragon. Until then lie quiet, remain dormant, and protect the magick.

The serpent had embraced the dragon. He had shared the magick with Cwen, and now he must protect her as well. His eyes grew heavy, and sleep drew him into a kaleidoscope of collective memories, the dragons' dreams.

Soaring over the rich, black earth of newly tilled fields, over glistening white palaces and busy trade centers, the dragons guarded Quondam.

D'raekn groaned within the dream as calm was traded for calamity. *Heavy nets, barbed to grasp scales and pierce deep into soft flesh, yanked dragons from their flight and filled the sky with bellows of pain and rage.*

"Karid," D'raekn snarled in his sleep as the nymph swept into the foreground of the shifting memories. Images sharpened and faded in a disjointed array of dragon thought.

So beautiful, so vile, Karid laughed and charmed the true king, married him, and made him worship her beyond reason, beyond the safety of his advisors' admonition. The vision turned deadly. *The warm palm of one deceiving hand cupped the king's face as Karid's other dealt the fatal blow, a cook's blade driven deep into the beloved ruler's heart.*

D'raekn's guttural grunts caused Cwen to toss restlessly, but did not awaken her.

The dragonspawn's dream slipped, took him backward. *Karid kneeling beside a dying man within the sacred wildwoods and taking a soul promised to the gods. Karid's angry words as she betrayed Flida, and the flash of the dark god who drove Karid into the realm of men.* His eyes shifted rapidly behind closed lids. *Karid stepped from the bathing pool into the king's waiting arms, promising passion.*

No! The dragonspawn's howl shattered the silence of his dream, but did not leave his lips. The scene shot forward. *Karid screamed and pointed to Malaia, sister of the king and blood heir to the throne of Quondam.*

"Mother, why did you fear me so?" D'raekn whispered aloud. His eyes opened, and he scanned the room, his gaze lingering on Cwen's dark form. He lay awake the remainder of the night, his mind tangled in the tattered remnants of a half remembered dream.

In the silent dawn, Cwen and D'raekn set the fire trap and then made their way back to Cwen's cabin.

Chapter 17: Visions

D'raekn's day was spent digging pits and setting additional traps along the path nearest the cabin. Cwen avoided him. She spent the day helping Aenzl construct a drying rack and tending the fire that smoke-cured Aenzl's offering of a scrawny deer carcass.

They shared an early supper around Cwen's table.

"Not a bad stew from such meager offerings," D'raekn mumbled around a mouthful of venison. "The smoking gives it a fine flavor, Cwen."

"Aye, even the stringiest flesh is better than bare bone soup," Aenzl agreed as he wiped his bowl with a finger and sucked off the last morsel of turnip. "Shall we share a bit of brandy before I head home?"

"No, no brandy." Cwen's voice was too sharp, and she looked away, embarrassed by her lack of courtesy to the old wizard. "I am sorry, Aenzl. I am just very tired."

"We will go then and give you your rest." D'raekn stood. "Come on old man, the woman wants a clear head, but you and I can share a swig on the porch before you leave."

Cwen cleared the table and washed up. When finished, she sat near the fire listening to the low drone of the men's conversation until hours later a sudden nod of her head startled her awake. It was dark and quiet now. She peeked out the door to find the porch empty. She stifled a yawn as she changed into her nightshirt and rubbed at the crick forming in her neck, and then she bolted the door, wondering if D'raekn had gone home with Aenzl.

Slick, cold sweat coated Cwen's body, and she tossed uneasily as the dream deepened. As always, it had begun in the gray of the glen with the great man rising to leave his fire and reveal his face, the dragon's shadow looming behind, but this time Cwen did not wake when his familiar face was revealed.

Footsteps pounded and hoarse voices cursed against a background of grating steel blades being drawn. Armed soldiers reached out and grabbed the man's unresisting arms, forcing him to the ground. They manacled his wrists and ankles, dragged him to a flat slab of rust-stained stone and forced his head over the edge. A gleam of light overhead caused Cwen to look up, and she screamed when the pale-haired woman turned and met her eyes before letting the axe blade fall.

"D'raekn!"

The groan and crack of splintering wood was accompanied by D'raekn shouldering his way through the door.

"Cwen!" His urgent whisper woke her. She gasped and reached for him as her tears broke with the relief of finding him alive. D'raekn gathered her close, touching her so for the first time since she had sworn she did not want him. He murmured soothing words against her hair and rocked her as if she were a child. When her heartbeat finally slowed to the match the rhythm of his own, he drew back a bit, smoothed her hair, and rubbed her chilled face with his warming hands. "What was it?"

She did not speak or look up, afraid to meet his eyes, but gave a slight shake of her head to let him know she had heard him.

"Can you not tell me?"

Cwen chanced a quick upward glance, and the compassion in D'raekn's eyes seized her. She wiped ineffectually at fresh tears trickling down her cheeks and laid her face against his chest. "It was you. They…you…died." She did not add her final thought. *And through it all you never looked away from me or tried to save yourself.*

D'raekn rubbed Cwen's back and whispered reassurances against the top of her head, "It was just a bad dream, nothing to fret about. It was most likely a result of my harshness. I have been pushing you too hard, and you have simply gotten even by killing me in your sleep. There is nothing to it, and you should sleep without worry now." He untangled himself from her arms, laid her back against her pillow and stood. "I should return to the porch."

"Please," Cwen held out her hand, "could you just hold me a little longer?" His uncertain expression caused her to withdraw her hand, bite her lip, and look away. "Please?" she asked in a softer tone.

D'raekn took a long ragged breath before sinking down on the bed beside her. When she snuggled against the warmth of his body he tensed for a moment, and then wrapped his arms protectively around her, pondering the dream and listening to Cwen's breathing as she drifted off to sleep.

Cwen yawned and stretched, then froze as her hand brushed against D'raekn's warmth. The nightmare flooded her mind as did the fact that she had practically begged him to hold her. Her cheeks flushed with the memory, and she looked up to find his soft gaze regarding her benignly.

"Did you sleep well?"

"Aye," she admitted, her hands twisting the blanket up beneath her chin. "I am sorry I woke you."

"It was nothing, though I fear I broke your bolt in coming through the door. I will repair it after morning training." D'raekn swung his legs over the side of the bed and stood, stretched and padded to the hearth to push the water over the flame. "Tea?" He grinned at Cwen's discomfited silence and her quickly averted gaze. "I did not fall prey to your bewitching in the bed." He pulled on his trousers and tossed her hers. "Even though you were quite bold," he paused and winked, "for a woman who does not want me. It was all I could do to fight you off."

"You lie!" Another wave of heat flooded Cwen's cheeks.

"By the gods, you are beautiful all flushed with your maidenly offense. Perhaps you should brew the tea while I gather a few more logs for the fire, for if I do not go I may not be able to resist you any longer."

Cwen leaned down from the bed, snatched up a boot, and flung it at his disappearing backside. "Beast!" she shot back, but her hiss turned into good natured laughter as she stretched again, luxuriating in the realization that just his presence had held further nightmares at bay.

They practiced the swords in the first of the heavy spring rains. Cwen slipped and tumbled to her back, sword braced against D'raekn's downward backhand.

"A drive to the gut is your only chance if you are lying on your back. Your arms are still too weak to hold the downward swing of a man's strength," D'raekn directed.

"I just held you off!" Cwen jerked away from his offered hand, rolled to her feet, and stood, muddied hair framing her furious scowl. "So surely I can hold off a nomad."

"You held me off because I pulled my sword. Had I not, your arm would have been cut off at the shoulder. You cannot take a man, Cwen, an inexperienced boy, perhaps, but not an armed nomad in a face-to-face fight. It is why your skill with the bow is so important. You must distance yourself from your enemies."

"Then teach me to beat an armed nomad. You know a day will come when they will be too close for the bow and only my sword will save me. I can do it, I know I can."

"The gods be damned! I can take you bare handed without breaking a sweat, and so can the weakest nomad. You try to challenge nature, Cwen, and be something you are not."

Cwen's chin rose in defiance, "Do it then. Toss away your sword, and try to take mine from me bare handed," she challenged, "without breaking a sweat."

He dropped his sword, knocked her down with a push to the shoulder, and wrenched the sword from her hand with a twist of his wrist. "Are you happy?" He let her sword fall from his fingers, his gut twisting at the shock on her face, her disbelief followed by shame and then anger, as he bent to retrieve his blade.

"Your grace and minimal skill have made you arrogant, and it will get you killed. Stand up. Bring your sword to guard. Now! Men will not wait while you flounder in the mud."

Cwen scrambled to her feet and reached for her sword. D'raekn placed his boot on her buttocks and pushed her face first into the slick, sticky mud. Cwen rolled and struggled, finally sliding to her feet, the sword clutched in an angry, white-knuckled, two handed grip. She swung—off balance—and he ducked away, coming up beneath her to grip her ankle and pull the leg out from under her. She fell heavily, the breath driven from her lungs. She struggled to her hands and knees and took deep, wheezing gasps trying to fill her burning lungs, but D'raekn pushed her down again with a shove of his boot to the ribs that flipped her onto her back. Cwen stayed down. Still breathless, she lifted the sword to ward him off and cringed away from the two-handed power of his overhand stroke. Steel crashed against steel. Her sword flew from her fingers, leaving her hands numb and empty and her body defenseless and shivering in the cold mud.

"You're dead, and you don't have sense enough to see it! Get up!"

D'raekn watched Cwen struggle to close an angry fist around a handful of mud, but her arm was too weak to lift it. He held her wrist with the toe of his boot and brought his blade point to her chest. "You cannot win against a man's superior strength, Cwen."

She twisted to her side and hugged her knees against her chest, ragged breaths still whistling through her open mouth, her words strangled as they conflicted with her need to breathe, "Aenzl said I would grow stronger because we...because of our..."

"You have not gained the dragon's strength. You are stronger, Cwen, but you will never win in a fair fight against a man's strength anywhere but in your mind. If you plan to take your revenge on the nomads, you had better understand that where you see one man, there will be five you do not see, and behind those five will hide another dozen. Now, come inside before you take a chill."

When the tub was filled with steaming water and Cwen had still not returned to the house, D'raekn stepped out on the porch to find her propped up against a tree and so cold that her teeth rattled loud enough to be heard from the steps. "Damn it, Cwen!" He jerked her up and dragged her onto the porch, pushed her against the rail and peeled her clammy, mud caked shirt up over her head. She pushed feebly at his hands, and he snarled, "Stop it! You risk your health deliberately. You won't listen to me." He jerked the drawstring and rolled her trousers down over her quivering hips, lifting her and pulling them off. He carried her inside and eased her into the tub, naked except for her socks. With a cloth he began to squeeze warm water over her neck and back, rubbing her arms briskly in an attempt to warm the bone-chilling coldness that had overtaken her body. Cwen raised a hand and took a slap at him, flinging droplets of water across the room.

"Leave me alone!"

"I should drown you!" His hands continued their work along her shoulders and up to encircle her neck.

"Then do it! We both know I could not stop you!"

D'raekn's breathing came faster, and his hands slowed as they traveled away from Cwen's neck, down her arms. "Damn you, woman." He threw the rag in the water, took the soap, and tossed it to her. "Wash yourself." Without a backward glance, he stepped outside and slammed the door.

Aenzl stood on the porch, staring at the pile of muddy clothes. "What did you do to her?"

"Nothing. I did not do anything. She is impossible!"

The old man looked out into the yard at the muddied and crushed grass. "You beat her?"

"No, she was…yes, I knocked her down in the mud, showed her she does not have the strength to fight a man. She was so damn arrogant, so positive that I could not take her sword. Do you know she believes she can take a nomad with a sword?"

"Oh, I am sure you showed her all right. You have grown too fond of her, and now she has burrowed under your skin like an irritating tick. You will not be able to protect her. She is stubborn, and I do not think she was ready for the burden you have placed on her." The elder shrugged. "I do not think you are ready either, and I know I am not, but it is too late to make it different. I will talk to her. You keep an eye on the sea—it appears the ice has broken against the far shore."

Cwen sat in the tub, eyes closed. She jumped at a scrape against the floor and looked up to see Aenzl dragging a chair to the side of the tub. He ignored her nakedness and captured her eyes with his worried expression. "You have to stop this foolishness. The jailors will be here by morning, and I cannot have D'raekn worrying about whether you are doing what he asks. He will make a mistake and get himself killed trying to see you safe. Is that what you want?"

"No." Cwen peeled off her soggy socks. "You know 'tis not."

Aenzl nodded. "Aye, I do know it, but he does not. I am quite sure you have not told him. Decide what you want, girl, and do it soon. If you are staying with him, tell him so and bring him in off the porch. If you plan on going and getting yourself killed, tell him that too. He needs a clear head to do what must be done, and you have done nothing but confound him. Do you understand me, girl?"

"I dreamt he died."

The elder sat silent, watching Cwen wrestle with the memory of the dream.

"He never even tried to save himself, just allowed that woman to take his life."

The elder nodded again. "In the glen at Stonetel, on the sacrificial block among the standing stones. I have seen this dream as well. His eyes never leave your face. Karid is his executioner. We can stop it, you and I, but not if you are not willing to accept who you are and what you must do."

Cwen gave a choked laugh and wiped at unshed tears. "Just who am I, Aenzl? Tell me, because I certainly do not know."

"I only know what D'raekn believes. He believes you are the woman promised by the nymph Flida. And this," he said as he traced the inky lines across her back, "this dragon spreading across your back may mean he's right. No matter what you choose, he has claimed you and marked you. There will be no other for him. I know your heart is like a stone, and you are afraid that accepting D'raekn's affection will somehow diminish you. You worry that you are not his equal, and yet you are. Woman and man, balanced in strength of body and heart. I see in here," he continued as he reached out and touched Cwen's chest, "the love that your mind won't allow you to give freely for fear of vulnerability. But your true strength—that which lies dormant within you—will allow you to open your heart and fulfill your role in this struggle. It is my hope that you will guide D'raekn, but the choice is yours, it always will be. If instead you choose to rush off in search of the nomads who tortured you, D'raekn will not stop you, but your death will break his heart and leave him incapable of fulfilling his destiny. That is how strong your influence is on him, Cwen, but I believe you already knew that." Aenzl stood, picked up Cwen's clean clothes, and dropped them on the chair. "You should dress. He will not be gone much longer."

It was a subdued, regretful D'raekn who returned to the cabin. Cwen was in the garden, digging out the early onions from the rain-damp soil and did not hear his approach. He stood, leaning on the fence, and watched the smooth roundness of her hips and the strong line of her thigh as she stooped to pull an errant weed.

"Will you forgive me?"

She stood, two onions dangling by their stalks in her left hand. "You are no more at fault than I. I challenged you."

"I would only see you safe, Cwen."

"I know that. Aenzl says I am afraid that caring for you will somehow make me feel weakened. It's true. I want to be strong, strong on my own, strong enough to fight my own battles." She stared at the earth, tugged her braid over her shoulder, and smoothed it with an anxious hand.

"You are strong, Cwen. You have survived things that would kill most men. I only ask that you not throw your life away on revenge. If you must hunt the nomads, plan to survive it and come home to me when it is finished."

Home. She looked toward the cabin.

"'Tis not in the wood and stone, Cwen, 'tis here within the heart." He climbed the fence and dropped into the garden an arm's length away from her. "Will you walk with me? There is something you should see."

She dropped the onions, brushed the dirt off her hands, and followed D'raekn around the house and down the winding path to the shore. They walked in silence, and when they stepped onto the sand, D'raekn pointed to the sea. Beyond the surf bobbed the merfolk, their songs wistful as they sighted Cwen.

Cwen slipped off her boots and waded out into the water up to her thighs, smiling with delight as the mermaidens drifted closer and reached out with webbed hands to stroke her skin. The male gave a low, soothing whistle and lifted himself to balance on the curve of his tail, bright black eyes shining with curiosity as he reached out to touch Cwen's coppery braid.

"He is Ewart, leader of the Umar mer-clan. Those with him are his wives," D'raekn called. "They remember you and have asked often of your health and your disposition."

Cwen spun around, her smile kindling a surge of hopefulness in D'raekn. "You can speak with them?"

"They speak here." He touched his head.

"But not to me." Cwen came back to the sand and sat cross-legged, watching the merfolk frolic in the water. They leapt and twisted, their voices lilting with their joyful songs.

"It was here they brought you to me." D'raekn sank to the sand beside Cwen, his warm hand curling around her cool bare foot. "I thought you were dead, but then I saw the life light in your golden eyes, and I knew you had been sent by my gods. You are strong, Cwen, but I could not lie to you and let you believe there is no risk in settling scores."

Cwen looked away and lifted a handful of sand, letting it sift through her fingers to be carried away on the breeze. "They left me with no self, with no memory of *me*. I cannot remember myself, but I cannot forget their stink. It clings to me, D'raekn, and I cannot wash it off." Tears welled in her eyes. "Each night before I go to sleep, I pray that I will remember who I was before they hurt me, before you found me on this beach. Do I not deserve some justice?"

"Justice will be yours. I swear it to you." He brought his hands to her shoulders. "But don't risk your life to see it so. Wait just a little longer for your justice, Cwen. You are a daughter of the House of the Serpent. I saw it in my dreams as clearly as I see you sitting here. Not once, but many times. I saw you run with the raven-haired woman you say spoke your name. I saw you flee together through the flames of a dying world beneath the burning symbol of the serpent embracing the dragon. Then you fell into Quondam, and I lost you to the nomads." D'raekn's hands rose to frame Cwen's face. "And I know you dream of me. Can you not trust your dreams?"

Cwen paled. Her dreams—a falling axe gleaming in a fog filled glen, D'raekn's eyes locked on her face as the blade took his head. The image stole Cwen's breath and left her quaking with its horror. *We can stop it*, the elder had told her. She would change the dream, save D'raekn's life. It would repay the debt she owed for hers. She would find

169

a way to kill Karid. Another shiver shook her, and D'raekn dropped his hands, believing his touch caused her sudden revulsion.

"If you do not care for me, I will not bother you again. I can understand that you might find my nature repulsive."

"No, D'raekn it is not that. It is only that I do not want to believe in dreams." Cwen brushed the sand from her feet and slipped on her boots. "Aenzl says the jailors will be here by morning. We should go home and rest, for it would not do if they caught us napping." She started up the path without looking to see if D'raekn followed, not seeing the pain and anger her sudden dismissal caused.

Supper became a strategic planning meeting between the three, with diagrams in charcoal covering Cwen's table.

"Cwen, you will lie in wait here." D'raekn's finger stabbed the drawing of a hillock above the dock. "When men enter the shack, you must use a fire arrow to light the line of black powder securing the threshold, thereby setting the brambles inside ablaze." He looked up with a fierce scowl. "You must not miss, for if you fail to trap them inside they will be on you within moments."

She gave a curt nod. Cwen had not voiced argument, nor questioned his course or command since returning from the shore. She listened and answered only when direct query demanded it. D'raekn dreaded the time Aenzl would leave him alone with Cwen to face another sleepless night on the porch, guarding a woman who found even his slightest touch repugnant. How could he have believed any woman, other than ones he paid, would desire his company?

The elder's voice suddenly interrupted his thoughts. "D'raekn?"

He looked up at the sound of his name to find both Aenzl and Cwen staring. "What?"

"You seem distracted, boy."

Forcing himself to regain focus, D'raekn continued, "Just stay on the hill until you hear my whistle. Aenzl, stay with Cwen. I doubt they will send more than a handful of men, two or three on horseback. They will not believe us capable of defending ourselves. And they will not know that we have weapons or that we planned ahead expecting their arrival. If we can catch a few in the burning shack, I can dispatch most of the others in traps or by the sword. Can I count on the two of you to follow directions?"

Aenzl bobbed his head and squinted at Cwen. "Aye, I will keep her on the hill even if it takes a head bashing and tying her in a sack."

Cwen stared at the old man with wide offended eyes but still did not speak out, only nodded her reluctant agreement.

Satisfied, D'raekn stood and said, "Good. Get some rest. I will call you when I see the boat."

"Nay boy, you rest, and I will keep watch. We will need your strength tomorrow." Aenzl gave Cwen a hard, warning glare and shuffled out the door, his staff making angry contact against the floor with every step he took.

D'raekn fiddled with the broken bolt, finally removing it and sitting down to form another. He heard the rattling of plates and sounds of dishwashing. Damn it, he wanted to look at Cwen, but instead he just banged the new bolt into the shaft and pounded in the dowel to hold it, scraped it up and down against the door several times and claimed it sound. "It needs only hold for this night alone, and if you do not wake me with your screaming, I will not be forced to break it again."

"Are you still angry because I challenged you?"

D'raekn turned around to find Cwen close and could not hide his sickness. His throat constricted, and he felt as if he teetered on a precipice above a vast darkness, afraid to speak, afraid to move lest he strike her, his expression consumed by the shadow of his angry hurt and wounded pride.

"It was foolish of me, D'raekn, but can you not forgive it?"

"Spare me your wide-eyed innocence and sweet tone," he growled, growing furious at what he perceived as pretense. "There is no need for your pretended compliance or concern over what I may think. Do you forget that 'twas only hours ago that you drew away in loathing at my touch?"

"But I—" Cwen began, reaching out toward him, but D'raekn abruptly interrupted her, throwing up his hands to avoid her touch, stabbing the air before her with an angry finger.

"It is only some perverse regard for your survival that keeps me from driving you into the sea from whence you came. Now, do not speak, just close your door before your beauty and the memory of your body drive all honor from my mind."

"Don't—" a soft throaty whisper.

"Damned if I won't." D'raekn closed his hands around Cwen's waist, the tiny sound she made enflaming him beyond reason. He cupped her buttocks and lifted her against him, his lips crushing hers, and his tongue stealing the wine-sweet warmth of her mouth. He tore the lace from her hair and speared the braid with his fingers to release the cinnamon softness. He grasped a fistful of her hair with one hand and backed her into the corner as his hand fumbled with the laces of her trousers. He growled with frustration and tore the fabric, lifting Cwen against him again as his tongue trailed along her neck to the hollow of her throat, savoring the intoxicating taste of her skin. One hand forced the torn fabric down Cwen's hips and the other explored uncovered warmth. Her soft moan sent fire coursing through his blood, and he ripped open his laces, pushing Cwen onto her toes in his eagerness to take her. He lifted her, and she wrapped her legs around his waist as he drove himself deep within her, all thought beyond the moment swept away by paralyzing sensation. He felt her arms come around his neck and was faintly aware of her speaking his name.

When the rush came, it left him drunk with its devastation, slick with sweat, and gasping to catch his breath. He gripped Cwen's thighs and held her to him as he leaned weakly against the wall. At last D'raekn opened his eyes to take in the destruction he had wrought on Cwen, only to find her staring at him with an expression that defied his understanding—not fearful or angry, but almost amused. Her hair was a tangled, sweat-dampened halo, and her lips were red and swollen, but her eyes sparkled, soft and drowsy.

Guilt pricked D'raekn's heart at the promise he had broken and the trust he had betrayed. He shook his head and tried to justify his actions. He had warned her. But damn it, she had not shut her tantalizing mouth not even when he'd warned her. Wordlessly he lifted Cwen away and set her on her feet, aware of the unsteadiness in her stance. She would be sore and bruised. What was a man to say to a woman he had promised to protect, yet had taken without invitation?

He had no idea. Aenzl had been right, D'raekn knew nothing of real women, and Cwen had certainly proved that.

Cwen had less trouble finding her voice. "Would you like a bit of brandy?" she asked in the same throaty whisper that had caused it all.

"Nay, I should go," he replied, his eyes locked on the floor.

"Truly?" her laugh forced him to look at her, and he swallowed against the dryness of his mouth, uncertain just what Cwen found funny beyond the fact that he stood there wearing nothing but his shirt, for his trousers had fallen down around his ankles.

"If that is what you want." Cwen stepped from the pile of pants, stripped her torn shirt off over her head, and pulled on her nightshirt.

The flash of her nakedness aroused him, and he wondered how he could possibly win her favor after the shambles of this night.

"I'll take the brandy." He felt unaccountably annoyed with himself, but he did not want to leave, so he reached down, dragged up his pants, tied the laces, and wandered over to sit at the table.

Why would anyone want such a difficult woman? He stared at her, watching her shapely calves as she stood on tiptoes to reach the brandy, and remembered the taste of her skin. She brought the bottle and a cup and set both before him. Then she knelt beside his chair.

"I should make you suffer, let you continue thinking you have committed an unconscionable act against me, for I can see it is what you believe. But in clear conscience I cannot. If you had only let me speak, you would have known I wanted you to stay. I only sought to say, don't go. You said I loathe your touch. How could you think such a thing?"

"On the beach you had such a look of disgust when I touched you," he grumbled.

"D'raekn, it was the memory of a dream that dismayed me, not your touch." She took his hand and held it against the side of her face. "It has only been memories that give me fear, never your touch."

D'raekn touched Cwen's hair. How could a woman infuriate him to mindlessness one moment and make him feel such tenderness the next? He would never understand Cwen, but perhaps it did not matter. All he knew was that he would do anything to keep her.

"You should sleep." He pulled Cwen up, turned her toward the bed, and pushed her gently. "Go."

Cwen looked back over her shoulder, the firelight's glow catching the shadow of a smile playing around her lips. "You would not join me?"

"I will drink my brandy, think about tomorrow for a bit, and then I will join you." D'raekn's thoughts were captured by Cwen's silhouette, but he shook his head, swearing silently that it would be only sleep he sought when he slipped beneath her blankets.

He dragged his thoughts back to the drawings on the table and sat there a moment wondering why he no longer felt afraid. In his mind he built the waterfront, the dock and hills behind, across the footpath. The shack would gain the jailors' attention with its locked door, and Cwen's arrow would turn it into an instant box of burning death. Above the path, an oil-filled stone mortar awaited the touch of a match to light Cwen's fire arrows, and braces of logs were tenuously stabilized, ready to fall at Aenzl's jerk of the rope. Again he worked the plan, envisioning the dozen Noors, three, maybe four on horseback riding straight for the cabin, another three searching the shack on the dock, and three on foot in search of Aenzl's cavern. The remaining men would stay with the boat, well within reach of Cwen's arrows.

D'raekn pressed against his temples, for a dull ache had taken hold behind his eyes. He bowed his head and closed his eyes, allowing the dragon dream to claim him.

Karid lay on her side, knees drawn up and arms wrapped around her swollen belly. She moaned and rolled onto her back and opened her legs to allow the beast its freedom. Neither dragon nor man, the deviant erupted from the false queen's womb, their voices joined in the agonized wail of unsanctified birth.

D'raekn blinked away the image. "My brother," he whispered, "so long you have suffered Karid's evil, but I will see you free and blessed by the strength of our father's seed."

With a rag he wiped away the charcoal drawings that evidenced their plan, snuffed the candle, and joined Cwen. She stirred at the movement of the blanket and, with a sigh, nestled herself against the length of D'raekn's body but did not waken.

It seemed only moments later that Aenzl's whistle woke D'raekn, and he whistled back to let the old man know he'd heard. Cwen slept beside him, and he wished they had more time, but they did not, so he gently shook her shoulder.

"Cwen, we must go."

The words were muted through the haze of her sleep. "Cwen," the voice persisted, and she forced weary limbs into a sitting position. She saw the flare of a match and candle glow and her clothes tossed on the bed.

"Hurry, there is not much time. We must be in position before they reach the dock."

They—the Noor jailors—were coming to take D'raekn and carry out the death sentence in a ring of standing stones in the fog-filled glen of Cwen's dreams. Cwen struggled with her clothes, an arm through the hole where her head should go, cursed and got it right. Trousers on, she slammed each foot into its boot, strapped the quiver to her back, shouldered the bag D'raekn had packed for her, and kept the bow in hand.

"I am ready." Cwen looked up, committing to memory the way D'raekn filled her doorway in case she should never see him there again.

Daylight was still an hour off, just a faint lightening in the dark of the eastern sky when D'raekn pushed Cwen down behind a fall of rocks overlooking the path to the dock. Three matches lay beside the oil-filled mortar, and Cwen sighted an arrow to the threshold of the shack's closed door.

"As soon as they enter, set it aflame. Your next arrows should be for the men on the dock and the deck of the boat. They will be confused over the fire in the shack and the burning deaths of their companions. Do not hesitate, Cwen." D'raekn's hand on her shoulder was light, the touch a reminder of her importance. "If they break and come up hill, release the logs—at the very least, legs will be broken. I have set pits along the path to your cave, Aenzl, so if they make it past me, the pits will take them. I will take the men on horseback and finish off any left below. Wait for my whistle before you show yourselves."

Aenzl and Cwen watched as D'raekn made his way into the underbrush. As he disappeared from view, Cwen heard the faint scrape of steel when he drew his sword. She wanted to run, to be back in her cabin held safe in D'raekn's arms beneath the warm covers of her bed.

"There is no need to fret. Today's battle will be won by the arrogance of our enemies. It is the battles of the coming days that will strain our skills." The elder patted Cwen's shoulder and chanced a peek above the rocks. "The boat lowers its ramp, be ready."

Cwen dragged a match across the stone, the scent of sulfur stinging her nostrils, the tiny flame feeling far too bright as she touched it to the oil-filled stone. She nocked her arrow and held the tip ready above the burning oil, her eyes riveted to the men on the dock below. Eight horses, not three or four, fought their way from the deck of the boat, rearing at the change in footing. Their shouts too far away to understand, the men swung into the saddles of their spinning mounts, jerked reins, and headed up the path. Two men ran toward the shack, and Cwen tore her eyes away from the mounted men, back to the task at hand. *Do not hesitate.* The memory of D'raekn's words rang in her head. Cwen watched as the first man kicked the door once, then again. The door slammed back against the interior wall. Dark inside, the windows had been carefully covered to hide the threatening brambles. The first man crossed the threshold, then the second. Cwen stood, touched the arrow to the flame, sighted, and let it fly. The *thwack* of the strike was immediately followed by a *whoosh* and blinding flash of flame. Men screamed. One ran out into the yard, rolling and emitting an ear-splitting howl as fire consumed him.

Cwen swung the bow toward a movement on the left. Two men ran down the wooden plank and out onto the dock, eyes focused on the burning man. The bow string hummed, and the second man stumbled and fell, an arrow through the heart, just as D'raekn had taught. The first man whirled about at the sound, and Cwen's arrow pierced his throat, strangling him in his own blood. She quickly scanned the scene below. Three bodies, one smoldering and two dead of her arrows, and the fourth had not left the burning shack. Four men dead and eight on horseback chasing D'raekn into the hills.

"Damn it, Aenzl! The numbers are not right! D'raekn cannot take eight mounted men alone!"

Cwen leapt up and slid down the slope on her backside sending a shower of rocks ahead of her. She hit the path running and ducked away into the brush before Aenzl's first words left his lips. "He's a dragon! He could handle twenty mounted men! And he told us to wait for his whistle!"

From the shadow of the boat crept another man, arrow nocked and tracking Cwen's noisy departure. Aenzl shouted and jerked the rope holding the first brace of logs, satisfied when the crashing ended in the sound of snapping bones and the archer disappeared beneath the weight of timber.

Aenzl made his way downhill, his staff bearing the burden of his lame leg. Down the path a horse screamed and then another.

Cwen raced ahead, lifted her bow, and aimed for a plunging horse's shoulder, her arrow bringing the animal to a tumbling roll, throwing its rider head over backside through the brush. A solid crack told her the man's head had met a stone, a second arrow through the horse's eye ended its struggles. She burst around the corner and let out a startled cry, backing away from the terror ahead on the blood-slicked road.

A monstrous dragon circled a Noor on a terrified horse. The dragon's breath scorched the earth at the horse's feet as its great tail curved to entrap it. Red and gold scales glittered in the roseate dawn of the rising sun, and the piercing glare of golden eyes gleamed above its snarling jaws. The long neck shot forward, great teeth locked across the rearing horse's shoulder and the rider's thigh as, with a triumphant roar, the beast ripped great chunks of flesh from its prey. Its eyes swung to fix on Cwen, who had dropped to her belly and was snaking away through the deep grass.

"Cwen!" D'raekn's voice stopped her movement, and she lifted her head, searching for him. "Cwen?" The dragon's bloody muzzle came to rest at her side, sending her scuttling away with a strangulated choking sound catching in her throat. Cwen jumped to her feet and stared in momentary disbelief before her blood suddenly stalled, failing to reach her struggling mind, and plunged her into unconsciousness.

Aenzl limped into view, shaking his shaggy, white-haired head at the carnage and pointing his staff at the dragon. "What did you do to her now, boy?"

"I did nothing, Aenzl." D'raekn's voice rumbled up from the dragon's chest. "She was merely overcome at the surprise of seeing me."

"Surprise! A bottle of brandy is a surprise, a bouquet of flowers is a surprise, a—"

"I get the point. Shall we wake her?"

"Not until you do something about this," Aenzl replied, poking D'raekn on a glittering scale. "You are quite fine looking, though. I had forgotten just how fine."

"Strip the remains of their gold," D'raekn said as he brought his dragon's body to a crouch. He closed his eyes, and the ancient whispered words brought a sudden chill stillness. The air convulsed around him, leaving his human form standing in the middle of the bloody destruction.

The old man bagged the jailors' gold and sniffed, "If I see that a million times, it will still amaze me."

He knelt beside Cwen and held a bit of foul smelling weed beneath her nose.

She slapped his hand away and sat up wiping dirt from the side of her face. Abruptly she scrambled to her feet and pointed toward the slain horses and riders. "There was a…a…a—"

"Dragon?" D'raekn finished.

Cwen nodded. Her eyes were wide as they scanned the bloody battlefield before her. "I thought it was going to kill me. It was crimson and gold, and it killed—"

"Well, I hope it didn't eat all the horses," Aenzl piped in wryly, "or it will be a very long while before we reach the village of Dragonfire."

"I don't eat hors—"

"It was you!" Cwen's thoughts spun dizzily at the recollection of his voice calling her name. She found herself on legs that would no longer support her and sank to the ground. "How could it be?" The earth continued to spin, and she lay back in the dust.

D'raekn dropped beside Cwen and tried to take her hand. She jerked upright, slapping him hard. "Don't you touch me!" She held up her hands. "Just—do not touch me!" Struggling to her feet, she staggered back down the path toward the boat dock.

"Well, that could have gone better," Aenzl quipped, pursuing his lips, "but I suppose you will figure something out."

D'raekn curled his lip in a snarl.

Leading three horses, D'raekn and Aenzl returned. Cwen got up from her seat on the dock. She opened her mouth to speak as D'raekn pointed a warning finger.

"Do not tell me not to touch you again."

She blushed. "I wasn't going to, but if you can change…if you can become…why do we need horses? Why don't you just fly?"

"I can't. Cwen, I am just a man with a bit of magick. I did not ask for it. I don't want it. I was just born with it. And for the past thousand years, I have not used it at all. It's a bit rusty, I can't control it, and I can't fly—at least not yet."

A frown creased Cwen's brow. "I saw what you did. It—"

"Happened out of fear for you. If you had done as I asked, I would not have changed, and you would not have seen."

"Damn you! Do not try to blame what happened on me! I did what you asked—set the shack on fire and burned two men to death. I killed two others by my bow. But there were eight on horseback, not three or four. I feared that with their superior strength they would kill you." Her words trailed off in a whisper as the remembered fear set her voice to trembling. "I was just afraid for you, D'raekn. I didn't know. You should have told me…" Her teeth worried a lip still swollen from the night's passion, and when he opened his arms she slipped inside their sheltering circle.

"I will take the horses aboard," Aenzl mumbled, pulling the reins from D'raekn's fingers.

"A boat! A second boat!" Aenzl's voice jerked Cwen from D'raekn's embrace, and they saw the elder frantically gesturing. "There!"

The small boat crested a swell, mermaidens leaping joyously ahead of its bow.

"'Tis B'rma," Aenzl shouted, "and the daughter of D'lana. I can feel their swords hum."

A young woman's excited cries drifted from the boat when she spotted the small, fire-haired woman. "Cwen! Cwen! You live!"

"Who are they? How do they know my name? Do I know them?"

"They are here to help us, Cwen. We will find out what news they bring of you," the elder explained.

The boat slid ashore, and a Noor man jumped out to pull it beyond the reach of the lapping surf. Two Noor women disembarked. The younger raced toward Cwen with arms outstretched, while the elder made her way to Aenzl.

Cwen backed away, coming to a halt against D'raekn's solid body.

"You are the daughter of D'lana?" D'raekn asked, closing his arms around Cwen.

"Aye, I am N'dia. Cwen? Do you not remember me?"

Cwen's eyes filled with tears, and she turned away in disappointment, mumbling, "I do not know you."

"Tell us what you know of Cwen. She has no memory of the past," D'raekn explained.

"And this? Do you remember this, Cwen?" N'dia held out the jewel Yávië had given J'var. "It is yours."

Cwen accepted the serpent encircled sapphire pendant, drawing the gleaming golden chain through her fingers and closing her eyes to recall her dream. A smiling woman, raven haired and violet eyed, beside a handsome man with eyes the color of the stone she now held, comforting Cwen's sorrows as she slept. "Yávië…?" Cwen whispered, opening her eyes to stare at N'dia. "Where is my aunt's body?"

N'dia looked away, toward the Noor man. "My brother, J'var, was with her when her soul departed. She asked that he give you this stone, the jewel of her birthright."

"The nomads killed her. I saw her fall, saw the blood."

"No, no, Cwen. She did not die in the wagon. J'var found her and brought her to our home. We searched for you, many seasons we searched for you. 'Twas only when we saw the signs and knew you were with the…" N'dia paused, her eyes locked on D'raekn.

"The beast?" he supplied without rancor.

"Aye. Then B'rma led us here."

"You said Yávië's soul departed. How did she die?" Cwen asked.

N'dia looked confused and again turned to look at J'var. He had not moved from his position near the boat. His eyes were shadowed beneath his scowl, and his gaze was fixed on the man embracing Cwen.

"J'var? Tell Cwen where Yávië is."

But J'var ignored his sister and asked D'raekn, "Are you the prisoner of this isle?"

"I am no more a prisoner, though once I was."

"The dragonspawn?"

"Aye." D'raekn nodded.

"But you are not—"

"A slavering, dragon-headed beast?"

J'var shook off his discomfort and came to stand beside N'dia, his eyes searching Cwen's face for any sign of recognition. "You truly do not know us?"

"Leave the girl alone." B'rma stepped forward and bowed her head respectfully. "My lord, forgive them their ignorance. D'lana was unable to prepare them before her death. They were too young to carry the burden." She glanced at N'dia and J'var. "It has become my task to educate them. We saw the signs of your awakening. We collected D'lana's sword, and we came here to find you."

"I only came to find Cwen," J'var said brusquely.

"J'var, we have found Cwen," B'rma replied calmly but firmly, "she is alive and safe, and the jewel has been delivered. Now we must go on to Dragonfire."

"I came to find Cwen," J'var repeated sternly, "and take her home."

D'raekn felt the shiver of Cwen's fear and drew her closer.

"Did you know me in the past?" Cwen's voice was small, frightened, as she formed her next question. "Were you one of my masters?"

J'var stood sullen, an unjustifiably jealous knot growing in his belly. Cwen's unanswered questions hung heavy between them.

N'dia swatted her brother. "Answer her! You torment her with your silence."

"No, Cwen. You were nothing to me, and I was definitely not your master."

Cwen felt D'raekn's heat and felt the rumble of his voice rising from deep within his chest, "Then why are you here, Director?"

Aenzl stared at J'var, then B'rma. "You've brought a member of the directorate here? To Dragon's Heart? To D'raekn? How could you?"

"He is N'dia's eldest brother, a son of D'lana."

"He is a director, a servant of Karid, and again I ask him why he is here." D'raekn released Cwen with a reassuring squeeze of her shoulder and stepped closer to J'var, the dragon's shadow flowing dark across the sun drenched dock.

"I am a director, and you are a prisoner of the directorate, bound to this island for the murder of a prime elder. If you leave this island, your life is forfeit, and your immediate execution will be demanded by the council. There will be no safe place. You and this old man have tangled Cwen in your hopeless dreams of freedom. Let her go. Let me take her to safety, and you can go where you will."

"No."

Both men's eyes shifted to Cwen when she spoke.

"Why do you do this if I am nothing to you?" she asked.

"That is a reasonable question," said N'dia, drawing a disgruntled glare from her brother. She slid between the two men and pushed against each with the palm of a hand. "There is nothing to be gained by this. I would venture you both seek the same thing—Cwen's safety and her affection." N'dia's pale eyes met D'raekn's. "Surely you cannot fault my brother for his concern, for no man can control the longing of his heart."

"You are wise beyond your years, N'dia, daughter of D'lana, and so I hope you will understand what I must do." Without warning, D'raekn's fist cracked against J'var's temple, and a quick second blow caught the Noor beneath the jaw, whipping his head back and sending him sprawling to the sand.

"Cwen, get on the boat with Aenzl. B'rma, if you intend to accompany me, go with them. N'dia, believe me when I say I do understand that a man cannot control his heart's longing, but I must leave you with your brother, for I cannot trust your blood. Too long your family has been held in the grip of Karid's madness without D'lana's counsel. Take your brother, and go home."

"I cannot go home!" N'dia called after D'raekn's retreating back. "My father will not take me back, for my beauty has been marred! Did you not notice this glowing handprint on my face? Someone calling himself a firefly mistakenly thought I was some kind of warrior! Now I will never find a husband, and I will have only you to blame! Is that the way you want to be remembered?"

D'raekn stopped and hung his head to hide a smile. "Are you always so annoying?" he called back over his shoulder.

"No," N'dia replied.

"Why do I not believe you?"

"Because B'rma has filled your head with lies about me?"

"She has not had time."

N'dia screwed up her face as if in deep thought. "My reputation precedes me?"

D'raekn laughed and beckoned N'dia to him. "You have a reputation?"

"Aye, for stubbornness," N'dia answered with a bit of pride.

"I would never have guessed—and what of your brother?" D'raekn asked, glancing at J'var.

N'dia grew solemn. "He is a good man, a compassionate man who believes he is responsible for our loss of Cwen. He cannot help what he feels for her anymore than you can, but he would not betray her trust, and if you are her choice, he will honor that against his desire. If you leave him here, he will only follow."

"I thought as much—another Noor with a reputation for stubbornness." D'raekn exhaled deeply and considered the unconscious man. "I might end up having to kill him, but since you refuse to take him home, I suppose knowing where he is will be preferable to wondering what he is up to. He is your responsibility."

N'dia nodded her understanding and headed up the ramp to join the others. D'raekn jogged back to collect J'var.

"You are a weighty bit of coin," he muttered, dumping the heavy Noor to the deck as the boat lurched against the incoming swells under Aenzl's less than expert management. "I hope you do not make me regret this." D'raekn turned to find Cwen watching him with a worried frown.

"You should have left him behind. He threatens you," she said.

"It will be better to have him in Dragonfire among my allies than left behind to lead my enemies." D'raekn lowered a pail over the side to catch the sea and flung the icy water on J'var.

The man coughed and spluttered and rolled his body so that he sat against the mast, rubbing his jaw and squeezing his eyes shut against the ache of his bruised head.

D'raekn squatted down before J'var. "You are here because your sister refused to take you home. She said something about her unsuitability for marriage. If you cause me any trouble, I will cast you into the sea. If I feel you threaten Cwen, I will cut your throat."

"Where is she?" J'var kept his expression blank, the ever inscrutable Noor.

"I warn you."

"Don't. Just let me talk to her."

"What is it you want?" Cwen asked, peering around D'raekn.

J'var held out the slender dagger Cwen had lost during her capture by the nomads, hilt first, watching her eyes.

She blinked several times, and her fingers twisted a strand of her hair. Her eyes lost their focus, finally closing as they tried to capture some shred of fractured memory. She swayed, collapsing beneath the flood of fire-filled images and terrified screams. Sobs choked her as the memories of searing death and screaming men brought back the truth of her life.

D'raekn pushed J'var back as he tried to touch Cwen, then gathered her in his arms and rocked her like a child, whispering his promise to protect her, to help her find justice for her losses.

When at last Cwen looked up, her face was filled with the deep pain of remembering, and she swallowed the bitterness of the past. She reached out toward D'raekn, and he took her hand. "I know who I am. I know where I came from. I have to find a way home. I promised I would find my cousin Sóvië, I promised my aunt Yávië. I swore it, D'raekn. I do not belong here." She turned to N'dia's brother. "You tried to warn me about the nomads, but I did not listen." The words spilled forth in an avalanche of sudden knowledge, tumbling forth in disarray. She buried her face against D'raekn's chest and whispered, "I have found myself at last."

"Tell me what happened to my aunt, J'var."

D'raekn squeezed Cwen's hand, and she looked up at him. "Will you be all right if I leave you while I go help Aenzl?"

"Yes, I need to talk to J'var." Her words carried no hint of uncertainty. "I need to know the truth."

He squeezed her hand again, brushed her hair with his kiss, gave the Noor a warning glare, and slipped away, leaving Cwen to sort things out with the sorceress D'lana's son.

Cwen looked after D'raekn for a moment before turning back to J'var. "Tell me of Yávië. N'dia said that Yávië released her own soul."

"She would not have done so without knowing you were safe. It is how I knew you lived. Cwen, never had I seen two people more at peace than when your aunt's soul was freed to join her husband. They are together, free, safe, and without worry. I promised her I would find you and protect you."

"As I healed, they came to me in dreams, comforting my tortured mind. Yávië whispered my name, for I had forgotten it."

"Cwen I am so sorry for…" J'var's throat closed, choking off his words.

"It was not your doing, J'var. You tried to warn me. Do not condemn yourself for the sins of others."

"Have you chosen *him*, Cwen?"

"I cannot allow myself to love him. I know, though, that my love is what he most desires. I do not know what I choose, but in D'raekn's arms at least I can sleep without the terror of dreams. With him I can heal," she said in a hushed voice, "because he is not part of my past. He needs me and I need him, J'var, and I owe him my life."

Just beyond the sound of their words, D'raekn worked alongside Aenzl, tying off a sail and pretending not to watch Cwen.

"J'var is no threat to you," came N'dia's certain whisper at his shoulder. "Cwen is yours."

"She gives herself to me for the moment, out of gratitude and pity," replied D'raekn, "but once beyond the sea, she may find my path no longer leads in a direction that suits her."

"More than one man's satisfaction has sprung from a woman's gratitude. Why should she pity you?" asked N'dia.

D'raekn stifled a bitter laugh. "I am a beast cursed by Karid and unloved by Man, one to be pitied rather than held against a true heart. You must know I risk you all in search of my own freedom."

"Cursed by a whelp of a flesh-bound nymph, but blessed by the nymph Flida. With whom does your faith lay, D'raekn? And the risk? We accept it willingly, but it would appear you wallow in self-doubt at the first hint of challenge," Aenzl badgered.

D'raekn shook his head in denial. "My strength wanes beyond the isle. Until we reach Shadowmaw, my strength wanes."

"'Tis why you have us, M'lord," B'rma called out jovially. "In her ageless wisdom, the nymph Flida found you worthy of having women to watch over you."

Her fearless irreverence brought a bout of laughter from D'raekn that drew Cwen and J'var.

"What is the jest?" J'var asked.

"There is no jest, Director J'var," D'raekn feigned dark displeasure. "I am reminded that my worth has been weighed and found wanting, therefore my fate is secured only by the strength of women."

"Aye," Aenzl grunted, "but oh what women they are! I believe a toast of blackberry brandy is in order for such a stroke of good fortune."

"Aenzl, break out your brandy. I think a toast would sit well with us all." D'raekn clasped the old man's shoulder.

Much later, alone, away from those who slept in the warm deception of brandy's comforting fog, D'raekn lay cold and sober on the chilled planks of the forward deck keeping watch on the stars enfolded within the deep cloak of night.

Oh, Flida, on the island it was so easy to accept Cwen as your promise, to forget that my actions would endanger others, to forget that a toll would be taken and the gods of death paid in the end. In her dark ambition, Karid has become Man's heartless mistress. She spoils all she touches. I have seen the visions of grass withering where'er she walks, horses taking colic, and cattle becoming barren. She will speak my name to common men and remind them of what I am.

As I pass among men, those gentle will call me legend as you once did, but those cruel—those loyal to Karid—will point fingers and call me cursed, for you know, nymph, it is they who have the most to lose. In my youth, C'thra sang the tales of Karid's war and the true king's fall beyond the safety of your woods. Men were paid by the withdrawal of death's sting and the promise of fertility for their daughters. Even D'lana's husband, A'bach, was purchased with Karid's promises. I do not know if the blood of D'lana remains untainted in N'dia and J'var, so long were they spellbound by the false queen's beguiling. I fear there is risk of betrayal, Flida.

A breath of breeze suddenly stirred where none should be, and a disembodied voice whispering her pledge lifted wisps of D'raekn's hair around his ears. "Do not fret, dragonspawn, have I not chosen you as heir to all of Quondam's magick?"

"Aye, nymph, it is your promise, but one I cannot claim."

"Have you not been freed by the heat of your coupling with the serpent's blood and the power of your name?"

Pain, bright and sharp as any memory of the burning brand, pricked D'raekn's heart. "I am more prisoner than ever, for the woman does not return my affection."

"Dear dragonspawn, you speak of love, but love was never offered," Flida gently explained. "Not even gods can promise love, for in the hearts of humans it is as illusive as a moonbeam or the rainbow's end."

D'raekn rose and stood gripping the rail, staring into the heart of heaven, "But I am not Man."

"No, my sweet prince, you are not. But the woman Cwen is born of Man. She was no more than a means to set you free, a gift with a soft voice and silken skin to warm your nights." The nymph shifted, and the air stirred again, sending a shimmer across the sky. "Cwen's is a heart so barren and broken it cannot even embrace your gift of the dragon's power. She is fearful of feeling more than she must, and her heart is a stone, for she has suffered the pain of loss too many times. The goodness of her soul is shrouded by a deep, angry, unyielding void."

"Then I will find a way to fill Cwen's heart and end the emptiness."

"Seek the wasp queen, D'raekn, and find the sorceress C'thra. Hidden somewhere within the mountains of the Shattered Spine is a gift of immense power that can only be awakened by one claiming Quondam's throne. You must find it before my sister does. Seize the power, purge the land of the Karid's false rule, and free your accursed kinsmen. By my command, that is your task. When it is finished, then you may choose your own path."

The nymph Flida reached out and, trailing particles of light, enveloped D'raekn's face, filling him with strength. "The stryvers have spoken, and soon the daughter of D'lana will lead an army of fire shields. The legend unfolds. Do not wander from its path because of a woman's flesh. Do not try to bind the foreign woman. It will bring you nothing but the heartache of failure."

D'raekn murmured to the silent, empty night in the wake of Flida's words, "Then I will suffer and I will fail, but Cwen's heart will be soft and she will be free of fear."

Below deck, J'var stood in a doorway watching Cwen sleep.

"I would not let him find you here," B'rma warned, casting a meaningful glance up the wooden ladder.

Perfect white teeth showed J'var's smile in the dim passageway. "There is hope for me. She told me she does not love the dragonspawn."

"Do not tell him that. Somehow I doubt it would please him. Did she say why?"

"No, but why is unimportant. He must know she does not, a man can feel such things."

"Oh, a man can, huh? You would be wise to remember he is not Man and that N'dia and I serve him, so keep your ideas for stealing his woman to yourself. Or better yet, come to your senses and decide you want the wisdom and experience of an older woman. I have always found you quite desirable, J'var. Now, go find a bed in a place that will be safer than outside Cwen's door." B'rma's fingers traced the handprint on J'var chest. "I mean it. Go!"

Another flash of teeth, a warm squeeze to B'rma's muscular backside and J'var turned away toward the safety of his bed, calling back quietly, "You are not so old, and I have always found you a rather luscious irritant, B'rma."

Back inside their room, B'rma found N'dia grinning.

"What? I meant it when I once told Cwen that women would kill for a man like your brother. I would."

"You exasperate him," N'dia cooed. "It makes him feverish."

B'rma rolled the tension from her shoulders and patted N'dia on the head. "He's feverish all right, and if we do not look after him, he may be dead. D'raekn may know that Cwen does not love him, but I can't imagine he will let go graciously. So watch J'var. Now, stop talking and get some sleep. Let me dream of D'lana's most handsome son."

N'dia's soft laughter was the last sound of the night.

Chapter 18: The Barrens

Wind, the gift of Flida, swept D'raekn and his company swiftly across the sea. They dropped anchor in a secluded bay deep within the barrens, midway between the trade city of Corusca and the ancient ruins of Eolia.

D'raekn, Cwen, and B'rma swam ashore with the horses and hobbled them near a clump of salt-rich dune grass before heading back to meet the others arriving in the dinghy. Together they dragged the small boat ashore, unloaded the supplies within the shelter of a small stand of stunted trees, and began to explore their surroundings.

They stopped where the sand ended, looking into a wasteland of pitch pines, thorny gorse, and carnivorous plants. The great barrens stretched beyond the shore as far as the eye could see, its sandy bogs hiding bottomless aquifers.

"It's hard to imagine that this no-man's-land was once part of the sacred wildwoods and protected by the one who has since destroyed it. 'Tis said a fire dryad now calls these barrens home," B'rma whispered, staring into the desolation that had once been consecrated ground, "and that the pines erupt in flames without warning—it is only the dryad's blaze that gives the barrens life. It is also said the soil is sweet as sugar, but eating it will make you mad."

J'var cocked his head and examined the tavern owner. "It is no wonder that my father forbade N'dia your company. You are a very odd woman, B'rma."

B'rma winked and shook her finger in his direction. "Just you remember, all I know I learned from your mother."

N'dia laughed and hugged her brother, laughing again at his raised eyebrow and pretended austerity.

"Did sorceress D'lana's teachings tell you if there was something besides sweet sand to eat?" Aenzl's brow puckered, and he held his rumbling stomach.

"Wizard, in the barrens you will find that if you misstep, you will have no need of food, for there are few safe paths across this wasteland," said B'rma, pointing to the nearby patch of watery sand.

"But for now we are safe, and I will cook for you all," Cwen called, returning to rummage through the nearby packs piled on the beach. "We may as well set off in search of death and the fire dryad with full stomachs and a good night's sleep."

D'raekn rubbed the back of his neck and frowned. There would be no safe places beyond this shore. "Aenzl, build a fire if it is your wish to eat. Keep the blaze high, and stay within its light. All of you, stay within the firelight."

"There will be no safe passage for the horses in the barrens. It will be best to set them free to find their way along the beach to Rider's Cross," B'rma shouted to the departing D'raekn.

"See to it then." He turned and walked past Aenzl, patting the old man on the back. "Do you need help?"

"Nay, I will have this gorse ablaze in no time. It is highly flammable you know."

"Aye, I will leave you to it then."

"Where are you going?" Cwen asked, looking up from a bag of dried stag and bannock, with a hint of alarm.

"I will be on the shore, just beyond the dunes if I am needed." D'raekn smiled to reassure her. "I promise I will not wander off into the barrens without you. I just need a bit of time alone."

"Shall I join you then, after I feed these hungry beggars?"

D'raekn watched, distracted as Aenzl's fire suddenly caught, flared, and touched Cwen's hair with its warm golden halo.

"D'raekn?" Cwen's voice pulled him back.

"Aye. Join me after they have been fed."

B'rma watched their exchange as she removed the tack from the horses. She threw up her hands and shouted to urge the horses down the beach toward the distant settlement. "Our lord is worried," she confided to N'dia. "Watch him closely. We cannot allow him to be distracted from his task by Cwen, or your brother."

D'raekn sat on the sand staring across the sea, back toward Dragon's Heart, oblivious to all except his own tumultuous thoughts.

Once the meal was cooked and served, Cwen left the others and brought D'raekn tea, settling herself between his knees, leaning back against him. "You are quiet. Why do you sit here all alone?"

Against his will, he found himself stroking her hair. "There is much on my mind. I cannot go home again."

Cwen swept her hand across the horizon. "It will all be yours. Aenzl says you will one day be king."

"Aenzl talks too much of things he does not understand. Why are you still here, Cwen? Here, instead of off seeking your revenge?"

She slid forward and turned to face him, her expression carefully controlled, hands folded in her lap. "Do you no longer want me? Are you sending me away?"

He held her eyes until at last she looked away. "I know you cannot give what I want. I know that, Cwen, for you have made it clear, but I want to understand why. Is your heart a stone as Aenzl and Flida warn? Is there truly nothing I can do to make you love me?"

"I do not want to hurt you, D'raekn…"

D'raekn touched his finger to Cwen's lips, bringing her eyes back to his.

"My heart is already scarred by the truth of it, and my soul slowly starves from the lack of it. I ache with the loss of love I never even had." He dropped his hand and looked away.

"I told you it was not love."

"Why, Cwen? Why has the nymph Flida sent a woman who cannot love me?"

"I have pondered this question myself, and I believe that in her great wisdom, she knows I do not threaten who you are or what you must choose. I cannot love you. If I did, you would stray from her and become lost."

"I am lost, fallen from grace at birth, punished with loneliness, tempted beyond my endurance, and now you deny me the greatest gift of all. What will I do now, Cwen? What can I do?"

Hoping to alleviate his distress, she spoke to him with words that pained her as she spoke them: "I cannot free my heart to love, though men have loved me." She grabbed D'raekn's hand and pressed it against her breast. "Although it beats, what sits within my breast is not a heart. It is a stone—a serpent's heart of stone, frosted with fear. And it is why I have been chosen to call you forth to freedom. Death holds no power over me. Take the gift your nymph gives, however fleeting, and let me care for you as best I can in the time we are allowed."

D'raekn wrapped his fingers around Cwen's hand and lowered his lips to her palm, trailing kisses from its center up the inside of her arm, finally drawing her close and pulling her down beside him.

In the distance, Aenzl muttered about "that damn woman" and D'raekn's badly chosen timing before herding N'dia, B'rma, and J'var closer to the fire with the promise of blackberry brandy and hot gall oil.

It was hours later that D'raekn lifted Yávië's jewel from the tangle of discarded clothing, examining the gleaming serpents that wrapped the sapphire dragon in their care before handing it back to Cwen. "Why do you hide its beauty within your bodice? Why do you not wear it?" he asked as he drew the drawstring of Cwen's trousers snug and tied it.

"It does not seem mine to wear. It is the jewel that bound a queen to her king, joined the houses of my aunt and uncle. Unless I avenge their kingdom's fall and their daughter's death, it is not mine to wear." She looked at the darkened stone, tucked it between her breasts, and allowed the cascading links of fine chain to follow.

As the two joined Aenzl, across the dying campfire B'rma leaned close and nudged J'var in brandy-bought carelessness. "From the look of Cwen's blush, perhaps love is not a necessary ingredient in their relationship."

J'var stared through a gall oil induced fog and caught Cwen's glance as it flitted across him from beneath her lowered lashes. "Then perhaps it will not take love to win her for my own."

"You will be winning naught but death if you do not change your course," N'dia warned her brother.

"They are all quite drunk. Now we will have to await the dawn," Aenzl hissed in D'raekn's ear. "I plied them with brandy and gall oil, and tales of past kings to keep their attention away from what you two were doing."

"And we thank you for it, Aenzl," D'raekn said with a serious expression on his face, "it gave us time to talk. We will take a bit of that brandy now."

They broke camp under D'raekn's sharp commands. His ill temper over a late, hung-over start earned curious looks from B'rma and N'dia and irritated glares from J'var. Cwen ignored D'raekn's impatience and gathered up the last of the supplies, distributing the weight evenly among her companions.

"It is your own fault we are late! So stop your cursed yelling!" Aenzl hissed. "Before I knock you unconscious and make you even later!"

D'raekn continued to fume. "Hurry! Light here is not long-lived. And watch where you step. Do not touch anything! No stone, no plant! There is no telling where danger may lurk within this godforsaken place!"

When at last they were ready, he led them forward along the only path in sight. He stopped suddenly and swung back to face them. "At all times, I want Cwen behind me and the director to follow last. The rest of you find a space between."

There was a moment of shuffling as they took their places, and then they set off again.

Dense fog shrouded the barrens, cloaking the travelers in its gray drifts, lending moisture to already shining eyes peering wide above cloth-covered noses and mouths masked against the bog gasses and venomous powdery particles emanating from the surrounding carnivorous plants. Each footstep was slow and precise as they attempted to remain secure on the slick, narrow pathways that wound their serpentine way among the pygmy pines and grasping gorse thorns.

Ahead, a flame flared in the crown of a tree and leapt, lifelike, to another and another, popping and hissing as it consumed dry needles and rich, black pitch and drew ever nearer to the walkers.

"You dare to walk the barrens?" crackled the dryad's smoky voice.

"We walk softly and with care and will leave naught but footprints on your soil, mistress." D'raekn's words were strong and sure, one fey to another.

Darkness settled and then fled in the flame as the dryad blinked her recognition. "Redeemer of magick, at last you come to free us of Man's covenant with Karid." Her voice was a sizzling hiss, the sound of water on hot coals

"Will you grant us safe journey through your barrens, milady?" asked D'raekn.

"There is no safe journey here, dragon, for the barrens are endlessly hungry and will take their own meal. Do not stop along the way when sleep beckons. Do not rest to take your sup. Be swift, and the barrens may leave you pass. Tarry and terror will overtake you, but I grant 'twill not be my fires that burn your flesh."

The dryad focused her bright gaze on Cwen. "And you, the dragon's chosen, born of the serpent's blood. Your path is the circle, your anger the death of men. When next we meet, you will be wearing the black cloak of sorrow, and my voice will join yours in grief's bewailing."

"And you," her gaze shifted to N'dia, "it is for you the hellwing flies."

"What do you mean?" N'dia asked, but the dryad's words faded away in a smoky coil that mimicked a serpent's spiral trail drifting in the misty gloom, leaving in its wake a lingering acrid aroma.

The travelers forged ahead, silent and thoughtful, each worrying about the dryad's declarations. The mist lifted and revealed an endless burnt-orange haze that warmed the land with golden tones and woke a horde of hungry soil-bound hunters.

A slither among the thickets brought tendrils bearing sharp barbs to test their boot-clad feet and calves, scratching leather in an attempt to garner purchase on the wearer's warm flesh. Mindless, petal-covered features followed their passage, shooting out venomous pollen to drift across any carelessly unmasked face.

N'dia, trailing the others by no more than a few strides, was caught in a disabling exhalation of plant dust and instantly blinded. She reached up to scrub at her swelling eyes and stolen sight. Screaming against the burning agony that scalded her eyes, she fell and rolled as the intensity of the pain increased with every contact. Thorn-filled vines rushed out from all directions, stinging and tearing as they vied for possession of her flesh. Gasping for air, N'dia dragged the mask from her nose and mouth but only succeeded in drawing more of the deadly dust into her lungs.

Swords hacked fleshy strands, thick as a man's arm, as D'raekn, B'rma, and J'var fought desperately to free N'dia. Viscous resin sprayed from every cut vine. It spread blisteringly across exposed skin and brought more violent thrashing, the furious shouts of shock and rage from the others adding to N'dia's terrified screams. Cwen held her bow ready, but there was no safe opening without risk of striking the struggling N'dia.

The vines curled and withdrew in the face of Aenzl's sudden destructive bursts of energy, but others swiftly took their places as the power of his staff was exhausted. Thick, sinuous arms coiled tightly to envelop the plant's terrified prey. The failing body was dragged into the dense thicket toward the great trumpet-shaped, acidic bath that would digest its latest meal. N'dia's hoarse cries trailed into silence as the toxins at last paralyzed her body and voice, and she disappeared from sight in a whisper of dry leaves against the sodden, blood-soaked soil.

J'var's bellows of rage and loss turned on D'raekn, but B'rma's sword pricked his chest. "More death will not bring N'dia back, and already other arms reach out to claim us. Run!" She jerked her sword away and slammed into J'var, spinning him around and pushing him forward as she jerked Aenzl in behind her. "Run!" she screamed again, casting a single glance behind to assure herself that D'raekn followed with Cwen.

They pounded down the narrow path, in and out among the pines, leaping over threatening vines and passing clouds of expelled pollen, their eyes closed and breath held, and when they could no longer run, they walked to catch a gasp of breath before running on again, never stopping, never looking back. Just when it seemed their lungs would burst and their shocked minds and burning muscles could carry them no further, a clearing opened to reveal the ruins of SuVgo, offering safety among the sacred stones.

They clambered up the massive steps and into the dark protection of the ancient temple, collapsing in the overwhelming numbness of disbelief.

N'dia's screams still afflicting his mind, J'var stood unsteadily and with slow determined steps made his way to stand in front of D'raekn and the shivering Cwen. The soft sound of drawn steel alerted him that B'rma had armed herself against him, and he held up his hand to wave her off.

"Is this what you wanted, dragonspawn? Is my sister's death sufficient repayment against the Noor for your imprisonment and Cwen's suffering? Are we even now, or do you still require my life as well?"

"J'var!"

"I will be heard, B'rma. You cannot silence me. N'dia did nothing to him. All she wanted was to find Cwen and see her safe. She was young and foolish, she wanted adventure beyond our father's house, but if there was blame for Cwen's suffering it was mine! Do you hear me? Mine! It was mine, not N'dia's!"

"Then why did you not heed my command? I told you to bring up the rear! If you had, N'dia would be alive and you—" D'raekn allowed the rest of the accusation to hang unspoken.

"Stop it! Both of you! There is no blame. Not for Cwen's suffering or for N'dia's misfortune." B'rma's feathery touch framed J'var's face, and her eyes suddenly filled his field of vision, turning him from Cwen and D'raekn. His huge muscles contracting tremulously, J'var's face collapsed in the agony of his loss, and he clutched at B'rma as his knees gave way, burying his face against her strength and stifling the wails of his lament.

She sank to her knees, and her arms enfolded him. "Leave us," she mouthed the words above J'var's head as D'raekn gathered Cwen against him and, beckoning Aenzl, moved away.

"I am sorry for N'dia's loss," Aenzl offered quietly, "but we would be wise to press on with morning's light, for with N'dia, we also lost the strength of D'lana's sword. I saw it glow a warning just before N'dia was stricken. It was inexperience as much as it was the vines that took N'dia. Now I will build a fire and boil J'var some gall oil and a sleeping potion to take the edge off his sorrow." He called back as he moved away, "And some bit of a meal for those who can stomach it."

"Why didn't the dragon save her?" Cwen wept from D'raekn's arms. "Why did you not call it?"

"I cannot control it, Cwen. I cannot simply light and quench it as if it were a candle's flame."

She struggled up, away from him. "Then what good is it? If it will not save us, what good is it?"

"It is good for naught," he mumbled as he watched her walk away. "If I cannot control it, it is good for naught."

"J'var sleeps?" Cwen asked B'rma.

There was a stony silence, and in her distress over losing N'dia, B'rma turned her rage on Cwen. "I wish it had been you instead of her," she snarled, inflicting steely, ice blue eyes on Cwen. "I truly wish it."

"I wish it too," Cwen answered honestly. "I wish I had died in the flames that consumed my home world, but death will not claim me, not even when the Emyutes cast me into the sea would death end my suffering."

B'rma pushed back a strand of white tipped hair and rubbed her arms against an imagined chill. "Sometimes the fates are cruel. If we reach Nestlewood, I will send J'var home. He should not be with us. Will you go with him?"

"But D'raekn—"

"It is my place to protect the dragonspawn, not yours. Your use has ended," B'rma spat. "You do not love D'raekn. You only worry him and make him weak. Go with J'var. Offer him what you have offered D'raekn—you owe him that."

"I am not some whore to be passed about, and I owe J'var nothing. I cannot afford the luxury of loving D'raekn. I have seen the pain love causes when it finally dies and must be swept away."

"It does not always die, Cwen. Some love is eternal."

Cwen snorted, "You could only believe that if your experience is limited. I have seen love and the havoc it wreaks, the boundless sorrow and the weakness it leaves in the wake of its dying. I do not love D'raekn. I can never love D'raekn."

"Then you are not the magickal serpent of D'raekn's dreams, not the woman we had hoped for him. Go with J'var, and free D'raekn to choose magick over Man. If he chooses a man's mortality to follow you, he will die by Karid's hand."

Long after B'rma had gone, Cwen continued to shiver from the effects of her baleful glare.

D'raekn wandered among the ancient stones in search of his gods or the nymph Flida. He sought some reason for the loss of the young girl, his thoughts a chaotic conflict of anger and apprehension. N'dia, daughter of D'lana, and the power of her sword, swept away in a moment of carelessness—how could it be? Why would the gods allow it? N'dia...so young, so innocent. If Aenzl was right and her loss was the fault of inexperience then they were truly doomed, for inexperience plagued them all.

N'dia...He reached down and grabbed a pebble and flung it forcefully against the wall, jumping back as the strike brought forth a shower of fiery sparks and a crackle of energy-charged air.

"You do not know your power."

D'raekn spun around, the speaker's flickering image assaulting his senses in disbelief. "Do I dream in wakefulness? Are you a phantom? A fabrication brought on by the madness of my guilt-ridden memories of you?"

The disembodied N'dia wavered like a midday heat mirage, trembling as if uncertain of its right to stand before D'raekn. "I don't know. I cannot feel my body, and I do not understand this manifestation except that it was caused by your calling."

"Are you dead? I did not call you."

"Aye, wrapped in a cloak of failure and fear your thoughts cried out my name three times. Do you not know the power in speaking a name thrice? As far as dead, I am not sure."

"I am not a wizard and have no power over names. Surely you must know whether you are dead or alive."

N'dia's smile brightened the gloom. "I know only that you woke me by calling my name. You are far more powerful than a wizard. Watch over my brother. He does not understand what he must do. And D'raekn, trust Cwen. She will make the right choice." The image faltered and began to fade until it became barely discernible against the stone.

"Do not go! Tell me what you mean! You aren't making any sense. We need your strength, N'dia. Your brother needs you."

"You need nothing more than what you have, D'raekn. My brother needs to listen. Quondam cries out, but Man does not hear. Karid's covenant with the directorate must be ended." The girl's image grew fainter. Her brilliant smile flashed once more, and then she was gone.

"N'dia? N'dia! N'dia!" D'raekn ranted her name, but her image did not return.

Aenzl led the sorrowing group, followed by J'var and B'rma. Cwen lagged a bit, still mulling over B'rma's remarks while D'raekn, deep in his own reverie of N'dia's ghostly image and mystifying words, tracked silently behind. They had chosen a wider path, one seen from atop the temple in the dawn's growing red-gold glow. They had not seen its end, but hoped it would lead them to the black waters of the Nigrous River. There they would bear north along the sandy shore until they reached the trade city of Nestlewood. Safety lay in reprovisioning and crossing the river into the Feverous Forest without being caught in the trawl of the directorate's net.

A sudden bout of cursing and Cwen's cry of "Aenzl!" caused D'raekn to push forward and find the aging wizard waist deep in a spreading quagmire of malodorous, sand-thickened water.

"Hold still, old man! 'Tis your movement that takes you deeper," J'var called out, dropping his pack and dragging out a length of rope. Swiftly knotting it, he tossed it across to Aenzl, but it did not drift quite far enough.

Aenzl struggled forward, slapping out repeatedly in an attempt to capture the end of the rope. With every thrashing movement, the wizard sank deeper into the swamp sand.

"Hold still, Aenzl," D'raekn shouted, "we will pull it in and toss it again. Just do not move!"

The wizard sputtered and spat out the gagging sand-filled water, finally quieting himself, neck deep in the gritty sludge.

Again J'var flung out the rope, but it was too far left of Aenzl. The old man floundered, shifting toward the rope, and lost his staff. "My staff! I've lost my staff!" Water flooded his open mouth, and with a wide-eyed look of surprise, he sank below the surface.

"Damn it!" D'raekn paced forward and knocked J'var away, handing one end of the confiscated rope to B'rma as he tied the other end around his chest and snapped, "Cwen, help B'rma!"

He waded ahead with his arms outstretched, feeling for the missing Aenzl, his weight quickly pulling him deeper and deeper into the lethal mire. He shouted Aenzl's name, diving headfirst into the bog, reaching ever deeper for the old wizard. B'rma, Cwen, and J'var dragged against the rope, bringing D'raekn to the surface for a breath of air.

"I cannot find him! Give me more rope!" Dread of what he might find gave a sharp edge to D'raekn's voice as he dove again.

B'rma pulled on the rope, bracing her feet against the thorny gnarl of gorse roots, and hauled back again. The rope burned her palms, and she glanced behind to see Cwen wrap the rope around her wrist to gain a better hold. But behind Cwen the rope was slack. J'var stood staring into the murk with a satisfied look on his face.

"No! J'var! Help us! J'var!" B'rma shouted.

Disinterested, J'var's gaze shifted to B'rma and back to the swamp. "Let him die, it will save the directorate the consequences of his execution."

Without warning the rope sagged and hung limply in the grip of Cwen and B'rma. The bog began to bubble as if in a sudden boil. The great red dragon shot skyward with the elderly wizard clasped in a talon. Sparkling droplets of waterlogged sand trailed from the glowing staff clutched in the old man's hand. Wings snapped open, and D'raekn settled to the earth, released the spluttering Aenzl, and turned about to face an awestruck J'var.

"You would see us dead?" the words rumbled forth as the dragon crouched. In a shudder of energy-charged air and a crack of thunder, the utterance of ancient words transformed D'raekn into his human form.

"How—?"

"Is it not what you came to see—the dragonspawn's beastly form? The murdering creature who your kind sentenced to the island? And now you would see me dead and my elder as well? Were you sent to carry out my execution, J'var?"

J'var took a deep, quaking breath and shook his head. "Nay, though your death would please me greatly. I came only for Cwen, but it would seem she has no need of me, and now that my sister is gone I have no need of any of you."

"Your sister is not gone, at least not completely. I spoke with her while you slept. She came to me, a spirit or a dream. She said I woke her."

"Has your tainted birth-blood made you mad? N'dia is dead. Gone! I heard her screams and watched her dragged away to be digested by some stinking plant!" J'var raged. "Telling me tales of ghostly visitations and lingering spirits will neither console nor appease me."

"She told me to watch over you, that you did not understand. I don't know what she was, but she *was* there! You need me to get you out of here, out of the barrens, and then you can do as you will. But I will not abandon you when I have been told to look after you by a spirit!" D'raekn's eyes flashed, and he moved a step closer to the furious J'var. "Conscious or unconscious, the decision is yours."

"How dare you threaten me, you demon spawn! I will see you dead! I will see Karid take your head!"

D'raekn backhanded J'var a staggering blow and waded into him with a jab to the gut, doubling the Noor over and dropping him to his knees. "Get up!"

"D'raekn, stop it! Do not hit him again. He is not himself. Can you not see? J'var bears the guilt of my torture and now that of his sister's death as well. And you make light of her death by pretending she is not gone! Can you not feel his suffering?"

Cwen knelt beside J'var and lifted the man's chin until his eyes met hers. "I need you, J'var. I need you to help me find my way home. Let D'raekn see us to the river, and I will go on with you from there. Will you do this for me?"

J'var's gaze shifted to D'raekn and back to Cwen. Without a word he got to his feet, wiped the blood from his mouth, and set a determined pace along the path, planting each foot cautiously as he edged around the quagmire that had nearly claimed Aenzl and the dragonspawn.

Cwen glanced at B'rma and acknowledged the Noor woman's approving nod with a less certain one of her own. The heart she had called a stone felt heavier than ever, and she could not bring herself to look at D'raekn, knowing he would see the feelings she hid.

N'dia's first indication that something was seriously wrong was her inability to move. She recalled pain and being entangled in thorny vines. She knew that D'raekn had called to her and that she had spoken to him since the attack, for she remembered the conversation clearly, though not the circumstance.

She opened her eyes to find herself neck-deep in what smelled like earth. She was buried in an upright position as if she had stood still while someone entombed her in damp soil. Only her head stuck out, and she could turn it as far as either shoulder—not that it achieved much. Wherever she was, it was dark.

Are you still in pain? The silent question resonated within her mind.

"Who are you? Where are you? I cannot see anything. Oh, no, I am not in any pain."

Tinkling laughter and the sound of scratching overhead preceded the next question. *Do you not know me? I once lived in your mother's garden, but no matter. I am glad the pain has gone.* Something soft, the feathery touch of a furred paw brushed N'dia's forehead. *The fever wanes, soon I can release you.*

"Where am I?" N'dia struggled to make out a shape in the dark but still saw nothing. "I cannot see you. How did I get here?"

After the fire dryad assured the thorny gorse that the stag was much more nutritious than a skinny Noor girl, the slow worm traded a rather large stag for your freedom. Then the worm dragged you into the cavern and stuffed you into one of his hidey holes. Together we packed the healing soil around you to draw out the poisons. And huzzah! Here you are, feeling almost good as new. Are you sure you don't remember me?

"I cannot see you, so how can I know if I remember you? Can you light a torch?"

Deep black became a muted green glow that disclosed a heavily cloaked figure, not quite human. N'dia stared open mouthed at the illuminated being. It was tall and dark, covered with a greenish gray growth that gave it a shaggy appearance but no more color than in the shades of soot. A faint glow emanated from feathery antennae set above wide spaced, lidless eyes.

"You were a fire shield in a story, not a real creature!" N'dia exclaimed. "You were something my mother made up. She called your kind hellwings, and she called you the she-shadow, ruler of them all. She described your race as creatures capable of hiding within the shadows of others. I must be hallucinating." N'dia laughed at a sudden memory. "Mother used to tell me you lurked within my father's shadow, spying on council meetings!"

And you did not believe her? Why would a mother lie to her child?

"My life has recently become very confusing. What once were faerytales are becoming my new truths." N'dia struggled against her earthen cell. "Will you let me out now?"

The hellwing hummed for a moment, and the earth around N'dia began to undulate. A shiny round face containing a row of multifaceted eyes and twitching mandibles appeared at her side. She jerked her head back as far as possible and gave a startled grunt.

It's just the slow worm, no reason to be frightened. He will loosen the soil and allow you to climb out.

Though the hellwing made it sound simple, it was hours before N'dia was able to scramble from her earthen sickbed. She pounded at her clothes in an attempt to loosen some of the soil still clinging to them, then sank to her knees to examine the scabbed remnants of puncture wounds, scratching the remaining itch.

They will soon fade.

N'dia stopped scratching and looked up at the hellwing. "Can you help me?" she beseeched. "I need to get out of the barrens. I need to quickly reach the village of Dragonfire."

Sleep. I cannot help you until darkfall.

Chapter 19: Among Enemies

"Icannot love you, and I can no longer stay with you. If I do, you will die. I have seen it, seen your death in my dreams over and over." Cwen moved around D'raekn trying to get him to look at her, but he just brushed past her and, with the help of several stryvers they had discovered waiting on the shore of the Nigrous River, finished tying off the last rope on the raft he was constructing. "I am not your chosen one! Can't you see that?"

D'raekn shouted, "B'rma! Find Aenzl and have the stryvers load our supplies. I want to be well downriver before darkfall. The stryvers say the wasp queen will take us to C'thra." Continuing to ignore Cwen, he began to drag the raft toward the riverbank.

"D'raekn, do not do this! Talk to me!" She stamped her foot, and he swung to face her, his hands reaching for her before dropping to his sides.

"Why do you deny me when you know I love you?" He wiped a hand across his eyes and shook away his hurt. "Just go, Cwen. Take your Noor director and go. Do what you must. I cannot stop you, and no argument I give will change your mind or make you follow your heart."

"J'var is not *my* Noor! There is nothing between us, and you know it! Please, D'raekn," begged Cwen, "I do not want us to part like this. I do care for you, I do. It is part of the reason I leave you. You need to focus on what lies ahead, and it does not include me. I do not belong here, D'raekn, not with you and not with J'var. You both deserve better."

A mist clouded D'raekn's vision, and he blinked and looked away. "You cannot understand. I have no choice but to love you. Aenzl was right. He said you would hunt death until it took you. And so you will. You care for no one, Cwen, least of all yourself. Go and take the director with you. There is nothing else to be done or said. You have chosen." Spotting Aenzl and B'rma hurrying along the sand with one of the stryvers, he murmured again, "You have chosen, and I cannot bear to watch," and went to meet them.

Cwen looked on as Aenzl and the stryver scrambled aboard, and D'raekn and B'rma pushed the heavy raft into the swift moving current of the river.

Eyes locked on Cwen, D'raekn clinched his fists as she turned away to follow N'dia's sullen brother. He saw her cast a single, brief look back over her shoulder before hurrying on. The acid of anger churned within D'raekn's belly, and something swelled painfully within his chest and brought a hot throb deep behind his eyes. What would become of Cwen now that she had left him? She clearly bore his mark. It was now completely formed across her back and shoulders. The image of the dragon marred her pale skin and shouted her betrayal of her own kind—announcing her as the human who had freed the dragonspawn.

The distance between them widened, yet Cwen did not look back again. She trudged behind the dangerous Noor director through the deep sand toward the distant, heat-distorted trade center of Nestlewood. When D'raekn could no longer see her, he poled the raft downriver toward the Obsidian Fan and the nest of the waspwomen.

In the darkness, B'rma's hand fell on D'raekn's shoulder, and he gave her a narrow-eyed glare.

"You fret needlessly. J'var means Cwen no harm, and she will be safer with him than with us. She will also keep his thoughts from you.

"We have work to do, D'raekn. The stryver brings word that the boak mines at Saedan's Sands have fallen to the nomads, and Queen Karid's assassins now camp at Stonetel awaiting the rest of her troops and the command to enter the Fungal Shroud. Other soldiers amass to the north, deep within the Dreadwoods. If they are allowed to join those in Stonetel, they number in the thousands...D'raekn, she grows strong. If you do not reach the bounty of the gods before Karid and her army cross into the Feverous Forest, we will not stand a chance of finding it first. She will use it to destroy the wildwood and all those within. Flida cannot stand against Karid without you and the hidden bounty."

D'raekn laughed. "You speak of the hidden bounty as if we knew what it was. What makes you think we will recognize it if we do stumble upon it? And how do we know it can destroy us or Karid for that matter?"

B'rma fumed, "We know because it has been promised by—"

"What other news? What is it you withhold?" D'raekn interrupted, his sarcastic disbelief suddenly turning to interfering curiosity.

B'rma bit her lip and rolled her eyes skyward. "By the gods I wish the stryver had not told me."

"But it did. Tell me what you know, what you hide from me," he demanded.

"There is rumor that another woman is held at Karid's palace in Serabia, one who shares Cwen's birth-blood."

Head cocked, D'raekn stared at B'rma. "But that is not the worst of it. I see the worry in your eyes, woman! What else is there?"

"An ambush has been set for you in Nestlewood."

D'raekn dove into the water and swam for the shore.

"No! You do not have the dragon's full power!" Aenzl screamed. "Do not sacrifice yourself! D'raekn, come back!"

D'raekn paused and shouted back to B'rma and the still screeching Aenzl, "Go! Find the wasp queen. She will lead you to the sorceress C'thra! I will meet you at Dragonfire!"

As D'raekn hit the beach the dragon's shadow darkened, and the air grew dense around him. Scales rattled, and the air was churned with the vibrations of his transformation. The dragon circled once above the raft before heading north, following the shore as he searched for his mate.

Nestlewood lay silent. Cwen caught the scent before J'var. She gagged, covered her face with her hands, and turned away.

Unwashed human flesh painted with oils and bitter spices. It was the unmistakable, unforgettable stink of Emyute nomads.

"Stay where you are, Cwen. Bow your head, and stay where you are." J'var took Cwen's weapons, gave her arm a reassuring squeeze, and felt her trembling. "They will not harm you while you are in my company. I am a high born Noor, a member of Karid's directorate."

The nomads rose from beneath the earth, throwing off the soil covered blankets that hid them within the pits. Not a small single clan, but hundreds of them moved closer amid sounds of clanking chains and the scrape of drawn swords. They surrounded Cwen and J'var, smothering them in an invisible cloud of choking stench.

Cwen whimpered. It was the small sound of a frightened animal, engulfed in fearsome memories of constant pain and terror.

Again, J'var gripped her arm and whispered, "Do not move, do not speak, and do not look at them."

A barely discernible nod was all Cwen could muster. She knew the rules.

A sharp guttural stream of Emyute spewed forth, but in her fear, Cwen caught only a word or two, barely able to distinguish J'var's voice in the cacophony of rapid fire questions and sharp, angry responses from the nomads.

Overhead the dragon D'raekn watched with growing alarm as the ground erupted and Cwen and J'var were surrounded by a swarm of nomads. He circled, catching J'var's angry threats and the nomad leader's disbelieving jeers. He watched the crowd begin to move. The swarm surged forward as if in some sudden agreement, heading north out of Nestlewood with Cwen and J'var captives in its center.

A roar of rolling thunder shook the ground. The nomads scattered, shouting and dropping into position, fumbling to let go a volley of arrows toward the diving dragon. The first volley fell short, and only a few arrows struck the tough scales before dropping to the ground. The second volley was more precise as the dragon was much closer.

D'raekn threw back his head and bellowed as an arrow plunged into the soft flesh beneath his right wing and another gouged a deep furrow along his muzzle before it skipped off a scale and ripped a hole in the already wounded wing. A final arrow buried its head under the scales of D'raekn's breastbone, and he launched a stream of fiery breath, rolling away and lifting skyward, out of range.

He swung back, searching for Cwen and J'var, but could not see them amidst the mass of milling nomads. He could not risk catching them in a firestorm. Suddenly aware of his own wounds, his loss of blood, and altitude, he turned back. He could not help Cwen if he was captured, and he could not help her if he was dead.

"Find its blood! Find its blood!" the nomads cried. "It was wounded! Struck in the heart! Find the blood!"

"What are they saying?" Cwen clutched J'var's sleeve and hid her face from the whirling nomads.

J'var looked up and searched the sky, but there was no sign of the dragon. It had been hit. He had seen it stagger mid-air and begin a wavering descent toward the distant shore.

"They believe the dragon was mortally wounded with an arrow to the heart. They are collecting blood evidence to give the queen. It will gain them great favor."

"J'var, it was D'raekn. We must go back. We must find him."

He gave Cwen a shake and hissed, "If I try to take you from this pack of wolves, the torture you remember will be nothing compared to what they will inflict. They will kill us both slowly if we don't go with them to Stonetel. The dragonspawn is dead or dying. Do not waste your worry on it."

"He is not dead. He cannot be dead! I never told him that I…he cannot be dead," Cwen's words quavered with an uncertainty that J'var did nothing to dispel.

"I saw him fall, Cwen. Right now the only concern is our safety. Your safety. Stay close to me, and do what I say. When we reach Stonetel, I will petition Karid for your freedom."

And so they marched, following the Nigrous River until they reached the southern tip of Elder's Lake. They threaded their way along the boundary of the Fungal Shroud and through the pass until they reached the city of Stonetel.

Karid's fire guards wandered the streets openly, clearly in control of the trade center, their sudden flares of heat indicating their displeasure with merchants or one another.

"How do the assassins control the power of fire?" Cwen asked J'var as they stood in line at a merchant's stall. "Yávië once thought they were Maraen, a race of fire women from my home world. But the Maraen are flesh and blood, and their heat comes naturally from within. These women create the fire somehow, but it is not their own. They only wear the image of the Maraen, like a mask. How do they do they do it?"

J'var ordered bread and wine, paid for it, and led Cwen away from the stall before answering. "They crystallize the dragon's fire and ingest it. They also make the powders that are used to burn away a woman's fertility and to blister flesh during torture, without killing the captive."

"How could you allow this? Allow this queen to enslave your people and devastate mine?"

"What should we have done, Cwen? Let the midwife destroy N'dia's fertility? Let Karid destroy our family? People do what they must to save the ones they love, and for us that meant bowing to Karid's will. It was enough she killed our mother. My father refused to lose us too."

Cwen's lower lip trembled, and she cupped J'var's face, her hands pale against the polished ebony of his skin. "I am sorry about N'dia. She tried to be my friend."

"She cared for you. She knew how much I cared for you." J'var shrugged, embarrassed by the admission.

"J'var!"

The Noor director stepped away from Cwen's touch, eyes widening with surprise.

"L'or?" J'var grabbed his brother in a hug that lifted the younger man off his feet. He slapped L'or on the back once, then again harder. "Where have you been? Where is Father?"

L'or remained grave and ignored J'var's questions while he appraised Cwen. "I am glad to see that you have been found. You look well. And my sister? She is with you?"

At Cwen's averted gaze, L'or turned to J'var. "Where is N'dia? Father assumed she was with you. We came to Stonetel in hopes of finding you here."

"N'dia is missing. We were separated while crossing the barrens."

L'or frowned and shook his head. "What were you doing in the barrens? The bar wench at B'rma's said you had gone off in search of Cwen." He swung on Cwen. "Weren't you held by the Emyutes?"

"Cwen was held captive by the dragonspawn, L'or. We were tracking it through the barrens when N'dia disappeared. B'rma stayed behind to look for her."

Cwen opened her mouth, but quickly closed it as her spark of interest died and the cold numbness of indifference returned. What good would the truth do L'or? His sister was lost and D'raekn most likely dead, so what did it matter if J'var lied?

L'or watched and wondered at Cwen's odd lack of response and general disinterest, for neither seemed to fit his recollection of the golden-eyed woman's pigheaded nature. Perhaps the nomads' abuse had left her with a captive's lethargy. When she still did not respond, L'or turned back to his brother.

"News from the north is not good. Karid's fire guards have killed many. The trade center at Quern's Crossing has been destroyed." L'or took a deep breath and swallowed the bitterness of recall. "Citizens were scorched, baked to death. Those who dove into rivers and canals for relief were boiled in the assassins' intense heat. After the firestorm, all that was left were twisted and melted household artifacts and burned out buildings. The fearsome cries of the dying could be heard for leagues." He reached out and gripped J'var's arm, his fingers biting into his brother's flesh. "Karid scours the land indiscriminately for the dragonspawn. Come, I will take you to Father. For the moment, we are safe in Stonetel, but that may not be true if we are discovered with Cwen. Come," he said, holding his hand out to Cwen, "you need rest, and we must keep you out of sight."

As L'or discovered Cwen and J'var in Stonetel, a band of Emyute nomads tracked the injured dragonspawn southeast of Nestlewood. They followed a blood spattered trail to a patch of trampled, blood soaked grass where D'raekn had rested, locked in the dragon's body and without the energy for transformation.

The Emyute hunters continued southward, the dragon's footprints becoming bloodied drag marks as it became weaker. Shouts from those in the lead announced the discovery of the fallen beast, and nets were cast to hold it. A runner was dispatched to share the joy of the dragon's capture with Queen Karid.

The nomads pitched camp and built a great fire, celebrating with huge quantities of greasy, green fermented gall oil, dancing and chanting their victory over the demon dragon.

Each time D'raekn regained consciousness, he was tormented by the pricking of the tender flesh between his scales and hot gall was thrown in his face, burning his eyes until they were finally swollen shut. The dragonspawn's struggles became more and more feeble, and his bellowing faded to a low moan.

Long after midnight, when the fire's blaze had waned to the flickering glow of embers, the celebration ended, and cool, fog-shrouded darkness cloaked the entrapped D'raekn and eased his burning eyes.

Seeing no need to guard the dying dragonspawn, the nomads snored in drunken slumber where they fell.

Chapter 20: Unlikely Allies

Illuminated by flickering torchlight from the passage beyond, Yávië's daughter squatted in the corner of a dank cell, her hands bound in coils of golden wizard's cord that hung loosely between her knees. Her head was bowed low. Her long tangles of oily, black hair curtained her tense features and hid her angry eyes.

Above the sound of dung flies droning around the stinking waste pail came a whisper of fabric against flesh. Sóvië shifted her gaze toward the barred door, curtailing her movement to avoid stirring up the unpleasant odor of her own unwashed body. Another rustle of fabric, but there was no accompanying rattle of weaponry or clank of keys. The one approaching was not a soldier. Around her the air grew warmer and announced the sudden arrival of a fire guard assassin.

The shimmering woman stood silent for a moment before grabbing onto the stout bars of Sóvië's cell.

"Cover your eyes," the young guard hissed.

Sóvië stood, her locked joints cracking loudly in the silence as she forced them into sudden service. "I'll look where I wish. What do you want, assassin?"

"Suit yourself, but this will sting."

The woman's deep blue skin paled as her core heat rose, spreading up and down the iron bars until they were aglow in her fiery grip. That which was solid became liquid, and the red-hot iron pooled at the woman's feet, popping and sputtering as it met the dampness there.

Sóvië threw up her arms against the growing heat, finally turning away and pressing her body into the cooler corner of the stone-walled cell.

"Come, we must hurry if we are to escape without notice. Your kinswoman is held in Stonetel, and we must reach her before Queen Karid."

"Why do you help me?" Sóvië asked suspiciously as she slipped through the opening and looked up and down the dim corridor.

"I want to use my name again and see my own face in a looking glass," the fire guard replied, looking anxiously up and down the empty passageway as she released the captive's wrists. "No matter what you may believe, I have killed no one. I did not choose this life but had it thrust upon me. It was either submit to Karid or watch my village burn. She must be stopped, and you and your kin can do it. You are the women of our legends, the chosen of the dragonspawn."

"How is this possible?" Sóvië asked in disbelief. "We are not even from your world. What is this legend of the dragonspawn?"

"There is something in you that Karid fears, and the only thing she fears is the fulfillment of the legend of the dragonspawn. I don't know what it is you and your kinswoman possess, but whatever it is, you will use it."

Bitter laughter choked Sóvië. "My cousin Cwen does not abide loyalty, and she possesses nothing but the shirt on her back and whatever weapon is in her hand. And I have no power here. The greatest mistake I have ever made was following you through that portal. My weapons are gone, and my spell-casting ability is nonexistent. The use of magick requires a source, a place of powerful energy. Do you know of such a place? In my world, it is held within a jewel."

The rattle of keys and crack of boot leather on stone brought panic to the eyes of the young fire guard. "Hurry! Follow me. I will answer your questions when we are safe." She grabbed Sóvië's wrist and pulled her down into a narrow opening between wall and floor.

Inching forward on their bellies, they crawled along a slime-coated floor and finally emerged into a room of hard packed earth with a trapdoor at its center. The fire guard knelt and placed her hands on the planked slab. Tendrils of smoke rose, and the wood began to smolder. She closed her eyes and increased the heat until the old door dropped out of sight in a cascade of glowing cinders. She motioned Sóvië downward.

"Wait. Before we die I would like to know your name and where we are going."

"Elle, my family calls me Elle. We are going to Stonetel to get your cousin. After that I don't know."

"And where is your queen?" asked Sóvië.

"She goes to arrest your cousin, but Queen Karid travels overland with her army. That large a group will move slowly. We will be swift, because we are only two."

"What is the charge against my cousin?"

Elle looked away, and heat distorted the air around them. She drew in a deep breath and allowed her body to cool. "She is charged with freeing the dragonspawn from his prison isle. The warrant is for high treason."

"Well, I suppose we have to save her, after all she is my kin. I'll need a weapon or an energy source if I am to use magick. Is there such a place?"

"Below us is the armory. You will find a weapon there and clean clothes and armor. I know of no such energy source on Quondam. Karid controls all magick here. Now, hurry. It is almost sunrise."

"Elle, yours is not much of a plan. But I suppose it is better than remaining in the cell."

Sóvië eased her body over the lip of the opening and dropped into the armory.

Elle landed softly at her side. "The soldiers sleep, but we must be very quiet, for not all are sound sleepers, and occasionally one stirs. The horns will blow for the changing of the guard just before daybreak. We must be beyond the outer walls by then," she whispered against Sóvië's ear.

They edged along the wall, step by cautious step, peering around each corner and crouching as they stealthily slipped past the huddled forms of sleeping men. In a storage room, Sóvië found a chain maille shirt and dropped it over her head, covering her body to mid-thigh. She chose a sword and wrapped it in straw from the floor to avoid the ring of the steel blade against the chain maille. Elle picked up a crossbow and quiver of bolts and held them tight against her chest to keep them from rattling.

They reached the outer wall without incident and had made their way through the postern and into the woods before a shout of alarm announced they were within a soldier's sight.

"Run!" Elle screamed. "Run and don't look back! Head southwest! There is a mine on the edge of the Alabaster Wastes. Ask for Tyne, he is my brother."

Sóvië ran, glancing back over her shoulder to see flames spreading out around Elle and smoke billowing against the rising sun. There was a deafening blast, and an aftershock's wave of tremors passing through the earth knocked her to the ground. Sóvië scrambled to her feet and raced away without a second backward glance.

The sound of stones being crunched underfoot brought Sóvië upright, and she pulled aside a branch from her makeshift shelter. Though several hours had passed since sunset, the moon was not yet high enough to provide much light.

"Sóvië?" Elle's hushed call sent Sóvië scuttling into the open.

"What happened? I saw the fire and heard the explosion."

"There is no going back now. I have single-handedly destroyed Karid's palace, though I only meant to set the brush ablaze. The crystals of dragon's fire were stored in the armory against the outer wall. Apparently they became sufficiently hot that they exploded. Anyway it was easy enough to escape in the confusion, and there are at least a few less crystals."

Sóvië took the flask Elle offered and poured water over her head and neck before taking a drink. "I need a bath," she said waving away her own body odor.

"Come, there is a spring not far from here. We'll camp there tonight and go on to my brother Tyne's mine in the morning."

"Tell me about the crystals," Sóvië said, falling into step beside Elle and listening intently as the young assassin began to explain.

"The crystals are created from the dragon's breath, refined and materialized by the queen's alchemist. No one knows where this task is performed. It is thought his workshop is hidden in an abandoned mine and guarded by the most loyal of Karid's fire guards."

"But how do they work?"

Elle pulled out a leather pouch and poured several fine crystals, each no larger than a pea, into her palm. "When ingested in large quantities, the crystals give a Saedan woman the ability to control fire."

"And other races, do they also have this power?"

"No, not even Saedan men are able to control the heat," Elle replied as she carefully replaced the crystals and brushed her hands against her trousers.

Sóvië built a steeple with her fingers and tapped it against her lips. "If the Saedan women are the only ones with the ability to use this fire as a weapon, why don't you just burn Queen Karid and be rid of her?"

"I am sorry, I thought you knew. Karid is immune to dragon's fire."

"Immune to the flames of the assassins? Even the great blocks of my father's fortress were misshapen by the heat of your attacks. How is it possible that your queen has such protection?"

"I don't know," Elle replied, "but I have heard others say that she takes a single crystal each day, and some believe that it is this constant treatment that toughens her against the flames."

"I suppose…" Sóvië grew pensive and was silent for a moment. "I suppose it is possible." She rubbed the hard surface of healing blisters on her palm. "Even the simplest task builds a callous over time."

After a moment's silent thought, Sóvië said, "Elle, we need to find that alchemist and destroy the crystals. We need to stop the assassins from taking anymore."

"We can ask my brother when he comes," Elle offered. "Tyne knows the mines within the Alabaster Wastes and maybe, just maybe, he has seen assassins where none should be."

"There," Elle pointed ahead of them, "is the stream. Why don't you wash while I prepare a bit of a meal?" She shrugged out of her knapsack and began rummaging through the contents. "Some old bread, dried hare, and a handful of herbs should boil up nicely."

Sóvië squatted beside the stream, which was little more than a rivulet running through a ditch. She cupped her hands and splashed the captured water over her face and rubbed. Her palms were left muddy, so she repeated the effort several times until her hands came away clean. She dragged her fingers through her filthy hair and pondered Elle's description of the fire crystals and Karid's uses of them. What would happen if Elle quit eating the crystals? What would happen if Sóvië took them herself to build up a resistance to a firestorm?

Finding a sharp stick and gouging out a small pool to collect a little water, Sóvië pulled her shirt up over her head, amazed at the dirt left beneath it. A rolled bit of grass became a washcloth and the petals of a nearby soapnut gave her lather. Once her body felt a bit cleaner, she let the water flow until the little pool was clear. She lay down, sticking her head in the hole, and scrubbed her hair.

At the sound of a rustle of leaves, Sóvië shot upright, flinging her hair out of her eyes and covering her breasts with her hands.

On the other side of the tiny stream stood a tall man, dressed in old leathers and knee-high boots with heavy soles. "Sorry," the stranger said, "I was expecting my sister."

"Then I'll hope you are Tyne."

"Aye, and you would be?"

"Sóvië. And if you'll turn your back, I'll put on my shirt and introduce myself properly."

Tyne grinned and turned around, speaking over his shoulder as Sóvië dressed, "Where is Elle? I smelled a stew and figured she had really come back. I can't believe she actually ran away."

"Oh she did more than run away. She broke me out of prison and blew up most of the queen's palace on the way. You can turn around now." She held out her hand and accepted Tyne's grip. "I am Sóvië of Aaradan."

"And I am Tyne, brother of Elle. Let's go see what my sister has in the pot. That girl can make a meal out of fog and blue sky."

"Tyne!" Elle threw herself into her brother's outstretched arms and let him swing her around several times before she pushed away and smiled. "I'm here, just like I told you I would be."

"So you are. What is your plan? Have you quit taking that poison Karid feeds you? It's an addiction—you have to stop before it's too late and your body can't let go of the fire."

Elle looked away as a flash of anger crossed her face and the air around them warmed. She jumped up and backed away from Sóvië and Tyne. "I'm sorry. I can't always control it. I'm sorry, Tyne, you're right." She pulled out the pouch containing the crystals and tossed it to Sóvië. "Don't give them back. No matter how bad my withdrawal is, don't give them back. It is the only way I will ever be free again."

"What will happen?" Sóvië asked, fingering the pouch and feeling the grains of dragon's fire.

"Elle doesn't know. It's why she won't trust me with the crystals. I'd give them back if I saw her suffering. But she is right. The only way to be free is to do without them. I think she would rather die than stay like this."

"I would, Tyne. I would rather be dead than be this...this creature Karid has made. I want to look in a mirror and see Elle. If I can't do that—"

"How long will it take before your body is free of the fire?" Sóvië interrupted.

Elle blew out a deep breath, hugged her brother again, and patted his cheek. "I don't know anyone who has ever tried to give up the fire. A fortnight, perhaps, for that is how it is with other poisons. The blue mushrooms or the stinging serpent nettle take about a fortnight to cleanse."

"Perhaps we should have a healer," Sóvië suggested, "in case it is not as easy as simply not taking the crystals. I mean, what if there are complications?"

"There are no healers here," replied Tyne, "and going into Serabia or Stonetel for a healer might raise suspicions. We'll stay in my mine, away from prying eyes until my sister is herself again."

"We cannot wait, Tyne," Elle refuted. "We need you to find the mine where the crystals are created and destroy them. By now, Karid knows that Sóvië is missing. We can't allow the queen to reach Stonetel ahead of us. Sóvië's blood kin, a cousin, is there, and she will be executed upon her arrest. Karid will use the announcement of a public execution to draw out the dragonspawn. Because of their numbers, the queen's troops travel slowly, Tyne, but they have four days head start and will be in Stonetel just after the next full moon. Sóvië and I will follow the coast. It is faster, and we can approach from the west. The executioner's glen is not guarded." Elle tugged at her brother's hand. "If you help us, we can leave in a day or two and arrive in Stonetel several days ahead of Karid. Just provision us, and supply us with mounts."

"Why do you risk yourself for strangers, Elle?" Tyne reproached. "Stay here with me, and I will see that Sóvië can find her way to Stonetel."

Elle shook her head. "I can't, Tyne. Sóvië and her cousin are the women promised in the legend of the dragonspawn. I have seen Karid's anger—anger born of fear—and I saw the look on the deviant's face. He recognized Sóvië when we passed through the mirror. That is only possible if the dragonspawn and the deviant have shared the same dreams. Sóvië and her cousin are the ones, Tyne. They possess the bounty of the gods. Together with the dragonspawn, they can defeat Karid and free Quondam. Free all of us."

"Wait," Sóvië held up her hand and waved away Elle's words, "just wait a moment. I do not understand most of what you are saying, but I do know that I do not possess any bounty. Traveling between our worlds has stripped me of my power, and you say there is no source for its replenishment. The deviant you mentioned—he is the beast I saw as I stepped through the mirror?"

"Yes. He is Karid's son, her attempt to create a dreamer, a searcher—one who could find the Daughters of Aaradan. But the union between Karid's womb and the dragon's seed was not sanctified. It failed, and the deviant could not find you but could control a mirror between our worlds. It's a long story, and I don't have time—"

"Oh you have time," Sóvië interrupted firmly. "I need to know exactly what is going on, and you can tell me while Tyne fetches supplies and mounts and takes a look around for a stockpile of crystals." Sóvië stared up at Tyne. "Are we agreed?"

The miner kicked at a clump of grass and walked away from the women. He stared south toward Stonetel and then north toward his mine. "At the least, Stonetel is a full moon's journey. Droms will be best for traveling the dunes to the western shore. I'll be going with you—be ready to break camp at daybreak in two days, and watch the northwest sky for the light of burning crystals." Without looking back at the women, he disappeared beyond the bracken.

"Now, you were going to tell me a story," Sóvië patted Elle's hand. "If Cwen and I are going to be your saviors, I need to know why."

When Elle finished telling the story of Karid's rise to power and the creation of the dragonspawn, Sóvië asked, "And this Flida is still a guardian of these sacred woods?"

"Yes, but the sacred woods fade," Elle responded solemnly. "As they grow faint, so too does the nymph Flida. She fears for her own existence. Without the dragonspawn's strength and the bounty of the gods, Flida stands no chance against Karid's authority. The gods have abandoned us, and in their place they send you."

"And the dragonspawn...?" Sóvië urged.

"D'raekn is his forbidden name. If he is free, then your cousin has spoken it."

"Elle, this is obviously more than just a tale to you. How do you know all of this?"

The reluctant assassin took a drink from her flask, licked the lingering moisture from her lips, and admitted, "My greatmother's greatmother is the sorceress C'thra, surrogate mother of the dragonspawn D'raekn."

"And Tyne does not know this?"

"He is not a woman."

"Obviously, but what does that have to do with it?"

"The males of all races have fallen prey to Karid's wiles. They could not be trusted with the truth until D'raekn was freed."

"And you believe that he is free?"

"Oh yes, I felt the earth move and have seen the many signs." Elle poked at the fire with a stick and offered Sóvië a cup of soup. "We should get some rest while my brother is gone. Tyne will be here early on the third day and impatient in his worry." She moved the cook pot from the fire, sipped her soup, and watched Sóvië. "You intend to take the crystals don't you?"

"I have been considering it. I would have a real advantage if I were protected against the assassins' fire storms. I think you should take one too."

"But, Sóvië, we don't know if the protection will work for either of us."

Sóvië shrugged and pulled the pouch from inside her shirt. "We don't know that it won't either." She shook a few crystals into her hand, replacing all but two of them, one she tossed into her mouth and followed with the last swallow of her soup, the other she gave to Elle. "Let us see what that does," she said, scooting nearer the fire and curling up on her side with the pouch of fire crystals carefully tucked beneath her.

Chapter 21: Crossroads

Cwen sat on the trade director's terrace in Stonetel, a cup of tea growing cold in one hand, while the fingers of the other twisted a strand of hair.

"Cwen?"

She started, surprised by J'var's presence. "I didn't hear you return."

"Look at me, Cwen. I need you to listen." J'var dropped into the chair at her side. Her eyes swept over him before darting off to the distant hills, the clouds beyond, and then to the vendors in the street below—her gaze lost and unfocused. "It is no longer a rumor. The nomad hunters found the dragon's body. Word has been sent to Queen Karid, and she will demand its head."

With great deliberation, Cwen extended her arm and placed the cup on the table. She stood, swayed, steadied herself with a deep breath, and smoothed the wrinkles from her borrowed gown. Once again she focused on the distance and crossed to the low balustrade. She held out her arms, leaned forward, and let herself fall.

"Cwen!" J'var leaped over the table and grabbed her ankle, dragging her back with an arm around her waist.

"Let me go!" she twisted and kicked out. "Let me go!"

"He is not worth your life!"

She quit struggling, and her words came, soft as down, "I loved him, and I did not tell him. Now I never shall."

"When the queen arrives, you must deny the dragonspawn. Tell Karid the union was against your will, that he forced you to accept him."

"Against my will?" Cwen pushed away, angry disbelief giving her strength. "Should I say he forced me? Held me down when I was dying, like the barbaric Emyutes! Should I tell your queen he strangled his name from my throat as he raped me? Is that what you want me to say? Then how will I explain this?" She dragged the gown down over her shoulders and turned her back. "That is not the mark of force. It is the mark of acceptance."

J'var pulled the gown up to cover the mark of the dragon. "N'dia wanted you safe, and I know no other way to save you."

"I denied him, and now he is dead. I will not deny him again."

"Then marry me."

"What?"

"Accept my proposal. It is the only other possibility. Perhaps Karid will honor our union and set you free now that the dragonspawn is no longer a threat. Cwen, if you do not want your life, if you care nothing for it, then give it to me."

"J'var, there is nothing left to give. Why would you want a woman who just told you she loves another enough to die for him?" Cwen covered her face and wept, silent sobs wracking her as she sank to the floor. "I thought I could save him if I left him."

"Do you think he would want you to give your life? Or, would he want you to win against Karid?" J'var sank to a squat beside Cwen. "He was a beast, a mutant with no race to call his own. He could not walk among men, and as a dragon, he would know no other of his kind. No matter what he chose, the dragonspawn was doomed to live his life alone. But I know he cared for you with passion, and he died trying to keep you safe. Would you waste his life by throwing yours away? Marry me, Cwen. Remove yourself as a threat to my queen."

"I would be no threat to your queen," Cwen said and looked away. She imagined herself close to this faceless queen and smiling before plunging a dagger into the woman's heart. Smiling with D'raekn's name on her lips before the queen's assassins burned her. There was nothing left but vengeance, but perchance the opportunity for vengeance was reason enough to marry J'var.

"I suppose at first Karid would watch you closely, but as the wife of a favored director, you would be no threat. I am sure that together we can convince her of that. Let me save you, Cwen. For those who have died protecting you, please let me save you," J'var begged.

Cwen struggled for clarity, for a plan to avenge D'raekn without betraying him again. "Publicly I would be your wife. Privately it could not be a real marriage. J'var, I am D'raekn's mate. He claimed me and changed me, and I denied him with my lies. Do you understand that?"

"But in time—"

"No," Cwen met the Noor's eyes, "eternity would not be long enough for me to forsake him again. I can only be your companion, J'var." Again the vision of Karid's bloody death swam before her, followed by her own death in the assassins' flames—murder and sacrifice, a fitting end for the two women responsible for D'raekn's death. "I can never physically be your wife, but I will stand by you. I will keep company with you until my death. If you can live with those terms, I will marry you."

"I have your promise that you will stay with me until your death?" J'var searched Cwen's face for signs of deception, but slavery at the hands of Emyutes had made her thoughts as unfathomable as any Noor's.

"You have my word."

"Then I will tell my father to petition Queen Karid for your hand. The sooner we are wed, the sooner you will be free of Karid's threat." He lifted Cwen's fingers to his lips, brushed them with his kiss, and stood looking down on her. "I would want you at my side under any circumstance."

Cwen watched J'var go, then she rose, returned to the table, and drank her tea, oblivious to its chill bitterness. Within her mind, she devised her plan to murder Quondam's queen.

The drom beasts carrying Sóvië, Elle, and Tyne slogged through deep sand and bawled their complaints as windblown particles blinded them.

Tyne adjusted the Emyute litham over the lower half of his face and squinted toward the horizon. Another week's journey and they would reach the standing stones and emerge from the endless sand into the safety of the woods. Mounted on droms and covered from head to toe in the nomads' traditional akhnif, they were indistinguishable from Karid's Emyute soldiers, at least at a distance.

Tyne's discovery of the alchemist's workshop had not led to the destruction of the stockpiled fire crystals. The mine was far too well guarded by the queen's assassins to allow the miner access. Without protection against the firestorm, there was no hope of infiltration, but he had made a map that might be useful.

Elle moaned, and Tyne eased his drom alongside hers. "Here," he said, giving his sister a single dose of dragon's breath and watching her toss it into her mouth with a trembling hand. Both women suffered from the chills and fever of fire sickness—Elle as she withdrew from the previous greater dosage and Sóvië as she continued to take a daily crystal in the hope of gaining immunity from the firestorms. When Sóvië had grown weak, Tyne had become their healer, the vigilant controller of the crystals. Though he also took a crystal each day and felt his blood grow warmer, he did not suffer the same debilitating illness as the women.

Tyne dismounted and helped his sister to the ground. Then he went to Sóvië, gave her a crystal, and asked, "Are you chilled or fevered?"

She slid from the drom, staggered, and caught herself with a hand on the stirrup. "Fevered, but not so fiercely as last eve, and Elle?"

"It comes and goes—the fever one moment and chills the next. But I have noticed that the false image of the blue woman fades."

"Aye." Sóvië dropped cross-legged next to Elle and pushed back the girl's hood. "I can almost see you Elle. Soon only you will exist." She turned to Tyne and asked, "How much longer?"

"A week, no more." He slipped a map from his pocket and pointed to a bump on the western shore. "See that outcropping, the one that extends into the sea at the southern mouth of the bay? It is there we turn inland to reach the glen of the standing stones just outside Stonetel. We should make a plan."

Elle drew a pinch of gulab flower powder from the pouch at her waist, dropped it beneath her tongue, and immediately felt the herb's cooling effect. She scrubbed her burning eyes and gave a grin. "You don't like *my* plan?"

226

Sóvië gave a rueful chuckle and said, "Well it needs a bit of fleshing out, or we are likely to be back in prison before we locate Cwen. Just walking into Stonetel and asking about her probably is not wise."

Tyne rubbed his sister's shoulder and then gave her a pat. "I think I should go into Stonetel alone, find the woman, and bring her to the glen. No one is looking for me—at least I don't think they are. It is unlikely Queen Karid sent soldiers to search the mine, unless she has discovered I am your brother."

"No, I don't think she knows. Assassins aren't allowed their own names, much less the names of family. She took everything from me, and now we will pay her back."

"Elle, you have a lot riding on Cwen's and my ability to challenge your queen," Sóvië said, "but as yet I have no power, none at all. Only this poorly crafted sword and a belly full of fire crystals. Don't be disappointed if all we manage is to escape with our lives."

"No, Sóvië, my trust is not misplaced," Elle replied. "I know the legend of Karid's fall as well as any, and I know you bear the bounty of the gods. You, or the one you call Cwen, already possess it. Karid would not be so anxious to jail you and execute Cwen if that were not true."

"But you don't even know what it is," Tyne's words held disbelief. "You are so certain that Sóvië or her cousin has it, but you have no idea what it is?"

"Yes, Tyne, I am certain. Not even the dragonspawn knows what the bounty is, but he knows as well as I that he cannot confront Karid without it. Why do you think he needs the women of Aaradan, if it is not for the bounty they hold?"

Tyne winked at Sóvië and laughed, "Because they are beautiful?"

Elle slapped at Tyne and reproached, "Beauty cannot save Quondam!"

Her brother stood and moved away mumbling, "But it certainly can't hurt."

Weakened by blood loss and pain, D'raekn struggled against the hunters' nets. His dragon jaws snapped at the stakes holding the mesh, but they were just beyond his reach. A sudden shift in the wind touched his ears and brought the sound of approaching death.

War cries—screams like nails on slate—woke the inebriated nomads. They staggered to their feet, stumbling in all directions as they fumbled for weapons, their minds rattled and incapable of lucid thought from long days and nights of celebratory drinking.

Overhead the impossible flap of leathery sails hammered their ears as giant wings beat the air. The Emyutes twisted and turned, squinting into the darkness, seeking the source of the new terrifying sound. When the first hellwing landed, a nomad's shriek of horror ended as his hands clutched his torn throat. Dozens of hellwings dropped amid the disorganized nomads. Their claws ripped flesh and their teeth ground bone until the Emyute campsite was a blood-splattered wasteland. The only thing left living within its circle was the dragonspawn.

On the ground, the hellwings resembled a gathering of cloaked men. Their great leather-like wings were folded, their claws hidden from view, as they surrounded the red dragon. N'dia stepped from beneath a shadowed wing and dragged the net away from the dragon's head. She knelt beside D'raekn and pressed her fingers below his lower jaw. "He lives, but his life force is weak. I need water. Send someone for a healer."

She splashed the proffered water over D'raekn's swollen eyes and wet his parched tongue until it retracted within his mouth and his jaws snapped closed, nearly taking her hand.

"D'raekn? Can you hear me? Do you recognize my voice?"

"I dream of N'dia," D'raekn mumbled. "Again, I dream of N'dia."

"I'm not a dream! The hellwings found me in the thorn thicket and healed me. I'm not a dream, D'raekn."

D'raekn tried unsuccessfully to lift an eyelid. "Are you a spirit? Hellwings...?" He shook his massive dragon's head. "The hellwings are cursed, forced to hide below ground. Like me, like the stryvers, they bear Karid's curse."

"They are free now." N'dia stroked D'raekn's muzzle and asked, "Where are the others? How is it you are alone, my lord?"

"And the daughter of D'lana shall lead an army of fire shields. Cwen...I lost Cwen."

"You aren't making any sense, D'raekn. Where are B'rma and Aenzl? Where is my brother?"

"N'dia?" D'raekn struggled to speak. "You told me Cwen would make the right choice. Why is my heart broken? Spirit of N'dia, my heart is broken, and I am very cold."

"Cwen will make the right choice. Just give her the freedom and the time to do so," N'dia soothed. "Right now, more damage has been done by the Emyute arrows in your flesh and the loss of blood than by a broken heart. Where are the others?"

"On the raft, I left them on the raft," D'raekn murmured. "The nest, I told them to go to the nest of the waspwomen and on to the village of Dragonfire. I am tired, spirit of N'dia. I am very tired. I cannot serve Flida until I have rested." The dragon's head lolled as D'raekn lost consciousness.

"D'raekn?" N'dia pushed against his throat and felt for a pulse. She gasped with relief when she felt it and shouted, "We can't wait for a healer! We must use the net and carry him to the nest of the waspwomen and seek the wizard Aenzl there!"

Beyond the sound of N'dia's voice a single surviving nomad watched. When the Noor woman stood, the Emyute hunter inched backward down the slope, leapt up, and raced away to report the escape of the dragon to Queen Karid.

Chapter 22: Roll the Bones

Karid snarled and swept the oracle's table clean. "What do you mean the dragonspawn escaped? He was dead!"

"Messengers, my queen." The old woman kept her eyes on the table and gestured toward the Emyutes waiting near the tent flap.

Karid ignored the gesture and continued to rant, "Messengers? Wasn't it a messenger who just told me that the dragon was dying near Nestlewood? A messenger delivered its blood as proof. Wasn't I promised its head would arrive with the next messenger? What kind of messenger dares bring news that the dragonspawn has suddenly revived and escaped? Bloody incompetence!"

Again the oracle pointed at the waiting men. The queen whirled around to face the Emyutes, raising an eyebrow at their disheveled appearance. One was covered in soot, and the other's clothing hung in bloodied shreds. "Well spit it out! I can't wait to hear your pitiful excuses."

"We were in the garrison…"

"They attacked from above…"

"You first." Karid indicated the soot covered soldier. "Were you caught in the dragon's breath?"

"No, my queen," he whined. "There was an explosion, the palace garrison was destroyed, and the guards discovered the woman prisoner missing. It appeared that her cell door had melted."

"So, you are telling me that in the time between my departure from Serabia and today, the garrison exploded and the Aaradan woman escaped? What pray tell were my soldiers doing?"

"Sleeping, Queen Karid, it happened just before the changing of the guard at dawn. The attack was well executed and—"

"Executed, an interesting choice of word," Karid shifted her gaze to the other Emyute. "And you? What horrific challenge did the dragon hunters encounter that ended in the dragonspawn escaping in less time that it takes my seamstress to fashion a new gown?"

The soldier glanced at his counterpart and began to babble in a high, nervous voice, sending his Adam's apple dancing, "It was dark, we could not see them clearly, but they came from the sky with a fearsome howling!"

"Clouds, a whistling dust devil? Surely your condition was not caused by inclement weather. You're going to have to do better than a howling from the sky!"

"The beasts were covered with great expanses of leathery wings that ended in long boney fingers and huge hooked claws. Their jaws were filled with rows of dagger-sharp teeth. My queen, they ripped the men's flesh and devoured them before we could even draw our weapons!"

"And why were my soldiers unprepared for this unexpected massacre?"

"My queen, it was the middle of the night! The men were sleeping!"

"Sleeping, again?" Karid picked a bit of lint from beneath a cerulean fingernail. "So, I am to believe that two of my captives are free, because all my soldiers were sleeping? Well executed indeed!" Karid exclaimed, her words dripping with deadly sarcasm.

A curl of the queen's fingers and a silent beckoning brought the fires of execution. Powdered dragon's fire scalded the Emyutes' eyes until they burst. As flesh blistered, their clothing was set aflame.

Shrieks and howls of searing pain fell on indifferent ears as Karid brushed a bit of soot from her bodice and focused on the old oracle. "Roll the bones, and tell me where my missing captives are. I want both of them at Stonetel when I execute the dragon's mate."

To the hovering assassin awaiting her command, Karid ordered, "Send the Emyute Lien ahead to arrest the red-haired woman. I want her in shackles when I arrive."

Chapter 23: The Nest

"Hellwings!" a stryver squealed and ran for cover beneath the trees, followed by the others.

"Do not be ridiculous!" Aenzl snapped, squinting and peering up at the fast moving cloud. "It's just a fog bank, or a wandering rain cloud. Now get back here and keep digging! I know the door's here somewhere."

"Aenzl?" B'rma watched the cloud draw closer and poked the old man with the shaft of her shovel. "It's not a cloud at all. It is a flock of giant bats or birds, and they are carrying something in a net."

"Balderdash! There is no such thing!"

Still too high to discern individual creatures, the shadow of the flock passed over them, but as it swung about and spiraled downward, B'rma heard a familiar voice.

"B'rma! Aenzl! I have D'raekn! He is near death and needs your healing!"

"N'dia…? N'dia!" B'rma sprinted for the descending net, grabbed it, and pulled as the hellwings settled. "D'raekn!" she cried. "Aenzl, he's full of Emyute arrows!"

N'dia jumped from the net and fell weeping into B'rma's arms. "I was so afraid we would not find you in time. Help him!"

"N'dia? How is it you live? We saw you die in the barrens!" Shocked, B'rma struggled to understand what she was seeing.

"That does not matter now, we have to save D'raekn. I found him quite by accident while looking for you. He said he lost Cwen."

Aenzl fumed and fussed over the net and shouted at the beastly hellwings, "Get it off! Get this bloody net off of D'raekn."

N'dia and B'rma joined them and dragged the net away to allow the old man to reach the wounded dragonspawn.

"Bring my bag! Bring my bag!" Aenzl screamed as he examined the short crossbow bolt embedded in D'raekn's chest. "I told you not to go after that woman! I told you! Now look at you! Where's my bag?"

B'rma dropped beside the wizard and dumped the contents of his knapsack.

"He's got to be a man before I can remove these damned bolts. I've got to know where his innards are before I start cutting up his flesh. Find the chiretta powder, the neem oil, and the bark oil of the arjuna! I've got to stop this bleeding, purify his blood, and protect his heart! Until that is done, transformation is out of the question! Hurry woman!"

B'rma frantically pawed through the wizard's herbs, popping corks and sniffing for the right ones. "Here!" she slapped the jar of chiretta powder into Aenzl's hand and watched him pack it into D'raekn's wounds.

"Now the neem and the arjuna!"

B'rma fumbled with the bottles, sniffed and sneezed at the heavy fragrances, then handed the wizard two flasks filled with oily liquid.

Aenzl leaned in close to D'raekn's head and whispered, "Drink these, boy—maybe they will work a wonder on you." Once the oils coated the dragonspawn's tongue, the wizard lifted the dragon's head and followed the herbs with water from his flask.

"Will he live?" N'dia fussed at Aenzl's elbow.

"I don't know. I cannot treat him until he gives up the dragon's body, but the herbs will stanch the flow of blood and keep his heart from seizing." Aenzl shook his head and added, "What am I thinking? It's good to see you, girl! We thought you were lost."

"The old hellwing, the she-shadow, saved my life," N'dia pointed to the waiting hellwings. "They helped me bring D'raekn to you. Without them neither of us would be alive."

B'rma hugged N'dia, tears of joy streaming down her cheeks. "We need to find Cwen and J'var. He was broken by your death. I sent Cwen with him to Nestlewood. D'raekn followed them when he heard Karid had an ambush waiting." She swiped at her eyes. "Now D'raekn lies here, and I do not know what happened to your brother or Cwen."

"Cwen—D'raekn says she broke his heart. Why would she do that? She loves him. It's as plain as the point on a pikestaff to everyone but her."

"And me," B'rma shifted uncomfortably. "Ah, N'dia, it was as much my interference as anything that made her go. When we lost you, I told her I wished she had died instead, told her she wasn't the one for D'raekn, and told her to leave him alone. N'dia, I treated her like a whore." She stared down at D'raekn. "I did this to him. If she'd still been with him, this would not have happened."

"Damn you women!" Aenzl suddenly wailed. "Quit your whining, and get over here! The bleeding's slowed, but his heart has too! If it slows much more, it won't be beating at all! He's dying, D'raekn's dying, and I do not know what to do!"

Petition the wasp queen.

As one they turned toward the hellwing at Aenzl's side—a female, a she-shadow as old as the plain beneath their feet. Lidless eyes stared back from a furrowed face and feathered antennae quivered with impatience.

You are nearly there. Only another meter of soil separates you from the dragonspawn's salvation.

"Maybe the hellwing's right. Dig!" Aenzl commanded fiercely. "Get back here you worthless stryvers and dig! If these beasts were going to eat you they'd have already done it. Now find that door!"

The stryvers slunk back to work, their sideways glances at the towering hellwings giving away their aversion and anxiety. Shovels rang against the occasional stone and dirt began to fly. Aenzl supervised with angry shouts. "Hurry! We've no time to lose to laziness or fear!"

There.

The she-shadow hellwing's word stopped the digging, and Aenzl's gaze followed the line of her extended claw.

"The door! It's the door! B'rma, open it!"

"Right," B'rma examined the waxy round plug that sealed the entrance to the waspwomen's hive. "Hand me a torch."

Slowly the wax dripped away until a hole appeared, large enough for B'rma's body. Cooler air from the depths of the hive whispered against her face, bringing with it the scent of fungus and wasp jelly and an angry hum of alarm.

"They are coming!" B'rma shouted and withdrew. "And I do not think they are pleased!"

The ancient hellwing pushed forward and blocked the hive entrance.

Kneel.

Her silent command brought fearful obedience from all except Aenzl. The deep drone of the irate wasps grew louder, but the old wizard stood his ground to the left of the she-shadow. The last of the wax was ripped away as the wasp queen's soldiers surged from the nest, forcing Aenzl and the old she-shadow back into the throng of stryvers and hellwings.

N'dia tilted her head and peeked between Aenzl and the she-shadow, blinking in disbelief at the strange creatures sliding out to challenge them. Women with four arms on either side of down-covered breasts poured out and surrounded the trespassers. Quivering antennae sat atop the wasps' angular heads, and glasslike wings vibrated to produce the angry hum. Their long, slender abdomens thrust forward between muscular legs, and their barbed stingers were armed with venom ready for battle.

"Hellwings!" hissed the commander of the waspwomen with a snap of her mandibles, ignoring Aenzl and those kneeling behind him. "You dare attack the hive?"

The hellwing spread her wings and exposed her tender underbelly in submission, silently offering the condition of her death.

We bring a gift. But if you do not await the dragonspawn redeemer as the hellwing do, then kill me.

She turned and extended a wing toward D'raekn.

The drone of the wasps deepened and spread among those still emerging from the hive, but less angrily and in the higher pitch of questioning. "You bring a dead dragon?"

We bring you the redeemer.

"He is hurt, not dead, at least not yet," Aenzl said. "I petition your queen for her healing sting."

The wasp commander pushed past Aenzl and the she-shadow and threaded her way among the kneeling supplicants to the unconscious D'raekn. "How do we know he is the redeemer?"

Aenzl urged, "Let your queen give her sting. He will die if he is not the redeemer."

What have you to lose, wasp? There are not enough of us to win against the strength of the hive. If we have lied, then the hive will have earned a feast. If we have not, you will have saved the redeemer.

"Do not think we will not claim that feast, she-shadow," the wasp commander warned. To a soldier she ordered, "Bring the queen."

They waited in uneasy silence for the vibrations that announced the approach of the wasp queen. She arrived on an immense litter of carved willow and woven grass carried by hundreds of attendants. Her tiny torso rested on a platform to ease the heavy pull of her enormous gravid belly.

"How can that sting anyone?" N'dia whispered and was hushed by Aenzl's wave. "Well she has not even got a stinger!" N'dia persisted a bit louder. "Or if she does, it is cloaked in the rolls of that shuddering fat."

"Dizzz-re-zzzzpect-ful," buzzed a wasp soldier at N'dia's side. "You would be wise to hold your tongue. Disrespectful can earn you a sting."

"I just don't see how—"

B'rma punched N'dia in the arm. "Wait and see. Your hellwing seems quite sure of the wasp queen's healing sting, and so does Aenzl. And do not forget, it was D'raekn who sent us here."

They watched the attendants maneuver the litter alongside D'raekn and saw the wasp queen reach out to stroke a scale. Then, with startling speed, her long, barbed tongue shot out and slipped in beside the arrow in his chest, delivering a massive dose of venom directly to his heart.

D'raekn lurched, his body consumed by the tremors of one violent seizure after another until at last they subsided, and his heartbeat became audible in the breathless silence around him.

Aenzl struggled in between the wasp queen's litter and D'raekn's side and looked for signs of change.

"His heart pounds with the vigor of my sting," the wasp queen hummed.

"Yes," Aenzl agreed, "it is strong, and soon his strength will return. Thank you."

"But it is not my sting you came to claim. It is knowledge of his surrogate mother's whereabouts that brought you here."

B'rma sidled up to Aenzl and stared up at the strange ruler of the waspwomen. "C'thra. He sent us for word of the sorceress C'thra. She raised him and knows how he can claim his heritage. Can you help us find her?"

The wasp queen folded her arms across heavy breasts and focused multifaceted eyes on B'rma and the ancient wizard. "She rests, long dead, and buried within a cavern on the great mount called Shadowmaw. Along the ridge of the Shattered Spine, you will find her there."

"Dead? C'thra is dead? Then Flida lied to us! How can C'thra help us if she's dead? She was to lead us and tell D'raekn what to do. What will we do now?" B'rma paced and fumed, "How was C'thra killed? When?"

"I do not know these answers, Noor. A stryver came and brought me this." The waspwoman reached into the folded flesh of her abdomen, brought forth a small threadbare cloth pouch, and held it out. "It is for one called Cwen, not for the dragonspawn."

"Cwen? C'thra knew of Cwen? How is that possible?" B'rma fingered the fragile pouch, afraid to open it.

"B'rma, I know how it is possible," N'dia soothed. "When I was dead, or dying, D'raekn summoned me somehow. He called on me, and my spirit joined him. I told him things that I did not know in my flesh, but I knew them as a dreamer. Aenzl, is that possible? Is that the way C'thra could have known about Cwen even before her arrival, through D'raekn's dreams? Cwen said her aunt Yávië came to her in dreams. Is it possible?"

But Aenzl was not listening. He sat beside D'raekn's head and whispered, "Come back to me, boy. The legend collapses in a mound of lies. I should never have allowed you to leave the island. I should not have let that woman live. This is my fault, and now I do not know what to do. Come back, boy, and tell me what you want me to do."

"Aenzl, stop it! None of this is your fault. I drove Cwen away. If it's anyone's fault it's mine," B'rma admitted.

"Why do you sorrow?" the wasp queen asked. "I have given the redeemer back his life and you the gift of the sorceress." She raised her hand, and her attendants lifted the litter and swung it back toward the hive. The queen called over her shoulder, "When the dragonspawn wakes, he will again be a man, allowing you to remove the arrows without danger and allowing the magick of his birth to heal him. Now I must go, already I have been gone too long, and the burden of motherhood summons me."

The soldiers followed their queen, and workers sealed the hive entrance with a thick door of wax. Those left outside gathered closer to the great red dragon and lit torches against the gathering gloom and growing chill.

"Aenzl?" the whisper broke the long, quiet vigil. D'raekn blinked and tried to focus on the old man. The surrounding air grew unstable, and thunder rolled as a flash of brilliant light brought transformation. "Where am I?"

"Lie still!" Aenzl pushed D'raekn back when he struggled to rise. "You are a pincushion of Emyute arrows, but now that you have shed that damn dragon's skin, we'll get them out of you. You are weak. I doubt that you can stand."

D'raekn's iron grip caused the old man to yelp. "I am strong enough to take you, old man! The Emyutes have Cwen." He glared over Aenzl's shoulder at the two Noor women. "Send B'rma and the spirit of N'dia."

"We will speak of this later. Now I need to give you a good dose of nightshade and dig those arrows out so your body can renew." The wizard made ready to blow the sleeping powder into the dragonspawn's face.

"No!" Fingers dug deep into Aenzl's shoulder, rendering the old man's hand useless. "Send them now! We promised Cwen! I promised

I would not let her come to harm. Send the Noors to bring Cwen back. Do not make me expend what little energy I have crawling to Stonetel!"

"D'raekn—"

"They bear the swords of the sorceresses! Send them! Tell them to return Cwen to me. They are all we have until I heal," D'raekn's strength waned, and his fingers loosened on Aenzl's shoulder, "which may be never if you do not obey me now."

"We go, my lord," B'rma shouted and dragged N'dia along behind her. "N'dia's hellwing will carry us! We can reach Stonetel by morrow mid-morn." To N'dia she hissed, "Tell your she-shadow we need an army."

Again D'raekn struggled to rise. "Hellwing?" He grabbed Aenzl's wrist. "The hellwing have risen as the dryad warned? It is said they are fire shields. If they have come, the war begins."

"Aye, they found N'dia in the barrens, and together they brought you here. The wasp queen's sting is all that saved you."

"The wasp queen spoke of C'thra?" D'raekn shook Aenzl when the he did not answer. "Tell me, Aenzl. What news is there from C'thra?"

Suddenly distracted by the storm of rising hellwings, he watched them until they disappeared beyond the tree line and then turned back to the old wizard. "The stryvers speak, and the hellwings rise from beneath the barrens. Aenzl the legend—"

"—is lies. D'raekn, it is all lies. C'thra is dead, long dead, according to the wasp queen, buried beneath Mount Shadowmaw. Flida lied to us, lied to you.

"D'raekn, the stryvers brought word of firestorms consuming the trade center at Quern's Crossing. Karid sent her assassins in search of you, and when they did not find you, they burned everything. Now the assassins are gathered in Stonetel, and Karid's armies march to join them. If Cwen is there, Karid's warrant will be served and its execution swift. And Karid will try to trap you."

"Flida would not lie," D'raekn insisted. "She did not say that C'thra lived, only that I must find her. We will go to Stonetel and then on to Shadowmaw—it is all I know to do."

"B'rma and N'dia may not find Cwen in Stonetel!" cried Aenzl. "It is thick with Emyute soldiers and the queen's fire guards! What if Karid is already there?"

"Until Cwen is safe, going to Stonetel is all that I can do. Give me the sleeping powders, and get these quills out of me so that my body can renew. Then we will go to Stonetel. If Karid is there, so be it."

Chapter 24: Arrival

Lien the Emyute fingered a pair of manacles and watched the Noor men leave the trade director's quarters. The house-girl had left earlier carrying a basket heaped with dirty linens. Lien was growing restless. The thought of the copper haired woman alone made him sweat with anticipation. Believed dead, this woman had brought him favor with the queen; alive she made him little more than a messenger, a servant with orders to return her to the shackles. Now, he would make her pay for crawling out of the sea. The chains made a pleasant jingling as he crossed the street and slipped into the scullery through an open window.

Cwen turned the page of a book but made no meaning from the words. With the support of L'or and A'bach, J'var was petitioning Queen Karid to allow his uniting with Cwen by handfasting. A'bach believed Karid would insist on being present for the ceremony and the celebration that would follow. Cwen turned another page and wrinkled her nose at a faint unpleasant odor—something rotting, perhaps, in the street below. She stood, marked her place with a dried flower, and left the book in the chair. Hunger nudged her for the first time in weeks. She would need strength to kill Karid.

Drawing a shawl around her shoulders, she started down the stairs. The bitter odor of rot grew stronger. Maybe the cook had thrown out some bad meat. A small sound like a chime made her look up, directly into the eyes of a nomad. Cwen turned and ran.

Lien leapt forward, knocking her to the steps, and dragged her arm up painfully between her shoulder blades. Cwen screamed and thrashed, desperately trying to retreat back up the stairs and relieve the pressure on her arm. Lien grabbed her hair and smashed her face against the edge of a step, blinding her with pain. She threw her head back and slammed into the Emyute's nose and mouth. He howled, let go, and rolled away, scrambling to gain a hold on her ankle. Cwen kicked him in the jaw with her free foot and staggered to her feet as his grip loosened. Lien lunged forward. Cwen screamed again and leapt to meet him, sending them plunging down the steps in a confused tangle of arms and legs until they landed, momentarily stunned, as their heads met the polished marble.

While Lien tried to gain his footing, Cwen snatched the dagger from his belt and struck him in the neck. The Emyute shrieked and clutched his throat. Again and again she stabbed the Emyute in the neck and face, raving with uncontrolled fury.

"You beast, you monster!" she screamed. "I smelled you! Demon! Pig! You raped me while I prayed to die! I smelled you! You threw me away like garbage! You beast! I smelled you! You filthy, stinking barbarian!"

Her breath came in great gasps, and she collapsed beside the dead man, still clutching the bloodied blade as she sobbed and wailed, "I smelled you, I smelled you…" She stabbed him over and over until he was unrecognizable.

Finally, depleted of energy, she struggled to her feet, then slipped and fell in the growing pool of blood. She sobbed, scrubbing at her streaming nose, oblivious to the blade of the dagger as it barely missed her eye and became ensnarled in her hair. Screaming in wordless frustration, she pulled the blade away, the tangled strand of hair coming with it. Still unable to keep her footing, she crawled up the stairs, dragged the coverlet from her bed, and curled up in the chair with her fist still locked around the hilt of the Emyute's dagger.

A cloud of dust accompanied Karid and her army as they arrived in Stonetel to the announcement that Director A'bach and his sons awaited an audience in her throne room.

"Seal the city! No one goes in or out!" Karid bellowed to the captain of her guards. Servants hurried ahead to open doors. The queen swept past them, shouted for tea and fruit, and wiped the dust from her gown. Dropping into the deep cushions piled on the uncomfortable stone throne, her scowl dissipated, and she smiled innocently at A'bach.

"You bring news from Achroma?"

"My daughter is missing."

"Daughter," she eyed A'bach's sons, "daughter...oh yes, the sorceress D'lana's daughter. I almost forgot you used to share your bed with a witch. Do you still miss your wife, Director?" she taunted, choosing a strawberry from the tray being offered by a cowering serving wench. She bit into it, licked her lips, and smiled at A'bach's silence. "You do. Of course you do, and now your precocious daughter is gone. What do you expect me to do about it, A'bach?"

"I would like permission to search for her. She was chased into the barrens by the beast that escaped Dragon's Heart."

"And your sons? Do they wish to search for her too?" She took another berry and paused with it inches from her lips. "I'm sorry, how rude of me. Would you like a berry?" She bit, sucked juice from her fingers, and ran her tongue around her lips before popping the rest of the succulent fruit into her mouth. "No? Are you sure? They are very sweet."

"Karid—"

"Karid? Karid?" she said, the feigned smile gone from her face. "How impertinent, A'bach, to call your queen by her given name. Are you trying to remind me that we were once...close? I was told a group of farmers already looks for N'dia. So why are you really here, pretending we are still friends?" She widened her gaze to take in J'var and L'or. "Do you bring me a gift?"

"Karid, don't."

She threw back her head and laughed, a nauseating braying that made A'bach cringe.

"Don't? You dare to make demands?"

"No, I make no demands," A'bach replied evenly. "I merely bring a petition before Quondam's queen. Will you consider my son J'var's petition to wed?"

"J'var has finally found a match. Good. Of course I shall consider it." She extended her hand and waited for J'var to step forward, kneel, and kiss her ring before she accepted the scrolled petition.

Silently the men watched Karid, awaiting her reaction. Petitioning Cwen's freedom to marry J'var was risky. It provided the queen with an admission of J'var's involvement with a woman warranted for execution.

Karid read the name and looked up, first at A'bach and then at J'var. "You have chosen to marry a demon? Is that wise?"

"My queen, Cwen is not a demon," J'var tactfully replied. "She was captured by the beast and enslaved until I found her and helped her escape."

"I am to believe that somehow this woman was forced to speak the name that freed the beast?"

"It was strangled from her. Queen Karid, Cwen feared for her life! She had barely survived her captivity with the Emyute Buul, and she was terrified the beast would kill her if she did not submit to him."

"And this is what the girl will tell me when my soldier delivers her?"

"Delivers her?" J'var remained calm, trying to conceal his mounting fear.

"Yes, J'var, I have sent a soldier—one I believe the girl already knows—to serve my warrant and bring her to me. I am surprised you were unaware of my order of execution against your beloved. It is widely known."

"I beseech you, my queen, to pardon Cwen. She is no demon, and any magick she may have had was beaten out of her by your Emyutes. As my wife, she will never go beyond Achroma's walls. I swear it. She is weak and timid. I wish to protect her."

"And she…what is her name?"

"Cwen, my lady. She is called Cwen."

"Cwen, a strange name for a strange woman—and Cwen has agreed to this…marriage?"

"Yes, Queen Karid, this very week Cwen accepted my proposal. I have been anxious for your approval."

"Hmmmm, I am sure you have," she mused. "And, L'or, what do you think of your brother's choice?"

"My queen, Cwen is no longer a threat. As J'var's says, she is fearful and docile. I think she will bear my brother strong sons. It is all a man dare ask of a woman."

"Will she, I wonder?" Karid tapped her nails against her teeth then rolled and tied the petition. She stood up and handed it back to J'var. "She may already be dead," she said lightly. "I don't believe the soldier serving my warrant is as appreciative of this 'Cwen' as you. However, if she still lives, your petition is granted. But I cannot allow this woman's freedom. If you cannot control her, if she is found beyond the borders of Achroma, she will be executed, and you will be imprisoned for noncompliance with the crown's direct order. Is that clear?"

"Yes, Queen Karid," replied J'var. "Thank you, Queen Karid."

As the Noor men bowed and turned to leave, Karid's voice stopped them.

"And I expect to be invited to this wedding."

"Of course, Karid," A'bach answered.

"At full moon, to assure the quick arrival of those strong greatsons L'or believes you will soon have."

"Yes, Karid, three days hence. The cleric is free, and the sacred stones will be bathed in moonlight."

"Excellent. I will have the crier announce the event and see that it is posted in the tel. And, J'var, tomorrow bring her to me, and I will counsel her and help her choose a gown."

"Aye, my queen. Tomorrow. "

Seeing them hesitate, Karid shouted, "Well? Go! What are you waiting for? Do you want me to reconsider?"

J'var raced ahead of A'bach and L'or, anxious to tell Cwen of his success. Shouting her name, he burst through the door. His second shout came as a disbelieving croak as he jumped back out of the red-black ooze that had once been a man's life blood. A nomad by his clothing, the face was shredded into ribbons of flesh and exposed bone, the hair separated from scalp and laid back like a filleted stag.

High-pitched, hysterical laughter and a mumbled stream of incoherent words reached J'var as he started up the stairs ahead of L'or and A'bach.

"Cwen?" he whispered as he followed the sticky crimson-brown trail that looked as if a broad washerwoman's swab had been dipped in paint and dragged up the steps. J'var paused in the doorway, fear choking him when he saw Cwen's body cloaked in the bloodied bed quilt and her hands and face bruised and smeared with blood.

"Cwen?" he whispered again, shocked by the fury in the eyes that met his.

"She sent him to kill me."

"Cwen, Karid has granted your pardon and given us permission to marry," he said gently, kneeling beside her.

"I smelled him, bitter and rotten," she said, her words dripping in disgust and anger. She slipped the Emyute's dagger out of sight alongside her thigh and beneath the chair cushion where she hoped J'var would not discover it. "He came to kill me! Your queen sent him to kill me. But I killed him. What will your queen think of that?" she spat.

"She will never know," A'bach answered from behind J'var. "L'or will get rid of the body. J'var, you need to go help him. I will wash away the blood. This never happened, Cwen. That soldier was never here.

"Tomorrow J'var will take you to meet Karid, and your deportment will be fitting of a Noor director's wife. You will not bring shame to my son," he said severely. "Go and wash yourself while we clean up your mess."

Cwen shifted her angry gaze to A'bach, and her expression softened as she said, "Yes, tomorrow I will meet your queen, and I will not embarrass J'var." She then silently added, *For I shall drive a blade through her heart before he has a chance to feel discomfited.*

Sóvië awoke suddenly, startled by the sound of approaching voices. She scrambled back behind a megalith in the executioner's glen near Stonetel and gestured frantically for Elle and Tyne to do the same.

The heavy thud of hammering was repeated several times, and a number of deep voices rumbled beyond the range of understanding. A sudden yelp of pain as hammer struck flesh, a snort of laughter, and then the drone of retreating conversation indicated the men had finished their task and were returning the way they had come.

When she could no longer hear them, Sóvië stepped out to discover a banner erected at the entrance to the glen of stones. Tyne reached it first, read it, and shrugged, "It is just a wedding announcement."

"Not just any wedding announcement. It seems my cousin Cwen is getting married," Sóvië said with a puzzled look.

"Why would your cousin marry a Noor?" Tyne's lip curled in loathing. "They have been in bed with Karid for as long as I can recall."

"Maybe she does not know, or maybe she is more at home here than I was led to believe. Do you know this man, Tyne? J'var, the son of Director A'bach of Achroma? Why would Cwen do this?" Sóvië asked. "She cannot possibly love anyone. She is far too selfish."

"This announcement bears the queen's seal, and Tyne is right," Elle agreed. "Director A'bach and his sons are favored by Karid. Perhaps Cwen has no choice. But we can use this to our advantage. We can hide among the guests while we look for your cousin. Once we find her, we can convince her to come away with us."

"I am not sure we should do that, Elle," Sóvië replied, frowning her puzzlement. "Why would your queen announce my cousin's wedding? Karid told me that I was bait to capture Cwen. Now all of a sudden she is throwing Cwen a wedding? What is really going on? The whole thing reeks of a trap."

"But for whom? Karid obviously controls your cousin. Do you think the trap is for us or for the dragonspawn?" Elle wondered. "Surely D'raekn would not come here. Those who protect him would not allow the risk. We have to try, Sóvië."

"Well, I guess if we are going to a wedding," Sóvië said as she lifted the edges of her coarse woolen robe, "we will need a change of clothing when Tyne goes into to town. Head coverings, something with veils, perhaps?"

Elle shrugged. "We may as well die celebrating. Look for browns and grays. The colors of old women will help us be less conspicuous. And loose fitting to hide Sóvië's—"

"Aye," Tyne interrupted, looked away, and grinned. "Old women you will be. I'll be back before nightfall." With a lift of his hand, he headed off toward Stonetel.

N'dia and B'rma watched the Emyutes erect a banner and then leave beneath the capstone and portals that formed the tel's ancient entrance. As N'dia started to rise, B'rma dragged her back, shushed her, and pointed. Across the glen three figures wearing the hooded cloaks of the Emyutes, but far too tall to be nomads, approached from behind the distant stones.

"They're too tall. They are not Emyutes," whispered N'dia. "Saedans, perhaps, or foreigners." She squinted in an attempt to see the faces within the shadows of their hoods.

Again B'rma held her finger to her lips and mouthed the word, "Wait."

"Who do you think they are?" N'dia persisted.

"Shhhhh!"

Fragments of conversation drifted toward their hiding place.

"...Wedding...Queen Karid...Cwen...D'raekn...trap...old women..."

"Who are they?" N'dia hissed. "They know of Cwen and D'raekn. Who can they be?"

Suddenly the tallest of three gave a wave and left the others.

"Come on!" N'dia stood and walked purposefully toward the remaining men. "Who are you, and how do you know Cwen?"

The nearest figure turned and pushed back her hood. N'dia stopped cold and shouted, "Yávië?"

B'rma cocked her head and studied Sóvië. "She is too young, and her eyes are blue, not violet."

"Who are you, and how do you know my mother?" Sóvië asked.

"Your mother?"

"Aye, my mother? Where is she?"

Elle tugged at Sóvië's sleeve and murmured, "They are Noors, and they are armed. We should run!"

"No, Elle, they could have already killed us from wherever they were hiding. They know Cwen and my mother." Sóvië again asked the Noor women, "Please tell me what you know of my mother. Is she with Cwen?"

"Your mother is gone, and we search for Cwen. She is in danger from Queen Karid. I am N'dia, daughter of D'lana. This is B'rma, a friend of my mother's."

Sóvïe ignored N'dia's introductions. "My mother is gone—as in dead or gone as in missing?"

"Her body rests in the city of Achroma. Her soul was freed to join that of her husband."

"My father? My father died in the assassin's fire. You are saying he was here? I saw his remains. He could not have been here."

"Not in the flesh. A soulbinder summoned his soul. I only know what my brother told me," N'dia explained. "Yávïe was all alone with no way home and was so sad, so wounded by the deaths on her home world. When the council of elders offered to let her join her husband, she chose to go, to be with him. I think she believed you were dead." N'dia paused, staring at Sóvïe. "You look so much like her."

"Aye, except for my eyes, I am her mirror image. My eyes are the eyes of my father, King Sōrél of Aaradan."

Elle peeked around Sóvïe, "Why do they search for Cwen?"

"Why do you search for Cwen?" Sóvïe repeated.

"We were sent by D'raekn. Cwen is his…" N'dia searched for a word.

"Chosen," B'rma supplied.

"Chosen for what?" Sóvïe asked.

"Oh! Sóvïe!" Elle exclaimed with sudden realization. "By the gods, these are the women who serve the dragonspawn, the sorceresses long hidden among the Noor."

"Chosen for what?" Sóvïe repeated, ignoring Elle's sudden outburst.

"As his mate," B'rma said. "She accepted him and spoke his forbidden name. It freed him. Now he awaits us south of Nestlewood."

"I don't understand." Sóvïe gestured over her shoulder to the queen's banner. "If Cwen is this D'raekn's mate, why is she marrying another?"

The Noor women stood motionless and dumbfounded at the news of the wedding announcement.

"J'var? How is this possible? There can be no doubt why Karid allowed it. She sets a trap for D'raekn. But why would Cwen agree?" N'dia wondered aloud.

"I don't know, and it doesn't matter," said B'rma. "This news will draw D'raekn like a siren's call. We cannot let him come here. He will be better off believing Cwen is dead than risking his life challenging Karid before he is ready. We need to get D'raekn to Mount Shadowmaw."

"I will go to my brother and bring Cwen back."

"No, N'dia, we need to go now! We have to return to D'raekn before he is well enough to follow us," B'rma snapped. "You, daughter of Yávië, try to talk some sense into Cwen. Take her with you. Take her home. Cwen must not be allowed to draw D'raekn into Karid's trap, and she cannot really want to marry J'var. Get out of here before it's too late, and take your cousin with you! There is a mirror below the palace at Serabia—"

"I know," Sóvië said with a nod. "I entered there. But what of the bounty? Elle believes Cwen has it."

"What do you know of the bounty of the gods?" B'rma asked, reconsidering the quiet Saedan beside Sóvië.

"The women of Aaradan possess it, and Karid fears it. Sóvië does not carry it, so her cousin must."

"You are wrong, Saedan. I know that Cwen has nothing. She was captured and tortured by Karid's Emyutes. They left her nothing. If this one does not have it, then it is still undiscovered." B'rma backed away, looking up at the sun. "N'dia, call the hellwing! We need to go now!"

N'dia paused, indecision holding her back. "Find Cwen, and take her home. Do not tell her you have seen us or that the dragonspawn still seeks her. It is too late and too dangerous for us to allow him such distraction." She reached out and squeezed Sóvië's hand. "I am sorry about your mother. She was my friend, and so was your cousin. They just wanted to go home, but I was too afraid to show them the way."

Elle rummaged in her knapsack. "Take this. It is a map. My brother drew it to mark the location of Karid's crystal stockpiles and her alchemist's workshop. You may find it useful."

"N'dia!" B'rma bellowed from beyond the distant bracken. "We need to go—now!"

"I wish you safe journey!" N'dia grabbed the map and ran.

D'raekn awoke and immediately rubbed at his chest where the Emyute arrow had struck. The area was slightly puffy, but the raw, open flesh had healed. The same was true of the wound beneath his arm, and when he fingered his jaw, there was no evidence of a wound at all. He was well enough to search for Cwen.

"Aenzl!" He threw off his blanket, stood up, and scanned the camp for the old wizard. "Aenzl! I am going to Stonetel. If you plan on joining me, do it now."

Aenzl shambled from the fire with a cup of tea and a bit of dried fish and offered them to the dragonspawn. "B'rma and N'dia should be back by nightfall. Why do you not wait for them before you go charging off into Karid's trap?"

"I have waited far too long and made too many mistakes where Cwen is concerned. She loves me, Aenzl, she simply fears telling me. I should never have let her go off with J'var. He would make a deal with death to have Cwen for himself, and I did nothing to stop him from taking her—nothing. Instead I just told her to go."

"D'raekn, Cwen is not our concern."

"She is everyth—"

"No, D'raekn, she is nothing. A key to your prison door is all that Cwen was meant to be. You need to go to Shadowmaw and claim the power of the throne before Karid reaches it."

"But you said it was all lies, that the legend was a lie. Why should I follow Flida into a legend of deception? Why should I not just find Cwen and return to Dragon's Heart?"

"Because Karid will never allow it, boy!" exclaimed Aenzl. "You know what I say is true. Karid wants you dead and Cwen along with you. She would have you both killed before you ever reach the isle. She may have already killed Cwen."

"No, she would not kill Cwen. Cwen is the only leverage Karid has. She knows that I will come for the one I have chosen."

"Aye, and she knows you stand no chance against her unless you possess the power of the royal blood and the bounty of the gods. If you believe Karid will not kill Cwen, then come with me and claim what is yours. We know the magick flows within you, and the throne is rightfully yours. We know that."

Suddenly the sky grew gray, and the sun hid behind a pulsating cloud of arriving hellwings.

As the flock drew near, B'rma hailed, "D'raekn! Aenzl! We could not find Cwen. Rumor says she is dead. You must go to Shadowmaw! If there is to be any chance of saving yourself, you will need to be strong enough to defeat Karid's army. The only way is to claim your power!"

D'raekn ignored B'rma and placed his hand on N'dia's shoulder. "And you, daughter of D'lana, what say you? Is Cwen dead, or does B'rma lie in an attempt to protect me?"

N'dia met his gaze and gave a shallow nod, "B'rma lies. Cwen is safe with my father and brothers. She is in no danger from Karid. And my lord, we have a map drawn by a miner that shows the location of Karid's alchemist and warehouses."

"Then we must begin." D'raekn swung about and strode to the mouth of the wasp queen's nest where he drew his sword and hacked away the wax. His action was met by an immediate roar from the ascending soldier wasps. D'raekn stepped back to make room for the surge of furious waspwomen that poured forth and surrounded those within the camp.

"Again you attack the nest!" the wasp commander exclaimed. "Mortal, do you have a death wish?"

"I am D'raekn, heir to the throne of Quondam. I need the army of the wasp queen, and I command your queen's obedience."

"And what proof do you have of this? Our redeemer is the great red dragon."

D'raekn reached into his knapsack and withdrew a ruby jewel, a glittering scarlet dragon scale. "A token of my promise, and the seal of your redeemer. I will await your queen's answer."

The wasp commander hummed. Her abdomen vibrated, and a drop of venom formed at the tip of her stinger. "If you are the redeemer, you should not fear my sting."

"I do not. My blood runs with the venom of the wasp, a gift from your queen." D'raekn held out his arm.

In a flash, the wasp struck, and venom oozed from the puncture in D'raekn's inner forearm. "If you are alive when I return, I will give you my queen's answer." The commander slipped through the opening to the hive followed by her soldiers.

"Does it hurt?" N'dia gulped. "You won't die will you?"

"It hurts, but I will not die. By the time the waspwomen return, only a shallow redness will remain. Now summon your she-shadow, for it is time she bestowed her gift."

"How do you know all this? How do you know what to do without C'thra's help?" Deep frown lines scored N'dia's usually unblemished beauty.

"C'thra taught me well, and my freedom brings a growing knowledge of my task. My sleep is filled with dreams that bring the wisdom of my dragon father. With the gifts of the wasp queen and the hellwing she-shadow, I will have the strength I need to see us into the mouth of the shadow upon the Shattered Spine. There I will claim my birthright and lead our army against the false queen." D'raekn paused and drew a deep breath. "Is that not what you want, daughter of D'lana? Freedom from Karid's false rule?"

"I am not certain. B'rma says that this is the legend that must be fulfilled."

"And B'rma? Do I walk the right path? Aenzl, is this your wish?"

Their whispered answers were lost in the cacophony of wing beats that brought the she-shadow and her hellwings.

Submit, my lord, the she-shadow's silent words commanded.

D'raekn tilted back his head, exposing the pounding pulse beneath his jaw, as he concentrated on keeping his heartbeat slow and steady to control the loss of his blood.

The she-shadow took his chin between the fingers and thumb of her left hand and sliced his jugular with a claw on the joint of her right wing. She forced the hollow talon at the tip of her right forefinger into the opening and released the poison of the hellwing. Then she licked away the blood on D'raekn's throat.

You are now one with the hellwing and we will serve you as our brother. In the days before Karid's curse, we wore another form, that of the shining ones. Together we will bring back those days and shake off the soot of our enemy.

A rattle returned their attention to the entrance of the wasp nest. The commander approached them wielding a sword in each of her four hands. "My queen accepts your command and delivers the force of the millions, the force of her army. One hundred soldiers will remain behind to ensure the security of our brood. When will we leave, Redeemer?"

"Now. We go to Shadowmaw now." The clearing pounded with the pulse of D'raekn's transformation and his shouted commands to his new army.

The dragon crouched and allowed Aenzl to clamber to a seat atop his withers, orders flowing smoothly all the while in his booming voice. "She-shadow, you and N'dia will lead your hellwings into the Alabaster Wastes. Locate the mines where Karid's alchemist creates the crystals from the dragon's breath and destroy them. The hellwings can hide within the shadows and enter the mines undetected. Destroy all the crystals. The assassins will suffer with the fire sickness and be useless against us.

"B'rma, take half of the wasp soldiers and secure the northern border of the Feverous Forest. It is the gateway into Flida's woods and must not be breached by Karid's army. Is that clear?" The massive head swung about, and the great dragon's eye fixed on B'rma.

"It is, my lord, but I—"

"You would be happier guarding the dragonspawn? Who is the rightful heir to Quondam's throne?"

"You are, my lord," B'rma said, grinning. "You are."

"Then do not question. Aenzl and I will join you as soon as I have taken the promised power."

D'raekn then swung his great dragon's head toward N'dia. "What are you waiting for? Go! I need those crystals destroyed, and only your hellwing shadows can do it!"

N'dia smiled, gave a small salute, and mounted beneath the wing of the she-shadow. Together they lifted in a flurry of leathery wings, circling in a dark funnel-shaped cloud before sweeping away to the north.

Amid a deafening roar, the wasp army rose and surged over the tree line as they headed toward the village of Dragonfire. Clutched in the arms of the wasp commander, B'rma rode at their head.

"Aenzl, do you know the location of the cavern we seek?" D'raekn asked.

"I only know that it is at the base of Mount Shadowmaw, and its entrance is most likely sealed."

"You say that I am not strong enough to take Cwen from Karid without the mountain's promised gifts. No seal will stop me." The dragonspawn cast his gaze across the remaining army of waspwomen and shouted, "To Shadowmaw!"

Together they flowed across the hills and into the mist that shrouded the Nigrous River and Elder's Lake beyond. In the East, across the river, towered the snow covered peak of Mount Shadowmaw.

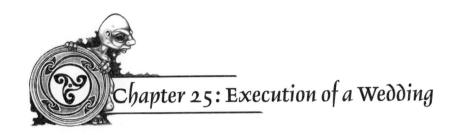

Chapter 25: Execution of a Wedding

Karid paced and watched the dragonspawn's woman. The girl—Cwen she was called—seemed calm and unafraid. That alone annoyed the queen, but even worse was her golden-eyed gaze, bold and challenging.

"You think he will come for you?" Karid asked.

"I think he is dead," Cwen replied.

"And if he is not?"

"He is, or I would not be marrying J'var, would I?"

Karid pinched the bridge of her nose and stopped in front of Cwen. "I have promised you to A'bach's son on the condition that you never leave Achroma. What good can that do you? You will be a prisoner in the Noor's home."

"I have been a prisoner for most of my time in Quondam. I am sure that J'var will be far kinder than Master Buul and less demanding than the beast of Dragon's Heart. What is it you fear from me? I am weaponless and without the power of my homeland's magick." Cwen covertly eyed the assassins stationed about the room. They were too close to give Cwen time to kill their queen. She would be burned before the dagger was drawn.

"I don't fear you at all. But if he lives, I do believe that your dragonspawn will come for you. Then again, he may be dead. Perhaps those who took him from my soldiers only sought to give him a proper burial before I could take his head. If he is not, he will be a most welcome wedding guest."

Karid lifted her hand, dismissing the conversation. "Come, we must find a suitable gown and have it altered to fit such a skinny girl."

The assassins moved in to escort Cwen. They were so close that she could feel their heat rising, a warning against causing provocation. In the corridor, J'var waited, his hands clasped nervously in his lap. He sprang up as Cwen approached, but Karid waved him back.

"We are off to choose a gown. I shall return your betrothed to you shortly. Until then why don't you see the oracle? Ask her to tell your future," Karid said with a grin.

J'var rubbed his sweaty palms against his trousers and returned to the bench. Having overheard much of their conversation, he muttered to himself, "I know my future. If the dragonspawn lives, it holds only death."

Cwen stood while Karid's seamstress pinned and tucked the ivory gown. While Karid appeared slim, Cwen was far leaner and slight of frame. The bust of the gown fell away as if it were empty. The young seamstress stitched quickly, her fingers nimble and knowing. Little by little the gown became snug.

"You will be well guarded in the glen. Any attempt to contact outsiders would be foolish," Karid warned.

"I do not intend to act foolishly. I simply intend to marry J'var and accompany him to Achroma, where I will live out my life in relative comfort. J'var is not an unkind man."

"Do you think I believe a word of that?"

Cwen shrugged and jerked as the movement brought a pin prick. The queen's clothier gasped and rolled her eyes toward Karid. "It was my fault," Cwen soothed, "not yours. While I doubt if your mistress minds you spilling my blood, I should not wiggle while you work."

"I will leave you now and let J'var know that you will join him shortly." The queen strode out followed by four of her fire guards, two remaining to watch over Cwen and the seamstress.

At the woman's urging, when the work was done, Cwen slipped out of the gown and stepped into the day dress. She began to tug it up over her slender hips.

"You really are his," the seamstress whispered, staring with wide eyes at the dragon emblazoned across Cwen's back and shoulders.

Cwen dropped the dress, flustered by the sudden question. "Aye, I was." She quickly drew the dress up to keep hidden the Emyute's blade currently bound against her inner thigh and to cover D'raekn's mark from the woman's scrutiny.

"Is he really dead?" the seamstress asked timidly.

Cwen glanced at the guards and spoke in a low voice, "I believe he is. He was seen wounded and falling, and then Karid's hunters tracked him to a glen where he is said to have died."

"And this saddens you?"

"Yes. He was very kind and gentle. Not a beast, like people say."

The girl gathered the wedding gown and draped it over Cwen's arm. "You will be beautiful on your wedding day," the seamstress said as she opened the door and ushered Cwen into the hall where she examined J'var for a moment before hurrying away.

"Orpins! Lowlife farmers and tailors," J'var snapped. "They act as if they have never seen a Noor."

"Maybe she never has. The Noor are quite striking and a bit unnerving to those who do not know them. You should be more accepting of others, J'var. Unfounded prejudice does not become you."

"You sound like my mother. Come, Cwen, and I will take you home." J'var held out his arm, and Cwen linked hers through it. "What did Karid say?"

"That she doesn't believe a word I speak."

J'var scowled. "She actually accused you of lying?"

"Oh yes. She can't imagine why I am marrying you. She thinks I am up to no good, planning to meet up with outsiders on our wedding day." Cwen gave a bitter laugh. "She forgets that nearly everyone I know is dead, and she has killed them."

"She will soon lose interest in you. Once we have gone to Achroma, her visits will become infrequent, and she will realize that you are not a threat. You are not, are you? You do not plan to do anything that will endanger yourself?"

"J'var, you are kind to me. I appreciate your concern." Cwen patted his arm and sighed, "How can I possibly be a threat to a woman who is surrounded by guards who will burn me to cinders at the mere wave of her hand? How can I be a threat? Now, no more talk of Karid for tomorrow we will wed."

⟨❧⟩

A'bach held out her cloak as Cwen shivered. She smiled and declined, "It is nerves more than chill."

"J'var will be a good husband. Will you be a good wife?" A'bach asked, searching Cwen's face for deception.

"I have sworn to stand by your son until my death," Cwen answered, keenly aware of the dagger's hilt now concealed beneath her gown against her right breast. It could be quickly drawn through the slit she had created in her wedding gown and thrown with great accuracy—as she had practiced every night since killing the Emyute Lien. D'raekn's words resounded in her mind each time she pulled the blade and hit the tiny circle drawn on the wall. *You cannot miss, Cwen. There is no longer room for error.*

For hours J'var and Cwen had been making polite conversation with hundreds of insincere well wishers while they waited for the moonrise that would signal the beginning of the handfasting ceremony. None knew the bride or groom, but Karid's official invitation was not something that dared be dismissed.

Two women approached in the slow shambling gate of the elderly, shoulders hunched and heads bowed, their faces hidden within the deep hoods of coarse robes. Poor old women, Cwen thought, forced to walk from Stonetel by a heartless queen's demand.

Cwen attempted a tired smile, but the smooth youthful flesh and the familiar ring on the extended hand with its painful grip caused her to look up into well-known, disapproving sapphire eyes.

"We need to talk, cousin," soft words belied the urgency of Sóvië's iron grasp.

A hurried glance at J'var showed him deep in conversation with his father and L'or and several white-robed elderman. J'var was nudging L'or as he said, "Marrying the dragonspawn's woman may bring our house to the throne. What would you think of that?" Deep laughter followed, covering L'or's response.

"Sóvië, you're alive!" Cwen whispered. "What are you doing here?"

She tugged against Sóvië's hold without effect. Sóvië merely squeezed harder. "Walk with us."

"I cannot! Karid is watching."

"Smile, and walk with us," Sóvië insisted through gritted teeth. "The queen will not mind you assisting a couple of old women. Just excuse yourself to your fawning men and escort us to seats beneath the awning."

Cwen frowned at Sóvië's snide tone. She jerked her hand away and turned to touch J'var's arm. "I am going to show these old women where they may rest. I will be right back."

J'var and A'bach glanced at the two crippled women. "Do not get lost," J'var warned with a meaningful look across the field toward Karid.

Cwen slipped in between Sóvië and her companion and linked her arms through theirs. She slowed her steps to match the shuffling gate Sóvië shammed. "You do a wonderful impression of an old woman, Sóvië."

"Playing an old woman is mild in comparison to much of what I've experienced trying to save your ass."

"Do I look like I need to be saved? What are you doing here? Who is that with you?"

"Saved? Yes, wearing that wedding gown you do. And Karid invited all the old women, so it seemed wise to take advantage of her invitation. This is Elle, one of the beloved queen's assassins, or at least she used to be. Now she is a free woman and my guide to Quondam's lore. It seems she believes our blood is of some importance."

Cwen looked around in search of Karid and discovered the queen was approaching A'bach and his sons. "She is looking for me. Get out of here before you are discovered, and we are all executed on my wedding day. Get out! Or I will scream and have you arrested."

"No, you won't. Not even you would be so cold to your last blood relative. Cwen, what are you doing? I know you—you would rather die than marry that man. Your hands are chilled with your deception, and your eyes are filled with fear and sorrow."

"You do not know me!" Cwen snarled. "Go, just go. Trust me to do what I must. Please, Sóvië, locate the mirror and go home! I promised Yávië I would find you if you lived and see you safe. Please go. Please."

"I don't need to find the mirror. I came into Quondam through the portal beneath Karid's palace in Serabia. Come with me, and we will go home together. I am alive, and Mother is dead. There is no reason for either of us to remain here."

"Yes, there is! I am going to kill Karid for all that she has done, and I do not want you caught in the firestorm that will follow. Now go, let me do something good for once, Sóvië. I know what you think of me, and you are right. I have been selfish, even ruthless, but this one act will give my life meaning and sweep the blackness from my soul. Please go." Cwen glanced over her shoulder to find Karid staring. She smiled and lifted her hand in greeting. "I must go now before she comes to see who I find so intriguing. Go!"

"You must give us the bounty of the gods," said the woman called Elle. "D'raekn needs it."

"D'raekn is dead, and I do not have anything, except this." Cwen's hand flew to her bodice where Yávië's jewel rested. "The jewel of your birthright, Sóvië, Yávië left it for you." Cwen lifted the serpent and dragon encircled stone from between her breasts and held it out to her cousin. "I promised I would give it to you. Now, go home and marry your humorless and annoying Xalin." She touched Sóvië's ring.

Sóvië blinked away tears and clutched the pendant against her heart, its sudden authoritative glow escaping through her fingers.

"It is the bounty," Elle gasped, pointing to the serpent embracing the dragon. "We must get it away from here before Karid finds us with it." She tugged on Sóvië's robe. "With its power we can win! Even if your cousin fails, *we* can win against Karid."

Cwen gave Sóvië a gentle shove. "Go with her. Please do not die here, Ædracmoræ needs you. Xalin needs you—he cannot lace his boots without your guidance. You are the Dragon Queen, Sóvië. The power of the House of Aaradan is yours."

"Cwen!" Karid's voice commanded, followed by J'var's anxious call.

Once more Cwen gave a gentle push. "My destiny lies here, if not today then very soon." She watched Sóvië's momentary indecision change to a brusque nod of agreement. "Kill her for our parents, for all of Ædracmoræ. Kill the queen of Quondam." Then she turned and limped away.

Elle reached out and touched Cwen's sleeve. "Don't die today. I swear to you, the dragonspawn lives. Do what you must to stay alive. He *will* come for you."

As Karid reached Cwen, the two old women were shuffling away.

"Who were they?" the queen demanded.

"Soothsayers who came to tell our fortunes," Cwen's eyes glistened with unshed tears.

"And this fortunetelling, it was good?"

"Yes," Cwen whispered as she covertly pushed the dagger back into its hiding place. "They said you would live a bit longer than expected."

Karid glared and gestured skyward. "The moon's glow bathes the stones. It is time we saw you wed."

J'var stepped nearer and offered his hand.

Cwen took a deep breath and accepted. If Elle was to be believed, D'raekn lived. Do not die today, do what you must to stay alive, the woman had said, and the only way Cwen could pacify Karid was to marry J'var.

Before the altar the cleric's words were blurred, a meaningless cant to Cwen. Her responses were mechanical, precisely as she had rehearsed. Her hand trembled when the scarlet binding cord touched her wrist, and J'var squeezed her fingers reassuringly. He did not know the words "bound until death" were now a lie, and the wife he took to Achroma still belonged to another.

Chapter 26: Shadowmaw

The opalescent mist eddied and swirled, its nacre drifts alternating between luminosity and a sinister, shadowy gloom that coalesced and then diverged to reveal the spirit of the souls. Flida the nymph sat in the shadows of the sacred woods, listening as the dark eternal god arrived.

"I have been patient, Flida. The joining of magick with the man's royal blood was a valiant effort, but it still may fail," the voice of death's god boomed. "Your sister has grown powerful, and your dragonspawn is weakened, distracted by his desire for the woman who brought him freedom. He cannot be allowed to fail, or all will fade. Flesh will conquer spirit. You and I will end."

"Can you not stop my sister? Will the gods not save the spirit woods? It was *your* curse that brought this upon us!"

"By the laws that bind me, I cannot. My careless curse sent Karid among the flesh-bound to make her way, and only one of flesh can end her reign. The dark gods may not interfere with the living, but if your flesh-bound dragon takes Karid's life, I can claim her soul and restore the wildwoods."

Flida brushed an ethereal hand across her glittering eyes. "It saddens me that even bound to the dragon's magick the flesh of Man is so weak. He approaches the Mouth of Shadows. To unleash his fury, D'raekn must believe his mate is dead, murdered by Karid's own hand. Only then will he choose magick over Man and bring Karid back to you. I am no longer strong enough to leave these sacred woods.

Will you see to this, my lord? Tell him that you have taken Cwen of Aaradan's soul?"

"I will go to Shadowmaw and deliver your deceit, but the weight of the lie is yours as will be the consequences."

With great wings curled and heavy hind legs thrust forward to slow his descent, D'raekn landed on a ledge followed by the army of wasp soldiers. Ahead, a great pile of rubble blocked the way into the cavern known as the Mouth of Shadows.

Aenzl slipped from the dragon's withers and tapped the nearest stone with his staff. A low rumble followed, and the smaller rocks skittered among the larger boulders to cascade into the emptiness below the ledge. "A slide may take this rock shelf and us along with it."

"Watch out!" D'raekn swept the wizard up in a talon as a slow shudder shook the earth. "What did you do, Aenzl?"

"Nothing yet," the wizard sputtered as he tried to extricate himself from D'raekn's grip. "Let me down so I can work!"

"Your work may kill us all."

Another tremor began, its reverberations sending the dragon staggering as the wasps took flight and hovered. With a sudden roar, the rock face erupted in an avalanche of flying debris and dust.

D'raekn threw himself backward, tucking his head and the wizard Aenzl into safety beneath his wing.

As if stretching and awakening from a long slumber, the earth again bellowed and quaked. Then, little by little the tremors lessened until the mountain was finally quiet.

Aenzl pushed his way out from under the dragon's wing and stared into the blackness of the heart of Mount Shadowmaw. "Well? What are we waiting for?" he shouted over the hum of alarmed and angry wasps.

D'raekn shook himself in a rattling of scales and a shower of dirt and stone splinters, then crouched and took the form of man. "Keep watch!" he called to the wasp commander. "Karid's soldiers cannot be far away."

Aenzl lit a torch and together with the dragonspawn set off in search of Flida's promised power.

Hours lost in darkness brought nothing but growing frustration. Blackness, dense and stale, surrounded them. There was no evidence of men, not even a footprint in the powdering of dust that coated the cavern floor and drifted through the air like flotsam with each footfall. No scorched remnant from a dropped torch or dampness from a spilled water flask—nothing.

D'raekn took Aenzl's torch, held it high, and squinted into the gloom ahead. He played the glow of the flame over the walls on either side and discovered a passageway to their left.

"What do you feel, old man? Where within these depths of desolation does our destiny lie?"

"I do not know, D'raekn. My lame leg hurts. I am hungry, and there is no sign of Flida's promise. I think we have been abandoned." Aenzl wiped dust and spider webs off his nose, then sneezed and grumbled, "I should never have let you leave Dragon's Heart."

"Aenzl! I must find the strength Flida promised and finish my business with Karid! Then I can claim Cwen from the Noors."

Dust floated down around them as a disembodied voice echoed through the cavern's passageways, "Cwen of Aaradan is dead, executed on the altar amid the standing stones near Stonetel by Queen Karid's own hands." The air warmed around them, and the dark god's image shimmered in the torchlight.

"You lie!" D'raekn snarled and launched himself at the god, thrusting the torch flame into the mist that swirled around him. "N'dia said she was safe!"

Aenzl gripped D'raekn's arm in restraint as he asked, "Who are you, and how can you know this?"

"I am one of death's dark gods, a collector of men's souls. I myself accepted the soul of your mate. I assure you that the blood on Karid's hands is not yet dry."

"You lie! It must be a lie." D'raekn's scowl deepened and his breathing became ragged. "I would know if she were dead." His voice broke with uncertainty, and he looked to Aenzl as he had when he was a boy. "Wouldn't I know if Cwen were dead? Wouldn't I, Aenzl?"

"The gods of death cannot create a lie. It keeps them from tricking foolish men out of their souls. You know that, D'raekn. This god could not stand before us and create a lie."

D'raekn roared and slammed into the wall, pounded it with his fists until they became bloodied. "I am betrayed by you all!" He howled and cursed the gods and swore eternal retribution to be paid by Flida, Karid, and Quondam. Terrified, Aenzl crouched behind an outcropping and covered his head.

With a final human wail of despair followed by the brilliant flash of transformation, D'raekn took the dragon's form and snapped angry jaws in the dark god's direction. "Tell me where my magick lies! Give me the power to challenge Karid! I will kill her with my bare hands!"

"You must choose, dragonspawn. Magick or Man, who do you serve? Whose kingdom will you claim—that of the dragon or that of Man?" the dark god questioned. "Once taken, the path cannot be changed."

D'raekn raised his scales in threat and rumbled deep within his gullet, "Do not play games with me! What path will bring me Karid's head?"

"Only magick is strong enough to win against Karid's flesh-bound spirit. A man alone would have no chance."

"Where is this dragon's magick?"

"In the tower." Death's god shattered the wall behind D'raekn and revealed a flight of stairs. "In the tower you will find what you seek."

The dragon growled, "Follow me Aenzl!" and squeezed through the opening, sending a shower of sparks where his scales scraped against the stone.

Flida's message delivered and the dragonspawn enraged, death's messenger murmured, "I would not like to be you, Flida, when he discovers your lie."

Images of Cwen swam before D'raekn. Her remembered scent filled his nostrils, and her first laugh rang in his head. How could she be gone? He raked his talons along the wall as he ascended the stairs and showered the trailing wizard with flakes of sharp rock and searing sparks.

"D'raekn! Do not do this to yourself!" Aenzl called out. "It's not your fault that Cwen is dead."

The dragon spun on Aenzl and snarled, "Don't say that she is dead! She lives in my mind, and if I find her blood on Karid's hands, I will shred the queen's flesh and eat her soul!"

He swung away from the old man and continued upward toward a growing luminescence, a sustained low pitched rumble giving vent to his anguish and anger. At the top of the stairs, he stepped into a large chamber, shook himself, and roared as new memories assailed him—Cwen's fear of loving, of trusting, of allowing another to share her burden. He had sworn he would see her fearless and her heart tender. Now she was gone. He shook his head to clear away the images that filled his mind, of Cwen standing in his yard, sitting on the sand, joyous as she met the merfolk. He snarled. He bellowed and raged as he crashed into the wall and caused a small avalanche of rocks from above.

Let her go, D'raekn. Accept your destiny. Take the power of the dragon, seek your revenge against Karid, and free yourself of this pain. Let go of Man, and take the magick of the dragon.

Flida's voice filled the dragon's mind, soothing him with the promise of freedom from his grief and heartache.

"Why are you not here beside me, Flida? How could you allow this to happen?"

Karid did this, not I! Karid took the girl's life. I know that you are in pain. I know that you are angry. Seek your revenge, and then come home to the wildwoods where you can be free from these memories of the flesh. Come to me.

D'raekn drew a great breath and pondered the future. What did it matter if he never took the flesh again, forgot the memories of warmth and love, the first swelling of his human heart when he had touched Cwen's dreams. What matter if he let Cwen go? It was then that he knew he was thinking about dying. A sudden quickening of his pulse, and he was ready to let go.

"Where is my promised power?"

You need only ask for it, and it will appear. The choice is yours, a life of flesh as king among men or the dragon's power over magick.

With his great head bowed, his voice boomed out and reverberated around the room, "Father Dragon, I beseech you, bestow the power of the dragon lords upon your sanctified son."

There was a tiny spark and then a muffled beat that grew until the chamber was filled with the pounding of the dragon lord's heartbeat. A pulsing orb appeared before D'raekn. Blue-white with flashes of deepest indigo, it was the dark emptiness of the frigid realm of dragonkin. D'raekn inhaled deeply and drew the raw power of ice and frost into his lungs. His body grew—twice, then thrice as large as it had been. Within his mind a flame of hatred sparked, and he bellowed his demand, "Where is Karid?"

"My lord…" Aenzl crept from his hiding place behind the fallen stones. "She leads her army through the mountain pass south of Stonetel."

"How do you know this, wizard?"

"I do not know, my lord, it is simply in my head, an image that came with your summoning of the power, but I know that it is true."

D'raekn lifted the old wizard and settled him amid the scales at the base of his neck. With a roar, the dragon smashed through the rock wall and soared high above the mountain's peak into the night sky. Snarling and snapping, he charged forward through the mass of hovering wasp warriors and swooped downward along the craggy face of Shadowmaw, a scarlet streak sweeping along the pass that opened onto the river valley.

The wasp commander came alongside in a surge of speed. "A messenger brings word from B'rma at the border of the Feverous Forest. She has been joined by humans. Farmers, herders, and some Saedan women somehow freed from the affliction of the fire crystals. Thousands have gathered to join in the fight against Queen Karid. And the valley fireflies lead the stryvers and the boak miners from the East. They will soon block the northern pass at Karid's back."

"And the girl, N'dia. Have she and the hellwings found the queen's alchemist?"

"They have. We are warned to be alert for fire in the sky. The hellwings have planted the black power of the miners in the crystal storehouses. They await your command to destroy Karid's supply."

"Send a messenger to N'dia with directions to blow the dragon's breath at daybreak, twelve days hence. It is then that I will take Karid's life."

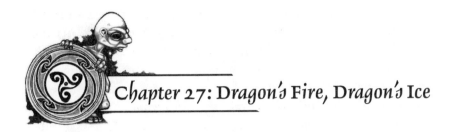

Chapter 27: Dragon's Fire, Dragon's Ice

N'dia hid beneath the sand no more than an arm's length from the nearest fire guard. As the shadows lengthened, she peered out through a slit in the trapdoor that kept her hidden from view. The hellwings stood among the shadows along the walls of the mine, unseen by the miners and assassins. Not even the alchemist himself was aware of their presence as they plagued his workshop and storerooms and scattered the explosive black powder.

To the east, the sky mirrored the early roseate opalescence that precedes the rise of the sun above the horizon. It was then that the hellwings would light the powder and destroy Karid's stockpile of dragon's breath.

N'dia heard a rustle to her right and turned to see the she-shadow, whose silent words anticipated her satisfaction. *Only a fool would store such a large quantity of flammable material in one location. The earth will shatter, and the sky will be ablaze with fiery destruction once the crystals combust!*

"Will they see it in Stonetel?"

See it? They will feel it! The whole of Quondam from Achroma to Dragonfire will shiver under our assault. The dust above will blaze as brilliant as noonday.

N'dia smiled and said, "Good. I would hate to think our efforts were wasted."

Humans are blind…except for the Noor, of course. The Saedan assassins pass within inches of us and see nothing, and they sense no threat. How can they be so oblivious to danger?

"They don't expect it. They have grown complacent under Karid's iron rule. They cannot believe any would dare to challenge her."

The redeemer grows strong. Do you feel it?

"Aye, she-shadow, and my sword hums with his new found fury. By tomorrow, Karid will be dead and Quondam freed."

And now we should go and join the dragonspawn. It would not do to be here when the mines blow.

The she-shadow drew N'dia beneath her wing and swept her away amid the swirling shadows of the rising hellwing flock.

On a small hillock overlooking Karid's camp, Sóvië, Elle, and Tyne watched the shadowed border at the forest's edge as daylight tinged the eastern sky.

"You should have done as Cwen asked," Tyne said with a frown.

"I am needed here." Sóvië fingered the glowing pendant, the jewel Elle called the bounty of the gods. "We need to make our way into the woods where there is movement beneath the trees and noise, like the hum of a hornet's nest."

"It is the waspwomen," Tyne said. "They bow only to their queen and the dragon lord. It tells us D'raekn is there, somewhere."

They moved forward stealthily, keeping to the shadowed side of the hill, running awkwardly in a half squat when they could no longer see the queen's encampment. They slowed as they reached the tree line and tried to determine the direction of the growing drone.

"There," Elle pointed and continued making her way deeper into the woods.

"What are you doing here?" A Noor woman stepped from deep shadow, backed by several well-armed wasp soldiers. "Didn't we tell you to take Cwen and leave Quondam?"

"We must see D'raekn. We have the bounty of the gods," Elle explained.

"She tells the truth," Sóvië added. "Apparently the jewel of my birthright is also the bounteous gift you seek. It is the amulet of the Dragon Queen, given to the women of Aaradan by the Sojourners who created Ædracmoræ, my home world. I am beginning to believe we share the same gods. Perhaps we should talk to your dragonspawn about his legend."

B'rma stared at the pendant in Sóvië's hand and muttered, "Cwen had it all this time. J'var gave it to her when we arrived on Dragon's Heart Isle. How is it that D'raekn did not know what it was?" She shook off a sudden feeling of unease and with it the realization that she had again underestimated Cwen's importance. With a glance at the lightening sky, she summoned, "Come with me. There is very little time. At daybreak, war will come to Quondam."

D'raekn's scales raised in annoyance at the sight of B'rma and the strangers. "I asked to be left alone!"

Sóvië stood silent and examined the halfling dragon as he returned her stare. She would not have thought such a union possible, and she had worked beside dragons all her life. She held out the pendant and watched confusion claim D'raekn's face.

"Why do you have Cwen's jewel?"

"Not hers, mine. I am Sóvië, daughter of Yávië and heir to the throne of the Dragon Queen. I am told by C'thra's greatdaughter, Elle, that it has some meaning here as well."

Elle peeked around Sóvië, drew nearer, and bowed. "I am Elle, and this is my brother Tyne. Our greatmother C'thra was your surrogate. She loved you very much and wanted you to have a life beyond the prison isle. This jewel is the bounty of the gods you seek. It began to pulse with life as soon as it was passed to Sóvië's hand."

"Passed by whom?" D'raekn asked. "When last I saw it...when last I saw it, Cwen of Aaradan carried it."

"Aye, and it was Cwen who gave it to me and told me to go home." Sóvië shrugged. "Obviously, I didn't do as she asked—too much curiosity about her...and you. So explain it to me. How did my cousin end up the mate of a dragonspawn? She's always had loose morals, but this is—"

D'raekn's tail lashed out and knocked Sóvië's feet out from under her. His jaws snapped a hand's breadth from her eyes, and his snarl rearranged the hair around her face. "Enough! You will not disrespect Cwen! Not now, not ever! Is that clear?" His foretalon slammed the ground at her side.

Tyne helped Sóvië to her feet, and she brushed the dirt from her clothes and smoothed her hair after picking out bits of grass. "It is abundantly clear. If you have such passion for her, why did she marry—?"

"He told you to shut up!" B'rma slapped Sóvië hard enough to send her staggering.

Sóvië rubbed her cheek and shouted, "What is wrong with you people? Is the truth simply beyond your comprehension?"

"Your truth will get us all killed!" B'rma glared.

An explosion with all the fury of a meteor strike prevented Sóvië from responding. The fire crystals in the mines below the Alabaster Wastes had been blasted. A blinding flash of light was followed by a towering, mushroom-shaped cloud of sand and smoke that raced out in all directions. From its midst rained earth and rock. Some boulders were as large as the isle of Endhaven. The heat from the blast liquefied the sand, fusing it into glass as it fell back to the ground and collapsed into a sinkhole as wide as a four day walk. The resulting shockwave rippled outward, and the ground beneath them began to move in the serpentine undulations of a storm at sea.

Wasps took to the air, as did the dragon. The earthbound humans were flung far and wide and lay hugging tree roots and clinging to bushes in an attempt to steady themselves.

Followed by the wasps and a horde of screaming humans, D'raekn surged across the open wetlands of the Fungal Shroud.

Karid stared in horror as the dragonspawn's wasp army struck with its unimaginably destructive force. The winged warriors blew through Karid's army as if it were made of fog. It was impossible to block out the deafening waves of sound that battered her, and her body vibrated with the wasps' aural onslaught.

The waspwomen landed, overwhelming Karid's army by sheer weight of numbers, slashing and stinging the queen's stunned Emyute soldiers, while D'raekn's icy breath immobilized the fire guards and allowed the mandibles of the wasp warriors to decapitate the remaining threat. Screeching humans fell on bodies still writhing in the agony of mortal wounds, pounding them to their death with pikestaffs and clubs.

Within minutes the battleground became a banquet, a feast, as the wasps dismembered the dead and dying, and workers arrived to carry off the flesh that would feed their queen's new brood.

Sóvië, Elle, and Tyne raced across the killing fields, slashing their way through Karid's wall of Emyute soldiers as they burst beyond the trees at the northern edge of the morning's heavy mist.

Ahead of the others, Sóvië slid to an abrupt halt and stared at the heat shrouded figure, an assassin that D'raekn's chill breath had missed. The woman's eyes narrowed, and the air around her burst into flame. With a flash of her hands, the fire swept forward, engulfing Sóvië and those arriving in her wake.

Instinctively, Sóvië, Elle, and Tyne covered their faces and flung themselves to the ground as the super heated air crackled and flamed. The surrounding woods echoed the firestorm's consumption of everything in its path, leaving behind the strangled hiss of dying vegetation and a rain of powdered ash.

Karid's assassin stepped forward to examine the soot covered bodies, a look of shocked disbelief widening her eyes as Sóvië's sword pierced her heart.

"Bitch!" Sóvië screamed, her trembling hands reclaiming the blood smeared blade.

"Thank the gods that low dose of crystals worked," her words tumbled out on shuddering breath.

"Aye," Tyne slapped her on the shoulder. "Come, we must find the dragonspawn." He grabbed Elle's hand and gave Sóvië a push in the direction that D'raekn had disappeared.

The dragon's keen eyes picked Karid out among the remains of her scattered soldiers.

The queen looked up when the dense shadow passed overhead, and then she turned and raced for cover. She ran, slipped, and fell, then struggled up and stumbled onward, the thunder of D'raekn's footfalls tracking her on the right. With each turn she made, the dragon countered, drawing ever nearer. As Karid tore through a stand of narrow saplings, the dragon thudded to the ground ahead of her, jaws wide and talon raised to strike.

"My power is far greater than yours! Your soldiers flee my winged warriors. Your assassins' flames are quenched by the chill gift of my father's breath! Today I take your life as you took Cwen's!"

Karid staggered back and grabbed an overhanging limb to keep from falling. "I did not kill the woman! Who told you such a lie?"

D'raekn stomped, and the ground around Karid trembled with his strength. "Do not toy with me, false queen. The god of death himself has sworn he took her soul, and unlike you, death's god cannot create a lie." Swift as a serpent he reached out and snatched Karid, a single talon piercing her flesh.

She struggled to catch her breath and screamed, "I do not lie! The woman was wed among the standing stones on fullmoon's eve! J'var, the son of Director A'bach, has taken her to Achroma as his wife! Would I lie in the face of death?"

"You would say anything to live!"

He closed his fist tighter, and Karid begged, "Take me to Flida! Make her swear before us that your woman is dead, that it was not a lie! Make her summon the god who cursed me! He will tell you the truth! He must! I did not kill Cwen of Aaradan!"

"It is true!" Sóvië shouted from above, repeating her words as the wasp warrior landed, and she leapt to the ground. "It is true! Cwen lives! She believed you dead and went along with the marriage plans in the hope of getting close enough to this so-called queen to drive a dagger through her heart. But Elle told Cwen you lived, and Cwen hesitated. The only way for Cwen to then save herself was to go through with the wedding. Everyone has lied to you. They have used your own obsession as a weapon against you. Evil as she may be, don't kill this woman for a sin she has not committed, although it would seem prudent to find out why your gods have lied."

D'raekn eyed Sóvië and the massive wasp army that landed behind her carrying B'rma, Aenzl, Elle, and Tyne.

"Don't mistake my words," Sóvië continued. "I want your queen dead. I would gladly rip out her heart myself, but not for a lie."

"She speaks the truth! I did not tell you for fear it would distract you from your task," B'rma acknowledged.

A deep frown forged a V-shape on D'raekn's scaly forehead. "What could be more important than the truth, B'rma? Aenzl—does Cwen live?"

The old wizard scrubbed his face with both hands and tugged at the age-white whiskers flowing down his chest. "I truly do not know. The greatdaughter of C'thra swears that it is so, as do Cwen's kin and B'rma. Why would any of them lie now? You hold the demon queen, and regardless of Cwen's life or death, Karid's crimes against Quondam

shall justify her execution whether here or within the sacred woods."
Aenzl reached out and stroked D'raekn's tense wing. "Boy, only Flida
can explain the choices of the gods, but if Cwen has accepted the
Noor, then she belongs to him."

D'raekn lifted Karid near enough that she felt her flesh stiffen
beneath the frost of his breath. "I will do as you ask. Flida will
decide your fate, and I will decide hers." To Sóvië and the others he
commanded, "Follow me." With a snap of leathery wings, D'raekn
lifted off to deliver Karid to her judgment in the wildwoods.

Chapter 28: Legend and Lie

Flida appeared in a twinkle of starlight, her evanescent features shifting with delight. The dragonspawn approached, and before him staggered the bruised and bloodied Karid.

"You are delivered, and by your death the wildwoods will be saved," Flida said to Karid. Then turning to the dragonspawn, she said, "You must kill her, D'raekn. For her sins are many and her crimes great."

The dragon's tail snaked forward and slid around his captive. "But she did not kill Cwen, did she?"

"D'raekn, why would you ask this?" Flida asked. "Did not the god of death tell you he took her soul? It is not possible for one of death's gods to create a lie. It is against the laws that bind him."

D'raekn leaned close and whispered in a deep, gravelly voice, "Did *he* create the lie? Summon him, and we shall see."

Flida's form grew more deeply shadowed, drawing in upon itself to create a more substantial presence. "You dare to question me, dragonspawn. I am your creator!"

"Summon the god!" the dragon's booming bellow scattered Flida's shimmering countenance, his frozen breath shooting across the distance between them and sending ice particles spinning in every direction.

Karid laughed out loud and said, "Your beast seems to have a mind of his own. If my servants were so insolent, I would have their tongues seared and fed to the dogs."

Flida gathered herself in a twinkle of motes and hissed, "I could crush you both!"

"Could you? Or have you lost the power to control those within the wildwood? Is your fear truly for the sacred forest or merely for yourself?" D'raekn prowled closer. "Summon the god of death—the one you say took Cwen's soul."

"Do you call me, dragon?" Overhead the heavens opened, and the dark god emerged from the swirling smoke-colored clouds.

D'raekn rumbled, "I would know the truth. Were your words a lie? Does the woman Cwen live?"

"They were no lies of my making. Your creator merely cast me as her messenger in the hope of seeing you complete your task. But I see the curse-bound Karid still lives in the flesh." A shake of his head covered those around him in a shower of heavy rain, and he reminded Flida, "I warned you that the lie would bring consequences. It seems you cannot control your dragon."

"Does Cwen live?" D'raekn repeated.

Flida allowed tendrils of her warmth to cloak D'raekn. "I did it for you, D'raekn. So that you could choose wisely, claim your rightful place here beside me in the wildwoods. Allowing you to pursue the woman would only have brought us failure," Flida admitted. "You must take heart that although Cwen is beyond your grasp, she is alive."

"You cannot keep her from me. I have delivered Karid as your legend requires. My life is my own now. I may choose Man or magick—that was your promise."

"You have already chosen, D'raekn. You can no longer take the form of man, and by the words Cwen has spoken—by the cord that binds her—until her death, she belongs to the Noor. There is nothing you can do. I know your heart is heavy, but I can relieve you of that burden, take those painful memories away. I can help you, D'raekn. If only you will kill Karid and free her from the flesh, I can help you."

D'raekn scanned the faces of those surrounding him. Wasp warriors waited as far as the eye could see—warriors that had followed the great red dragon, the redeemer of legend who would free those cursed by Karid. B'rma stood expressionless and stoic, and Aenzl wrinkled with his worry and distress. The Saedans, Elle and her brother Tyne, so positive that Cwen's jewel was the bounty of the gods, stared anxiously at D'raekn. The dark daughter of Aaradan, Sóvië, had asked if truth was foreign to the inhabitants of Quondam, and it seemed it was, for not even the gods were above deception.

"Remove her flesh yourself. I am not the beast of your legend. I am not the redeemer of the cursed or the king of men. You have lied to me and taken all I cared for. I am free of you." D'raekn held out his open palm to Aenzl. "I am going home, will you come with me?"

The old man looked at D'raekn with sad eyes, and his lips trembled as he replied, "Aye, boy, there is nothing for you here."

"I suppose this means that I may leave?" Karid suggested, looking hopeful.

"Hold her, sorceress!" Flida ordered B'rma. "Her separation from the flesh will come at the order of the eldermen she has corrupted. Take her to Stonetel and bind her over to the director there. Send a fleet of hellwings or waspwomen to summon the council of elders to the executioner's glen."

Beyond the throng, unseen and shadowed by the hellwings, N'dia watched as the rightful king of Quondam and his wizard broke free. The loss of Cwen had stripped D'raekn more thoroughly than all the years under the scourge of Karid.

N'dia swung to the she-shadow. "Do you recall my mother's garden?"

I know it well, young sorceress.

"We need to undo a grave injustice and free Quondam's king."

The hellwing leader swept out a wing and pointed skyward.

All hope has been abandoned by our redeemer, our king. He has not lifted the curse that covers us. Flida's legend fails.

"Yes, but I know where the true legend lives and hope resides. Flida and the dark god have overlooked the greatest magick, the mystery of the heart. Take me to my mother's garden."

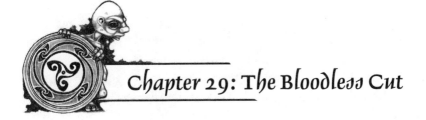

Chapter 29: The Bloodless Cut

Cwen was as good as her word. At home she shared her husband's meals and conversations, walked with him along the shore, and allowed the touch of his lips against her temple. She accompanied him to public functions, smiling appropriately and feigning interest in matters of state and the trade directorate.

When wild rumors surfaced of cataclysmic ruptures in the mines beneath the Alabaster Wastes, and when battles waged within the Fungal Shroud led by the dragonspawn, J'var called them lies intended to inflame those loyal to the queen. He swore that the dragon's head had been seized by Karid's soldiers and mounted on Stonetel's parapet while the body was left to rot and feed wild scavengers.

Cwen's sorrow deepened with each dreamless night as she wished and prayed to see the hooded man in her dreams once again. Unbeknownst to J'var or his father, she sought solace in the moonlit shadows of the forbidden gardens of D'lana the sorceress. Every night from midnight until the first blush of dawn's light, Cwen wandered aimlessly among the overgrowth of the gardens to avoid the emptiness of her sleep.

She whispered to D'raekn in the darkness, "Where are you? I search for you within my mind and listen for the whisper of your soul, but still you hide from me. Why, why do you hide? I do not fear death, D'raekn. I would join you in your eternal sleep if only you would say you want me." Another wave of sorrow, this one sharp as the blade that sliced the loaf at A'bach's table, cut through her.

"He cannot." N'dia slipped from the darkness of the she-shadow's wing. "He believes you are lost to him. First, he thought you dead, and now he believes you belong to my brother. But my brother can no longer hold you with lies."

"N'dia? Are you the spirit that visited D'raekn at the ruins of SuVgo? Shall I summon your brother so that he might find comfort in your apparition?"

"Comfort is not what I wish for J'var. He lied to you, Cwen. So many times he has lied to you. D'raekn has fled with Aenzl, sorrow stealing the dragon's strength and sending him into the dark, and look at you, you are a frail specter of the woman the stryvers found and brought to me. My brother has done this, and I will not allow it to continue. Quondam needs a king."

"If you are not a spirit, how is it that you live?"

"You are not listening to me, Cwen!" N'dia pinched the flesh of Cwen's upper arm and twisted until the woman cried out. "Can a spirit do that?"

Cwen rubbed the reddening welt and blinked several times as she attempted to untangle the confusion within her mind. "D'raekn lives?"

"Yes, D'raekn lives. That is why I have come. He has abandoned the legend, because without you there is none. He basks in self-pity and hopelessness, just as you do." N'dia reached into her knapsack and withdrew a circlet of scarlet cord—endless, the binding cord of Cwen's marriage to J'var.

"I cannot be free unless J'var cuts the cord, and he will not," Cwen said, her voice trembling with sorrow. "Even though I do not love him or give him any physical pleasure, he will not let me go. He has told me as much, that until my death I am bound to him by the words of promise and the handfasting."

"We will see about that." N'dia smiled and took Cwen's hand. "You cannot be held by lies, Cwen, though no one in Quondam seems to remember the power of the truth." She gave a little grimace and added, "Your kinswoman has made note of that on several occasions."

"Sóvië remains in Quondam?" Cwen asked with concern in her voice. "I thought she went home. I told her to go home. Is she safe?"

"Along with her companions and B'rma, she tidies up in the West. She and B'rma guard Karid in Stonetel until the council convenes and sanctifies her execution. It seems that with the jewel of her birthright and B'rma's sorcery, they have formed a barrier from which Karid cannot escape."

"My cousin must go home, she is promised to a Xavian empath, and together they will rule my home world with wisdom and courage."

"She will return when her task here is complete. She knows the way." N'dia wrapped the handfasting cord around her forearm and made her way toward the garden gate with Cwen in tow.

"You have grown very wise, N'dia."

"Aye, with the acceptance of my mother's sword and the freeing of the dragon's power, my fate is sealed, and I will serve Quondam's king. Now, come and we will show my brother the future of his servitude."

"J'var?"

J'var rubbed sleep from his eyes and scratched his head as he peered into the gloom. "Who is there? Cwen?"

"Aye, it is Cwen and another. Have you so soon forgotten me, my brother?" asked N'dia.

The Noor shot up from his bed so quickly that he slipped on the corner of the bedcover and went sprawling. He rolled, sprang to his feet, and spun around toward the moonlit balcony where N'dia stood with Cwen.

"Why have you come to haunt me, sister?" J'var managed to choke out through his fear and disbelief.

N'dia pushed Cwen ahead of her and lit the wall torches with a twig from the fireplace. "I am not a spirit, although everyone I meet seems to think I am. I did not die in the barrens, J'var. An old friend of our mother's saved me."

"N'dia," J'var dropped before his sister and held her, relieved sobs coming in great gasps. "I thought you gone forever."

"I can tell. Without my guidance, you have lost your way. What is this?" She pulled free of J'var and held out the handfasting cord.

J'var wiped his eyes and stared. "How did you get that? It is mine."

"Yours?" N'dia shook her head. "Rightfully it belongs to D'raekn, or at least it should. How could you do this? How could you lie, just to have a woman? A woman who does not even love you."

"She will in time. When the pain of loss fades, she will come to love me. I am good to her, kind and generous."

"There is no loss, J'var, and I believe you know that," N'dia accused.

"He is dead, the dragonspawn is dead," J'var claimed desperately. "The Emyutes brought word that they found his body and that Karid demanded his head."

"J'var, Cwen knows he lives. And I know that you cannot hold her. By the laws of marriage, you cannot bind a woman with deception. Cut the cord, and set her free."

"No!" J'var held out his hand to Cwen. "Do not leave me. I will give you anything if you will stay."

"I cannot love you, J'var. I told you that even when I believed D'raekn dead. I must go to him."

"Then you will be arrested!" J'var yelled, dropping Cwen's hand. "It is against Quondam's laws for a woman to leave a marriage without the consent of the husband."

"What is going on? Your shouting woke me," A'bach's voice called from the doorway. His gaze fell upon N'dia, and he blinked in disbelief. "Daughter? N'dia?" A'bach said, his voice softening. "I thought you dead. We searched but did not find you. I thought the dragonspawn had killed you!"

"Father!" N'dia rushed to her father and buried her face against his chest. "O, Father, it is so good to see you."

He held N'dia out and gingerly touched the firefly's handprint on her cheek. "Your mother wore that mark, the mark of magick. N'dia, what have you done?"

"Compared to J'var, nothing of consequence—I helped the hellwings blow up Karid's fire crystal supply and arrived within the wildwoods in time to see B'rma take charge of the captive Karid. Then the lord D'raekn denounced his birthright and slunk off with the old wizard Aenzl." N'dia narrowed her eyes, thinking about J'var's sins. "My brother, however, has broken every law of love and marriage. He has stolen another's woman through deception without a moment's remorse. And now, when I call him on it, he denies it and threatens her with arrest. What kind of son have you raised, Father?"

A'bach rubbed a hand across his eyes and sank into the nearest chair. "What is N'dia talking about J'var?"

"I don't know. She crept in here in the middle of the night and started spouting some nonsense about Cwen deserving to be released from her vows. I believe that witch B'rma and the demon dragonspawn have somehow bewitched her."

"You are a liar!" Cwen screamed and flew at J'var with balled fists, pounding futilely against the stony muscles of his chest. "You hate D'raekn, and you would do anything to steal the throne. I heard you say to L'or that the dragonspawn's woman would lead you to the throne. Do you deny it?"

"It was nothing, a joke…" J'var threw up his hands.

"L'or!" A'bach bellowed toward the hallway. Turning to the others, he commanded, "Sit down! All of you sit down! I will not have my house turned on its head by the accusations of a foreigner, even if she is the wife of my son. Now, sit down."

"Father," N'dia began.

"Sit down!"

"Yes, Father." N'dia dropped to a stool next to Cwen and reassured her, "Soon they will understand. I promise that they will."

Cwen tried to smile but merely managed to look even more miserable and tired.

L'or arrived, looking sleepy and confused, but the sight of N'dia brought a grin, and he lifted her up over his head and spun her about. "What's this?" he touched the handprint on N'dia's cheek. "Why didn't someone call me when they found you?"

"No one found her. She brought herself here with some unbelievable tales along with that brand on her face and serious charges against your brother. Put your sister down and sit. I will not have this chaos before my morning tea," A'bach said. "Answer me this, did your brother tell you he was marrying Cwen of Aaradan in hopes that it would lead to a promotion?"

"He wanted D'raekn dead! He wants to be king!" Cwen stood, fury overcoming caution. "I heard him tell you. And now that N'dia has told me that he lied, he threatens to have me arrested because I want to be free of him."

N'dia held up the binding cord and twirled it about. "He needs only cut it to do the right thing."

"Well, L'or?" A'bach glared at his youngest son.

"He made light of it, but it was his plan. To marry Cwen and keep her hidden until the dragonspawn killed Karid and the council executed him. A new king would require a vote of the council." L'or shrugged. "I would have suggested that you recommend your firstborn."

"All of you have used me!" Cwen cried. "What you have done is far worse than anything Karid or the Emyutes did to me. You are wicked and without honor." Cwen walked to the door. "Have me arrested. I would rather rot in prison than stay another day in this house."

The sound of a sword being drawn was loud in the sudden shocked silence. N'dia stood before J'var and held out the glowing crystal sword, hilt first. "Set her free. Set Quondam's legend free, J'var—the legend of our mother. Do you not love me enough to give me this gift?"

"N'dia, I…" he met his sister's eyes, saw the spirit there, and accepted her sword.

She lifted the handfasting cord and slipped it over the blade point. J'var looked to the emptiness where Cwen had stood a moment before and slashed the cord. Once cut, the cord disintegrated and drifted to the floor.

N'dia reclaimed her sword, slid it into its scabbard and framed her brother's face with her hands. "I love you, J'var, and so does B'rma." As she headed out the door, she called to her father and L'or, "I'll be back after I go see a dragon."

"N'dia!" A'bach bellowed.

But a backward glance and a blown kiss were all N'dia spared her father.

"Cwen," N'dia shouted and raced to catch up with the dragonspawn's mate.

"I don't care, N'dia. He can have me arrested, or have me killed. I just don't care."

"He cut the cord."

Cwen stopped and turned to N'dia. "What?"

"J'var cut the cord, just like I told you he would," N'dia eagerly replied. "You are free. So what will you do now?"

"I do not know." Cwen looked small, frail, and uncertain. "First, find Sóvië, and see that she goes home."

N'dia grinned mischievously. "A good start. You will find her in Stonetel. After that, after your cousin is safe, you should really go see a dragon about an island." She winked and walked back toward her mother's garden and the waiting hellwing.

"Where are you going?" Cwen called after her.

"To find a mother who is still lost."

"I don't understand! Will I see you again?"

N'dia picked up her pace and waved back over her shoulder. "I suppose that depends entirely on you." She hurried on, anxious to search for C'thra within the Mouth of Shadows.

Chapter 30: The Surrogate

"We have to find C'thra!" N'dia shouted above the wind.

The she-shadow nodded and circled the base of Mount Shadowmaw. *There is the entrance to the cavern. From the cloud of frost above the mount, I would say our redeemer rests within.*

"And his elder, I suppose. Why is it that everything is so difficult? Why can't a legend just unfold the way it was told?"

Tricksters every one. Gods and men are all tricksters, and our dragon lord is young...

They landed in soft snow at the cave entrance. With the hellwing's words echoing in her mind, N'dia lit torches and handed one to the she-shadow. "Let's find C'thra. Only she has the power to see us through this maze and out the other side. Even in death, she will know what to do to save D'raekn."

"Someone's in the tunnels!" Aenzl smacked the sleeping dragon on the muzzle. "Who could it be? Karid's soldiers come to kill us?"

D'raekn snorted and opened his eyes. "Go away, old man, and let me sleep. Karid awaits her death in Flida's chains," he said despondently.

"Aren't you curious?"

"No! Now go away. Why don't you go down the mountain and return to the island. I do not need you anymore."

"You need me more than ever. You can't just sleep until you die! Why aren't you out hunting for Cwen? You could kill J'var and take her back."

"Aenzl, she is bound by the laws of men. I am no longer Man, and to take her by force would only result in my death—or hers. Besides, what could I offer her if I did take her from the Noor? Look at me! I thought I was a beast when I was neither Man nor magick, but now? What could I offer a woman?"

"There has to be a way."

"There is no way. C'thra is dead, and Flida wants no part of me unless I allow her to strip my memories from me."

"You did the right thing. Not killing Karid."

D'raekn nodded and sighed. "It was the right thing. I could not kill her simply because of another's mistake. The god made her flesh. The god made her what she is. Like Flida made me what I am."

"But Karid is wicked, really evil—someone should kill her."

"Get out Aenzl before I eat you!"

The old man muttered and shuffled off in search of the intruders, his staff at the ready and his rheumy eyes swimming in the dim torchlight. "It's cold in here. Least you could do is light a fire!" he shouted back toward the resting dragon.

Tipping and tilting, Aenzl kept one hand on the wall and squinted into the passageway ahead. He held his breath and heard a distant voice and the scuff of boots on the earthen floor. One step at a time, tiptoeing to avoid making any sound, the wizard crept forward with a torch in one hand and his staff raised aloft in the other. As he rounded the corner, the shadows blurred and shifted, and he slammed his stick into their midst.

Shrill howling preceded deep wailing and snarling, and the old man cast a spell of aversion and backed away.

"Aenzl!" D'raekn's deep bellow echoed off the walls, and the shudder of the tunnel brought the thunder of his heavy steps. "Where are you, old man?"

"Here! Here!" Aenzl shouted. "There's an army of them 'round the corner." He grabbed hold of D'raekn's scales and shimmied himself up to the dragon's withers. "A whole army, I tell you! Right around the bend."

D'raekn poked his nose around the corner and sniffed. "Smells like a woman and by the sounds of her, one in quite a bit of pain."

He stuck his head around a bit further.

"N'dia? What are you doing here?" He slipped into the corridor and lifted the girl to her feet.

She brushed herself off and looked up. "What was that? Suddenly something crashed into us, and then a charge of energy came out of nowhere and gave us a terrible shock."

"That would have been Aenzl. And I suppose you are the army he refers to?"

"Army? It is just me and the she-shadow." N'dia looked behind her, suddenly realizing that the hellwing was missing. "She-shadow, where are you? Are you hurt?"

The ceiling bulged and swayed, and the she-shadow dropped to the ground. *Insane old man…*

"Not really, but I fear he grows bored, and a small noise creates a large image in his feeble mind. Now, why are you here, N'dia?"

"I am looking for C'thra."

D'raekn scowled. "The sorceress C'thra is dead."

"Aye, perhaps, but didn't Flida tell you to find her? You never did. So, I thought I would see what I could find. I did not expect to find you two here."

"I await death, and Aenzl has chosen to annoy me until it comes," D'raekn despaired.

"Cwen is free. I thought you would want to know. She's gone after her cousin Sóvië, and then I guess they will go home."

D'raekn tilted his head and studied N'dia. "You are not as clever as you believe. It does not matter where Cwen is or what she does. In a moment of fury, when I believed Karid had killed Cwen, I chose magick. There is no future for us. She is flesh, and I am…well, even a young and inexperienced woman like you should see the problem."

"Where is the pouch that the wasp queen gave B'rma?" N'dia asked. "It held a gift for Cwen. Do you know what happened to it?"

"I don't know what you are talking about," D'raekn said with growing annoyance, "and changing the subject does not change my plight."

Seated amidst D'raekn's scales, Aenzl shifted and admitted, "After the wasp queen gave you her sting, she gave B'rma a small tattered pouch. She said it contained a gift from C'thra and that it was for Cwen, not for you. I guess we forgot to tell you when you regained consciousness." Aenzl raised an eyebrow. "As far as I know, B'rma still carries it in her satchel. We were all afraid to look inside."

"Why would C'thra leave a gift behind for Cwen?" D'raekn asked. "In all her teachings, she never spoke Cwen's name. She only told me that a woman would come to release me—the woman born beneath the sign of the serpent. That was Cwen."

"Well it could have been her cousin," N'dia suggested. "Maybe you chose the wrong woman."

The dragon shook his head. "I did not dream of her cousin. I shared my dreams with Cwen."

"You should share her dreams now. She is so alone and lonely."

"Go about your business, N'dia, and leave us alone." D'raekn turned to leave.

"She needs you!" N'dia called after him.

D'raekn moved off down the corridor, back the way he had come. "She needs a man, and I am not a man."

"She does not care! Are you really that stupid?"

D'raekn crashed against the wall as he swung back to face N'dia. "What can you possibly know about it? I love her. Do you understand that? I love her, and so I let her go."

"Legends," N'dia spat. "I have seen more intelligence on the underside of a mushroom. What must I do to make you see?" Her eyes watered, and she swiped away tears. "She loves you too! It doesn't matter what you are. She loves your soul, D'raekn. She loves your soul. And no amount of leaving her will ever change that."

"Cwen cannot even speak of it. She is too damaged to let herself love. She told me so," D'raekn insisted. "She said she could not love me and did not want me. She said the reason Flida chose her was because she would not distract me from my task."

"She doesn't have to say it, for it's as plain as the glow on that wizard's staff. Her heart aches with grief, just like yours. And Flida is wrong. She might be able to take Cwen from your mind, but never from your heart. I may be young and inexperienced, but I know love. Help me find C'thra," N'dia begged. "Take a chance. Quondam needs you, and without Cwen you are useless."

"He's not useless!" Aenzl argued. "He is just contrary and a bit cantankerous because he hasn't—"

"Aenzl! Watch yourself," D'raekn interrupted. "I am also quite hungry, and even a skinny old wizard may soon begin to sound tasty." To the hellwing standing silently at N'dia's side, D'raekn remarked, "You are awfully quiet, she-shadow. What do you think of N'dia's quest for the sorceress C'thra?"

The hellwing stretched and allowed her wings to flutter for a moment before folding them again. *I think that humans lack sagacity and harmony. If they did not, I would no longer wear the gray of Karid's curse.*

"I am not human."

Ah, but you are, and more than you know.

"Will you help us find C'thra's tomb?" N'dia asked.

D'raekn's expression softened. "You waste your time, young sorceress. I have seen C'thra's tomb. I have rested beside her through the night in the hope of some consolation. There is nothing there but a silent sepulchre and the cold emptiness of the cavern."

"Will you show me? I cannot walk away without seeing for myself."

"You are strong willed, daughter of D'lana." The semblance of a smile lifted the dragon's lips. "There can be no harm in it. Come and I will show you."

Together the four made their way along the twisted passages, in and out among the ancient stalagmites that had mated with their stalactite counterparts above to create great columns. They skirted a deep pool that glowed with the activity of phosphorescent algae and the fish that fed on it. As they descended, the air grew colder, fuelled by the mountain's heart of ice.

The dragon paused before a slab of stone. He gripped it with his foretalons and, using his massive shoulder, gave it a shove to slide the barricade to the crypt aside. "C'thra rests here."

N'dia entered, followed by the she-shadow. D'raekn remained beyond the door, head lowered in reverence to the woman who had called him son. "She was my mother, the only one I knew."

"Aye, and I cannot believe she did not leave you with a gift. Perhaps the gift left for Cwen is yours also?" N'dia wondered.

"N'dia, C'thra would have told me. She spent many hours sharing her belief that I was part of a legend and that I was meant to rule

Quondam. She told me a woman would love me. C'thra was wrong, and Flida was right. My place is within the wildwoods, among the hidden, with the nymph. I will go to her, beg her forgiveness and let her end my sorrow."

"D'raekn—"

The dragon held up a claw. "I know that you want to believe in a faery tale, but the beast they created was only a tool used to save a woodland nymph from death at the hands of a sister. There is no magickal legend, N'dia. Stay as long as you like. I will light a way to the exit before I leave for the wildwoods. I wish you good journey and long life, young sorceress."

N'dia watched the dragon leave and turned to the hellwing. "Help me raise the lid on the casket."

They shoved, and bit by bit the heavy stone moved and revealed the bones within. There, on the breastbone, rested a small ivory dragon. In its side there was a small notch, the promise of another piece.

"I knew it was here! I knew C'thra would never abandon the dragon's child to the wood nymph's whimsy or a god's foolish mistake." Firelight set perfect teeth agleam in N'dia's wide smile. "Now, let us go to Stonetel." She patted the she-shadow's wing. "We don't want to miss out on Karid's separation from the flesh!"

Chapter 31: Stonetel

Cwen's horse stumbled and dropped to its knees. She encouraged it with soft commands, and it struggled to regain its feet, but exhaustion won over her silken urging, and it collapsed and rolled onto its side. Cwen cursed and struggled to escape the crushing weight, kicking against the horse with her free foot and dragging herself away when the beast made a lackluster attempt to rise.

"I am sorry," she whispered as she drew her blade across the bulging vein in the muscular neck. Cwen held the horse's head until life faded from its eyes, and then she stood and shouldered her pack from the saddle and began the long walk into Stonetel.

While waiting for the barge in Quern's Crossing, Cwen learned that Karid's execution—her release from the flesh, the man had called it—had been ordered by Quondam's council of elders and was scheduled at midday at moon's dark in six days, too soon for a woman on foot to reach Stonetel. Under her relentless demands, the horse had given all it could for five days, and now Cwen needed to find another. She raised a hand to shade herself from the afternoon glare and stared, alert for any movement that might indicate a traveler. A shimmer in the distance made her smile, and shouldering her bag once again, she set off at a steady run, keeping to the tireless pace that D'raekn had taught.

An hour later Cwen was close enough to distinguish three Emyute riders, one on horseback and two on droms. They moved along at a comfortable jog, seemingly in no hurry. Cwen crouched and slipped toward them in a stooped run, ducking behind each low patch of sulfur brush and rock that was large enough to act as camouflage.

The nomads stopped and dismounted. One began the arduous task of digging to release a bit of water from the scorched earth. The others hobbled their mounts and began to set up an awning for shelter and build a cook-fire.

On her belly, Cwen crawled forward, dropping her head each time the men looked in her direction. Hidden behind a clump of sagebrush, she lifted her bow from her shoulder, nocked a bone-tipped arrow and let fly. The arrow slammed into the nearest man's back and knocked him face forward into the awning.

Her skin turned to gooseflesh as she rose and sighted her second arrow. It left the bow with a hiss and caught the man tethering the mounts high in the shoulder as he swung around in alarm at the screams of his uninjured comrade.

"Demon! The dragonspawn's demon!" bellowed the third Emyute, charging toward Cwen. He crashed into her, hands circling her throat as they fell. Cwen thrashed beneath him, clawing at his vice-like grip. She bucked and butted him with her head twice and then slammed her knee up between his legs. The man howled, drew back, slapped Cwen hard, and grabbed her hair with both hands.

Cwen drew in a wheezing breath and saw the man's dagger out the corner of her eye. She screamed and slammed against the sides of the nomad's head with balled fists. As he pulled back out of her range, she grabbed the dagger two-handed and plunged it into his thigh. He threw himself back. Cwen jumped to her feet, stepped backward as she heaved in great gulps of air, and dragged an arrow from her quiver.

The Emyute rose to his knees with a roar, pulled the dagger from his leg, and staggered to his feet to make a charge at Cwen. She whirled away and drove the arrow into the side of his neck as he passed by. His hands flew to the shaft, and his howls became garbled as his blood blocked his windpipe and filled his lungs. Still he would not fall and continued to lurch after Cwen.

Cwen tripped and the nomad collapsed atop her as she fell. "Get off me!" she screeched, pushing against the heavy man, then rolling him away and lurching to her feet. With hands on her knees she dragged in great gulps of air. She forced herself upright and scanned the makeshift camp. The nomad with the shoulder wound was trying to mount one of the droms. Cwen raced across the sand and clubbed the man across the back of the neck with a double fisted overhand blow. He dropped and rolled onto his back. Cwen kicked him in the head. She backed away and looked around again. When nothing else moved, she rubbed a hand across her bloodied mouth, released the hobbled horse, and dragged her exhausted body into the saddle. A kick to its sides sent the horse leaping forward with ears laid back and tail lashing. Cwen loosed her hold on the reins, crouched low over the animal's neck, and urged it faster with a rider's whispers. Daylight tomorrow would bring them to Stonetel.

The streets of Stonetel were filled with humanity rejoicing over Karid's capture. Hellwings and wasp warriors ferried wounded soldiers to healers and apothecaries. The trade director opened his home to house the remaining Saedan assassins as they began to suffer the fire sickness of crystal withdrawal.

N'dia and the she-shadow lurked outside the barracks where a local tavern keeper had said that Sóvië and B'rma spent their nights. The hellwing drew her wings around her against the evening chill and settled from sight among the shadows. N'dia picked at a fingernail and watched the street.

"Why don't they come?"

Perhaps they are eating supper, something we could stand to do.

The young sorceress dug in her bag and pulled out a dried loaf, broke it, and passed half to the she-shadow.

I wonder just how long a human can live on crusts of bread.

N'dia choked off a laugh and said, "I know you need meat. I promise we will eat a proper meal just as soon as I talk to B'rma. I must have C'thra's gift to Cwen."

If you do not need me, young sorceress, a feast remains upon the killing field. I could join the others feeding there.

The Noor woman grimaced and waved away a vision of slashing wasp mandibles and the hellwing's ripping teeth. "Go. I will find you should the need arise."

N'dia sank to a squat and folded her arms across her knees. She yawned and rested her head on her arms. The exhaustion caused by lack of sleep and the excitement of discovering the ivory dragon finally claimed her.

At the sight of N'dia huddled against the wall, B'rma remarked to Sóvië, "Will you look at that? It's a good thing Karid no longer rules these streets or I know a little Noor sorceress who would find herself in a bit of a sticky situation." B'rma laughed softly and knelt beside the sleeping N'dia. "Wake up," she whispered and patted N'dia gently so as not to startle her awake.

N'dia opened one eye, yawned, and gave a sudden smile of recognition. "Where have you two been? I have been waiting here for hours."

"Where is that hellwing who is supposed to guard you?" Sóvië asked.

"She was starving, so I sent her off for a meal." N'dia shuddered and made a nasty face. "She went off to feed with the wasp soldiers." Suddenly remembering the reason for her waiting, N'dia stretched and stood. "I need the gift that the wasp queen gave you for Cwen. Do you still have it?"

B'rma looked puzzled, then reached inside her tunic and brought out the soft, threadbare bag. "This?"

"Aye," N'dia reached out and lifted it from the palm of B'rma's hand. "It goes with this." She pulled the delicate ivory dragon from her pocket.

"Where did that come from?" B'rma asked.

"C'thra. It is D'raekn's gift from C'thra. I found her tomb on Mount Shadowmaw, and this was buried with her. She knew that he would one day find her and claim it. Trouble is she didn't know just how stubborn he would become. He has grown sullen and obstinate, given up and gone off to hide within the wildwoods." N'dia shook her head. "But he didn't count on me."

"Hold it." She dropped the ivory carving into B'rma's waiting hand and loosened the drawstring on the little cloth bag. She peered inside, grinned and tipped the coiled ivory serpent out into her palm. Gently she lifted the dragon and snapped the serpent into place. "Cwen embracing D'raekn—C'thra always knew."

"What do you intend to do with those?" B'rma asked.

"Oh, I don't have to do anything. Cwen will do it all."

"Cwen is here?" Sóvië asked.

"If not, she will be. She's coming to make sure you go home and get married to your empath."

Sóvië's eyes twinkled. "So she's been talking about my Xavian empath has she?"

"Indeed. She says the two of you will be fine rulers for your home world."

"I want her to come home too. There is no reason for her to stay here now, and I can use a strong woman like Cwen. She is quite adept at magick and weaponry and could frighten off a regimen with her fierceness." Sóvië paused for a moment and pondered, "Though it may be difficult to make her listen or to get her to swear loyalty to any cause. She's never been one to admit the good in swearing allegiance."

"Her allegiance is here." N'dia glowered and her voice took on an edge. "I will fight you if you try to take her from him."

"What are you talking about, N'dia? The dragon is gone. We all heard the nymph tell D'raekn that he is no longer a man. Cwen cannot...well, you know. It isn't even a *bad* plan. It is no plan at all."

"Do not cross me on this, Sóvië. I am warning you as a guardian of the redeemer of magick and the king of men. Do not cross me."

"B'rma?" Sóvië looked to the older Noor for reason, but B'rma was staring at N'dia.

"You feel it here." B'rma patted her breast with her fingertips. "You feel the calling here."

"Aye. He is the king of men. I know he is, and Cwen will set him free."

"What about your brother? Doesn't he have anything to say about losing his wife?" Sóvië snapped. "Or can a woman just walk away from her vows on this forsaken world?"

"J'var is proud and foolish, but he knows the laws of marriage do not allow him to bind a woman through deception. He freed her. Severed the cord and gave her freedom."

B'rma laughed and said, "You have become most masterful at the art of persuasion, N'dia. I believed I would be forced to kill J'var before he let Cwen go."

The shrill whinny of a horse caught their attention as Cwen of Aaradan brought her mount to a sliding halt and dropped to the ground on unsteady legs. She held the reins and stood speechless as N'dia stepped forward and embraced her. "I found something that belongs to you." She took Cwen's free hand and slipped the ivory serpent into it. "And this one belongs to D'raekn. Will you give it to him when you see him next?" she asked before handing her the tiny dragon.

"Is he here?" Cwen's voice trembled, and she blinked to keep from weeping at the sight of the ivory totems.

"No. He and the old wizard have given up on the legend and retreated into the wildwoods to make peace with Flida. That dragon totem is a gift from C'thra, his surrogate mother. I am sure he would like to have it. B'rma and I will not be free for many months, so I thought maybe you would take it and leave it with the nymph—"

"I don't know—"

"—before you journey home with Sóvië. She could remain here with us until you return."

"Cwen, I want you to come home with me now," Sóvië insisted. "Ædracmoræ will need you. I will need you. We can leave as soon as the power of the jewel of my birthright is no longer required to hold Karid. Tomorrow, after she is freed of the flesh and returned as nymph to the sacred woods, we can leave. Quondam's legend will have been fulfilled, and they will have no further use of us."

Cwen brushed her hand across her eyes, the leather reins tickling her face. She suddenly felt faint as the smell of horse sweat closed in around her. "Sóvië, I don't know what I want. I should stable this horse, and I need to rest. Tomorrow I will see Quondam freed of Karid. I have seen what she has done. Here, just like on Ædracmoræ, she has poisoned the people and destroyed them in the assassins' fire. I saw the villages, I saw the trade center at Quern's Crossing—all were burned, everything was dead. When Karid is no longer a threat, then I will go with you to Serabia and see you safely through the portal. But I do not know if I can go with you to Ædracmoræ."

"Why not?" Sóvië's words were sharp, causing Cwen to jerk and her horse to shy and stomp.

"There is nothing there for me," Cwen answered, stroking the restless horse and whistling soothingly. "Sóvië, there is nothing there for me."

"And there is something here?" N'dia watched Cwen's fingers play over the ivory dragon and serpent still clutched in her hand, noticing how she snapped the pieces together and then pulled them apart.

"Dragon's Heart," Cwen replied.

"There is no one there," B'rma reminded. "D'raekn has gone to Flida. Why would you go to Dragon's Heart now?"

"It is...my home." Cwen turned away. "I need to find a room. I will join you in the executioner's glen at noon on the morrow, Sóvië. After that we will decide what to do."

The three women watched Cwen lead the horse toward the stables, and N'dia smiled, slapping B'rma on the back. "She will go to him. I know she will."

B'rma nodded to end N'dia's chatter, but in her mind she voiced the silent truth: But it will be too late. By now, if Flida has had her way, D'raekn will have no memory of Cwen.

"Cwen looks terrible." Sóvië gave a shake of her head. "I don't believe I have ever seen her look more miserable or uncertain, and neither of you made her feel any better. You are quite a piece of work, N'dia!"

N'dia lifted her shoulders and stuck out her lip. "Is there an empty bed in your barracks?"

"I think we can provide you with a bit of space." B'rma threw her arm across the shoulders of the younger Noor. "Tomorrow should be an interesting day."

Cwen lay awake in a room at the inn, unable to look away from the ivory totems on the bedside table. She tucked her hands up under her cheek and, in the flickering firelight, watched as the lustrous swirl of color moved across the surface of the ivory. The dragon totem sat a finger space apart from the coiled serpent, at an angle that let Cwen look into its eyes.

"I did save you," she whispered. "You did not die in the glen of stones as threatened in my dreams. Tomorrow Karid will be taken from her human form and returned to the wildwoods. Quondam will finally be safe. Do not hate me, D'raekn. I only wanted to see you safe." Her eyelids fluttered and closed, as heavy as her words.

The startling brilliance of the sunlight seemed incongruous in the executioner's glen where, under the watchful eyes of Quondam's citizens—human and beast alike—the council of elders convened to approve the sentence that would be delivered upon Karid.

"Who charged this woman?" the prime elder asked, pointing a withered hand at the prisoner who stood between B'rma and Sóvië, the Dragon Queen's pendant holding Karid within its spell.

"I did." Flida's image shimmered in the midday sun—a pulsing array of light and shadow, shifting and changing as elusive as moonlight, as tantalizing as sunlight on sea. "Within the bounds of flesh, the nymph Karid has betrayed us and committed crimes against both men and gods. She killed your rightful king and ascended the throne falsely. In the flesh, she has brought a curse upon us all, stolen magick from men, and brought the sacred woods to near ruin. The god of death, who locked her in this human body, admits his error and swears to accept her soul upon its release from the physical form."

"And what consequence for this soul would you ask us to approve?"

"Return her soul to solitude within the wildwoods, eternally bound within the heart of the great sacred elm, never to wander, never to be free. This is the petition brought before this council of men."

"It is a farce!" Karid shouted. "My sister only seeks to save herself. Did I not protect this council and those loyal to the crown? My only crimes were against foreigners and freaks!"

"This...this *woman* lies." Cwen shook off her cousin's warning hand. "She sent assassins to my world where none had done her harm and destroyed us. She burned our cities to the ground and killed indiscriminately as she sought the blood of the women of Aaradan. Even now, if she was free, she would murder me where I stand."

"You fornicated with the beast! You bear his mark! You set him free!" Karid shook her fist and ranted. "This is the demon you should be executing! The dragonspawn's mate," she spat. "Demon! Demon! You are the one who loosed evil on Quondam!"

A sudden breeze rustled Cwen's clothes and set her hair dancing about her face as the nymph Flida drew near. "Prime Elder, my sister speaks the truth. The dragon soars free because this foreigner spoke his forbidden name. What this foreigner does not tell is of her own suffering. Karid had her tortured by the Emyutes and then cast into the Sanguine Sea when they believed she was dead. The only kindness this girl has known is at the hands of D'raekn, the dragonspawn, and the sorceresses who serve him. Justice is all we ask, Prime Elder."

"Bitches! Scheming with one another to take the throne! It belongs to me! I deserve it! It was I who was strong enough to take it from the hands of humans! I hold the power of the dragon's fire! I control the army of the Emyutes! It is all mine!"

"Enough!" the prime elder raised his voice to be heard above Karid's snarling tirade. "This council has found you guilty of the charges and grants justice to the victims of your wickedness. Flida, sentinel of the sacred woods, your petition is granted."

Flida bowed before the authority of men and faded from their sight.

To the waiting executioner, the prime elder commanded, "Bind her to the stone."

Sóvië and B'rma dragged the wailing Karid to the altar stone, lifted her up, and held her as the executioner tried to manacle her wrists.

"Is it my fault I loved the flesh? Is it? Is there no mercy for the cursed? Damn the gods of heaven! Damn the council of men and the spirits of the wildwoods! And damn you most of all, Cwen of Aaradan!" Karid shrieked and flailed, her boot striking B'rma a vicious blow to the jaw and her nails raking the executioner across the eyes. She jerked free of Sóvië's hold and kicked the hooded man a wallop to the groin, grabbed his axe, and shot up off the altar stone.

As a single entity, the crowds surged backward, away from Karid's threat.

Cwen ducked beneath the axe blade as it whistled overhead, trimming tendrils of her copper hair. She rolled away and regained her footing beside a stunned N'dia. Cwen snatched the sword from N'dia's scabbard and, with a strength born of fearless fury and hatred, charged at Karid and drove N'dia's sword deep into the queen's midriff. As the axe cleaved Cwen's flesh, its great weight drove her to the ground. She fell and lay still. Karid dropped to her knees, hands clutching the hilt of the sorceress's sword, watching transfixed in horror and disbelief as the glow of its crystal blade radiated outward over her body and disintegrated her flesh. The odor of burning filled the glen as cinders of blackened skin and muscle drifted like dark snowflakes upon the wind.

Overhead a flash of lightning rent the gathering dark clouds, and from their whirling vortex emerged the dark god. Eyes fiery with intent, he approached the dying Karid. "I have sworn to right this wrong. To take your soul and bind it within the sacred elm where it will forever feed the wildwoods and keep them free of the blight of flesh. "

From Karid's blackened and screaming lips the god of death snatched the writhing soul and held it out for all to see. "This is a wickedness that is only fit for fodder," he said, his voice booming across the glen. "I free each of you from Karid's curse! From this day forth, no seed of Man will suffer the failure of the gods." With Karid's screeching soul in hand, the dark god brought an image of the sacred elm before the throng and, with a cast of his hand, melded the black soul with the glistening purity of the heart of the ancient elm tree. "It is done."

His words lingered as an echo among the standing stones as he disappeared from view. Nothing remained but N'dia's sword and a growing puddle of blood around a fallen warrior.

"Cwen?" Sóvië knelt at her cousin's side and brushed blood-matted hair away from her eyes. "Cwen, can you hear me?"

Lashes fluttered and unfocused eyes stared for a moment before they closed again. "Go home, Sóvië." Cwen's hushed command made Sóvië smile.

"Not yet, cousin. Not quite yet."

Chapter 32: Homeward Bound

Cwen cradled her arm, rolled her shoulder and watched the puckered scar ripple across the wing of the dragon emblazoned on her back. Her arm remained useless, but the painful tingle of a thousand needles told her it would heal. She replaced the sling and slid the arm inside. With her good hand, she bunched up the woolen cloak, stuck her head in the opening, and gave a shake to settle it into place. She brushed away a wrinkle, and her hand paused over the ivory totems tucked against her heart.

She glanced around the room and allowed a bitter laugh. Here in the bombed out palace of Serabia, Karid's deviant son had saved Cwen's life. It was odd how the fates worked. Today she would go home with Sóvië and try to forget the sorrows of Quondam.

Turning around, Cwen opened the door to find N'dia there, her hand raised and about to knock.

"Sóvië waits in the hall of mirrors. Elle and Tyne are with her."

Cwen nodded. She was glad that the Saedans had decided to accompany Sóvië back to Ædracmoræ, for they were strong and loyal to her cousin. A new queen could use friends like Tyne and Elle.

N'dia linked her arm through Cwen's, and together they started down the staircase to the lower level.

"Cwen, is there anything I can do?"

"You've done enough." Cwen clasped N'dia's hand and squeezed. "Without your hellwing's speed and the deviant's healing power, I would have died. Karid would have won."

"The deviant has chosen a name for himself—Gush'an. It's Emyute for healer. It suits him, I think. My father has offered him sanctuary in Achroma, but I think he may ultimately choose the magick over man and take the dragon's form."

Cwen withdrew her good hand and patted her damaged shoulder. "He has my gratitude. To think that all the years he spent locked in that room, opening and closing portals for Karid, he learned healing from the oracle's daughter. It is amazing what the human spirit can overcome right beneath the nose of evil."

"He's not human, Cwen."

"Aye, but there is more humanity in him than in many pure of blood. I have discovered that the human condition is something more than birthright."

They reached the chamber, and N'dia paused and placed her hand on Cwen's. "Aren't you going to ask?"

Cwen swallowed and looked away. "No. It would not matter."

"He soars free over the sacred woods. Rumor says he has forgotten the woman he once loved."

"Stop."

"Why? Don't you want to see him? Don't you want to know the truth?"

"My truth is here, with Sóvië. I want to go home."

N'dia took a deep breath and blew in frustration. "I don't understand. Karid is gone, and Quondam is free. Even the hellwings have shed the cursed gray of Karid's hatred to shine again. You are both alive, and you need each other. Why don't you go to him?"

The threat of tears gave Cwen's eyes a sparkle that belied her pain. "It is too late, N'dia." She turned and entered the hall of mirrors and called out cheerfully to Sóvië, "Are you ready to return to your handsome empath?"

"Aye, it seems a lifetime since I last stepped through this mirror. And N'dia, I did not have a chance to thank A'bach for delivering my mother's body. She will rest better with her ashes beside my father's on Ædracmoræ."

"I will thank him for you." N'dia kissed Sóvië on the cheek and hugged Elle and Tyne. "Safe journey to all of you." As Cwen passed, N'dia whispered to her, "You are like a sister to me. I will miss you."

"Good-bye, N'dia. Tell B'rma…when you see her, tell her I said thank you for seeing D'raekn safe."

N'dia could only nod. "Gush'an? It is time."

The deviant son of Karid shuffled from the darkness, his misshapen face screwed up into a smile. "B'rma says this is the last time the portals will be used. The chamber will be sealed when you are gone. I am sorry I will not see your wound healed, Cwen of Aaradan."

"It heals well, Gush'an. I have begun to feel the prickle of healing in my fingers. Thank you." Cwen hugged him and watched a flush spread across his deformed features.

"Send them home," N'dia said as she waved and swung away so they would not see her tears.

Under Gush'an's magick, a mercurial spot grew on the wall ahead, and when it was large enough, Tyne and Elle lifted the casket containing Yávië's body and stepped through into a new home.

Sóvië gave the deviant portal keeper a gentle hug and whispered, "Thank you, healer," and reached for Cwen's hand. Her eyes narrowed when her cousin balked.

"Cwen!"

"I cannot go," Cwen said, backing away from the portal.

"We've been through all this, a thousand times over!" Sóvië cried. "It is all we talked about while you healed. Cwen, do not be stupid. There will not be another chance to come home. You heard Gush'an. This room will be blasted and sealed, and Gush'an is never to open a portal again, never. Come home, Cwen."

"I cannot." Tears flooded Cwen's eyes and streamed down her face. "I am sorry, Sóvië, but I just can't. All the real happiness I have ever known is here."

"No, Cwen, only heartbreak and sorrow follow you here. I have watched you suffer. At home you will have a chance at life."

Cwen's head shook, and she choked on sudden sobs as she wiped a stream of mucous from beneath her nose. She pushed Sóvië ahead of her. "Go, Sóvië, go home to your empath. He will make a great king. Go home and be the Dragon Queen."

Sóvië clutched Cwen's hand and started through the portal. Her face crumpled, and she wept as Cwen withdrew her fingers.

"Good-bye, Sóvië, safe journey."

When the linking mirror closed behind Sóvïë, Cwen looked up at Karid's deviant son, "Gush'an, get me out of here."

The hulking Gush'an lifted Cwen against his chest, patted her and broke his promise to the sorceress B'rma. He opened a portal and carried the weeping Cwen into Flida's sacred woods. He settled her on the soft moss, smoothed her hair, and gave her another comforting pat before turning back into the mirrored portal. After closing it behind him, he hurried to tell N'dia what he had done.

The crackle and hiss of damp wood burning woke Cwen from tearful sleep. She found it hard to catch her breath and stood up slowly, gasping for air. Sparks cascaded around her. She looked up into the familiar flame of the fire dryad's eyes and covered her ears against the grief-contorted wail.

"Where are we? Why do you scream?" Cwen asked.

"I clear the sacred forest of deadwood. We all suffer with your pain." The fiery spirit howled again, and this time other voices joined her from deep within the woods.

"Stop it!" Cwen covered her ears against the anguished cries.

"What are you doing here?" A sudden wind swept the embers of the dryad away and silenced the howling. "You bring discord to the wildwoods. Why?"

Cwen eyed the glimmering nymph as she swirled about trailing sparks of starlight.

"You are the sentinel, Flida. D'raekn's creator?"

"Ah, you remember me. Now, why are you here?" Flida asked again.

"I do not know how I got here. Where is D'raekn? Is he here?"

"A dragon calls these wildwoods home, but he is nameless."

"Why? Why would he give up his name?"

Flida pulsed, the equivalent of a shrug, and replied, "Tales abound. It is said he was once a man. That a selfish stranger broke his heart."

"Tell me the truth. Where is D'raekn?" Cwen fingered the totems against her breast. "Where is he? Why do you play games?"

"Cwen, what do you want? He has no memory of you. No memory of Man."

"Is he happy?"

The nymph swirled around Cwen. "What do you care?"

"I care."

"He no longer suffers. He has found peace. What would you have me do? Let him remember you? Reawaken the pain?"

"No. No, I do not want him to suffer." Cwen bit her lip as a shudder of regret tore at her heart, and she cried out again, "No!"

"Then go, and leave him alone."

Cwen turned and ran several steps before she glanced back and asked, "And Aenzl? The wizard? Is he here as well?"

"I know nothing of the wizard."

Cwen ran blindly, surrounded by the lament of forest spirits, sobs tearing at her chest, tears burning her eyes. When she could run no more, she stumbled against an embankment and curled up beneath a bough that spilled from an overhang of earth, weeping herself numb.

The dragon soared and watched the woman below. She seemed injured and smelled of fear, the salty smell that came with human sweat and tears. When at last she stumbled and did not rise, he circled and landed in a nearby clearing. He padded toward the stream, the scent of water masking that of the woman. As he drew nearer, he slowed and stalked ahead in the crouch of a hunter—silent and alert to the danger of weapons.

He sniffed and snorted at the scent. It was somehow familiar, yet he could not place it. Ahead the dragon saw the frail woman huddled under an earthen overhang, her small sounds of distress interrupted by the shudder of gasping.

"Woman," his voice boomed.

She screamed and clutched at her legs with her good arm.

Cwen sobbed harder. The sight of D'raekn, along with the realization that he did not recognize her, brought another sudden and agonizing burden.

"Are you sick? I can take you to the wizard. He is a competent healer."

The woman did not answer but emitted a wordless keen that made the dragon flinch. He lifted her gently, a deep scowl rearranging the scales of his forehead. "Who has done this to you?"

The dragon surged upward into the air and flew along the tree line at the edge of the Feverous Forest, searching for the distant island where the old wizard lived.

Chapter 33: Heart Song

"**B**y the gods, not again!" Aenzl screeched, spittle flying, as he stormed out of the cabin. "Where did you find her this time?"

The dragon slunk back to avoid the wizard's lunacy and the flash of energy emanating from the flailing staff. "She was wandering the woods. What do you mean, again?"

Aenzl leaned on his stick and sputtered, "You really don't know do you? Flida's done a magick number on you! And you allowed it!"

"Wizard, calm down," the dragon said evenly.

The old man shook his head, sat on a step, and held his head in his hands. "I can't be responsible for her! You found her, you deal with her!"

"She just needs a bit of healing. Her arm appears injured, and her brain is a bit muddled."

Aenzl jumped up, ran forward, and smashed the dragon across the snout with his staff. The dragon bellowed and released a cloud of soot and ash that covered the old wizard and left him coughing and choking.

"Why did you strike me? What have I done?"

The wizard shook his fist at the sky and kicked the dirt. "I am too old to do this anymore! You are free, fly away!"

"You are not making any sense, old man."

"You have got to remember, that's all there is to it!" The wizard pushed open the cabin door. "Look at her!"

"I see her." The dragon peered at her through the doorway. "She is a human. A woman."

"Why did you bring her here?"

"I told her you would heal her."

"You talked to her? What did she say?"

"She did not say anything, elder. She made tears and was having trouble breathing."

"She was crying! You know, it's what people do when they feel sad."

"I do not know why you are so angry. You have the healing herbs. You could at least look at the wound." The dragon snaked its head inside the cabin and eyed the woman. "Is she sleeping?" He rested his muzzle on the foot of the bed and breathed deeply of the pleasant scent.

"She is unconscious, cried herself senseless, I imagine. You know, you used to be a man. What happened to you?"

"I chose magick. That is what Flida says."

"And what else does Flida tell you?" Aenzl muttered a curse under his breath and squeezed past D'raekn and into the room. "You don't even remember your name."

With a sigh, Aenzl looked down on Cwen. "And what are you doing here, missy? I thought you would be long gone by now." He took a blade from the bed table, slit up the length of Cwen's shirt and peeled back the edges to expose the dragon's mark and welted scar. "Looks like somebody slashed her pretty good."

"What is that mark?"

"A dragon gave that to her. Marked her, so he wouldn't forget who she bloody well was!" the old wizard snapped. "Fools, the lot of you!" He snatched up a jar of salve, smeared a handful across Cwen's scar, and covered it with a clean bandage. "How can you stand there starin' and not know who she is?" He slammed a fist between the dragon's eyes and shouted, "You have let that wood nymph addle your brain! That's what you've done—and all because you're a big ninny!"

"Wizard! Do not strike me again! Just tell me who the woman is."

"Nay."

"Why not? You obviously know."

"Go on, get out of here. You're breathing up all her air, and you're useless to her."

"I saved her! Do you forget it was me who brought her here?"

The wizard waved him back, and the dragon withdrew into the yard.

"I am not likely to ever forget it was you who brought her here. Go see the merfolk, maybe they can help you."

"Help me what?"

"Aenzl?" Cwen's voice was hoarse, her throat raw from crying, and her eyes swollen from tears.

"Go! Shoo! Sit on the shore and commune with the merfolk." Aenzl waved the great dragon off without success.

"Aye?" The old wizard rushed inside and slammed the door against the dragon's intrusion. He sank down on the bed beside the girl and rubbed her good shoulder. "Just rest. You are quite a sight for these old eyes."

"I saw him, in the woods. He does not know me, Aenzl. What am I going to do?" Her words stumbled over one another, and her face collapsed in sorrow as she wept into her hands. "Help me! Help us!"

"I cannot, you know I cannot. I do not have the power to undo what Flida's done. What he's allowed her to do. I wish C'thra were here, she'd put that nymph in her place."

Cwen struggled up, slipped the ivory figures from her shirt and held them out to Aenzl. "She gave us these. They are gifts from C'thra."

The old man took them, rubbed his finger over them, and felt the groove where they snapped together. He put them together then took them apart and handed Cwen the serpent. "Wait here."

She watched him leave and looked around. She was home, in the cabin D'raekn had built for her. She stood up, supporting her aching arm, kicked off her boots, and went to the cupboard, tiptoeing to reach the bottle of sweet brandy and a cup. She sat down at her table and poured a generous slug, downing it with one gulp, gasping as it burned her raspy throat.

"Girl!" Aenzl shouted from outside the cabin.

She padded barefoot to the door and stepped onto the porch. "What, Aenzl?"

"He's waiting on the beach."

Tears brimmed and threatened to overflow.

"No crying! You've got to stop that, it's not fitting," Aenzl said gruffly. "You're tough, remember. You belong to the dragonspawn."

"But he no longer belongs to me." A single tear escaped beneath her lashes. "I love him, Aenzl."

"I know, now go before he forgets to wait."

Cwen raced along the headlands, down the path that led to the sea. The spectacle of moonlight on the great red dragon resting on the sand stopped her, and she clutched the tiny serpent and prayed to the ancient gods before hurrying on. "Please, please let him remember. I'll never ask another thing if you just let him remember me."

The merfolk caught sight of Cwen and danced joyously among the waves, leaping and twirling, calling with happy songs.

As the dragon watched the merfolk, a tickle of memory touched his mind, and he looked back over his shoulder. The woman stood there. Her fragrance eddied around him on the shore breeze, and his eyes closed in pleasure as she came closer.

"I like the way you smell," he rumbled from deep within his chest, a purr of welcome.

"It's my skin. You always liked it. You told me once that it was intoxicating."

"I remember you from the woods. The wizard told me this was yours." He opened his foreclaw and exposed the ivory dragon. "Is it?"

"It would be if it were joined with this one," she showed the serpent. "Will you wait for me, while I go to see the merfolk?"

D'raekn nodded and kept his eyes on the girl as she walked away and waded out into the water up to her thighs. The mermaidens drifted closer and reached out with webbed hands to stroke her skin. The male gave a low, soothing whistle and lifted himself to balance on the curve of his tail, bright black eyes shining with curiosity as he touched Cwen's coppery braid.

In his head, the dragon heard Cwen's heart song. It pounded like the surge of water breaking on the sea stacks, a song of fear and sorrow, and the merfolk sang along inside his head, soothing the girl. *Joy and goodwill, Cwen of Aaradan...*

D'raekn turned the tiny ivory dragon over in his palm and stood and made his way into the pounding surf. "Show me the serpent," he bellowed, and Cwen's eyes grew wide. "Show it to me!" He thundered toward her, covering her with foamy spray as he lowered his head to her eye level. "I need to see it again, please."

Her tears were hidden by the salty sea spray, and she held out the serpent totem.

"Show me how they are joined," his voice was gentler, his expression kind.

Cwen lifted the dragon and snapped the serpent into place. "I love you, D'raekn. I should have told you long ago. What you have become does not matter. If only you will remember me, I will be happy."

His gaze shifted from serpent embracing the dragon to search Cwen's face. He watched her wipe away a tear, bite her lower lip, and close her hand around the ivory.

"Please, D'raekn, try to remember. Flida cannot hold you with a lie. No one can hold us with lies. I am free, and so are you. Please." Her arms reached out and encircled his neck, and her breath mingled with his as she kissed the corner of his mouth.

He snorted and pulled away, knocking Cwen down. "I am a beast."

"No!" She fought to rise and gritted her teeth against the pain of her shoulder. "You are a man forced to wear a dragon's skin. It doesn't matter, D'raekn. Close your eyes and remember your dreams." Her fingers danced along his scales, her touch sure. "You told me our dreams never lied. Close your eyes and dream of me."

His eyes grew heavy as he found himself seduced by her voice, and he lay down in the surge of the sea.

"Dream of me," she whispered, her breath warm and sweet, her touch feather light.

He saw her in the age-old dream, where she stood in the distance beyond a campfire. He rose and went to meet her, pushed back the hood of his cloak, and revealed himself to her. "Cwen…" He opened his eyes and murmured, "Cwen." The earth trembled under the dragon's final transformation. He pulled her up against him and folded human arms around her, savoring the flood of memories. "Cwen…" He kissed her eyes, her lips, and wept against her throat.

"Speak your name to me," Cwen whispered. She tightened her arm around his neck, laid her head against his chest, and felt the power of his voice as he spoke his name to her.

"I am D'raekn…conceived in the royal womb of the woman Malaia…from the seed of the dragon lord Brug…and reared by the sorceress C'thra and the wizard Aenzl."

Across the land, a million night birds took to the air in a sudden storm of wings as brilliant lightning flashed and thunder reverberated around a turbulent sky. Deep within Quondam, against the sacred heart, dragons woke and filled the night with their songs.

On the headlands, the old wizard smiled and watched as the dragonspawn became the king of men.

Glossary

A

Aaradan [AIR uh dan]—ruling house of Ædracmoræ

A'bach [A bawk]—a Noor director, father of N'dia, J'var, and L'or

Achroma [uh KRO ma]—a Noor trade center, home of A'bach and his children

Acolyte [AK oh lyt]—a student or apprentice, often of an arcane order

Adumbra [uh DUM bruh]—a western trade center located near the Sanguine Sea

Aenzl [AIN zul]—a wizard, D'raekn's friend and teacher

Akhnif [AWK neef]—hooded Emyute cape

Alchemist [AL-kuh-mist]—a person who is versed in or practices alchemy

Alchemy [AL kuh mee]—any magical power or process of transmuting a common substance, usually of little value, into a substance of great value

Arjuna [AR joo naw]—an herb to calm the heart and protect against seizure

Augurer [AWG uh roor]—a wizard or soothsayer

Æ

Ædracmoræ [DRAC mor]—world of Yávië, Cwen, and Sóvië's birth

B

Bane boar [beyn bor]—large, foul tempered, inedible beast whose name is often used as a curse

Bannock [BAN uk]—flat bread, also called morning buns

Barrens [BAR uhnz]—tract of unproductive land, often with a scrubby growth of trees and pitted with quicksand

Beorn's Freehold [BEE ornz FREE hohld]—an estate in land, inherited or held for life

Boak [bohk]—incendiary mineral used for fuel

Bounty of the Gods [BOUN tee uv thuh gawdz]—a powerful gift promised to D'raekn by Quondam's gods

B'rma [BUR muh]—tavern owner and sorceress, a guardian of the dragonspawn

Buul [bool]—an Emyute leader

C

Caen [kayn]—Cwen's lover, killed by Lohgaen of Lochlaen on Ædracmoræ

Chiretta Powder [SHE ret ah POW der]—herbal coagulant and blood purifier

Cloister of Belasis [CLOY stur uv BAY lah sis]—training center for thaumaturgy

Corusca [kor OO ska]—a trade center

C'thra [KATH ruh]—a sorceress, surrogate mother to the dragonspawn

Cudge [kuhj]—an Orpin farm woman in Achroma

Cudgel [KUHJ uhl]—a short, thick stick used as a weapon; club

Cwen [kwin]—daughter of the sorceress Näeré and the guardian Nall, niece of Yávië the Dragon Queen

D

Daughter of the Serpent [DAW tuhr uv thuh SIR pent]—woman promised by the nymph Flida and the sorceress C'thra to free the dragonspawn

Directorate [di REK ter it]—Quondam's ruling group of Noor tradesmen

D'lana [dee LAHN uh]—Abach's wife and sorceress mother of N'dia, L'or, and J'var

D'raekn [DRAY kin]—the dragonspawn's forbidden name

Dragon's breath [DRAG uhnz breth]—element used by Karid's alchemist to create the crystals ingested by the fire assassins

Dragon's Heart Isle [DRAG uhnz hart ahyl]—island prison of the wizard Aenzl and the dragonspawn

Dragon's milt [DRAG uhnz milt]—seminal fluid of a dragon

Dragon Queen [DRAG uhn kween]—female ruler of Ædracmoræ and the Seven Kingdoms; Yávië's birthright. Sóvië is heir to the throne of the Dragon and the Serpent.

Drom [drahm]—Emyute beast of burden

E

Elders [EL durz]—Quondam's ruling council of humans

Elle [EL]—young Saedan woman, a fire assassin

Emyute [EM ee oot]—a nomadic race, Karid's henchmen

Endhaven [END hay vun]—island home of the council of elders

Eolia [ee OH lee uh]—ancient temple ruins

Equus [EK kwus]—magickal steeds bound to the House of Aaradan

F

Feie [fay]—a race with magickal abilities

Feverous Forest [FEE ver us FOR ist]—sacred wildwoods, home of the nymph Flida

Fire crystals [fyr KRIS telz]—crystals created from dragon's breath and ingested by Karid's fire assassins

Fire dryad [fyr DRI ad]—fire elemental charged with cleansing the barrens and the sacred wildwoods

Fireflies [FYR flyz]—small winged men, bound to the dragonspawn

Fire sickness [fyr SIK nis]—sickness suffered by fire assassins when they withdraw from the fire crystals

Flida [FLEE duh]—nymph, guardian of the sacred wildwoods, Karid's sister

Fount of Sorrows [fownt uv SAR ohz]—hidden cavern beneath the Hall of Hallows where Yávië is reunited with Sōrél

Fungal Shroud [FUN gul shrowd]—broad expanse of heavily misted land just to the north of the Feverous Forest

G
Ga [gah]—a firefly
Gall oil [gahl oyl]—bitter, fermented gall consumed as an intoxicating drink
Glen of Silence [glen uv SY lentz]—sacred glen at the Cloister of Belasis where the messenger delivers word of Cwen's friends' deaths
Great War [grayt wor]—war following Karid's murder of Quondam's rightful king
Grumbleton [GRUM bel ten]—Ædracmoræ's wizard; Yávië's, and later Sóvië's, advisor and teacher
Guardian [GAR dee un]—one called into service to protect and defend a person or world; guardians are given conditional immortality by the Ancients who call them into service.
Gulab flower powder [Goo lob FLOU er POW der]—an herb used to break a fever.

H
Hall of Hallows [hahl uv HAL ohz]—meeting chambers of the council of elders, located in the cathedral in Endhaven
Head Knock Narrows [hed nok NER ohz]—northern entry point of the Sea Beyond Us into the Sanguine Sea
Hellwing [HEL weeng]—winged being capable of disappearing into the shadow of another
Horsfal [HORZ fal]—owner of Horsfal's Tavern, Cwen's lifelong friend
H'san [he SAN]—Noor family responsible for guarding the dragonspawn prisoner living on Dragon's Heart Isle
House of Aaradan [hows uv AIR uh dun]—ruling house of the Kingdoms of the Serpent and the Dragon

I
Indigo [EN dee goh]—Maraen woman believed to be responsible for the fiery deaths of members of the House of Aaradan
Ip [ihp]—a firefly
Islander [AY lan der]—name used to refer to the dragonspawn imprisoned on Dragon's Heart Isle

J

J'var [je VAR]—a Noor director, son of A'bach, N'dia's older brother

K

Karid [KAIR ed]—a flesh bound nymph, the false queen of Quondam

Klaed of Drevanmar [klayd uv DREV an mar]—Cwen's friend, killed in the assassins' fires on Ædracmoræ

Knotwood syrup [NOT wud SIR up]—the clear sap of the knotwood tree, used as a natural sleep aide

L

Lien [leen]—an Emyute soldier promoted to clan leader after Buul's death

Litham [LEE tam]—Emyute veil for the lower half of the face

Lohgaen of Lochlaen [LOH gan uv LOK lan]—noble imprisoned on Ædracmoræ for attempting to overthrow the House of Aaradan

L'or [lor]—a Noor director, son of A'bach, younger brother of N'dia

Luminora [LOO men or uh]—a trade center

M

Malaia [muh LAY uh]—biological mother of the dragonspawn, a member of Quondam's royal human bloodline

Maraen [MAR ayn]—a race of fire women found on Ædracmoræ and originally believed responsible for the assassination of members of the House of Aaradan

Magick [MAJ ik]—the art of conjuration and spell-casting practiced by witches, wizards, and sorcerers

Merfolk [MUR fohk]—a race of beings adapted for life in Quondam's sea.

Mirror [MIR er]—refers to the ancient mirrors used to move back and forth between Ædracmoræ, the Seven Kingdoms, and beyond

N

Näeré [nair UH]—a sorceress, twin sister of Sõrél, Cwen's mother

Nall [nawl]—a guardian, Cwen's father
N'dia [IN dee uh]—only daughter of A'bach and the sorceress D'lana, destined to serve the dragonspawn
Neem [neem]—an herbal blood purifier
Noor [nur]—race responsible for control of Quondam's trade centers

O
Orpins [OR penz]—race responsible for farming on Quondam

P
Pikestaff [PAHYK staf]—a foot traveler's staff with a metal point or spike at the lower end
Portcullis [powrt KUHL is]—a strong grating, as of iron, made to slide along vertical grooves at the sides of a gateway of a fortified place and let down to prevent passage.
Postern [POH stern]—a back door or gate, a private entrance hidden from the main one
Prime Elder [prym EL dur]—leader of the council of elders

Q
Quern's Crossing [kernz KRAHS eeng]—barge system constructed across the northern end of Head Knock Narrows
Quest [kwest]—to perform a prescribed feat within the constraints of a prophecy
Quondam [KWAHN dum]—the dragonspawn's home world, world ruled by the false queen, Karid

S
Saedans [SAY dinz]—one of Quondam's races, its men are miners and its women have been enslaved as Karid's fire assassins
Sanguine Sea [SANG gwin see]—large inland body of water surrounding Dragon's Heart Isle
Sea Beyond Us [see BEE ond us]—seemingly endless oceans that lie beyond Quondam's landmass
Sign of the Serpent [sahyn uv thuh SUR pent]—an icon under which Sōrél, Sóvië, and Cwen were born
Slitherwort [SLITH er wort]—a noxious weed, a word often used as part of a curse

Soapnut [SOHP nut]—an aromatic plant whose sap is used as a cleansing agent

Somerbane [SUM ur bayn]—a trade center

Soothsayer [SOOTH sey er]—a person who foretells the future

Sōrél [soe RELL]—king of the House of Aaradan, twin brother to the sorceress Näeré

Soulbinder [SOLE byn dur]—a wizard capable of locating lost souls

Sōvië [so VEE uh]—daughter of Yávië and Sōrél, future queen of Ædracmoræ and the Seven Kingdoms

Span—measurement of length or height based on the average width from outstretched thumb to tip of fourth finger of a man's hand

Stonetel [SOHN tel]—a trade center located next to the Glen of Execution

Stryvers [STRY vurs]—ancient race, enslaved by Queen Karid after the Great War

T

Talin [TAHL en]—lifelong friend of Cwen, killed in the assassins' fires on Ædracmoræ

Tyne [tyn]—a Saedan miner, brother of Elle

U

Ud [uhd]—a firefly

V

Volites [VOH lyts]—race responsible for the care of Quondam's herd animals

Vows of promise [vowz uv PROM is]—words spoken under the direction of a wizard that bind a man and a woman as husband and wife

V'ran [vrahn]—a Noor director who wishes to marry N'dia

W

Wasp Queen [wahsp kween]—leader of the waspwomen, sole mother to the millions

Waspwomen [wahsp WIM in]—a race consisting of millions of half-woman half-wasp beings who join the dragonspawn against Karid's army

Wildwoods [WYLD wudz]—a sacred tract of land within the Feverous Forest overseen and protected by the nymph Flida

X

Xalín [ZAHL in]—an empath, Sóvië's betrothed

Y

Yávië [YAH vee uh]—Queen of Ædracmoræ; a Dragon Queen

Y'ithe [yth]—A Noor prostitute sent to serve the dragonspawn

Turn the page for exciting excerpts from other books in the
Ancient Mirrors series.

Dragon Queen
The Wrekening
Damselflies

Synergy Books are available wherever books are sold.

Dragon Queen: An Ancient Mirrors Tale

Dragon Queen: An Ancient Mirrors Tale *contains the first two Ancient Mirrors books,* Into Abaddon's Abyss *and* The Dragon Queen, *merged into a single story, the prequel adventure to* The Wrekening.

Imagine being summoned from the slumber of death, awaking in a shattered world you do not recall, betrayed by sibling, parent, and lover…imagine your search for the truth. *Dragon Queen: An Ancient Mirrors Tale* is a legend of magic, adventure, and courage set in the mythical world of Ædracmoræ; a tale that explores strength and weakness, hope and fear, and what it means to be a guardian in a world where peace hangs by a fine, golden thread.

With the discovery that she was born of the Dragon Queen, Yávië is given knowledge of the powerful artifacts that will reunite the shattered kingdoms into a single world.

However, with the rebirth of Ædracmoræ will come the opening of doorways that bring chaos and shadow to the new world—an evil that may be far worse than the original destruction of the realm of the Dragon Queen. It is within this darkness that the guardians and their young queen struggle to gain control of what they have unleashed upon the kingdoms.

Excerpt from Jayel Gibson's
Dragon Queen: An Ancient Mirrors Tale

To walk into a dragons' flyte was an overwhelming experience. Cavern walls towered over all. The sleeping ledges were vast fields of stone and at the far side of the chamber, Sybeth and Sygarnd lay relaxing on theirs. Eonis padded on dripping feet to stand in front of his parent and Matriarch, lowering his Huntress to the floor before her.

"The Prophecy of the Men is coming to pass. The strength of your flyte is needed. A mortal has overstepped his bounds, causing the death of the firstborn of Ilvaria and Ilgrond. He has also placed machines beneath the sea that are a threat to this flyte. They are shielded with sea dragon scales. Which of you allowed this?" Rydén asked.

Sybeth drew herself up to her full height, towering above Rydén. This was a serious accusation, for the law of the Ancients forbade the use of dragon scales by any save dragons or Guardians.

"Why do you think it was allowed? Why could the man not have stolen them from the scale pile?" Sybeth challenged.

Rydén shook her head. "I may have been captive in a crystal, but I was neither blind nor deaf. I heard a dragon's voice freely give the scales, Sybeth, and I saw Maloch take them from a dragon's claw."

"And did you recognize this dragon's voice, Huntress?" prompted the great dragon.

"Nay, but I am certain that you did," Rydén replied sharply.

Sybeth moved from her ledge, allowing her tail to brush Rydén's legs, causing her to stumble.

"What if I did, Guardian?" She put her face up close to Rydén's.

Rydén steadied herself. "You will mete out a swift punishment to any involved, or see this flyte destroyed."

From within her cloak Rydén drew a crystal, round and clear as glass. Holding it out before her, balanced on three fingers, she asked, "Do you recall this, Sybeth?"

Sybeth pulled back her head and bellowed in terror. It was a creation crystal, capable of entrapping an entire dragon flyte.

Hearing the dragon's thoughts, Rydén chuckled, "Oh, not just any creation crystal, Sybeth, but the Sea Dragons' creation crystal. It will destroy your flyte without harming the others. You choose. The traitor…or the flyte."

With an anguished roar, Sybeth's mate, Sygarnd, sprang from his ledge and closed his great jaws over Eonis' neck, twisting and snapping, leaving Eonis broken and bleeding on the sand of the flyte's floor.

Rydén knelt near Eonis' head. "I have time for that apology now," she whispered into his ear as the last of his light ebbed. There would be no one who dared to gather this dragon's heart shard.

"Call the flyte, Sybeth. I will explain my plan," Rydén commanded.

The Wrekening: An Ancient Mirrors Tale

In *The Wrekening*, an ancient evil is discovered lying deep beneath
the earth, waiting to be awakened by those possessing the Wreken wyrm
shards. The Dragon Queen of Ædracmoræ and her guardians realize the
shards must be recovered before they fall into the wrong hands—they
turn to Cwen of Aaradan, fierce warrior and estranged daughter of
the guardian Nall. Cwen reluctantly agrees, and she and her band of
renegades set off on a perilous quest to reclaim the lost shards.

Cwen's male companions, Talin, Caen, and Brengven the Feie
wizard, journey with her on an adventure that tests both strength and
honor. Cwen, who submits to no man, is endlessly pursued by Caen, a
thief by trade who truly cares for her. However, Cwen's inner demons
prove more difficult to overcome than any dragon or thralax creature
the group of friends encounter. In this tale of magick, adventure,
romance, and deceit, the fate of Ædracmoræ hangs in the balance.

Excerpt from Jayel Gibson's
The Wrekening: An Ancient Mirrors Tale

As Cwen, Talin and Caen reached the canyon floor they noticed
the silence. The deathawks and klenzingkytes had flown away and
no evidence of last night's death remained beyond the blood-stained
earth.

"It would appear that something larger and hungrier than the birds
feasts here," Talin said, looking around for drag marks that would
indicate the direction in which the bodies had been taken. Finding
none, a flicker of unease crossed his face.

From above, sand drifted toward them, dusting their clothes. A sudden grinding sound caused them to look up just in time to see the large stone that had been balanced on the short spire topple forward. Talin shoved Cwen and leapt after her as Caen threw himself backward. The stone struck the ground, sending up a cloud of dust as the pieces settled to the ground.

"Did you see that?" Cwen asked. "The firedrake?" She pointed above, but it was gone. "It leapt to the other stone and sent this one tumbling down. I saw it. It was the color of the stones with a red underbelly about as long as you are tall," she said, indicating Talin.

Beyond them another slab of stone fell crashing to the sand below and then they saw the reptilian form of the firedrake slipping back toward them. Its body was elongated and the head wedge-shaped. Short legs carried it quickly over the sand and its forked tongue flickered as it sought the scent of its prey.

Talin drew his axe but Cwen cautioned him with a shake of her head. "Do not get close, for they have the gift of .re. The crossbow will end its life swiftly and without danger to us if you will lift me to that ledge and offer yourselves as bait." She laughed at their expressions. "I shall not let you die today, and you know I never miss."

Talin lifted her up until she could reach the ledge and pull herself up. Then, as she slowly walked along its length, he and Caen started up the canyon toward the firedrake.

Cwen heard the firedrake's low growl and saw it in the shadow of a tall, monolithic column. With the swift nocking of a bolt, she aimed just behind its front left foreleg and whistled. As the creature looked up, she sent the arrow straight into its heart and watched it collapse with nothing but a twitch before death. Nocking another bolt, she glanced down toward Caen and Talin.

"Cwen, above you!" Talin's voice cracked with urgency.

As Cwen looked up, a second firedrake launched itself across the void from the top of the pillar in front of her. Falling back, she let the arrow loose, catching the animal in the throat and dropping it to the canyon floor where it lay thrashing and exhaling its fiery breath in its death throes.

"Well done," Talin called up to her. "Now I suppose you want me to get you down?"

Without warning the rocks of the canyon wall behind her gave way and Cwen was jerked backward into the dark.

Talin raced to the ledge and tried to leap up and grab the lip but it was just out of his reach. Caen interlaced his fingers and created a step to boost Talin up to the ledge. Reaching down, Talin pulled Caen up behind him and they charged into the opening. Rock and dust still sifted down, but there was no sign of Cwen.

Cwen regained consciousness in dim torchlight and reached for weapons that were no longer there. Her captor sat across from her, an immense man-shaped creature covered in fine, pale hair. Its eyes glittered as it raised its face to gaze across the wide cavern at its newly acquired meal. The face was hideous, flattened and slightly blue; the flesh of its forehead was loose and fell in folds across the heavy brow. Two large openings served as a nose, the surrounding area moist and glistening in the flickering firelight. A gaping mouth held large canines that extended beyond loose and flabby lips.

"I'll not eat you until the morrow, for I am full from feasting on the dead. Most men wish to spend their last hours talking to their gods," the deep voice explained in a matter of fact manner.

"I have no gods," Cwen responded, examining the creature more closely. The muscular arms ended in three fingered hands with opposing thumbs. The digits ended in blunt black nails, not claws that could rip and tear.

The creature licked blood from its lips and tossed the slender forearm bone it had used to clean between its teeth into the pile at the edge of the room. Cwen's eyes rested on the pile of clean white bones bare of any flesh. "Have you no soul?" the beast asked, the flesh of its brow forming a 'v' as it frowned.

"Of course I have a soul, but it is not burdened by the superstitions of the timid," Cwen answered, looking around for an exit. The only openings were in the walls near the ceiling—large enough for a man's passage but far too high to reach. Along the walls rested piles of bones and treasures carefully separated by kind. Long bones, skulls, vertebrae, and short bones—all carefully sorted and stacked. Rings, cups, medallions, books, staffs, lule, and weapons rested in their individual lots.

The creature cocked its head as Cwen eyed the stock of weapons. "While I prefer my meat fresh I can also eat it slightly ripened. The choice is yours."

Cwen laughed in spite of her growing fear, "I shall choose life until the morrow and then I shall make you work for your meal."

A coarse cackle came from deep within the beast's gullet. "You are not like most men. They cower and beg, offering great riches if I will only spare their lives."

"I am not a man," Cwen spoke truthfully. "And my life is not of sufficient value that I would be forced to beg to save it."

The beast gave another low hoot. "And you hope that the two men creeping through my tunnels will reach you before you become my excrement."

Cwen grimaced at the unpleasant thought.

"Your companions will wander in search of you for days, lost among the passageways. Eventually I will prey upon them as I hunger, for I have found that men offer little challenge to a hunting thralax."

"It is obvious that you are thoughtful, and aware that men are as well. How is it that you eat others…"

"Who are self-aware?" the thralax finished her thought as another bout of laughter shook him. "I learned from men. Are they not the ones who hunt the dragons, the Equus, and the Great Wyrms who live below the earth? Do they not kill and skin us for our scales and hides and shards? They even defile their own kind, for I have seen it in their camps. At least there is purpose to my killing. Are you not the one who killed Fa'ell and his soldiers as they slept?"

"We kill to avoid being killed or to defend the defenseless. We are not murderers."

"No, you are merely food," replied the thralax with a sigh. "If you do not wish to pray to the gods of men, perhaps you could remain silent so that I might rest." The great creature gave her one last look before closing its eyes as if in sleep.

Cwen stood and wandered around the large cavern, examining the treasures that lay against the walls. She ran her finger along the blade of a long sword, glancing over her shoulder to see the thralax watching her with one open eye. Shrugging, she moved on to a pile of rings, lifting them and placing them one by one on her fingers. At least she would die well adorned. The pile of lauds was quickly pilfered and she filled her pockets with the coins. At the small pile of books she sat down and pulled one onto her lap. It was a book of tallies, sales, and purchases from some bookkeeper who had become excrement. The thought brought a shudder. Next was a journal kept by a poacher, a list of Equus and dragon deaths so long she was grateful to know he was dead. A tightly rolled scroll caught her eye and she untied the leather binding. Carefully unrolling the parchment she frowned at the long rows of symbols—symbols she had seen before on the surface of the G'lm's shields in the cavern below Révere. Looking toward her captor she saw that he was wide awake and watchful.

"Property of one who escaped my digestion," the thralax said quietly, pointing to the scroll she held. "A good tale if you should choose to hear it."

"I have nothing else to fill the hours until my death," Cwen said, turning to face the storyteller.

"I knocked him from the back of a dark dragon—a tall man, pale and nearly hairless. He wore the cloak of a wizard and attempted to kill me with bolts of magickal lightning. Obviously, he failed." The beast laughed at his own cleverness. "I dragged him here and tied him with the wizard binding chains because he would not abide by the rule regarding weapons. He struggled and fought until he was covered in blood. The scent of it brought me great pangs of hunger even though I had recently fed. As I removed his chains and drew him forward to be devoured, he screamed words I could not understand and disappeared in a flash of blue light. The heat of his magick left me this." The thralax turned his face to the light showing a deep scar running from the corner of his mouth to his left ear. "I have promised myself if I ever catch him again, I will eat him while he is still chained."

Drawing the small disc she had retrieved from Caen, Cwen held it up. "I also possess the unknown words."

Moving swiftly for one so large, the thralax leapt across the distance that separated them and grabbed Cwen's wrists in one great hand, quickly wrapping her in the coils of the wizard's chain he kept on his belt. Drawing a hefty lock he snapped the ends of the chain together and dropped her to the ground. With the grimace that passed for a smile he reminded her, "Then I will eat you while you are still chained."

Cwen lay silent, awaiting the sleep of her captor. As she saw his head fall forward onto his chest and heard the deep snores of his slumber, she touched the small pouch that rested against her heart and with her thoughts used her gift to meld into the links of the wizard's chain, leaving nothing visible but empty coils.

Damselflies: An Ancient Mirrors Tale

Legend: real or imagined? In their demon-bound minds, fearful and powerful men consider Arcinaë, the last damselfly, a threat to their race. Hunted by those men, Arcinaë must set aside her docile nature to learn the skills of weaponry and war if she is to protect her unborn offspring and ensure the future of her race.

With the help of Ilerion, an embittered nobleman, and his manservant, Nilus, Arcinaë races against time to stop a vicious warlord set on cleansing the world of the damselflies' potent magick.

Spanning two generations, *Damselflies* sweeps you into a tangled web of twisted legends and broken promises, desire and deception, fear and fallacy, and the endless struggle to control the minds of humankind.

Excerpt from Jayel Gibson's
Damselflies: An Ancient Mirrors Tale

The hunters dismounted their gryphons and cautiously approached the scorched remains. Intermittent flames flared as the last of the settlement's dry wood was consumed and cinders, caught in gusts from the light spring wind, scurried and hissed over the final drifts of snow.

"Harpies," Nilus spat, kicking at a smoldering body with disgust.

"Nay, I do not think so. They do not bear the talons of the harpies. See? The feet appear human," Ilerion said as he examined the charred remains, "and the harpies do not build bothies, only stick eyries."

Squatting next to another burned corpse, Ilerion reached out and touched it, testing for heat. Finding it cool enough to handle, he reached under and turned it over to examine the vestiges of the amputated wings. The blackened flesh came away in his hands and the delicate bones crumbled beneath his touch. Moving, he lifted another and discovered its wings had also been severed.

"Check the bodies beyond you," Ilerion called to Nilus. "It appears that the wings were severed from each body."

Using the toe of his boot to lift the remains of several of the bodies, Nilus shouted back, "Aye, I have not found a single one with wings attached."

Wandering from corpse to corpse, Ilerion checked each one. None had escaped the blade of the butcher. It was impossible to tell if the wings had been amputated before or after death, but he hoped the butchery had only been on those already dead.

A high pitched keening shattered the silence of death and brought Ilerion to his feet with sword drawn, eyes searching for the source of the wailing. Atop a small knoll stood an apparition so covered in gore and ash that it was impossible to determine its identity. A second scream echoed through the smoke-filled glen as the body crumpled and fell backward to the earth.

Ilerion raced forward and dropped to his knees beside the fallen creature. It was a woman, naked and blood-smeared. Her features distorted by swelling and dark bruises. Pulling the cloak from his shoulders, Ilerion covered her before placing his fingertips below her jaw, feeling for the pulse of life. It was slow and faint, but it was there.

"Out of mercy finish it off," Nilus said from behind him. "It will not live long, if indeed it lives at all."

"She lives," Ilerion said, gathering the woman into his arms and lifting her to his chest. "If we can reach the healer before the life fades away, there is hope that she may continue to live."

"Ilerion," Nilus's face darkened with concern, "it is not a woman, for there are great bloody wounds in its back where wings grew. It is...a beast. Ananta will chase us away if we bring her such a creature."

"Not a beast, Nilus," Ilerion said, his eyes warning against speaking further of beasts. "Without wings she is simply a badly beaten woman. The healer will help us." Squatting, Ilerion laid the unconscious woman across his knees to examine the gaping wounds high upon her shoulders. Pulling a shirt from his pack, he tore it into pieces and stuffed them into the holes to staunch the bleeding. He then lifted her and placed her gently over his shoulder as he whistled for his mount.

As he mounted Grundl, Ilerion heard the gryphon's question in his mind, "Whose life do we save today, Hunter?"

"I do not know her name." Ilerion answered.

Shaking his head at his master's foolish risk, Nilus leapt to his own mount and urged it skyward, banking toward the outskirts of Lamaas and the healer, Ananta.

About the Author

Jayel Gibson is the author of the Ancient Mirrors fantasy series. From the tip of her Marto of Spain sword to the hem of her fifteenth century reproduction Italian gown, her effervescent enthusiasm encourages a belief in enchantment. A student of Celtic history, folklore, and faith, she spins the magic of timeless adventure throughout her tapestry of tales.

Ms. Gibson lives on Oregon's southern coast with her husband, Ken. They share their home with a Molluccan cockatoo and five sugar gliders.

She is currently at work on her next book.